– Book 3 –

Shadowed Space

SHADOW BEYOND THE REACH

Lucinda Pebre

A K DUBOFF

Published by Dawnrunner Press
Cover Copyright © 2020 A.K. DuBoff

ISBN-10: 195434435X
ISBN-13: 978-1954344358

0 9 8 7 6 5 4 3 2

Produced in the United States of America

TABLE OF CONTENTS

THE CADICLE UNIVERSE

Tarans are the predominant race in the Cadicle Universe; humans are a Taran sub-race. Most of the Taran sphere falls within the purview of the Taran Empire, governed from the planet Tararia by a council of High Dynasties. Earth is one of several rogue colonies on the outskirts of the Empire, separated so long ago that they have forgotten their Taran ancestry.

The Tararian Guard is the primary military force for the Taran Empire. Its counterpart, the Tararian Selective Service, includes a specialty branch with Agents gifted in telekinetic and telepathic abilities. The TSS is headquartered in Earth's moon, and its iconic Agents are known in Earth lore as the mysterious 'men in black'.

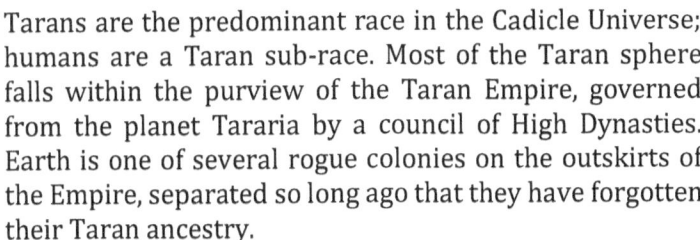

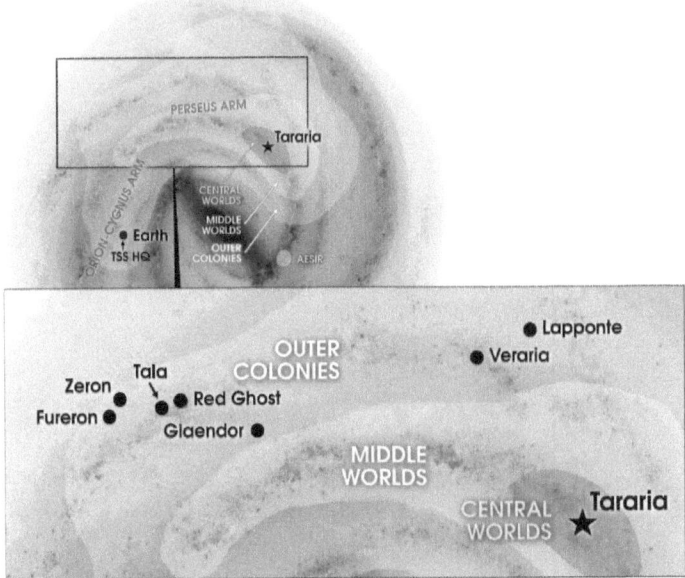

KEY TERMS, CAST, & LOCATIONS

KEY TERMS

Taran – The race of all people in the Taran Empire; synonymous with human

Tararian Guard – The primary military force for the Taran Empire

Tararian Selective Service (TSS) – A quasi-military organization with Agents specializing in telekinesis; a complement to the Tararian Guard

Jump – Faster-than-light travel through subspace

Beacon Network – The navigation method for subspace jumps, maintained by SiNavTech

High Dynasties – The seven ruling families of the Taran Empire, collectively a governing council

Lower Dynasties – Influential families throughout the Taran worlds, second only in power to the High Dynasties

CAST

TSS Agents
Kali Wietris – Newly graduated Agent, born to the Wietris Lower Dynasty
Andy Renteria – Experienced field Agent; Kali's former internship proctor and advisor

The Bruisers Band
Mika Hendri – Owner, captain, and lead engineer of the

Sepiantia; Tregaren's son
Owen Bruiser – Lead singer and guitarist
Vaira Destitutty – Drummer
Caryanne Westby – Lead Guitar
Honk Da Moog – Keyboard/Sax player

Additional Key Characters
Treva Marsh – 15-year-old son of Marco Steyn, from Glaendor
Anissa Marsh – Treva's mother
Joelee Hendri – Mika's mother
Herja – Pirate captain of the *Hyperion*
Gosta – First officer of the *Hyperion*
Marco Steyn – Crime Boss
Andrei Steyn (a.k.a. 'Commander') –Head of the Steyn family crime network
Pyra – Assistant to Andrei Steyn
Vaughn – Captain of the *Vector,* one of Marco Steyn's ships
Pesta – A sentient weapon (a.k.a. 'the destroyer of planets')
Jon Del-Awai – A guard with Avon Security on Glaendor
Tregaren – Ex-Priest who independently pursued illegal genetic experiments (deceased)

Ships
Sepiantia – Owned and captained by Mika Hendri
Hyperion – Pirate ship, captained by Herja
Vector – Owned by the Steyn family, captained by Vaughn

LOCATIONS
Tararia – The capital planet of the Taran Empire

Glaendor – Tourist-catering world in the Outer Colonies
Tala – Primitive planet in the Outer Colonies
Red Ghost – Private planet in the Outer Colonies where criminal activity is suspected.
Space Station Spadrosi – Subspace near to Red Ghost
Fureron – Border world near Zeron

CHAPTER 1

THE ECHO OF footsteps prompted Owen to struggle into a sitting position on the hard cot. He'd seen the cramped cell briefly, and it wasn't worth a second viewing; chiseled stone walls on three sides and a door with thick metal bars. Eyes open or closed, he couldn't tell the difference in the dark that was as black as the space between the stars.

The boots clattering on stone steps were light—perhaps from the only woman who knew where he was, since she'd been the one to betray him. His initial anger had first faded to embarrassment for not seeing the trap, and then had been beaten out of him. The fists of Diamond-Boy's goons had started to break his spirits, but it was time in the dark, utterly alone, that had made him question his future.

Where did it go wrong? Standing up to these criminals wasn't his mission. He was just a singer in a band, not an Agent in the Tararian Selective Service like Kali. But, he had felt compelled to help when he'd discovered the kidnappings hadn't stopped with Tregaren's death. Sick bastards, all of them. Helping to carry out the vision of a dead madman. Whoever was now running the show behind the scenes needed to pay.

Owen was in no position to do anything about it now,

though. Battered, bruised, starved, and thirsty, it was everything he could do to sit up straight, let alone think about fighting back. They certainly wanted him like that. No doubt, they were professionals at making people behave how they wanted. Though they were doing a bomaxed good job whittling away at his psyche, he wasn't broken yet.

His captors hadn't believed his pleas of innocence, not even when he'd explained how the band played Earth music in the Outer Colonies. When he'd demonstrated his amazing vocal range, they'd locked him in the cell.

Chief interrogator, Diamond-Boy, had asked if Owen had any regrets. How could he explain that while he was sorry to be captive, he'd do the same again? For Luca! Diamond-Boy would never understand why anyone would take risks for someone else.

Luca was a bomaxed hero. Killed while trying to protect one of Tregaren's victims. His best friend's courage had shaken Owen and changed everything. How could he continue drinking every night, waking with a different woman when he might have been in Luca's place? It made him want to do something and so, here he was. He'd rather be a captive than have taken no action at all.

With effort, he held in a burst of laughter that had nothing to do with amusement. If he let rip, it might frighten away his approaching visitor. Even if the footsteps didn't belong to Narda, he didn't want to be alone any longer; he needed some interaction—even if it was another beating—to break up the monotonous darkness. Perhaps in one of the 'interrogations, he'd learn something useful about his captors that he could use to fight back in a meaningful way.

He opened his eyes to a flicker of light. It hurt after so long in the claustrophobic darkness.

One set of footsteps. If he was wrong and it wasn't Narda... He tried to take a big, steadying breath but his throat was too tight to let in much air.

If Diamond-Boy kills me, I will foking haunt him. Bravado was all he had. If he'd truly been brave, he would have tried to escape instead of being too scared to move.

A figure turned the corner of the corridor, light held out in front, but he couldn't make out any detail. He wobbled to his feet and went to grip the bars, squinting as he tried to take in anything.

"You been down here long enough?" Narda's lilting accent bounced off the walls.

Owen's shoulders dropped with relief and a little air escaped in a laugh. "Yeah, let's do something else now." It was a wonder that the words came out as casually as they did. In actuality, deep fear and a looming despair that he'd never see daylight again pressed against his mind.

The pretty woman stood well out of reach, and he scowled. "What do you want?" He didn't mean to sound so cold. While he couldn't forget that it was her fault he'd been caught, he needed a way out.

"Owen, you know I never had a choice. You wouldn't want me dead, would you?"

She cocked a hip to one side and it occurred to him that she'd done it to remind him of her lush body. She was treating him as gullible. Perhaps, responding to the troubled and charismatic delinquent he portrayed on and off stage.

"I'm having difficulty believing anything that comes out of your mouth." *Don't antagonize her. She's your only way out of here.*

Narda pouted, untroubled by his attitude. "That's not nice. You've forgotten the good time we had together?"

Owen wasn't convinced he could tell what was real and what was an act. She'd used him in the same way as he'd used her, but she'd taken it a step further, turning him over to be locked in the dark.

She shined the flashlight on his face, causing him to blink rapidly. "I didn't know you had freckles." He caught a whiff of her crisp, clean perfume, inhaling deeply, glad of some respite from the dirt that permeated the air.

Self-conscious, he rubbed his face. He didn't explain that he usually covered them up; a luxury he didn't have at present.

"Steyn sent me to get some information," she turned her head to one side as if not wanting to look at him any longer.

Owen didn't recognize the name. "Is that your boss?"

"Sort of. He's the Commander."

Be careful, Owen, be nice. This cold air will ruin your vocal cords if you don't get out soon.

"So, you're nothing more than a whore for him?"

The light fell to her side as she stepped toward him. Still nowhere near enough for him to reach her. It turned out that Narda wasn't stupid.

"Why do men have such double standards?" He felt her glare even with her face in shadow. "It's no worse than what you did."

Owen shook his head. "Hey, I never said I wasn't a whore. Everyone knows it—just ask around."

Narda's laughter rang harsh and false. Owen's survival instinct finally kicked in and even though it was the last thing he felt like doing, he forced out a smile.

Narda stopped abruptly. "The thing is, Owen, I was sent for information and that's what I'm going to get." When he opened his mouth, she held up a hand. "It's not your fault that you don't know how lucky you are to deal with me rather than anyone else, but if I don't get the answers..." She trailed off, raising the light, which caused him to turn away. "You won't like what comes next. Talk and we both get out of here."

Owen was so desperate that he was willing to believe her. There had to be something he could tell them, not about Kali and the TSS because Luca would never have betrayed his friends and neither would Owen.

Before he could speak, Narda said, "If it's loyalty stopping you, it might help to know that your friends left while we were together."

Was that pity on her face? It was impossible to tell in the low light.

Diamond-Boy had said the same, but Owen had thought it a ploy to get him to talk. It was harder to doubt Narda.

He hadn't expected everyone to leave the foking planet. The *Sepiantia* had been seized; locked down. "How?"

She shrugged, either she didn't know or she couldn't be bothered to explain.

A cold rock settled in Owen's chest It wasn't being abandoned that bothered him, it was the thought that nobody was left to search for him.

Narda altered the angle of the light so that the center of the beam hit the wall, and he had the sense she was smiling. She probably did this sort of thing all the time. The thought made him nauseous.

"Tell me about the band."

Owen hadn't expected that. "What do you want to know?"

"Perhaps they aren't what they appear to be. A bit like you."

Owen let out a breath, knowing that he would fail on the first question. If he told the truth and said the band was just a band, she wouldn't believe him. Owen was not prepared to make up lies and condemn his friends to save himself.

"I hope they are far from Red Ghost."

There was a few seconds of silence before Narda shook her head. Auburn hair glided over the shoulders of her leather jacket as she sighed.

"It's been nice seeing you." He didn't know how he kept his voice steady when his insides were in turmoil. "I'm sorry..." he couldn't finish.

"I was sure you'd talk to me." She turned away, causing shadows to swing across the walls. "I wish things could be different."

Owen pressed his lips together to stop from saying

something he'd regret and slid down to crouch on the cold floor. He closed his eyes so that he didn't have to watch the light fade. An opportunity to get free would come another time. He hoped.

CHAPTER 2

KALI PACED THE grey and white lounge while Mika stared at a wall-mounted viewscreen showing a live feed of space. They had dropped out of subspace ten minutes ago. While it felt wrong not to be on the flight deck, with TSS' resources stretched, they hadn't wanted to wait when directions to a small moon near Elwansa came through on a coded channel.

The message had to be from Herja. She must have retrieved their contact details from the *Sepiantia's* internal files. The moon was probably far from her real destination. So, they'd hitched a ride on Captain Zumartra's transport ship, destined for Elwansa. She'd agreed to drop them off and pick them up, if necessary, once she'd delivered her cargo.

Every few seconds, Mika glanced at his handheld. The *Sepiantia's* tracking device should pinpoint the ship's location when they were near enough. Then they could land as close as possible. One ankle lay over the other despite the bulky material of his EVA suit. The moon had a breathable atmosphere, but there was no information about other environmental hazards.

As Kali passed his chair, Mika gave her a lazy smile. There was no sign of worry as he'd spent too long hiding how he felt to let anything slip. Unfortunately for him, the truth came through their shared connection. It made her wonder if Tregaren had been able to read him as easily. *It's no surprise that he doesn't trust anyone.*

Mika jumped to his feet. "I have a signal on the nearside to the planet."

Rather than use the comm unit, he went to speak to the captain in person while Kali gathered her dark hair into a ponytail in preparation for landing. She continued to pace until Mika returned. He slumped into the same position and stared at the signal as if afraid it would disappear.

When he glanced at her, she met his green bioluminescent eyes. "I'm trying to work out what's bothering you the most."

He looked away. "It's hard to believe that we found Mother amongst the captive women on the subspace station. She might not have regained consciousness from stasis, but she's in good hands."

Kali knew that Mika had wanted to wait at the medical center on Fureron for her to wake. He'd been told that it might never happen and if it did, it would take time. With the antiquated equipment used to keep her in stasis, it was unrealistic to expect anything else. After everything Mika had been through, it would be awful if she died.

He continued, "I don't know if anyone in the band is even alive and I'm worried that the pirate might have damaged the *Sepiantia*, flying it like she did."

Kali stopped pacing. "She attacked the station to buy us some time."

"Maybe she just wanted to test out the *Sepiantia's* weapons." He straightened. "We will see, but if she's harmed my ship in any way, I will track her down and make her pay."

Kali raised an eyebrow, knowing he was serious, but before she could delve any deeper, the captain's voice came over the comm, "Arrival in five minutes."

Reluctantly, she dropped the conversation and pulled

her EVA suit over her arms and located her helmet in preparation to leave. A few minutes later, she jumped the short distance from the open hatch to the ground. Mika landed behind.

The ships thrusters kicked up so much red dust that Kali couldn't see anything. Her helmet protected her from breathing in vast quantities of filth as the ship rose before shooting into the black sky.

"They didn't hang around," she complained.

Mika wiped his visor with a grimy glove. "We shouldn't either."

The jagged horizon of the moon's landscape was dark with a distant sun casting an eerie low light over the reddish soil. As expected her helmet's readings confirmed that the atmosphere was breathable, although, the temperature was dangerously low.

Having failed to clear his visor, Mika removed his helmet to peer at his handheld. "I have a signal." He immediately set off. "It's not far."

Kali removed her helmet and followed. The dust had settled but enough persisted to make her cough, and the cold quickly numbed her cheeks. She looked around at the barren landscape. *I hope that signal is accurate.*

They trudged over uneven ground, skirting boulders and sliding on scree for forty minutes until Mika broke into a run. It took Kali a couple of seconds to see why. Ahead, a blurry object took on an ugly, elongated shape with a bulbous head and a pointy snout. Gradually, Kali made out the distinctive brown paintwork and the single word— *Sepiantia*—emblazoned in white across the nose of the ship.

Suddenly nervous about what they might find but not wanting Mika to discover anything distressing alone, Kali ran toward the abandoned ship.

Three figures emerged from the *Sepiantia* and raced to meet them. Laughter sprang out of Kali on recognizing Vaira's long legs and Caryanne fighting to run in a long skirt. Honk's zombie-like gait brought up the rear.

Mika reached Caryanne first and locked her in a hug. Honk's expression became mildly alarmed when Mika turned in his direction.

Kali grinned. She hadn't realized how much she'd worried about the three band members until she saw them alive and well. Now, if only they could find Owen on Red Ghost, things would be back to normal. Except, technically, they'd fulfilled their mission. Kali pushed the thought from her mind. *The mission's not over until every member of the team is safe and accounted for.*

Shivering, Vaira strolled over with a scowl. Before Kali could move, the woman pulled her into an embrace. "Glad you made it," she said in a thick voice.

Kali squeezed back. "This doesn't mean I like you."

Vaira pulled away, chuckling. "Understood."

Kali clasped Honk's arm. "Where's Mac and Pesta?"

"They went with Herja on the *Hyperion*. Seems they were in a hurry to dump us and the *Sepiantia*," Honk said before hurrying to the ship.

Kali frowned. Half the sector was searching for them. They must have lost the *Vector* but did that mean Herja planning to use Pesta? It was possible, she was a pirate after all.

Mika listened to Caryanne talk about an idea for a song and the worry that had been tight across their bond loosened a little. He caught her eye and winked. It was so unlike him that she burst out laughing.

Vaira wrapped her arms around herself and looked from one to the other. "What's going on?"

Kali shook her head, not wanting to explain. "Nothing."

"I don't know. Are you two... you are, aren't you?"

Kali reddened. "Of course not."

Mika pretended he hadn't heard. "Is the *Sepiantia* okay? If not, we'll need to get in touch with Captain Zumartra to pick us up."

Caryanne wore one of her vacant smiles. "Shall we go and check?" She linked her arm with Kali, startling her. "I'm so happy to see you."

Kali studied her face, trying to work out how much Caryanne knew about where they were and what had happened. She had probably been through a lot even if she didn't remember, so Kali didn't try to free her arm until they were safely on board. *It's not because I missed any of them.*

Honk was first on board, triggering the ship's sensors and initiating a hum of power. A bright colorful interior was in stark contrast to the featureless landscape outside. The cushioned floor sucked at Kali's feet. It took a couple of steps to reacquaint herself with the sensation.

Mika jogged to the flight deck and jumped into one of the blob seats, which flowed around his body. He leaned forward and planted a loud kiss on the console. It was the only outward sign that he was pleased to be reunited with the ship he'd built with his mother.

Vaira nudged Kali. "He's not looking like much of a catch now, I grant you, but I'm sure you'll be very happy together."

Kali ignored her and went to scroll through a list of the ship's systems on the wall-mounted viewscreen.

"Herja mentioned you'd found the women, but that's all she'd tell us." Vaira scowled.

Kali outlined what had happened on the space station, leaving Mika free to check every section of the *Sepiantia* to ensure that she was fully functional.

"We need to go get Owen from Red Ghost," Honk said, searching his pockets.

Kali shook her head. "The TSS is all over Red Ghost, and they know to look out for Owen. Hopefully, he'll be waiting by the time we get back."

Mika continued to pet the ship until at last, he started the pre-flight checks. Caryanne drifted off the flight deck as if following something only she could see. *Stars, how does she function? Perhaps she doesn't, not without considerable help.*

Vaira lounged in the doorway. "We need Owen to start practicing again." She gave Kali a meaningful look.

Kali stared at her, open-mouthed. "You are trying to arrange a band practice as if it's just another day."

Vaira flashed her a look that said, 'so what.' "That is commitment and besides, you need the practice."

Kali rolled her eyes, not caring that Vaira saw. She let out a sigh of relief when Vaira and Honk left the flight deck. Honk muttered something about swinging by the kitchen to get food.

Mika had his chin tilted down so she couldn't see his face, but he had the most expressive hands that she'd ever seen. They hovered as if he was about to play a masterpiece on a piano and she sensed his excitement as they swept over the controls. He had flown the *Sepiantia* alone for a long time and didn't need her help.

Kali thought about Vaira questioning their relationship and, for the first time, wondered what it would be like to kiss Mika. *That would be a really bad idea.*

Mika looked up, and Kali quickly returned her attention to the viewscreen. She should let Andy know what was happening and when they were likely to arrive on Fureron. When she glanced at Mika, the tips of his ears had gone red, making her wonder how much of her thoughts he sensed.

A dull quiver ran through the vessel as the primary thrusters fired, slowly lifting the *Sepiantia* off the surface. The background noise deepened before returning to the steady thrum that signaled they were through the moon's atmosphere and out into space.

The sound of Vaira screaming, "Hooonk," came through the open door. Along with Caryanne giggling like a teenager. Kali considered ways of getting in touch with Herja to ask her to return for the band. A minute later, it went quiet, and Kali let out a breath. She sensed that the three had retreated to their cabins.

Mika started to hum a tune that Kali didn't recognize. She hoped that it wasn't one of the Bruiser's songs that she should have known backward.

She headed toward the door. "I'm just going to check over the ship."

"What for?" Mika sounded distracted.

"I just want to be sure that we don't have any surprises." Perhaps she should trust Herja after she'd risked her life for them, but it was better to make sure.

Mika's attention didn't waver from the console and in the next second, Kali felt the dampening of subspace. It might have been her imagination but the effect on her ability didn't feel as pronounced as usual.

Engineering was exactly as she remembered with nothing out of place. She checked the rest of the ship for good measure. Though she told herself it was to make sure the pirates hadn't done anything illicit to the vessel, it was really to give her time away from Mika. Instead of fading, the feeling of closeness to him had become more pronounced the more time they spent together. *It will be fine once we have some time apart.*

They reached Fureron in two hours and thirty-four minutes. Kali dealt with security to enable them to dock at the hastily erected but fully functional new TSS base.

She still felt guilty for abandoning Owen on Red Ghost and had hoped that he would be waiting. She would miss the band when they went their separate ways. There was no reason for the TSS to keep them together now they'd rescued the missing women. Besides, their cover was well and truly blown, and while Kali remained an agent in the TSS, the others were not.

"Two minutes to docking," an automated voice reminded her that time was short.

There was no sound from the internal cabins and so Kali looked at Mika. "Lock the door and let them sleep for a bit longer."

He raised an eyebrow. "Is this what it's like to have kids?"

She grinned. "I think it's exactly what it's like."

Mika brought the *Sepiantia* to dock and they stepped out of the airlock into a quiet area set aside for civilian ships. The base had been designated solely for TSS use and most ships were on Red Ghost so it was quiet.

Despite the grey sky overhead, it was good to be on a planet with a life-sustaining atmosphere. It reminded Kali of home, and, for a few seconds, she wondered what her younger brother was doing. Then she saw the figure, standing a short distance away, clearly waiting for them. Kali only partly relaxed when she recognized Andy's tall, muscular frame. She had a sinking feeling. *What could have brought him away from the myriad of crises?* He didn't smile as a breeze ruffled his dark hair. Something was definitely wrong. Mika slowed, and Kali felt his apprehension.

She swallowed. "Whatever it is, let's get it over with."

Mika reached for her hand and squeezed once before letting go, which only made her feel worse.

As they got close, Andy said, "I've a room where we can talk." He looked at Mika. "Do you want Kali present?"

She scowled. "Of course, he does."

"It sounds serious," Mika said to her telepathically. *"Perhaps you should go."*

The skin around Andy's eyes tightened on sensing their telepathic communication but he didn't comment, only looked around. "Did you pick up the band as well as the ship?"

"They're sleeping. It's better to leave them," Kali answered, wondering how she sounded so calm when her heart was hammering. She wanted to get the talk over with, while at the same time wondering how long she could delay the potentially life-changing conversation.

"Good." Andy set off, clearly expecting them to follow. "Have you thought about where the band are going to stay?"

Mika frowned. They had talked about it on the return trip but not come up with a solution.

Kali asked, "Have you found Owen?"

"No. I'll give you the details when we are somewhere private." Andy walked quickly. "Treva returned to Glaendor, where Avon Security offered assistance. Given that they missed Steyn's activities for so long, on top of the kidnapping case that they insisted wasn't a kidnapping, I suspect they are trying to make amends. I'm inclined to let them find accommodation for the band."

Kali supposed that forcing Avon Security to deal with the drunken drama surrounding the band would be a fitting punishment. One glance at Mika's serious face and she agreed that they weren't in a position to babysit.

They crossed an open area dotted with a handful of sleek TSS ships. The people they passed were too consumed preparing the ships for flight to pay them any attention.

"Is there any news about my mother?" Mika asked.

"I'm sorry, there's no change in her condition." Andy turned into a hangar and their footsteps echoed off metal. "I'm told that Treva's mother, Anissa Marsh, is recovering well," Andy's voice softened, "but she hadn't been in stasis as long as yours."

Kali frowned. "Why put them in stasis at all? I understand how Tregaren might have wanted Mika's mother out of the way, but what about the others?"

"The medical experts think they were kept there, ready for transportation to somewhere else."

They entered a corridor with harsh, unforgiving lighting that smelled of old fuel. A couple of TSS Militia soldiers made room for them to pass. Kali realized that she hadn't seen any Agents. When Andy went through a grey door, they followed.

"I suppose immortality is an attractive incentive..." Kali drifted off as she stared around.

It wasn't a room like Andy had said; it was a massive space within the hangar. Their footsteps reverberated as they crossed to the one table and six chairs at the center. When Kali sat, she wondered how anyone could have manufactured such an uncomfortable design.

Andy perch on the edge of a chair. "Unless the women can tell us anything, we might never know."

Mika paused, still scanning the interior while pulling out a chair. The metal legs scraped across the concrete floor with an ear-bleeding shriek before he sat.

Kali winced. "Has something else happened?" When Andy didn't acknowledge the question, she asked, "What is this about?"

Andy glanced at her before staring at Mika. "I should be speaking to Mr. Hendri alone."

Mr. Hendri! Since when does Andy refer to Mika in that way?

Andy looked at Mika squarely. "I have to arrest you."

Kali closed her eyes for a second. It wasn't a surprise, but knowing it was her fault made it worse. *Would she report Mika again?* Her head and her heart gave different answers.

"I have to formally charge you for the unauthorized use of invasive telepathy on Tala." When Mika didn't say anything, Andy added, "You signed documents to agree to limit the use of your abilities."

Kali's mind raced as she tried to come up with a way out. Could she retract the report? Maybe, but she couldn't lie, could she? No. Aside from the immorality of lying to the TSS, they would know.

Mika was too calm. "What now?" He sounded as if he'd known this was going to happen.

"We will go through the charges, and you will be taken to TSS Headquarters for a hearing."

"There's no need for a hearing. I'm guilty of looking into that criminal's mind to find out what I could about the missing women. It was necessary. Kali wasn't going to do it."

She grabbed his arm. "Mika, don't say anymore. This will be recorded."

Andy's eyes hadn't left Mika's face. "In that case, it

should be straightforward."

Kali could walk away. It would solve the problem of their newly formed connection. Suddenly, she was sure that's what Mika expected her to do.

"I'll go with him."

Andy frowned. "You can't make that decision."

"I just did."

Mika put a hand on her arm. "He's right, and it won't change the outcome."

"Perhaps not, but—"

Andy's handheld let out a piercing shriek. His face drained of color.

Kali stood, trying to see the screen. "What is it?"

"There's been an attack on the TSS outpost of Antaris."

Kali shook her head. "Why would anyone attack Antaris?" But even as she asked the question, she knew the answer: it belonged to the TSS.

CHAPTER 3

"WE CAN HELP." Mika's voice was steady. "Make use of us."

He dared Andy to accept. At least, it would delay his transfer to TSS Headquarters and distract him from thinking about Kali's offer to go with him. He didn't want to read more into that than he should.

Andy didn't seem to have heard as he gave orders via his handheld, but Kali had. He felt her attention on him and had no idea what she was thinking. He checked their surroundings again, aware that there weren't any comm units or any other equipment in the vicinity. *They really put this place together in a hurry.* When he caught her gaze, there was an unspoken question—*what are you doing?*

There was no point pretending that he hadn't understood. *"I'm not expecting it to help my case. It's just... something to do."*

Kali's eyes narrowed. She clearly did not believe that he had a pure motive. He smiled. She knew him too well. *And yet, she would go to Headquarters with him.* Not that he'd let her.

"I'm sorry for dragging you into this mess." Still, he wasn't sorry he'd done it. His focus had been to find those women and since nine had died when the technology used for stasis had turned out to be old and unstable, he felt justified. Although, he was ultimately responsible for those deaths. He could no longer blame his actions on ignorance. Whatever Tregaren had wanted with those women, it was obvious that it had not been good. Mika wished he could have killed Tregaren long ago.

"I'm sorry, too. Perhaps..." She looked away.

Mika knew Kali would never lie to the TSS and it made his heart ache that they had her complete loyalty. While he could only imagine how it would feel to deserve her devotion, she didn't owe him an apology.

Andy shouted orders from the doorway before suddenly swinging to face Mika. "We don't have the resources, not when we're fighting in other quarters." He straightened. "We need the *Sepiantia*."

"Okay, but I will pilot her." Andy paused, and Mika added, "Nobody can fly the *Sepiantia* without a neural link."

He braced for rejection since Kali had a neural link, but Andy just said, "Stay with Kali. Listen to orders."

Mika nodded, not daring to speak in case Andy changed his mind. He had a knack for saying the wrong thing to the Agent.

Andy was already halfway out of the door. "Since I don't have time to arrest you, it's better that I know where you are."

Catching his retort in time, Mika let out a long breath. Kali raised her eyebrows as she left, allowing Mika to follow one step behind them both.

"What do you have?" Kali asked Andy.

"Children were injured, possibly killed, in the initial attack." Andy was grim. "There are more families than usual at the outpost due to the time of year."

"Who would do such a thing?"

Was this the beginning of civil war? The end of the Priesthood had resulted in a power vacuum, which could prove to be dangerous.

Mika blinked. Caryanne, Honk and Vaira filed from the *Sepiantia*. He had forgotten about the band. Vaira was the only one who would have known how to unlock the ship from inside.

Andy was saying, "Our priority is to save as many people as we can."

Mika decided not to tell the band about the current crisis. They would want to come, and Vaira would worry. Although, Honk would be inebriated, if he wasn't already, and Caryanne wouldn't remember.

"No time to explain," Kali said as they passed.

Vaira and Honk looked confused, while Caryanne waved. *They'll be fine on Glaendor until Owen joins them.* That meant that he might not see them for a long time.

Mika shouted over his shoulder, "I'll call you."

They stopped at a small group where Andy gave orders, before speaking to Kali, "Take the *Sepiantia* along with," he pointed to two people not much older than Kali, "Senior Troopers—Sabrina Allongi and Ted Grenna."

Mika didn't want anyone else along but he kept quiet, knowing it wasn't a battle he would win. He idly wondered how strong Andy Renteria was and whether he could win a fight, not that he would do it. Kali wouldn't like it if he hurt Andy. She was fond of him for some reason that Mika couldn't fathom.

Once on board, Kali started the pre-flight checks. Mika wouldn't trust anyone else but found that he didn't mind her messing with his ship. He directed the two Militia personnel to the lounge area where they could don their gear out of the way.

Kali's forehead wrinkled in concentration as she double checked that the hatch was closed. Even with her rich chestnut hair pulled into a messy clump, she was beautiful. He pushed the thought away, afraid she would pick up on it as she turned her attention to a map of Antaris on the viewscreen.

He hurried to the console. Nothing felt real. It was a good thing that Kali was present, since she served as his anchor to reality.

Cleared for launch, Mika took the *Sepiantia* straight up. The neural link made take-off effortless. His knowledge of the ship allowed him to compensate for every quirk without conscious thought.

One of the Senior Troopers appeared wearing a bright neon-green suit with a pile of more neon-green clothing and two helmets in her arms. "Sorry to disturb you, but these protective suits offer some defense in hostile terrain."

"Why do we need spacesuits?" It felt increasingly natural to speak to Kali telepathically.

Kali nodded to the woman. "Thanks, Sabrina." She took the suits and passed one to Mika. *"They aren't spacesuits, and we need some protection from the burning, crumbling structures."*

Fire! It was the first time that Mika had really thought about what they would encounter. Just the word took him back to the shock of blistering heat and the way that he lost his mind every time Tregaren burned him. He'd been ten years old when he'd understood that it was only in his mind, but somehow, that hadn't made the pain any less.

Mika's life didn't have a great deal of value, but he wouldn't have volunteered if he'd known that Kali would be walking into danger. *Fool, where did I think we were going—a party?* There was nothing he could do about it now. Kali had a one-track mind when it came to her job. Then there was no more time for regrets because they had arrived.

They exited subspace closer to Antaris than the safe zone reserved for jumps, and Mika had to quickly alter course to avoid a collision with a shuttle leaving the planet. Kali gave him a reproachful look but he shrugged; it would have taken too long to navigate regular space.

Mika turned his attention to the planet. He counted seventeen ships of varying size dashing around above the base. As they got closer, smoke and flames became visible through the viewport.

Mika hurriedly climbed into the protective suit despite the garish color, trusting Kali to land the ship. Now that he knew there was going to be fire, he would take any protection he could get against the flames. The smell of burning flesh made him want to bring Tregaren back to life just so that he could kill him again.

Kali executed a decent landing on one of the external pads designed for emergencies. One side touched down slightly before the other, causing an unnecessary jolt, but it wasn't bad. Kali didn't know that the landing gear needed a gentle bang on the console to get it into the exact position.

"Mika, put on your helmet," Kali shouted as she initiated the sequence to open the hatch.

He ignored her because despite the risk of getting singed, he wanted a feel for the planet before dulling his senses. Without a bridge to link the *Sepiantia* to the planet, the ramp would deploy across the short distance. Since he wanted to be first, Mika raced for the hatch as soon as it was open and dropped to the ground.

The stink of burning plastic hit first. Smoke billowed from multiple points, making his eyes water before the breeze changed direction for a blessed couple of minutes relief. A wave of nausea had him fist his hands before hurriedly pulling on the helmet and locking it in place. It fit snug to his face, molding to his forehead and chin, creating a moment's extreme claustrophobia despite that it allowed him to breathe more easily.

Once in place, the helmet hardly obscured his vision. He had a moment where he wished it had as he took in the damage. Wherever he looked, there were piles of burning timbers, belching black into a once bright silvery sky. Patches of flames showed through the edges of the heavy, dirty smoke. Beams of metal glowed dark red from a fire that licked the remains of the main structure. The bones of it rose into the sky as big as a city. What was left defied gravity. Mika sensed a large number of people trapped inside.

Teams of rescuers worked at the edge of the inferno, but they didn't dare get too close in case the building collapsed. They wouldn't feel the flickers of life that fought to endure unless they had an ability.

Kali landed beside him, having also chosen not to wait for the ramp. That didn't surprise him. Not wanting to let the side down, the two Senior Troopers joined them a second later.

Mika shared a look with Kali, knowing that she could feel those trapped as clearly as him.

Kali's visor reflected the red glow of the fire, but he could make out her grim expression. *"Can we support the building together?"*

He swallowed and stared up at the enormous structure. Exposed floors stretched into the sky in a vertical city. Everything in him wanted to run from the flames but if Kali stayed, so would he.

A life slipped away. On impulse, Mika attempted to catch it, but it was like trying to hold onto water. Kali needed him to do this and besides, when Tregaren died, Mika had vowed never to be weak again.

Mika looked at her. *"Let's try."*

She nodded, and he felt a wave of determination emanate from her. Kali would help those still trapped, no matter what it took.

Mika didn't want to warn her that, if they did this, their connection would grow, but he wouldn't hide anything from her. *"You know that I might go to prison, and if I do—"*

"I know. Hurry."

Mika let the words go. Knowing that he could be selfish when it came to her, he had tried. It wasn't his fault that she wouldn't listen.

Kali outlined the plan to the Senior Troopers, while Mika fed energy through their bond to her. They hadn't agreed that she would take the lead, but it made sense since she had trained for these types of situations, while Mika had trained for something very different.

As soon as he'd given her everything he could, they joined the medics on the outskirts. Mika didn't look at the flames, which were visible for the few seconds that the smoke cleared. They were mostly silent expect for the occasional crack as another section of the building failed.

Shouts from the surrounding people added to the confusion. It was only after a few seconds that Mika noticed there was order in the chaos. Everyone was focused on their particular task with grim determination.

He glanced at Kali who, was staring at the vast structure as if she could force it to cooperate.

"Who are you?" The shout came from a man five meters away whose helmet was so covered in dust that Mika couldn't make out his features.

Before Mika could respond, the man was gone, racing to intercept a figure lurching from the building. Mika gasped and clutched his chest as a violent tremor shook him.

Kali spoke without looking away from the structure, "I'm doing what I can to strengthen the walls and floors."

It's only her telekinesis that I feel. With relief, he ignored the sensation as it grew stronger.

As if he had the authority to give orders, he spoke to the Senior Troopers, "Three people are alive about fifty meters that way." He pointed at the rubble. "Down to two now. Go, see if you can reach them."

Neither soldier hesitated before running into the smoke. Mika wished he could remember their names.

With visibility growing worse and now less than an arms-length away, he realized that they wouldn't find anyone without his help. Mika had no choice but to follow them into the burning building. His mouth was so dry that he could barely swallow, and with the heat and all his energy going to Kali, it was his worst nightmare.

With only his hands to pull away rubble, he set about freeing people. The suit protected him from the worst of the heat and dust. The first person he found was covered in so much debris that she appeared to be part of the rubble. Mika pulled her out, carrying her ragdoll body until he reached the first medics.

At that point, the Senior Troopers were far away, helping the people that remained trapped in one section. Kali was out of sight. The thought of plunging into the flames alone made Mika's heart raced until he couldn't feel his body.

He looked around to see that the medics had helmets but nothing like the protective suit he wore. With nobody else to go, he knew what he had to do. Kali would be in there, if she could, until every last person had been rescued. Better that it was him than her. He forced heavy legs toward the nearest life, focusing only on what he had to do next.

Mika staggered out with the injured, one by one. Each time he went back in, he fought against a yearning to run back to the *Sepiantia* and hide.

He couldn't see anyone that he knew, only medics, waiting just out of range of the worst of the heat and danger. He was alone, just like when he'd been a boy.

Mika wasn't aware of the passing time. All that mattered was getting as many out as he could. It was sometime later that he looked up and realized with relief that Kali was there, directing energy into reinforcing the building. Without a word, he joined her and they sifted through the rubble with their combined telekinesis.

A warning came through the helmet that there could be another bomb, but Mika didn't see any point worrying about it. They couldn't leave now, not even if they died.

Every cell of his body felt depleted and yet, Mika supported a man with his telekinesis until a medic took him. Then it was as if every last drop of energy had drained from him.

Kali stepped through a patch of smoke. *"There's another and then we're done."*

They were down to the last life. He could do it one more

time.

One of the medics shouted to someone inside the rescue vessel. "How many dead?"

Mika couldn't hear the answer but knew it was too many. Sweat ran down the inside of his suit as he headed back into his own personal nightmare. He glanced back to see Kali dropped onto her knees.

She gasped. *"I can't hold it much longer."*

Mika felt her exhaustion as the last life slipped away, and he changed direction toward her. He had become slow and sluggish but eventually, he reached her side and sunk down, at the point of collapse.

"Gone," even her telepathic voice was quiet, *"everyone is safe or dead."*

Mika wasn't sure whether it was a statement or a question. *"The building is clear."*

He tugged on her arm, knowing what was going to happen. Neither of them had the strength to support the building any longer. Kali struggled up, which was good because he couldn't have done it otherwise. Together, they reached the medics which was when he felt her let go.

Nothing happened for a long moment. Then the top of the building swayed, giving Mika time to worry that they were still too close, before it sunk in on itself in a cloud of toxic dust. Mika couldn't see anything, but his shoulder pressed against Kali's and their minds remained connected.

Hands pulled them into one of the rescue vessels. Mika was aware of her close as someone helped him strip off his outer suit before allowing him to lay on a cot opposite her. Kali's eyes were closed, but he knew that she was aware.

Andy's voice came through a comm unit in the rescue vessel. "All rescuers accounted for." Mika opened his eyes to see Andy's pale face on a screen on the wall and realized that he was talking to them. "Well done. I don't know how you did it, but we couldn't have had a better outcome." Despite his words, Andy looked as drained as Mika felt.

"We need to talk about that at some point," Kali said in a croaky voice. "How many did we lose?"

Andy paused, before saying, "All one hundred and five individuals working at the top for certain, and there may be more, but a lot less than everyone anticipated. The incendiary device took out the upper two floors."

"Who planted it?" Mika asked, not sure that Andy would respond to a question from him.

Mika must have earned an answer because Andy didn't hesitate. "An organization, calling itself SPEAR, has taken public responsibility. It happened soon after the bomb went off, and so there's not much doubt that it's them." He looked from one to the other. "You both look terrible. Get some rest." The screen went blank.

There were too many seriously injured for them to take up space in the rescue vessel when they only needed rest, so they picked their way toward the *Sepiantia*. As they crossed an area that was far more open than it should have been, Kali pointed to the side of a building untouched by flames. Emblazoned on the smooth paintwork was an image of a giant spear with a letter 'S' at the center. The area around it was blackened and below were the words "Revolution, Join Us."

As they were in a TSS stronghold, someone would have reported it if it had been there for any length of time. SPEAR operatives must've finished putting up the graffiti seconds before the bomb went off.

Mika wondered if SPEAR's failure to kill greater numbers and thereby, gain extensive exposure, would incite it to further acts of violence.

CHAPTER 4

ANDREI STEYN STARED at the display, ignoring Diamond-Boy standing on the other side of the table. He had given instructions for all trace of his betraying nephew to be scrubbed from the Blue Pixie before his arrival. Yet, there was a picture of Marco's bratty son on the desk. The know-nothing kid who'd destroyed his space station. Although, they had the same intense, brown eyes and dark complexion, that was where the familial similarity ended. Treva had inherited his father's strong facial structure and lean frame, whereas Andrei was broad like their father. He would have Pyra remove the picture later. For now, all that mattered was the data stream.

BREAKING NEWS!
At least one hundred thirty-seven military personnel have died, and dozens were injured during a terrorist attack on the TSS outpost of Antaris. On Sunday night, SPEAR claimed responsibility and promised further devastation unless their demands were met. The nature of those demands are not known at this time.

Andrei felt a tiny sense of satisfaction that his operatives had escaped, and then he frowned. SPEAR needed a significant victory to be taken seriously. A body count of one hundred thirty-seven was not enough. All serenity disappeared as he concluded that, overall, the attack had been a failure. The next target would have to be big enough to establish SPEAR as a threat to the Outer Colonies, or else his plan would fail.

The door opened to reveal Pyra with drinks that Andrei couldn't remember ordering. He watched the little man stumble over the threshold, making Diamond-Boy jerk back as the tray almost flew from his hands.

While Andrei liked to make his secretary nervous, the resulting clumsiness could be irritating. Somehow Pyra made it across the room without dropping anything, and Andrei resisted biting his head off. When Pyra removed the cups from the tray, he sloshed coffee close to the viewscreen.

"Just set down the tray and take a seat. I'll need you to run some errands," Andrei spoke through gritted teeth before turning his attention to the willowy Diamond-Boy. "Any word on Pesta?"

"No, Commander. I mean, the *Vector* was close behind but lost them near Zeron," Diamond-Boy said. "There is a rumor that your nephew might know something." When Andrei didn't respond, Diamond-Boy paled. "He did spend time traveling on the *Hyperion*."

"Warn Vaughn that I will replace him as captain of the *Vector* if he fails me."

Diamond-Boy opened his mouth and shut it again before tapping at his handheld. "We know that the pirate captain is the leader of," he smirked, "a city-ship located somewhere in or near the Outer Colonies."

"I don't want her life history," Andrei snapped. "I need something useful."

Diamond-Boy hurried to speak, "Her people are refugees from Roana." He avoided Andrei's eyes. "I know it's a coincidence, but..."

"How?" Steyn stared into space before saying more to himself than Diamond-Boy, "We made sure that nowhere would accept the survivors. They should all be dead."

"Nobody survived Roana, so they cannot know what happened to their home planet."

"And they can never find out."

"What is a pirate doing with a bunch of refugees?" Andrei wished Diamond-Boy would tell him something he could use.

"She was military, and they live on the city-ship. Vaughn said she came back for her crew at great risk to herself. She must have a vested interest in the wellbeing of her people."

Finally, some useful information. "We need to find this city-ship and then we have her. It doesn't sound hard so, why haven't we done it already?"

"That's what Vaughn is working on, Commander."

Was there a hint of defiance in Diamond-Boy's tone? Andrei might need to remind him of his role but not now, he had more important things to do.

Andrei steepled his hands. "We need control of Pesta for the plan to work." He scowled, this simple matter should have been sorted already.

The silence was interrupted by Pyra tapping on a tablet he'd produced from somewhere. Andrei's eyes narrowed. What notes was the little man taking since Andrei hadn't requested a record? He would check—sometimes Pyra was one step ahead and could be too smart for his own good. Nobody knew SPEAR's real goal, and Andrei intended to keep it that way.

Andrei's attention returned to Diamond-Boy. "Are we ready for Stage Two of the attack?"

"Yes, Commander."

"Let's make sure this one does better than the last."

Diamond-Boy dropped his chin. "They were lucky last time. That won't happen again." His forehead glistened in a sheen of sweat.

"Good. I'm going to take that as a personal guarantee of success."

— — —

Treva had an awful sinking feeling. It was like he'd stepped into a parallel universe. Everything was familiar and yet different.

Most of the kidnapped women had been transported to a TSS facility. While he was still reeling from everything that had happened, Glaendor had been the only place he could think of when asked where he wanted his mother to receive treatment. Then he'd remembered that the main hospital had an excellent reputation, which meant he'd made the right decision.

He'd wanted to go see her straight away, but the doctor said that there would be no point. The medics were as certain as they would admit that she was going to be okay. But, what if she woke to find him so changed that she didn't know him? Stars, he almost didn't recognize himself.

At first, he hadn't known where he would sleep, since it never occurred to him that he might inherit his father's apartment. Why would it? He'd only known Marco Steyn for a short period. His throat tightened as he wished for the millionth time that they'd had longer together. The luxurious apartment was more than he could ever have wished for, even though it had never felt like home during his short time there. It was so very different from the little place he'd shared with his mother. At least it was somewhere private so that he could try to make sense of his father's death and work out how much was his fault.

The heaviness in his chest grew now that he was alone, ascending in the elevator. The fancy chrome finishes were an achingly familiar taste of what was to come. When he reached the top floor, the biometric scanner read his palm print and the door beeped on opening. He went inside and locked the door behind him, staring at the scanner for much longer than necessary.

Treva had wanted to know his father from the first time he'd discovered that children had two parents. Despite that, Marco Steyn had remained a stranger. It was difficult to know someone who hid so much and yet in the end, he'd sacrificed himself to save Treva. There was so much he wished he'd said. He would not make the same mistake with his mother. Unfortunately, it would be hours, or possibly days, before she was awake enough for a conversation.

The entry corridor was longer than he remembered. All he wanted was to sleep, but he instead headed to the kitchen to see if there was any food. There the viewscreen displaying a pink background with a list of contact details from food delivery to deep-cleaning services.

Treva's eyes rested on a breakfast table where his father had drank his first cup of coffee every morning. The aroma of his favorite blend made the memory more vivid.

A noise made Treva turned to face the door. He blinked twice. Familiar ice-green eyes stared back at him.

"Ava?" Treva said her name before he'd made sense of what he was seeing.

As graceful as ever, she stepped into the kitchen. "I'm sorry, I didn't mean to startle you."

Ava had paid Nash and him for picking up packages he now knew contained drugs. What felt like a lifetime ago, she'd said that there was no such thing as coincidences. She'd been right because as it turned out, his father had been responsible for his mother's disappearance Despite that, he'd never trusted her.

What does she want now?

"I bet you weren't expecting to see me here." She laughed. "I wasn't sure about waiting for you, but I thought it'd be wrong to let you return to an empty apartment after..." she trailed off.

Treva wondered how she'd gotten past the security

downstairs. Should he ask her to leave? Ava was beautiful, but he wasn't crippled with fear like he'd once been around pretty women. A lot had changed in a few weeks, and he felt much older than the boy who had left Glaendor.

Ava's presence suggested that she knew what had happened with his father. How could she? There was so much he didn't understand and he needed to be careful. Whatever she wanted, he couldn't deal with it now.

He passed her. "I'm tired."

"Of course you are," she said with sympathy. "But, there's something I want to tell you." She followed him to the bedroom. "Your father and I... were... well, how do I say it?"

Perhaps because he was so tired, Treva was irritated by her reluctance to spell out the obvious. He stopped in the doorway, resisting the temptation to help her so that she'd leave.

Ava eventually said, "I was your father's girlfriend."

Treva didn't know how to respond. He wasn't shocked or upset, having guessed there was more to the relationship than what his father had told him.

Sighing, he gave up trying to work it out. "What do you want?"

She frowned as if confused and yet, Treva was sure that she understood well enough. "I don't want anything. I thought you might need someone to welcome you home." Her sultry smile was more than Treva could deal with.

Does she mean what I think she means? She was my father's girlfriend. That's just so wrong. He didn't want to play her games.

With one hand on the doorjamb, he faced her. "Can I deal with this tomorrow?"

"I wanted to... never mind."

She must have seen the impatience in his expression because she said, "I'll leave." She strolled to the front door.

Treva watched, wanting to be sure that she left before he went to bed. He had just started to think that she really had only wanted to make sure that he was okay, when she turned. "When you're ready, call me. I was your father's business partner as well as his..." She laughed again. "You *will* need to talk to me." Before Treva could respond, she pressed her palm against the scanner and he heard the soft sound of the elevator.

Treva thought of the drugs. They had belonged to his father, but had become Herja's problem when she stole them from his father's ship. There might be more shipments, which he would have to intercept. It was too much to think about tonight.

His handheld warned of an incoming communication. *What now?*

He noticed the name on the call IT. *Vaira!* "Hello."

"Hi Treva, I don't know if you remember me. We only met briefly."

He forced a smile. "Of course, Kali's friend."

She grinned. "Oh good, that makes it easier. We, as in the band, are on our way to Glaendor and need somewhere to stay that doesn't feel like we're in custody. Can you recommend anywhere?"

Treva didn't know them, but this was one of the few decisions that was easy to make. "You can stay here—there's plenty of room."

"Great. I hoped you'd say that. We'll be there by tomorrow evening."

Treva leaned back on the bed, hoping he wouldn't regret the impulsive decision. One more night and then he wouldn't be alone if Ava returned.

CHAPTER 5

HERJA SIGHED AND wrinkled her nose at the sheen of condensation coating the walls and dripping from the ceiling as a result of the thinning hull. Pools of water filled as soon as they were cleaned away and the smell of the repair substance polluted the air, leaving a nasty taste at the back of her mouth. To top it off, somehow she'd forgotten the way the dim lighting gave everyone a jaundiced cast.

The metal walls had pressed in as soon as Herja had stepped onto the city-ship. It usually took days for the feeling to creep up on her, and she couldn't help thinking it was strange that the *Hyperion* was so much smaller and yet, never felt as cramped. *Storm's Breath* was their temporary sanctuary, when it didn't feel like a prison.

An ominous clank sent vibrations through the hull. Herja hoped it had nothing to do with the reason Gosta had called her to Engineering.

Hopeful faces turned in her direction as she marched down the corridor. She kept her stride purposeful and avoided eye contact. People had managed perfectly well while she'd been away, but as soon as she returned, they'd looked to her to solve every little problem.

Herja was a leader—just not the sort of leader who

could find somewhere for what was left of her people to live. *I'm more warrior than queen.* Which was why she couldn't wait to leave.

Herja reached Engineering and stood in a space about two meters square, while a wall of pipes and circuitry rose in front of her, ending at the ceiling. There were gaps that would allow someone small and agile to pick their way through the chaos, but she had no intention of stepping into that maze. A small shelf to the side of the door overflowed with smaller circuitry and a couple of chairs.

Gosta was talking to Peter, who had to be the oldest engineer she'd ever met. People joked he'd been around since the start of the Priesthood. There was no way it was true, but he was wrinkled enough to make it seem plausible. Both men stopped talking as soon as they noticed her. Sensing an ambush, she took a deep breath but didn't retreat.

Peter smiled, displaying worn teeth—a sure sign his medical nanites needed a boost. There was little chance of that happening on *Storm's Breath.* Although things might be different if she could find a way to get her people off this death-trap.

Peter cleaned debris off the capacitor housing. *Where did that come from?* She looked up to see that the ceiling had rusted away in layers. They would soon be closer to the stars than anyone wanted.

A new clanging started, sending Peter off to release a valve. If anything happened to Peter, she doubted they'd be able to fix anything on the ancient ship.

"We are taking good care of him, aren't we?" When Gosta didn't respond, she looked at him. "What's with the pained expression on your face?"

"Repairs are needed, and food is running out, as usual." He tried to wipe a screen with a dirty cloth. "Besides, what's there to be happy about?"

"I don't need you to spell out the situation. Within the first two minutes of our arrival, I was fully briefed on the doom report." Herja didn't need to be told that they needed a miracle.

Gosta pretended to be engrossed in something on the viewscreen, which just irritated her more.

"Get on with," she frowned, "whatever it is you're supposed to be doing. I'm sure that you shouldn't be in Engineering."

"You asked me to explain…" Gosta trailed off, mumbling under his breath so she couldn't make out the words.

He wants something.

"And you asked me to come down here. Why?"

His gaze snapped to her. "I wanted you to see how urgent things were."

Ah, that's what he's up to.

A loud crack reverberated off the metal walls. Startled, Gosta stepped back. The rag dangled from one hand as he stared at a broad crack running across the screen he'd been wiping a second before. He twisted and glared at her, like somehow it was her fault.

Herja raised an eyebrow, not feeling the need to point out that he had broken the screen. This was one of those moments where if she started laughing, she might not stop.

One glance at Peter's distressed expression from across the aisle destroyed any vestige of amusement. Instead, she crossed her arms and waited for Gosta to speak. There would be no avoiding it and so, it was better to get it over with.

Gosta folded the cloth and placed it on top of the viewscreen. "You know we are gonna have to do it in the end."

Herja knew exactly what he was talking about but she hadn't reached the same conclusion. There had to be another way to make the credit they needed. She wondered if any of Marco Steyn's ships were still operating before immediately dismissing the idea, since it would involve stealing from Treva, not Steyn. She wasn't comfortable with betraying friends. She hadn't sunk that low. There had to be another way, and if anyone could find it—it was her.

Her eyes narrowed. "Why don't you look at me and say what you mean so we can have a discussion like adults?"

"Alright." Gosta paused. "We need to sell the drugs in the hold because they certainly aren't good for anything else. They've pushed us to this." He waved his arm vaguely, but she knew he meant all those planets that had refused to help them.

"Not yet." She folded her arms. "See, it wasn't difficult to talk to me, was it?"

He turned furious eyes on her. "Look at this place. They're all going to die unless we get some substantial credits soon." Deflated, he added, "And, we should have kept the *Sepiantia*."

Herja shook her head. "Great idea, and then we could have run from the TSS for the rest of our lives." She let out a breath, forcing herself to calm down because this was not Gosta's fault. "I'm fully aware of our circumstances, but we have always had limits and we need to be extremely cautious about crossing those. If you think that makes me a terrible leader, so be it."

"I never said that. You make a great pirate."

She scowled at him. "Don't call me that."

He almost smiled. "There's no hiding from the truth."

She resisted the urge to poke at his chest. "One thing you got right is that we need to find some credits and get off this rust-bucket." She made a decision. "We are going to steal some cargo."

If I'm a pirate, I may as well behave like one.

She felt better now that she had decided. When Gosta opened his mouth to point out some logistical problem, she hummed something that was almost a tune.

Both of their handhelds pulsed with an alert at the same time, and they scrambled to find them. Gosta got to his first.

"What is it?" she asked.

He looked up, face pale. "The *Vector* has found us."

No, it was impossible. They'd checked and double-checked that nothing followed them before returning home.

Herja's mind was already considering the possibilities. It would take thirty minutes to get to the *Hyperion* and longer to power her up. They didn't have time. The city-ship had little in the way of defenses. They relied on staying out of sight and looking like the poor pickings they were.

Think, there has to be a way out of this!

Herja needed to be on the flight deck before she tried to reason with Vaughn.

"They want Pesta." Gosta said. "It would be best to hand Mac and the creature over."

"Pesta is more like an entity than a creature."

"What?" Gosta scowled. "We should hand them over."

Easy for him to say since he'd argued that from the start. Herja wasn't so sure. What was to stop Vaughn destroying everyone once they'd handed over Pesta? She was their only bargaining tool.

CHAPTER 6

A BULKY SECURITY guard stood by the entrance to the Blue Pixie. Treva didn't recognize the man who wore a modified version of the over-the-top uniform that was standard for Avon Security.

As Treva approached, the guard stepped into his path. "It's okay." He was about to add, *I own this place*, but the words stuck in his throat. He'd recently made a silent promise not to get involved in his father's dishonest dealings, which he suspected included the night club. "I'm supposed to be here." When the guard continued to stare at him, Treva said, "Ask Ava. She'll tell you that it's okay."

"Ava is busy," the guard said at last. Then he spoke into his handheld, squaring his shoulders as if expecting resistance.

A figure slipped out of the club and Treva suppressed a groan because it was the last person he wanted to see. "Nash? I thought you'd have gone." Even as he said it, Treva didn't know why he had believed that, except he'd wanted it to be true.

Nash grinned. "Still here, doing the same old, while your star rises in the world." The bitterness in the older boys words was obvious, and while Nash had shown jealousy the last time they'd spoken, a lot had changed since.

The security guard finally stepped aside as if Nash was important enough to vouch for Treva. Nash opened the door, deliberately inviting Treva in, as if the Blue Pixie belonged to him, before disappearing into the darkness.

Treva ground his teeth, wondering what his father would think. He had a horrible feeling that if he'd tried to assert his authority, Nash would have watched him fail spectacularly.

With head held high, Treva straightened and strode into the Blue Pixie. He was missing something, but there was nothing new about that. He couldn't see much as his vision adjusted to the gloom. Soft music played, without the usual buzz that accompanied opening time.

"What are you doing here, anyway?" Nash asked close to Treva's right ear.

Treva pulled back, heart hammering. "Why hide behind the door?"

It had been a mistake to come. Something's happening, and I'm not a part of it.

"Treva has come to see *me*." The smooth, feminine voice carried from the bar.

Surprised, Treva spotted Ava sat in shadow with a cup by her left hand, holding a tablet in a pool of light. Heart-shaped bottles filled the shelves behind her and two bowls containing small fish sat on the bar. Flashes of red caught his attention every few seconds as they circled within the glass.

Ava cocked her head to the side, and he wondered what she saw. He felt nervous, but it wasn't the usual anxiety that stemmed from his fear of doing something stupid. It was more serious—an awareness of being at a disadvantage in a potentially treacherous situation.

Nash slipped away, still wearing a smile that said he knew more than Treva. He hardly noticed as Ava's ice-green eyes scanned him from the tip of his toes to the top of his head. He hoped that she couldn't see his burning face.

Ava crossed one unnaturally long leg over the other, displaying red shoes with dangerous heels. Her blonde hair was piled on top of her head, except for a few wisps that framed her face. A skirt hugged her thighs and, if the memory of the previous night wasn't fresh in his mind, Treva might have stared more than he did.

He swallowed and asked a question he'd been avoiding, "You know about my dad?"

"That he died—yes." She lowered her eyes. "He didn't like you seeing us together. It was understandable, I suppose."

Treva had to think before he realized that she meant the night she'd given him a cryptic warning about coincidences. She hadn't lied. Marco had been responsible for his mother's disappearance.

"Why?" He worked out the answer before she answered.

"He didn't want you to know that we were in a sexual relationship."

He looked away even though he liked that Ava was at last treating him like an adult, "Oh." He wondered if she wanted to shock him. "That was silly."

She shook her head. "Never mind, it's in the past." She held out a hand as if they hadn't met before. "I'm Ava Funshi, your father's business partner and former girlfriend."

Treva thought it was a bit sudden for her to let things go, but he shook her hand anyway. "Thank you for helping me with... Nash." He didn't want her to think he needed rescuing. "I mean, I can handle him. It's just, I'd rather not..." It was easier if he didn't look at her while talking. "Why are you helping me?"

He glanced up, catching an unguarded moment. For a split second, her expression was calculating before she smoothed her face back into a pleasant mask. He was suddenly certain that Ava was not going to help him but, in fact, wanted something from him.

It felt like there were predators circling. His heart clenched as he realized that his mother was even more vulnerable.

He would let Ava see what she expected—a naive boy. Not someone who had escaped a hostile ship, made friends with pirates, and seen his father murdered. She didn't know him. Neither did Nash; he could use that to his advantage.

Treva looked through long, dark lashes at Ava. "Can you help me understand what's going on? I know Dad left things to me, but... well, I thought it would be different."

Such as being able to get through the door of my own club without being accosted by Nash.

Ava smiled, showing a slither of perfect teeth. "I'd be happy to, Treva. How can I help?"

"Well, I've been here loads, but would you show me around as if it was my first visit?"

She frowned. "You want me to show you around the club."

He smiled. "That would be great. I just want to see everything again"

Her face cleared. "Ah, I understand. You want to see things from a new perspective" She gestured to the bar. "What about a drink to take with us?"

Treva blinked. He didn't think she meant fruit juice, but he wasn't sure what answer she expected. *Act like I would have before Mom went missing.*

"Sure." His grin widened as he frantically tried to think of the name of an alcoholic drink.

It didn't matter because she didn't ask what he wanted. There was no bartender, so she just slipped through a hatch to the other side of the bar and poured something into a glass before sliding it across the counter. Treva caught it in one hand while she poured a matching one for herself.

She took a sip before saying, "There are three bars. All

serve the same selection of drinks."

After making her way back through the hatch, she led the way through an archway to the other side of the club. Treva didn't tell her that he'd explored when he'd first arrived. Instead, he let her chat about revenue and client expectations while pretending to sip the fiery liquid that made his lips numb. It was easy in the low light to tip a little liquid out, here and there .

Once around the bar area and the kitchens and she said, "There isn't much to see."

He almost agreed just to keep the peace but wondered how she could have forgotten. "What about the back room?"

She stared at him while a tension grew until it felt physical. Treva wanted to take the words back, but at the same time, he tried to work out what Ava's reaction meant.

She forced a smile. "This way."

"It's okay, I've been there loads."

"Have you?"

By attempting to repair the damage, had he'd gone too far? "I got the packages with Nash, remember?" Of course she remembered. It was only a few weeks ago that he'd last seen her with his father.

Ava raised an eyebrow, but he couldn't tell what she was thinking as they continued down the narrow corridor that led to a fire exit. Treva had never noticed before that the office door was invisible until they were directly outside.

Ava knocked, and when there was no answer, she tried the handle. "It's locked."

The way she looked at him, Treva knew at once that she'd lied. Why? He had to know.

"It's a shame," Ava turned to go.

Treva grabbed the handle, twisting and pulled. Ava's stilettoed shoe blocked the door from swinging wide and her vicious expression confirmed Treva's fear that she had something to hide.

"I think it was stuck," he said, striving hard to pretend there wasn't a problem.

Ava scowled, peering into the room while Treva stayed quiet, not daring to push his luck any more than he already had. Her shoulders relaxed and she went inside, leaving the way clear for Treva to follow. He was half-disappointed that whatever she'd been trying to hide, wasn't there. Something told him that Ava wouldn't react well to being caught out.

The room was exactly as he remembered, complete with Ava's perfume permeating the claustrophobic space. The only light came from an idle holodisplay over the huge desk and two small lamps on one wall.

Treva's eyes went to the internal door to the left and then the other next to it. He'd always wondered what was on the other side.

Ava saw him look. "The other half of the cellar, before it was bricked up." She gestured to the door on the right. "Let me show you."

Treva nodded even though what she said made no sense. Why would anyone brick up half a cellar? If he'd needed further confirmation that she was lying, he remembered his father appearing from the door on the left, although, he couldn't find the courage to challenge her. He would check out where that door led another time.

He followed Ava into the cellar, but halfway down the steep steps, he became worried that she intended to leave him in the dark. With no idea where the thought had come from, he raced to the top of the stairs.

At the door, he turned. "Sorry, never mind."

She laughed. "Afraid of the dark?"

He stared past her. The cellar was large but not as big as it should be.

"What's wrong?" She was halfway back when she turned to look.

Treva forced a laugh. "Nothing. I just saw a ginormous spider."

Ava smiled. "Better shut it in, then."

Treva's racing heart had just returned to normal as the door to the office opened. A small, unassuming man froze with one foot over the threshold as if torn about which direction to go. He mumbled an apology.

"Pyra, sorry we were just leaving," Ava said as she shut the cellar door.

The man cautiously continued into the room with eyes downcast. He skirted around Ava as if trying not to draw her attention. Treva had never seen him before but there was no point asking for an introduction since Ava had already said his name.

Ava was talking. "I'd forgotten that you were involved in collecting the...er, packages."

Annoyed at her conspiratorial tone, Treva said, "I know what's in them."

She laughed. "Those packages were tamperproof. I seriously doubt that you *know* what was in them."

"Actually, I saw them on the *Hyperion*." Too late, he realized what he'd said. The last thing he should do was talk about Herja or her crew.

Ava's eyes narrowed. "That's right, you were on the pirate ship."

"I had to get to Red Ghost to look for my mom somehow," Treva said, watching Pyra move to the desk.

He didn't pay any attention to them as he took a small device from the drawer. Treva couldn't see enough in the dim light to make out any detail. Then, Pyra started toward the door that Ava had claimed was bricked up.

Her head snapped to him and them Treva. "We need to leave. I'm too busy to waste any more time."

She headed out, and Treva followed because even a little bit of resistance felt too dangerous. Besides, he was now certain that there was something behind that door that Ava didn't want him to see.

Once they were in the corridor, Ava relaxed. "Do you want another drink?" She seemed to have forgotten that she was supposed to be in a hurry.

Surprised to find that he had an empty glass in his hand, he shook his head. "No, thank you. I need to go home to change before I visit the hospital. They wouldn't let me go until this afternoon." For some reason, he didn't mention the band coming to stay with him.

"Oh, yes, your poor mother. I do hope she's feeling better." Ava's voice was sickly sweet, telling Treva that she didn't mean a word. "I'll get you transport home."

"No, thank you."

Treva was determined to walk. It would give him some much-needed space to try to work out what was going on at the Blue Pixie.

Ava must have seen that he meant it, as she didn't argue, but she didn't look happy. He couldn't work out why it mattered. Despite her claim to be busy, he felt her eyes burn into his back as he'd left the club. Even when he reached the walkway with both hands in his pockets and his shoulders hunched, he felt as if someone was watching.

CHAPTER 7

MIKA'S THROAT WAS parched and he wished he'd had time to shower. Fortunately, the protective suit had kept off most of the grime, so he didn't look as unclean as he felt.

The hospital's smooth lines and tranquil colors did nothing to reduce the anxiety that was like a living creature under his skin. He'd searched for his mother for years and would not accept that he might lose her now that he'd finally found her.

Hurried footsteps echoed in the empty corridor. *Kali! What's she doing here?*

She didn't shout for him to wait but he did, feeling unaccountably grateful that she'd ignored his order to leave him alone. Instead of turning to face or acknowledge her, he stood in the middle of the corridor. Her footsteps slowed as soon as she realized that he wasn't going to run away.

A few seconds later, she placed a palm in the middle of his back and it was like an electric current going through his body. "That was low, Mika, sneaking off while I was cleaning up." There was no anger in the words.

"I didn't want you here." There was no point pretending when she already knew, but that was the problem; she saw and understood too much.

It wasn't a surprise when she didn't take offence. "Well, the thing is, you don't always know what's good for you, and that's where I can help."

Mika started to walk. The same corridor that had seemed endless when he'd set out, turned out to be way too short. Upon reaching the critical care section, he announced their arrival to the intercom and the double doors swung open. They were greeted by a medic in the standard grey uniform of the facility. She was young and athletic with short silver hair and a harried expression.

Kali hung back, making it clear who was important. Mika wished that she would stay by his side.

"Mr. Hendri, we're expecting you." The medic held her right hand horizontal to the ground, palm up, in the customary Taran greeting.

Mika reciprocated and asked, "Has she woken?" even though he already knew the answer.

"Sadly, no. Although her vitals are adequate and her body has accepted the nanites working to rebuild some of her neurological pathways."

Mika nodded. "So, why isn't she awake?"

"We think that parts of her brain experienced low perfusion while in stasis and didn't receive the nutrients necessary to sustain life."

That sounded serious but he knew that medical facilities like this could fix almost anything. Still, the medic was not exactly giving off happy vibes.

"What are her chances?" he asked.

Mika saw her hesitate and could identify the point where she changed what she was going to say. "If you push me to give a number," she hurried on noticing his expression, "I'd say fifty percent."

There was no point talking further since he knew the hospital was doing everything they could. "I want to see her."

Do I really? He wasn't so sure that he did, but this wasn't something he could hide from.

The medic pressed her lips together as if holding back something while she led them to a white door. "Go in when you're ready. There's no need for any special precautions, and she might know you're here."

Was she just saying that to give him hope? Mika was too tired to ask.

Kali slid a hand into his. The unexpected warmth was a shock to his system, and he dared to glance at her. She faced ahead as if she wasn't offering him the comfort she thought he needed. Stars, who was he kidding, comfort he *desperately* needed.

He stared at the plain, white door. It didn't have a window to show what was waiting for him inside.

The medic had said there wasn't any need for special precautions, so why did it feel as if there should be something before he opened the door to his mother?

Mika shook his head to clear it. He'd wanted this for so long, but what if his mother had changed and wasn't how he remembered her? What if she blamed him for everything that had happened? After all, he couldn't help blaming himself and couldn't explain some of the things he'd done. Part of him wanted to cling to memories rather than face the future. After the attack on Antaris, he suspected that they hadn't yet uncovered the extent of his father's legacy.

Loitering in the corridor wouldn't achieve anything, and if he didn't hurry, Kali was liable to shove him in there in the same way as he'd pushed her on stage in the past. The thought almost made him smile.

There were too many questions about the future swirling in his head, but one thing was certain: he had to be braver than this. He pushed the door open and stepped inside. Kali came in but stayed just inside.

Joelee Hendi lay pale on white sheets, with her head tilted to the window as if that was where freedom lay. He remembered with a jolt how she preferred dark colors as they warmed her skin tone. Perhaps there were a few more wrinkles, but most of the lines on her face were exactly as he remembered. He tried to swallow down the emotion that clogged his throat.

If she wakes, will she know me?

One hand was on top of the sheet. Perhaps it had been positioned there by a nurse who knew that he would need to check that she was real. Mika touched her tiny, cool fingers.

Even though he felt foolish, he spoke, "I'm sorry." He took a breath. "There is so much to tell you." Then, when he couldn't find the words, he just held her hand.

— — —

"SPEAR claimed responsibility!" Kali gazed over at Andy. "What do we know about them?"

Andy looked up from where he was fiddling with a newly installed viewscreen that hadn't been in the room when he'd almost arrested Mika twenty-five hours ago.

Mika sat opposite with his head resting on both arms on the table, and if she hadn't known better, she would have thought that he was asleep. He hadn't said much since they'd visited the hospital, but having some idea of what it had cost him, she understood.

Andy nodded. "Not a lot. There'd been no mention of them except in your report, detailing what you saw in Marco Steyn's mind."

Kali should have felt a sense of urgency, but she felt nothing. Perhaps she'd reached her emotional limit. One thing was certain, she needed a break. Andy must be just as tired but he didn't look like he was planning to rest anytime soon.

Abandoning what he was doing, Andy wandered over. "It's confirmation that the attack was linked to what happened at the space station." He pulled out a chair and sat. "The loss of life was less than it might have been," he glanced at the top of Mika's head, "thanks to both of you, which leads to my next question."

Mika opened an eye. They both knew what was coming next.

"Don't you dare leave me to explain everything," she said telepathically.

"I'm a wanted man. What do I have to offer?"

Andy cleared his throat. "When you've both finished. Mika, I would appreciate it if you joined in the conversation."

Mika lifted his head. "Hey, I left school years ago."

"Not as long ago as me." Andy looked from Mika to Kali. "Now, someone needs to explain how you held up that structure." When neither responded, he added, "It isn't like I don't know your CR score, Kali."

Mika propped his head up with a hand. "What are you talking about?"

"CR—Course Rank—is the official measurement of an Agent's ability, taken at the end of their training and immediately before they graduate from Junior Agent to Agent," Andy smiled. "Even though it was many years ago, I remember my own Course Rank Test."

Mika frowned but Kali sensed his interest. "How can anyone reliably test ability?"

"Through a multi-phase examination, part of which involves directing telekinetic energy into a testing sphere. The magnitude of energy focused during the exercise is the primary factor that dictates an Agent's CR."

Before Mika could ask, Kali said, "My score was 9."

Mika shrugged. "Is that high?"

Andy answered, "In general terms, yes. But not enough to explain what you just did. That wasn't just a matter of raw power, but of complexity."

Kali flashed Mika a warning look. "I didn't have time to tell you before we ended up on damage limitation and had no choice but to use it." Kali didn't know why it felt like confessing to a crime. "When we were under attack on the space station, we linked our abilities somehow."

Mika raised an eyebrow. "We didn't know what we were doing." Mika shook his head slightly. "It seems our combined ability is a lot stronger than each individually."

"Interesting that you left that out of the report." Andy looked at Kali. "And now?"

Kali shrugged. "We don't know." She frowned, "I didn't deliberately leave it out of the report. I didn't know how to explain what we'd done, and was still trying to make sense of what happened..." She trailed off, feeling awkward.

Andy sighed. "Try to explain."

Mika sat up straight, glaring at Andy. "We haven't separated."

"So, you're still linked now?" Andy's eyes widened. "No wonder you insisted on returning to Headquarters with Mika."

Kali shrugged. "I was going to tell you, but there wasn't much chance with the speed that everything happened."

Andy looked at his hands. "Have you... you know?"

"What?" Kali frowned.

Mika said, "No, we haven't even kissed."

"No!" Kali glowered at Andy. "I cannot believe you asked that."

"Well, it would only be natural," Andy studied her and probably read more into her reaction than he should.

"I... we didn't want to make things worse... more permanent." Why was she struggling to get her words out? Perhaps because she hadn't had a conversation with Mika about it yet.

Mika stared at her with a raised eyebrow, not at all embarrassed as he said, "Quite frankly, I wouldn't be too worried if it happened."

"Mika, stop. Now." Kali did not need Andy or those above him, hearing any of this.

Andy shook his head slowly. "This isn't good, but we have bigger things to worry about." When nobody spoke, he continued, "Look, there's not much love for the TSS out here in the Outer Colonies. That means there's a danger the population might find SPEAR's offer attractive." Standing, he started to pace. "The TSS is already dealing with a threat at the other side of the sector, but this smacks of organization and planning."

"Andy, will you sit down please." He was making Kali feel as if she should get up and join him. "Surely, nobody is going to side with an organization that carries out attacks on innocent people."

"Not in the Central or Middle Worlds, but out here, they don't always see us as a force for good, and they don't like sticking to the rules. You've seen that for yourself." He met her gaze. "We need to find SPEAR and neutralize it quickly."

Kali frowned, not sure she liked the way he lumped all the worlds in the Outer Colonies together. The TSS's priority had to be preventing more deaths, but her instincts told her they were missing something big. She looked at Mika whose head was propped on both elbows again. She felt a soft vibration in their shared link that came from his inner tension.

"Are you going to offer to help?" Mika asked in her mind.

"Of course not, I'm going with you to Headquarters."

"I hate to say it, but they need you, Kali."

Although the driving need to stay with Mika was down to their connection, Kali didn't know what to do about it. Andy was staring at her, and pointedly ignoring Mika. She felt a wave of irritation. The TSS needed Mika as much as her.

She shook her head in an attempt to clear it. "Sorry, I was—"

"Having another telepathic conversation with Mika." When she opened her mouth to say—what? She didn't know—he added, "I feel the buzz when you talk to each other."

She shrugged. "I was just letting Mika know that I was still going to Headquarters with him, that's all."

"I'm sorry, but we need you here."

His tone was uncompromising, which made her push

back immediately. "I've done enough." He wouldn't order her to stay after everything she'd been through—survived. She had earned some time off and would not abandon Mika.

"I think you will." He put up a hand when would have argued. "You know how we sent people down to Red Ghost to secure the planet?"

Kali leaned forward because she hadn't forgotten about Owen. She was vaguely aware of Mika shifting in his seat. It was evident that the news would not be good.

"Just tell us, Andy."

He took a deep breath. "They found nothing. No sign of Owen Bruiser."

"Did they check underground?" Mika pressed his hand into the table. "There was an installation of some sort under the city."

"There was no city."

"It was abandoned..." Mika's voice trailed off.

Kali pictured Owen as she'd last seen him. He'd been focused, as if he'd discovered a new purpose. She tried to remember what they'd talked about, but she was too tired.

It didn't feel real. Owen couldn't have just vanished. When they'd abandoned him, it was supposed to be temporary.

She found herself asking, "Did they find any remains?"

Mika's response was sharp in her head. *"He's not dead."*

She didn't bother to point out that he couldn't know for sure. It was difficult to imagine Owen gone forever, and she hadn't known him that well.

Kali half-turned to Mika. "We need all the facts."

Andy threw up his hands. "We need to focus on the thousands, perhaps millions of lives relying on us to eradicate SPEAR."

Kali stood. "If I stay, then Mika stays." She saw that Andy was going to refuse. "We are effective together. There's no way I can repeat what we did today without him. You know that."

Andy paused and thought before saying, "I can't make that decision. I will have to speak to the Lead Agent." He stared at Mika and then Kali. "You have to realize that this is just the beginning of what could become a civil war."

Kali couldn't help retorting, "Then the last thing we should do is imprison our best fighters."

CHAPTER 8

ANISSA YANKED AT her wrists but her arms didn't budge. Too weak and helpless, she tried not to give into the voice in her head screaming to escape. The panic came in waves. She concentrated on breathing because losing her mind was not going to help.

The only thing that frightened her more than been trapped at the mercy of Marco Steyn and his people was losing herself and becoming someone who reacted without reason. She would not go there again.

Anissa concentrated on the restraints. If the material hadn't been so soft, she might have had a chance of squeezing her tiny wrists out, but it clung no matter how she twisted. There was nothing she could do. Better to accept that fact and find another way out.

Trouble was, her head felt so fuzzy. It must be the drugs they'd pumped into her, but she couldn't give up. She had to get back to her Treva.

Anything could have happened to him since they'd taken her. She didn't even know how long it had been since she last saw him.

Heat burned the back of her eyes. *I will not cry. Not until we are safe.*

— — —

Treva stared up at Glaendor City Hospital with its central dome surrounded by five arcs of glass that made it look more fairy castle than medic facility. That wasn't the reason for Treva's reluctance to walk through the entrance; it was the fear of what he might discover once inside.

With a deep breath, he stepped up to the retinal scanner that controlled the main doors.

After a couple of seconds, an automated voice announced, "Welcome, Mr. Steyn."

The door slid open. *Why does the system think I'm my father?* Not wanting the door to close before he was through, Treva hurried into the building.

The corridor was wide and flooded with natural light thanks to the glass ceiling. He was half-aware of bird song playing in the background while the smell of freshly cut plants made his nose itch. Flowers didn't grow naturally on Glaendor, which made the scent popular in the more exclusive hotels. Treva felt as if they were trying too hard to force people to relax.

Since he had the directions to his mother's room on his handheld, he swerved past the information consoles near the entrance. He'd been told that the list of visiting times was individual to her particular needs and that these would be strictly enforced, whatever that meant. He hurried to the fifth floor, his heart thudded against his chest as he tried to understand why he felt so raw.

"Can I help you?" A tall, thin man in a medic's uniform walked toward him. Treva opened his mouth but before he could respond, the man smiled. "Sorry, I didn't recognize you, Mr. Steyn. I'm Doctor Haeloni."

Treva jerked at the use of that name again. "I'm not Steyn. That was my father's name. My name is Treva Marsh." When the Doctor Haeloni expression remained puzzled, Treva said, "My mother is Anissa Marsh and I am Treva Marsh."

Stars, it's not that difficult to understand.

Doctor Haeloni smiled again. "Yes. You are here to see your mother. She's doing remarkably well physically, but we have some concerns about her cognitive state."

The constant anxiety that had been present since they'd return to Glaendor spiked. "What do you mean?"

"Perhaps it's nothing to worry about at this stage, but she's paranoid that someone wants to hurt her. It's taking longer than we anticipated for her to accept where she is." He nodded toward a door. "Perhaps your visit will help."

After everything, it didn't sound like paranoia to Treva. *Perhaps the hospital doesn't know the circumstances that led to her coma.* But surely, they'd have the full information so that they could treat her.

Then, something Doctor Haeloni said registered. "I thought she'd only just woken," Treva said.

"Ah, she has been awake for a little while, but we were... erm... busy stabilizing her condition."

Treva frowned. "Her life was in danger and nobody told me?"

"Nothing as serious as that." Doctor Haeloni's smile was strained. "We contacted you as soon as we had permission."

Treva stiffened. "Permission?"

"Sorry, I've said too much." Doctor Haeloni turned to go.

Treva thought about following him and forcing him to answered his questions but his need to see his mother overrode his desire to find out what was going on. "Can I go in?"

Doctor Haeloni was already walking away. "Of course, just don't expect too much."

It was only once he'd gone that Treva thought that he should have tried to explain that his mother had been kidnapped and put in stasis. It felt as if it had been years since he'd seen her. Biting down on his lip in an attempt to stay anchored in the present, he stepped through the door.

— — —

Anissa heard the door open. Panic made time stand still and she craned her head to see what new horror was coming.

Marco Steyn wins. He's finally driven me mad.

Treva stood in the doorway with a worried expression, except he couldn't be here. He couldn't be real despite that one strand of hair that always stuck up no matter how he had it cut or how many times he flattened it.

Illusion or not, the tears that had burned the back of her eyes earlier now fell in streaks down her face.

The imaginary Treva stepped toward her, his face blurred through her tears. "I'm so sorry, Mom."

It sounded like him. Then he reached her side and burrowed his head in her shoulder. He was too solid to be an illusion created by her damaged mind.

It really is Treva. He was warm, real, and here.

Forgetting about the restraints, she tried to hold him but couldn't move. Tears came faster. She didn't know if she was crying with relief that he was okay or frustration that she was trapped and unable to hold him.

Treva pulled away to stare at her hands. She blinked the worst of the tears away. He examined the restraints and it was in her mind to beg him not to, but she didn't get the words out fast enough. Warm fingers tugged her wrists free.

His eyes met hers. "What?"

"Stop." It was too late.

He froze but her arms were already free. The relief at being able to move her hands was overshadowed by fear of what they might do to him for helping her.

She swallowed. "I don't want them to hurt you."

Treva frowned. "Who?"

Doesn't he know where we are or who is watching?

There would be surveillance. Someone was always watching and reporting back to Marco. Anissa had to be careful. The stakes had just become much higher. Why else would they let her see Treva unless they planned to use him against her?

Anissa whispered, despite knowing that it wouldn't do any good against sophisticated surveillance. "You have to get out of here."

Treva's face cleared and instead of listening, he smiled as he sank into the chair next to the bed. "It's okay. You are in hospital." He patted her arm before looking down at the white sheet. "Dad's dead."

Her fuzzy brain tried to make sense of what he was telling her. *Marco's dead?*

Treva clearly believed what he was saying and was upset. He'd always had an annoying obsession with his father, which was her fault. She'd been so careful not to let him find out anything about the man. It was unfair the way Treva wanted Marco when she'd been the one making sacrifices to ensure he had everything he needed growing up, but that was an old hurt and wasn't important now. All that mattered was to make sure that Treva was safe. To do that, she had to understand what was going on.

"What happened?" Her voice was thick and it hurt to speak, probably because of all the screaming she'd done when she'd woken in this room with its green walls and grey blinds.

The last thing she'd seen as they held her down had been the faces of medics, and it had been the first thing she'd seen on waking. She hadn't known what they wanted before, and she didn't now.

Treva looked at her. "I'll tell you when you're better."

She grabbed his arm, saw him wince and loosened her grip. "Just tell me." He had to understand how important it was that she know everything. Neither of them had a chance unless they knew their enemy, and Treva didn't have all the facts. She'd made sure of that.

Treva must have seen how important it was to her. He took a deep breath before starting with Marco's betrayal, explaining how his father had arranged to have her kidnapped and put into stasis. It wasn't a surprise. Marco would never have understood her reasons for running away with their son all those years ago. He'd always chosen not to see the danger of his lifestyle and the threat his mother posed.

When Marco had found them, she should have grabbed Treva and left, but it hadn't been so easy. Treva was almost an adult and wanted to know his father, and she hadn't had the resources to disappear.

The rest of what Treva said was hard to follow. There was talk of stasis and being Gifted, clones and space stations hidden in subspace. She hoped to make sense of it all later.

She interrupted Treva. "Please, be careful. They are bound to be listening."

"You aren't with them anymore. You're in Glaendor City Hospital."

She was so tired, but frustration helped fight the overwhelming need to close her eyes. *Treva doesn't believe me. He thinks we are safe. I have to make him understand that it isn't just Marco but his entire family.*

When he opened his mouth to continue, she said, "What about them?" And pointed at the restraints, which dangled against the side of the bed.

Treva frowned. "Perhaps, they were trying to keep you safe." At her glare, he hurried to say, "I don't think Doctor Haeloni knows what happened to you. I get that you were scared when you woke up, but the staff here don't know about any of that." He dropped his voice, hand plucking at the sheets. "It's fine, Mom. All of Dad's businesses belong to me now."

Ice traveled down her spine. "No, Treva. You can't. That's not how it works." She had not fought for her entire adult life only to let the Steyn family have him.

Treva forced a smile. "Don't be silly. You'll never have to work again. Everything is going to be fine."

"Marco ran a criminal business for his family—"

"I know, but we don't have to do anything illegal."

He doesn't understand. How could he? Marco had never been the entire problem.

She fought to stay awake, but her eyes were getting heavier by the second. *Drugs,* her mind screamed. Even knowing that, she would lose the battle.

"Treva, you have to listen." Were her words slurred? "It isn't your father's business; it belongs to his family. They're not all dead, are they? I can't stay awake any longer, but you have to listen." She knew she sounded weak, but Treva had leaned forward. "We need to get out of here." Through half-lidded eyes, she saw doubt on his face. "You have to know what I'm telling you is true."

Treva glanced at the door. "How? I mean, you can hardly keep your eyes open. How are we going to get out and where will we go?"

Thank the stars. He was thinking in the right direction. Anissa was more comfortable with her eyes closed. She let them stay shut this time. *I can talk without looking.* She reached for his hand and felt a reassuring squeeze.

"Not now, but promise me. You will start preparing for when I get out of the hospital…" The words ran together. She knew what she wanted to say but nothing was coming out right.

Anissa felt warm lips on her forehead. Her boy, kissing her goodbye. She drifted off while hoping that he stayed safe.

CHAPTER 9

KALI SIPPED COFFEE, thinking about how much had changed in the short span of time. It was like being on a runaway starship.

Since there was no peace on the hastily set up TSS base on Fureron, she'd walked a short distance to a local coffee shop. The weather was grey but mild, so she'd sat at one of the few of tables outside before realizing that she might as well stayed on base with the large number of Militia soldiers coming and going. Too many eyes looked her way. *I'm becoming paranoid.*

Andy emerged from the crowd. "Do you mind if I join you?"

Kali sighed, cradling her cup in both hands. "I can't stop you."

"I'll take that as a grumpy 'yes'." Andy pulled over a chair from an empty table. "You know it's not my fault, don't you?"

She stared at him, determined not to let him off too easily, even though she knew she was being unfair. After all, Andy didn't have any choice, in the same way as she hadn't had any choice to report Mika.

Eventually, she sighed, unable to let him think that she was angry with him when it was the situation that she hated. "I know, but better to be annoyed with you rather than have to look at the part I played in Mika being arrested."

"Yes, but you're TSS through and through. I'm quite proud of that fact."

Her chest filled with something that felt like emotion. "The truth is that I don't know what to do. My head is messed up, and I'd give anything for a few minutes break."

Andy leaned into her space. "I completely understand why you did it, but opening yourself to Mika was incredibly dangerous." He grabbed a glass, pouring some water from a bottle on the table. "My personal view is that you should do what it takes to reverse the process." Kali wanted to argue, to explain that she didn't know how. "But professionally, we need your combined abilities."

Kali stared at him. "You want to use our combined ability?"

"Your bond will strengthen over time and," he hesitated, "Mika is not a good man."

Everything in her rebelled at the statement. "Why does everyone seem to forget that he was a defenseless child when Tregaren first invaded his mind?" She pressed her lips together not wanting to say something she would regret.

Andy watched her for a long moment, eyes cool and assessing. "What about now that Tregaren is dead?"

She looked down, unable to lie to him no matter how much she wanted to, finally admitting, "He could go either way."

"You should have separated automatically." She felt his eyes still on her but refused to meet them as he said, "How do you really feel about Mika?"

Kali's impulse was to dismiss the question, but she could see that Andy had a theory and wanted to know what it was. So, she said the first thing that came into her head, "I can't live without him." She stopped, unable to believe she'd said that aloud, never mind to Andy.

He nodded, not looking surprised. "What do you know about bonding?"

"That it's something that happens to other people." She glanced around to make sure nobody was listening. "Or it doesn't exist at all."

"Oh, it exists alright. It's a deep, telepathic link that can happen at first-sight. For others, it takes time to develop and requires an intentional commitment."

"There's nothing intentional about this, let me tell you." Even as she said it, she wasn't sure it was true.

"Perhaps not, but you and Mika must be well matched, which complicates things."

"You think?" She didn't bother to keep the sarcasm from her voice.

Kali took a deep breath because losing her temper with Andy was not an option when he knew her too well.

A group of TSS Militia walked past. When they drew level with their table, they stared at her as if she was a rare, exotic species. Surely, they'd seen enough Agents in their training to be used to her bioluminescent eyes. It went against everything in her to wear contact lenses or shaded glasses when she didn't have to, but next time she would just to get some privacy. Then, she noticed that they didn't look at Andy despite his exposed eyes.

"Why aren't they staring at you in the same way?"

He glanced up from his handheld and grinned as if their earlier serious conversation had never happened. "You really don't know?"

She scowled, getting annoyed again. "I wouldn't ask if I did."

He paused, obviously enjoying himself. "Because I'm not the one who casually held up one of the largest TSS buildings while working to save every single casualty from the rubble. It has led to some curiosity. I'm surprised that you haven't received any marriage proposals yet."

"Oh, please tell me, you are joking."

He tapped his handheld. "The media have only just

worked out who you are." He transferred an article from one of the Sensationals tabloids to her device.

She opened it to find a blurry image of her on Antaris. "Oh, no." This was the last thing she needed.

She was still reading the article when Andy shot to his feet, sending his chair flying across the tiles. "SPEAR has announced a new target." He was already running back toward the base.

Kali was after him before she'd processed the meaning of his words. "Where? And why would they?" She matched his stride as he negotiated base security, heading for the ships. "I mean, we expected another assault, but why announce it?"

"Mika, hurry, there's another attack. Meet me at the Sepiantia.*"*

There was a brief pause. *"On my way."*

"To taunt us, while causing as much disruption as possible." Andy shouted orders before saying, "It's the transit hub in the Kaldern System."

"How long does the warning give us?"

"Three hours."

She froze—it would take them that long to reach the hub. "They know TSS resources in that area are already fully subscribed and that it will take us that long to make it from here."

"The timing is unlikely to be a coincidence. They want us helpless to save anyone."

"We'll be there." She turned towards the *Sepiantia.*

She used her handheld to check the location. Two hours and forty-five minutes to the Kaldern System. Perhaps the extra fifteen minutes was to give them time to sacrifice themselves in any blast.

Part of her couldn't help thinking it was a genius place to attack. The planet of Kaldern had been taken over by Bakzen telepathic influence within the population's living memory, and resentment toward the TSS continued to the current day.

"Kali!" Andy shouted.

Oh, no. Kali knew he wasn't keen on them taking the *Sepiantia* alone. *He hasn't changed his mind, has he?* She could see Mika in the distance, almost at the *Sepiantia*.

"I have to be here to coordinate our defense. Be careful."

She nodded, relieved. Her mind was trying to work out what to expect when they reached their destination. Now she ran to the *Sepiantia*, knowing Mika would meet her on the ship. Indeed, she sensed him on the flight deck as soon as she arrived. No doubt he was going through pre-flight checks.

After climbing through the hatch, she closed and secured it before negotiating the inner door. It was as she was slammed the internal locking mechanism into place that it occurred to her that there was only the two of them on the *Sepiantia*. Mika might want to run. Even Herja hadn't kept the *Sepiantia* because the ship was too distinctive. Plus, she would have been stuck with the band and they were high-maintenance, which was enough to give anyone second thoughts.

Kali paused, one hand remaining on the door. *"Mika, are you okay?"*

He didn't respond at first. The floor sucked at her feet, holding her in place. It always took a minute for her brain to adjust to the environment on board the *Sepiantia*.

"I'm fine."

"It's just..." She didn't know how to ask without insulting him.

"I've thought about running. But we won't."

Her heart picked up speed. She should have known that he'd guess what she was thinking.

"People would die and..."

She waited, wanting to know what could be so important as to risk imprisonment?

"You love the TSS too much," he said.

Silence, while she considered his response. *"We're going to the transit hub in the Kaldern System."*

Kali walked into the heart of the ship. Had Mika just put her first? Something had changed, but she couldn't think about it now.

The colors and patterns on the psychedelic walls transformed as she moved. In the next second, she felt the dampening effect on her abilities, which meant they'd already entered subspace.

"Hello, *Sepiantia*."

Mika had changed the name of the ship's onboard computer from the standard CACI. It wouldn't surprise her to discover that he thought of the ship as sentient.

"Welcome, Agent Wietris. Please enjoy the journey."

Kali barely registered the inappropriate comment as she was already thinking about what they might find when they arrived at Kaldern. The door automatically slid open, and she stepped onto the flight deck. Mika turned and she felt an unexpected jolt of connection. *That bomaxed link!*

"There's no point worrying that the attack will start before we arrive. There's nothing we can do about it while we're in transit."

He was right. She could make better use of her time. Mika didn't need help flying, and they wouldn't receive any communication while in subspace. She checked the viewscreen: one hour forty-five minutes until arrival. It should take longer than that.

Mika saw her puzzled expression. "We made good time getting away and entered subspace quickly."

Kali nodded and shared everything she knew about the mission. They didn't talk about their connection, and she wondered if a permanent bond was inevitable.

She stared out the front viewport. "They might not stick to the deadline, but if they do and we're early, we risk being caught up in the blast."

"It might not be a bomb this time?"

"We won't know anything until we leave subspace. One thing is certain, there will be destruction and loss of life. SPEAR wants the publicity."

Mika nodded from the middle of a chair that looked like a giant blob of goo. "I agree. The larger and more devastating the attack, the quicker they achieve their goal."

"They hold the advantage. We are forced to react to whatever they have chosen to do." Kali sat on the nearest chair, sinking as it took her weight. "While we can't prepare for everything, we'd better keep an open mind and put on those protective suits." She pressed the leaver that made the chair release her and stood.

Andy had supplied the same multi-hazard resistant protective suits that they'd worn previously. The first ones he'd given her had been neon green, but Kali had requested an exchange for black. While it made sense to be visible in a disaster zone, they were going into hostile territory where it presenting a luminous target to the enemy might be dangerous.

Mika scowled. "They're resistant to heat, cold and microbes but so are our flight suits."

Kali liked hers as it was supple and didn't impeded movement. "They're a lot lighter than an EVA suit."

Since there was no point in wasting time going to somewhere private, Mika stripped off to get into the suit she handed him.

Kali had never noticed how much his body resembled that of a dancer. Layers of lean muscle made each movement precise and controlled. She leaned toward him, trying to identify the smell that came from him. It was like old wood and—

She pulled back, finally noticing the amusement on Mika's face. There was that whole bond thing that made it difficult to hide her inner world, but there was no need to broadcast her feelings. She cleared her throat and banished all unprofessional thoughts, determined not to give into her biological drive. Kali hurried into her suit. She had no idea whether Mika peeked or not since she dared not look at him and blocked anything he might be broadcasting.

The rest of the journey sped by before they exited

subspace close to the Kaldern System. The black of space replaced ribbons of blue-green, and a sprawling space station filled the front viewport.

Kali only half-heard the comm unit chime as she tried to detect anything unusual about the hub. It appeared whole and functioning from this distance.

Andy's voice filled the flight deck. "Good, you're there already. Do not approach." There was a pause before he added, "We've identified a large device in a storage area. There may be others, possibly rigged to go off at the same time."

Kali's eyes met Mika's as their worst fear was realized. Thousands of lives were at risk. In which case, Andy's orders made complete sense, but he couldn't feel the vast number of vibrant minds on the station like they could.

"How big?" She asked because it felt the right thing to say, not because she wanted hard numbers.

Mika interrupted, "If we go closer, there might be something we can do."

Andy's response was sharp. "No." His voice softened. "I know it's hard, but sacrificing your lives won't help anyone."

They couldn't just hang out here, waiting for a bomb to snuff out all those minds. *Think! Stop panicking and think.*

"There are things we can do." Mika sounded as controlled as Andy, except where Andy's calm was forced, Kali sensed that Mika's emotions were entirely under control. Unlike her, he'd immediately shut away any feeling and was utterly focused on the task. Kali wondered whether the calm was a result of what he had been through—whether he'd trained his mind to deal in situations where there was more than it could cope with. She pushed the thought away, not wanting to think about the cause of Mika's pain right now. She didn't want Tregaren in her head when she needed to concentrate.

Mika was still talking and at first, his words washed over her. "If we get closer and you directed us to the exact position of the bomb," she tuned in to what he was suggesting, "we might be able to contain the force of the explosion."

Is that possible? Perhaps together, they could build a barrier that was strong enough to contain the force of the blast. It would depend on the size of the explosion, and they couldn't know their limits until they tested them. *It's risky.*

"That's why they warned us." Kali suddenly understood. "There isn't enough time to evacuate even a fraction of those people."

"We're trying," Andy sounded tired. "But the warning went out to the media at the same time. You can imagine the chaos and panic down there."

Kali stared at the floor without seeing anything as the enormity of what SPEAR had done sank in. It was as much about the fear they could generate as slaughtering large numbers. People trapped on the hub would know what was happening. They would cry out to their loved ones and pass on last messages, which would be shown across the system for weeks.

"Let's try it." She looked up to see Andy watching her through the viewscreen, and Mika nodding to her left.

"It's too dangerous..." Andy trailed off and then said, "Do you think you could do it?"

"Yes," Mika and Kali said at the same time.

"I must be as mad as you two because I'm tempted to give you a chance." Andy muttered, "Okay. I'll send you the precise location in three minutes." He disappeared, but neither Mika nor Kali made any attempt to end the link.

Kali didn't need to ask if Mika was sure as she met his eyes. "This is the most dangerous thing we've ever done. Nobody would blame us for changing our minds."

Mika shook his head slowly. "Diving out of an airlock into space with a god-like maniac bent on killing you still wins hands down."

Kali laughed. She couldn't help it, because he was right. *This should be easy in comparison.*

Andy reappeared. "Okay, I'm referring us all for psych

evaluations if this works and you survive. Just me, if you don't." He looked down at something, and then a holographic map sprang up next to his face. "This is a detailed map of the area under threat."

A red line circled part of the central station. Of course, it would be in the middle where it would cause maximum damage. Kali had hoped there would be another way but seeing the cold hard facts, she realized that there was only one option.

"We have to go down there," Mika's voice was emotionless. "We need to be close enough to act with precision."

Kali used her finger to draw a second rough circle inside the first. "The initial pressure wave will cause most of the damage. When the bomb explodes, one of us needs to be there to contain it." She looked at Mika. "The other needs to be outside the blast area to create a shield around the one inside to protect *her* and make sure she lives long enough to do the job."

Mika frowned. "I never agreed that it would be you."

"It has to be."

"Why?"

"You don't work for the TSS."

Andy interrupted their staring contest. "I'm going to leave the details to you two because I can't ask either of you to do this."

"The easiest way for me to get into position," Kali said, pointing at the edge of the station, "is to run the two hundred meters from the docking point." When no argument came from Andy or Mika and with the clock counting down, she continued. "Once the area is clear, and Mika has a shield around me," She tapped the inner circle, "I'll detonate the bomb early. If I can release the energy gradually, everything will be fine. Understood?"

Andy and Mika stared at her as if she was crazy and she couldn't argue with them.

CHAPTER 10

MIKA DOCKED THE *Sepiantia* without incident, thankful that Andy had smoothed their way. Nobody questioned their sanity for arriving when everyone else was fleeing. They secured the ship to the station in record time. Most of the personnel were probably trying to calm the hundreds of passengers and crew still trapped on the station.

Mika stood beside Kali at the exit hatch of the *Sepiantia*, waiting for the door to release. He'd left his helmet off, planning to put it on at the last minute in case they needed to deal with any officials. He was well aware that they couldn't allow anything to slow them down. From the moment the *Sepiantia* attached to the docking clamp, their greatest risk was the bomb detonating before they were ready.

"We've got this," Mika told Kali.

He could see through the helmet of her suit that she was pale and yet, her expression was determined, not that he expected anything different from Kali.

"Mika, I don't want you to stay when the bomb goes off."

"What? I'm supplying the shield."

"You know what I mean."

He did, but he had no intention of leaving so that he wouldn't experience her death. The way he felt, he didn't know what he'd do if anything happened to her.

"I need you to agree."

"Okay, I agree."

Kali stared at him for a long moment before she must have decided that she was wasting her time. She was right. He wouldn't leave, no matter what she said.

The hatch door swung open to reveal an enormous Enforcer. He blocked their exit.

Mika felt the buzz of telekinesis as Kali duck around one side. She pounded down the gangway before either of them could move.

The man turned. "Wait. I need—"

Mika took advantage of the Enforcer's unsteady footing, stepping through the larger gap and hurrying after Kali for a couple of paces. He stopped. From his elevated position on the walkway, Mika could see that Kali wasn't going to get very far, very fast.

If he was to put his helmet on, Mika could bring up an image of the station's map against his visor, but he didn't need to, he held a perfect image in his mind's eye. As the point farthest away from the bomb, they had docked where the entire station was headed. The volume of people moving in their direction blocked Kali's route, and they were running out of time.

The Enforcer was talking, but Mika didn't hear as he used his telekinesis to move people out of Kali's path. She must have been shouting at them at the same time because some attempted to scramble out of the way.

Kali would never have thought to use her telekinesis to move civilians but if they didn't make way, everyone was dead. If the TSS didn't like it, they could rage at him later if anybody survived.

Mika started to follow Kali. The Enforcer remained glued to his side.

Mika glanced at him. "You don't want to go where I'm going."

"I spotted your ship and want to know who you are and

what you're doing. We need every vessel for the evacuation," the man said.

Mika couldn't quite believe his stubbornness. "We're TSS," which was almost true, "and we're going to deal with that bomb. Don't touch that ship."

When the man didn't move, Mika had him speak to Andy. He moved off grumbling, leaving Mika alone. *Just the way I like it.*

The lie was automatic, something he'd told himself often since his mother's disappearance. Except, this time, Mika struggled to believe it. Kali could not die, but if he was going to save her, he had to get into position.

What if the bomb goes off before we're ready? Then we both die, and I won't know life without her. Not a bad result.

Mika had less trouble getting through the crowd than Kali; perhaps people understood what was expected now, or maybe they sensed that nothing was going to stop him from getting where he needed to be.

If they were too slow getting out of his way, he used telekinesis to move them. There were screams and gasps, but Mika ignored them. Wrapped in his suit and knowing precisely where the threat was, he ploughed through with a singlemindedness the band had never noticed that he possessed. It took minutes to get to the point where the crowd thinned to stragglers, and then he could run.

Ahead, a small girl stood crying in the middle of the corridor while people flowed around either side of her, either not registering that she was alone or not caring. Instead of passing her by, Mika swept her up, carrying her toward danger.

She stopped crying, either shocked, frightened, or grateful. He didn't know why he hadn't left her to fend for herself when his priority was to get to Kali. Without him to form a shield, she would become one of SPEAR's thousands of victims.

An Enforcer, smaller than the one who had been waiting when they'd arrived, ushered stragglers toward him. The corridor was wide enough that he was able to dodge these easily.

As he got nearer, he saw that the Enforcer was female and her eyes were on him, no doubt assessing whether he posed a threat. His outfit made him stand out as either military or a terrorist. Before she could point a weapon at him or demand an answer, Mika dumped the toddler in her arms and ran past.

"Hey!" she shouted.

Mika didn't slow, unconcerned that she might shoot him with the knot of anxiety was growing in the pit of his stomach. *Is Kali ready and waiting for me?* SPEAR might see her and detonate the bomb. Out of time, the bomb could go off as planned, and he wouldn't be there.

He quickly left the Enforcer far behind. The corridor was silent, except for Mika's footsteps echoing off the walls. Two figures stood by double doors at the far end. Not Kali, he knew without needing to reach out with his mind. Still in a flat out run, Mika jammed the helmet on his head. Information immediately scrolled across the visor, telling him that his target, a storage area, was beyond the doors.

As he got near, one of the figures, who was wearing a station uniform, pointed. Mika scanned his mind to check that he wasn't a terrorist. Rather than the expected healthy dose of fear, his mind was full of curiosity. Mika ignored him, only caring about getting to Kali.

Bursting through the double doors, Mika found himself in a large chamber. He stood on a wide ledge that ran around the outside of a storage pit, five meters below. A variety of different sized containers were stacked on top of one another. The smell of sawdust was overpowering despite a suspended ventilation system.

His brain, which was usually so logical in the face of stress, wasn't working so well. The danger to Kali must have overloaded his neurons. Their whole plan suddenly seemed like a terrible idea. Mika didn't care about any of these people, but Kali did. She was so much better than him, which was why she could not die.

They should've stayed on the *Sepiantia* and arrived at the station when it was all over and the only risk came from collapsing structures, secondary to the blast. They could have helped evacuate the survivors, rather than chance being caught in the primary explosion.

Mika saw a lone figure in the vast chamber—*Kali!*

We can do this, he'd said to her earlier but now, he had to believe it. They would only have one chance, and Kali needed him to get this right. Movement made him turn his head sharply to the left where he made out a figure, climbing between the crates near to where his visor told him the bomb was located.

"I'm waiting for him to get out of the way." Kali's voice in his head startled him.

Mika barely resisted the urge to rip the figure clear of the area. While the TSS might accept such an action as a necessity under the current circumstances, he knew without asking that Kali wouldn't. Mika knew precisely where her line lay.

The figure was past Kali and moving up the ramp to Mika. Without pausing, he was through the doors and running away.

Mika stepped to the edge, making sure he kept a fix on Kali. The plan included her detonating the bomb using telekinesis. As far as he knew, nobody had done anything like this before and they had no idea whether it would work.

It was pointless, but he had to ask, *"Are you sure you can contain the blast?"*

"No," she replied. *"Are you ready?"*

Mika pushed down his panic just enough to concentrate. He began to construct a shield around her, far enough away that it had some give in it. Inside, he did what he could to maintain enough air to cushion her, while questioning whether his understanding of physics was sound.

Not happy with the result, Mika asked, *"Should I start again?"*

Kali's flash of impatience woke him to the danger. The timer on his visor counted down to their best guess of the detonation time from the information SPEAR had provided the media. Thirty seconds to go! It could be sooner.

"I'm ready," he lied.

Twenty-four, twenty-three, twenty-two...

Mika put everything he had into the shield and braced himself, thinking how it was like learning to fly by jumping off a building.

Nineteen, eighteen...

In the next heartbeat, searing heat hit. Flames licked up the invisible barrier around Kali with the closest a meter from his face.

Mika's brain screamed to get as far away, as fast as possible, but he didn't. One lapse in concentration would kill them both and so, he didn't move.

"Kali, can you breathe? Are you okay?"

There was no answer. Mika felt hundreds of minds flash red in panic, shattering with the onset of agony. They flickered out all at once.

CHAPTER 11

TREVA SAT ON his bed in the apartment and thought about calling Idra. Would she still be on the *Hyperion?* He'd never discovered where the pirates lived. It wasn't as if he hadn't asked but nobody ever gave him a straight answer.

It might be better to call her later. He didn't want to have to end their conversation because the band had finally arrived.

He went to check the front door. Everything was quiet and yet the hairs on the back of his neck rose. He turned in a full circle but nothing was out of place. After the first night, when he'd found Ava in the apartment, whenever he'd been out, he always checked to make sure nobody was hiding in one of the rooms.

The band was late. It was possible they'd had second thoughts and gone to a hotel. Glaendor City had loads to choose from, although most were pricy. He rubbed his eyes, trying not to feel disappointed.

Treva didn't care that he'd only met the band for a short period, because on Red Ghost, they'd been loud and funny. He wasn't sure what his mother would think of Honk, but that felt like a small problem.

Treva made his way to the kitchen where he warmed up a spicy potato snack and slumped into a chair to eat. He sighed. It had taken ages to clean up his mess, but it hadn't been a waste since his mother was about to be discharged. He'd have to tell her the band wasn't staying, but since he hadn't exactly warned her what to expect, it might be for the best.

The comm unit chimed. "Hello."

"It's Security, Mr. Steyn." *There's that name again.* "We have some people here who claim you invited them."

Treva pushed down the surge of irritation; the man was just doing his job. "I told you to expect them. They are guests."

Treva hated having anything to do with the new security people. He hadn't minded the ones that guarded the apartment when his father was alive but these were something to do with Avon Security, like the guard at the Blue Pixie that had refused to let him into the building.

"The problem is," there was a pause as if he was about to deliver bad news, "I didn't think you were allowed guests."

Treva froze when too many responses clambered to get out all at once—*says who? It's* my *apartment. I'll say who comes and goes. Who do you think you are to tell me that I can't have guests?*

"They are here at my invitation," he said, managing to sound calmer than he felt.

"Right. I'm sorry, sir, but I'll have to authorize it."

"With whom?"

The Security Guard cleared his throat. "You can probably tell that I'm new. Forget I said anything." He ended the call.

Treva went cold as he stared at the comm unit, trying to make sense of the conversation. One thing was certain, whoever had order security not to allow guests had to be someone important. What did he do? Accept what was happening because he was too scared, or fight it?

Treva headed to the door. This had been his father's apartment; now it was his. They kept calling him 'Mr. Steyn', so nobody should need reminding. He hadn't reached the end of the long corridor before the house computer—Zoro—announced that he had a visitor. He was so annoyed that he didn't check before authorizing the door to open.

Three unruly individuals and their bags swept inside, arguing and laughing. Treva had never been so grateful to have the quiet so thoroughly destroyed.

He remembered the woman with blue hair the best—Vaira. He'd had to look their names up. The way she moved made him want to stare at her for hours, with those long limbs, she shouldn't be so graceful.

"What happened to your eyes?" He blurted out. "They've gone hazel."

"Blue is for onstage." She battered her eyelashes. "You don't like brown?"

He felt his face flush. "They're beautiful."

Honk laughed. "Quit it, Vaira. Let's not get thrown out before we've unpacked."

Treva's eyes widened. "I wouldn't do that." They didn't know how glad he was to see them.

"Honk." The man held out a hand in an unconventional greeting.

Treva shook it. "I remember." It occurred to him that Honk might not. "Sorry, it's Treva."

Honk nodded at him. "Didn't think we'd get past security, but the guy called someone after he spoke to you. What was that about?"

Treva could only shake his head since he didn't understand it either. "I'll show you around. The kitchen's this way. Are you hungry? I'm always hungry after traveling." Treva didn't know why he was rambling. Two days alone and he forgot how to speak to people.

"Have you got anything to drink?" Honk asked, peering down the corridor as if having trouble seeing.

Treva frowned, knowing that Honk meant alcohol but he hadn't thought about it. "I don't know."

"I'm Caryanne," the other woman said, "and don't

worry about him. Honk is always off his head. The rest of us can manage without a drink for a couple of days."

Wow, a couple of days!

"There's always the Blue Pixie."

Honk swung to face him. "That sounds like a club."

"It is... it was my father's place. They have alcohol there." *What a stupid thing to say. Of course, they'd have alcohol.*

"Do they have live bands?" Caryanne asked.

Before he could answer, her eyes lost their focus, and she turned away.

"Caryanne can be a bit odd," Vaira said, nudging his arm and whispering, "doesn't remember much, but she's harmless."

"I heard that," Caryanne said without any heat in her voice.

Conscious they were still in the hallway, Treva led the way to the kitchen, pointing out the other rooms and where they could sleep. They each claimed a bed like children and dumped their luggage.

"Nice place." Honk grinned. "You should see some of the dives we've stayed in."

"Thank you for inviting us," Vaira said, "Let's look at the kitchen."

"Afterward, can you direct us to the Blue Pixie?" Honk asked with a grin.

Treva cleared his throat, embarrassed but wanting to be honest. "I had a few problems getting into the club last time."

"We'll sort that out," Honk said with such confidence that Treva wondered if he meant by using violence. Then, he added, "The ladies can be very persuasive when they want to be."

Treva laughed in relief. If the club was busy, he might get the chance to check out that forbidden door in the back room. Honk, Vaira, and Caryanne were likely to create a good distraction. While exploring the club wasn't a priority, he couldn't get over the feeling that he needed to find out what was going on before he'd be able to get back to a normal life.

Tonight, he was just happy to be around people who weren't anything to do with his father. He would sleep better with them in the house. Besides, if his mother had her way, this would only be their apartment until she was fit enough to travel. He thought about trying to explain all of that to them but didn't know where to start. Besides, they'd only just met, and that seemed like a pretty deep conversation to have with new acquaintances.

He frowned, realizing that the apartment didn't feel very secure. His mother's paranoia must be rubbing off on him. Though there might be some surveillance in the apartment, who would care what he did? But, his mother had been right about his father. Did that mean that she was right about the danger? Treva just hoped it wasn't too late to get away.

—   —   —

Herja used every curse word she could think of, and when she started to make them up, decided it was time to do something constructive. So, Vaughn had somehow tracked them, despite all their precautions. For now, it didn't matter how he'd managed it.

Gosta was staring at his handheld as if someone was going to call and tell him it was a bad dream. They had to act to save their people. There were only a few thousand left and most were on the rotting city-ship.

Herja slapped Gosta across the back of the head. "Move. We need to get to the flight deck." She set off at a jog, cursing again because everything was so far apart on *Storm's Breath*. She put a call through to Idra. "Take Kinder and get the *Hyperion* out of range now."

The girl's face was pale. It wasn't surprising since Idra knew firsthand how cruel the universe could be, and her entire family, including a very new baby-brother, clung to existence on the floating hunk of metal.

Herja forced down the empathy that threatened to derail her plans. "Before you ask, there's no time for goodbyes. Go, and that's an order." Herja's tone was uncompromising. "I have to stay to *negotiate*," she spat the last word out, "but don't give up yet."

Herja ended the call. She couldn't leave and they needed the *Hyperion* somewhere safe. A vague plan started to show itself but she didn't have all the details yet. One thing was certain; she would show Vaughn that they were not easy prey.

People in the corridor parted to let them through. Everyone suddenly seeming to need to be somewhere. Didn't they know that nowhere was safe? *Storm's Breath* couldn't survive a sustained attack and nobody would rescue them.

"We don't even have weapons," Gosta said from a few paces behind, "and, our shields are rubbish."

She wanted to laugh at how everyone panicked to the point where they couldn't think. It was as if they didn't live from crisis to crisis all the time. *This is why I'm a great leader. I'm no good with the little stuff, but I can deal with a threat to our survival.*

"That's right, Gosta. No weapons, except for a foking entity that can wipe out vast numbers!"

His footsteps faulted. "That's right. We have Pesta."

"Yes, and can you remember what Mac told us. Pesta is a threat to anyone within a large radius, and space is no barrier to the disease." She grimaced; the concept was unnatural. "I need you to bring Mac and Pesta to the flight deck."

"Yes, Captain."

"Gosta," she called as he veered off. She waited until he had turned before saying, "Time will be short. Fill Mac in on the situation."

He nodded before disappearing down a branch tunnel. A few people stared after him, probably wondering why he wasn't going to the flight deck. Herja ignored anyone looking for reassurance. She had none to give and was too busy scrolling through the options in her head.

They couldn't outrun this threat. No, their only chance was through a semblance of negotiation, and while it wasn't her strong point, she'd had plenty of practice over the years. For now, she ignored the knowledge that Vaughn wanted them dead. If she could get him to agree to a deal, they might yet survive.

The flight deck had been impressive when it was first built and housed state-of-the-art equipment. While it was still vast, with everything on a larger scale than the *Hyperion*, it was unfortunate that the instruments were either out of date or broken.

A couple of teenage pilots checked readings, attempting to prepare the ship for movement. While fighting was impossible, she couldn't help wondering if the city-ship would shake itself to pieces in flight. Not that they had anywhere to go. It had taken them weeks to find this hiding place, and that was before she had put them on the TSS radar.

On reaching the central console, Herja took a deep breath and activated the viewscreen. She closed her eyes so as not to get annoyed about the length of time it took to fire up. She was about to initiate contact with Vaughn when an alarm sounded. The *Vector* had locked weapons on them. Vaughn would target the flight deck.

"Just foking great," she muttered. To the pilots, she said, "You, get out now." It probably wouldn't make any difference if they were on the flight deck or elsewhere when the ship came under attack, but irrational or not, Herja didn't want anyone nearby when she made Vaughn angry enough to react. Besides, they were too young and inexperienced. If she was going to fly *Storm's Breath*, she needed Kinder or Gosta.

On their way out, one of the pilots looked back, probably to check if she was serious. Herja ignored the woman until her colleague tugged her away.

Something hit the side of the ship, throwing Herja backward. At the same time, the comm connected. With nothing to break her fall, Herja landed hard on the metal decking. In danger of skidding the length of the floor, she rolled and scrabbled to her feet. Thankfully, her brain hadn't time to register the pain of the impact.

She steadied herself on the edge of the console with both hands and spoke calmly into the comm unit as if her coccyx wasn't throbbing, "Hello Captain Vaughn. *Storm's Breath* would like to negotiate."

At first, there was only the sound of static, and Herja gripped the console tighter. Vaughn had to want Pesta, else they were all dead.

Vaughn's hated face appeared in the viewscreen, smiling from where he stood on the flight deck of the *Vector*. When he saw her, his smile widened as if he already had what he wanted.

Outwardly, Herja stayed calm, while her mind raced to come up with a way out of the situation that didn't involve giving over Mac and Pesta. She rejected most ideas immediately as impractical. Vaughn had to have chased them across the sector for a chance to retrieve what he'd lost.

"So, this is where you've been hiding." If Vaughn's smile got any broader, the top of his head was going to fall off. "A nest of pirates." He tutted. "I might get a medal if I destroy you."

Herja dismissed the idea of appealing for the babies and children on board. Truly out of options, there was only one thing left to do so, she met his soulless eyes. "Do you want Pesta or not?" She didn't have much patience, which was sometimes a weakness. "Because I was thinking of killing it and taking you down with us. After all, I don't have anything to lose."

Vaughn leaned forward as if to study her face.

Desperation gave weight to her expression. Stars,

killing them all had been the first unsavory option that had come to mind.

Vaughn might have believed her because he said, "We won't attack, if you give us Pesta and its handler."

It hadn't been long ago that Treva had announced to Vaughn that Marco Steyn was his father before trading himself for the lives of the *Hyperion's* crew. Vaughn had then taken Treva while planning to kill everyone on board the *Hyperion. Does he think I've forgotten?*

She forced laughter. "Captain Vaughn, you are not a man of your word. Why would I trust you?"

"You have no choice."

"There are always choices. I've given you one."

He shifted in his seat, perhaps sensing that the conversation was going nowhere. "There's no way to guarantee that I won't attack."

"You have so little imagination." Herja didn't sit. There was too much tension in her body, but she forced her shoulders to soften a little. "You could start by powering down your weapons and allowing my people to get on with their day."

They stared at each other. Herja projected strength, even though all she had was a threat of suicide that would take down her enemy. She was vaguely aware of Gosta arriving on the flight deck with Mac and Pesta, but she didn't dare take her eyes from Vaughn. At least, Gosta had enough sense to keep the others out of sight.

Vaughn sighed. "Okay, consider it done but I want to see them."

Inside, she cheered. "I will arrange to have them brought up."

"You have thirty minutes."

She thought about arguing for longer but he wouldn't compromise and she didn't want to waste time when she had a plan. Thirty minutes might be enough. It had to be. She ended the call. *Now to deal with Mac and Pesta.*

CHAPTER 12

KALI GASPED AS hundreds of lives were extinguished at once. They'd failed, so why wasn't she dead?

Reason came back slowly. There had to have been more than one bomb—smaller devices that nobody found, until it was too late. SPEAR must have detonated them at the same time as the one she now contained.

Mika was safe. She felt him like a light at the other side of her shield but couldn't see him—*because my eyes are closed.* Her body was still there but she couldn't feel it. No, that wasn't right. Sensation *was* coming back and with it the strain of holding so much. Her mind had expanded beyond the shield and now held the force of the bomb.

Kali enfolded the bomb's energy, which had the potential of a nuclear explosion. It fought her containment, battering her shield in a relentless barrage. With a dawning horror, she realized that she was trapped and couldn't hang on for much longer.

"*Mika, can you hear me?*"

"*Thank the stars.*" She felt his relief.

Tears formed at the corner of her eyes, although she didn't know why it mattered so much, but she was glad not to be alone.

Mika tried to pull back a wave of emotion but some

reached her anyway. *"I thought for a moment that it was too much. I couldn't…"*

She'd thought that, too. Just for a second, when the wave of energy had first touched her. She hadn't known if she could hold it.

"What about now?" she shifted from foot to foot. *"You're tired, I feel it. I'm not sure we thought this through."*

His shield might be smaller but he held the same amount as her. She didn't understand how either of them had been successful. Surely, stopping a blast of this magnitude required more strength than they had combined. Although, now that she thought about it, Mika had never been tested. They didn't know the limit of his strength, and it was probably best not to dwell on it right now.

"Tell me what's happening." Andy's voice came through the audio in her suit.

Had he told her the comm system was there? She couldn't remember but found the interruption distracting when she was trying to think.

"We're fine."

He responded immediately. "Define 'fine'."

Kali couldn't. She'd stopped the energy expanding and was sort of stable, even if she couldn't hold it for long. But she had no idea what to do with it now that she held it. If she let go, it would travel on to destroy the station, and since that was what they were trying to prevent and they were standing on the station, that didn't feel like a good option.

"I'm in the middle of a bomb-blast," she found herself saying to Andy.

"Where's Mika?"

She finally opened her eyes to see Mika twenty meters away, appearing as though there was nothing between them. "He's close, holding a shield around me." She reached out with her fingertips and touched a solid wall. "The shield is about a meter from my face. I would have preferred more space."

Andy let out a breath. "Right, I'll have a word with him about that," he spoke slowly, "for next time." There was a pause. "Mika, can you hear us?"

"Yes."

Kali grimaced at Mika's abrupt response. He hadn't forgotten that Andy had arrested him, no matter what he said.

"Actually, I've changed my mind. Neither of you are doing this ever again. Whatever you've done." Andy's voice sounded strained. "It shouldn't even be possible."

At the periphery of her awareness, Kali felt panicked minds. She was conscious of the structure of the station. Most remained solid but there were weak spots where the secondary blasts must have detonated. People tackled two blazes. She couldn't help them while contained by her own shield. So many would die if she didn't find a way to disperse this energy.

"Can you channel the blast anywhere?" Mika asked, moving closer.

"I'd need help to move it." She laughed nervously. *"It would be a shame if it slipped out and killed us after we've gone to so much trouble."*

"Okay, but I am not letting go of the shield around you."

"I think it will be okay." She had no idea whether that was true but staying trapped for hours or days or... she couldn't hold it that long. Perspiration coated her forehead.

"We can't be sure what will happen. I'm not chancing it."

"There's a lot of it." Kali considered releasing the energy slowly. Anything to escape the relentless pressure. *"I can't hold it for much longer."*

"If I let my shield go, your organs will fry. I'm not doing it."

He was probably right but she couldn't stay here much longer. *"Mika, you are the only one who can help."*

"I think Wil Sietinen might have a chance."

"Go fetch him." She tried to lighten the mood but didn't

smile. *"Could we channel it into space?"*

"What are you two planning?" Andy's voice cut in. He had to have guessed they were using telepathy because there was no way he could sense it over the distance. "I know you're up to something."

Kali took a breath, not wanting to sound as desperate as she felt. "We're holding a lot of energy and are trying to work out how to get rid of it without causing further damage." She was proud that she sounded calm.

Mika was silent. He had to sense her desperation and probably didn't want to tell her that they'd never be able to force the energy into space. Even if they did, what would happen to it then? It wouldn't just disappear.

"Andy, give us a couple of minutes to work something out." If there was anything to work out.

"We need to try something," she said to Mika.

"Not unless it's safe."

"Mika, you're killing me."

"That's harsh."

She wanted to laugh and tell him that she hadn't meant it literally, but it was too much effort. *"How could we channel the blast into space?"*

"Too dangerous."

"Why?" Pounding had started at her temples, making it hard to concentrate. *"Are you afraid we'll hit a ship?"*

"No, more that it would punch a hole in the side of the station in the process, which we'd have no way to plug." He sounded normal but she felt the buzz of his anxiety. *"Everyone's been told to stay away from this area. I remember us being told the same thing. It's a shame we didn't listen."*

"I can't hold on much longer."

"Let your shield out a little to reduce the pressure."

If she did that, where would it end? Then, she had an idea. "Mika, can you let a little of the energy through your shield to me?"

"What are you going to do with it?"

"Vent it." When he stared at her as if she'd lost her mind, she said, *"Send it into subspace—create a spatial distortion around me."* She wasn't proficient at it the way that some Agents could 'stop time', as they called it, but she had gotten close enough to achieving the feat during training that she felt confident in her ability to generate a localized spatial distortion. The energy would want to follow the path of least resistance, so it should naturally flow into the distortion and leave her unharmed. Hypothetically.

Mika didn't acknowledge her request, but then every one of her hairs rose as the atmosphere inside her shield became charged.

This is crazy. She concentrated on controlling the energy, causing everything to tingle. In her mind's eye, she saw the spatial distortion forming around her—grazing the edge of subspace like a ship about the jump. This was more than she'd ever been able to achieve on her own, no doubt thanks to her enhanced abilities while linked with Mika.

Slowly, the energy from the blast began to flow into the spatial distortion. She wasn't sure exactly what was happening in the exchange, but it was the same principle as many Taran ships used for exhaust venting of the pion drives used for the sub-light propulsion.

"It's working. I feel okay."

Mika was silent as he allowed more energy through. The pressure dropped more than it should when she hadn't done anything.

"Mika?"

"If you can vent it, so can I."

She stared at him but couldn't make out his expression across the distance. He looked okay. The amount she'd taken was miniscule to the drop in pressure. Mika had to be directing the vast majority of the energy. How was he doing that?

It's working—that's all that matters. The pressure around her dropped and Kali felt all right—well, sort of all right. Her body vibrated but it didn't feel as if she was going to die. Her shield was shrinking and as it did, Mika followed it until they stood a meter apart.

Was he glowing? It might be an effect of the lights. His eyes were so bright that she couldn't see the amber flecks that she loved so much.

The energy had almost been completely vented. Though Kali was exhausted from the exertion, a thrill ran through her as she realized that they were going to make it out alive.

Mika said, *"Let go."*

"When you do."

"On my mark—three, two, one."

Kali released her shield and a second later so did Mika. She popped her helmet off and dropped it on the floor. "You cheated."

He grinned as he took off his own helmet. "I thought you would have anticipated that." He raised a hand to her face but didn't make contact. "You're glowing."

She gazed into his eyes. "So are you." While he wasn't *actually* glowing, there was a new brightness to him—though she couldn't be sure if it was only in her head. Heat radiated from him.

"You're too hot." She put a hand on his chest.

"It only happens when I'm with you," he breathed the words close to her ear.

She should laugh at the cheesy line and perhaps, she would have done if they hadn't just achieved the impossible. His chin reached her forehead where she felt the bite of stubble on her oversensitive skin. They fit well together.

It was his scent that muddied her brain as he lowered his head. His mouth found hers. She considered pushing him away but couldn't find the will. Then it was too late; her brain checked out.

CHAPTER 13

ANDREI STEYN SAT in a dark corner of the Blue Pixie, studying the people at the bar. It didn't matter if anyone saw, but the shadows suited him. Besides, it gave him a chance to covertly watch the club's routine. Since the Blue Pixie had belonged to Marco, Andrei had never paid it any attention, but that had changed with Marco's death.

So far, nothing had interested him. The staff were efficient, restocking the bars and accepting deliveries. Their thoughts were mundane, and despite one young man speculating about getting away early, there didn't appear much deception.

Andrei kept trying to work out what it meant that Mika Hendri, Tregaren's son, had rescued people on Antaris. *With that sort of power, he's working for the wrong side.* Andrei's sole loyalty was to the Steyn family, but Tregaren had understood him in a way nobody else had. If he got the opportunity, he would make Mika an offer that he couldn't refuse.

With that decision made, Andrei was thinking about returning to his hotel when four people entered the club. His lip curled on recognizing his nephew and he instinctively leaned back in the booth. Whoever was on the door had let them in without warning. He or she would not be providing security at the Blue Pixie after he had a word with Raffia, the head of Avon Security.

Unfortunately, Andrei's telepathy did not extend far enough to read the minds of the people with Treva.

Nash had assured him that Treva didn't have any friends in the city and so this must be the band who were staying with him.

Well, what a coincidence. He'd just been thinking about Mika Hendri when the band he managed walked into his bar. Andrei loved it when the universe lent a helping hand.

A pretty young woman broke off from the group and wandered across the polished floor with such a vacant expression that Andrei thought she must be under the influence of something. As soon as she was in range, he scanned her mind.

As a child, Andrei's mother had thrown him in their private pool. He couldn't remember the events leading up to the incident, but the shock of being submerged had stayed with him. Arms and legs whipped, he sucked in mouthfuls of foul-tasting liquid instead of air. He hadn't known which way was up, and it was likely he would have died if his mother hadn't had a rare moment of clarity and got help.

Thrashing about in this woman's mind brought back the memory. Something dark ate his thoughts. It happened so fast that he almost forgot who he was before he could pull himself out.

Andrei withdrew, shuddering at how he'd almost lost his identity. It was the closest he'd come to dying since the swimming pool when he'd been four years old.

The woman drifted across his line of vision, oblivious to his presence, or so he initially thought. She paused and glanced around. Tiny frown lines creased the middle of her forehead and she turned to wander back in the direction she had come.

Andrei saw that the group had disappeared while he'd been fighting for his memories. Treva must have taken them into the office.

Some impulse made him rise. "Excuse me," he said before she could go in search of her friends.

She turned with a smile. He'd thought she was pretty but when she faced him, he saw he'd been mistaken and she was actually stunning.

Andrei held out a hand, not in the traditional greeting but he was curious to see what she'd do. Her response would tell him something even if she refused to touch him.

She smiled and took his hand in a grip so soft that her hand almost slipped from his. "I'm Caryanne Westby."

Not highborn, then. Although, her eccentricity and the way she didn't focus on his face suggested otherwise. She clearly had no idea who he was. The vacancy in her eyes wasn't the sort of thing anyone could fake, and he knew from his experience in her head that any thought passing over the surface of that mind sunk without a trace.

"Do you know who I am?" he asked, wondering how he could use her particular talent.

She shook her head, frowning. "I don't think we've met before."

Andrei smiled. "I thought that you might have heard of me. I own the Steyn Corporation."

Her face cleared. "Oh, I don't remember people unless I've actually met them. There's something wrong with my brain." She let out a high-pitched giggle.

He knew that she wasn't nervous, but for some reason, she wanted him to believe she was. A defense mechanism, perhaps. Some women were so intimidated by the world that one way to cope was to appear non-threatening like a child.

"Call me, 'Commander'."

This time her laughter was genuine as if he'd told a joke. Normally, he'd use telepathy to find out what she was thinking, but he had to rely on mundane methods with her.

She sobered. "So, are you a Commander?"

He nodded slowly, watching to see if she could process

what he was saying.

"Okay, then." Without missing a beat, she smiled broadly. "I can't remember what I was doing when I wandered over here."

"Why haven't you sought medical treatment for your brain condition?"

She didn't take any offense. "Nobody is sure why it doesn't work." She leaned closer to whisper, "I think, it's because I don't want it to."

He thought a moment before asking, "Does that mean we'll have to start again next time we meet?"

She stared at him, and he had the sense that she was checking to see if he was serious. Andrei wasn't sure, and for the first time in a long time, he found that he liked this woman—brain-damaged or not.

"No, I remember some things. I always remember people once I've properly met them, or at least as much as anyone else. It's like I remember the emotion attached to the meeting and so I will know that you were nice to me. Repetition helps."

Andrei wanted to keep her. If for nothing else but to experiment on that black hole of a mind. It might lead to a breakthrough in his other research.

He was about to ask her to join him when Pyra appeared. Caryanne stepped out of the way as the little man bent toward Andrei in a move meant to convey privacy.

"I'm sorry to interrupt, Commander, but there's a call I think you are going to want to take."

For someone so clumsy, Pyra could be silent when he wanted. It was a shame he was too useful to get rid of, for now.

Caryanne looked around as if she had forgotten what she was doing and where she was.

How does she cope on her own?

"If you don't mind, I have things to do." Pyra had reminded him that he couldn't afford distractions today.

"Sorry, you look like a busy person." The emptiness had returned to her eyes and when he scanned the surface of her mind, making sure not to get sucked under, it was as empty as before.

From the direction of the bar, glass broke, followed by "whoops" and a man staggered toward them. It was one of Caryanne's companions.

"Hello, Honk. How long have you been drinking?" Caryanne didn't sound bothered.

At least Andrei knew where to find the lovely Caryanne. He wondered what she'd say if he told her that her friend was beneath her feet. Would she remember? That would be an interesting experiment when he had time.

— — —

When Treva had arrived with the band, it had felt like releasing wild animals into their natural habitat. Each had gone in a different direction. Honk had shaken his head and smiled before setting off to the bar with a swagger that suggested he was already drunk, while Caryanne and Vaira had wandered toward the seating areas where other patrons were congregated.

Even with the band present, Treva felt uncomfortable in the Blue Pixie in a way he hadn't when his father had been alive. He couldn't help thinking about the way the security guard had treated him at his last visit. Then Nash had barely bothered to hide his loathing. Thankfully, there was no sign of Nash. The relief made Treva feel like a coward.

He was trying to figure out how best to slip into the back area of the club when his handheld chirped. When he checked the screen, the contact card for Doctor Haeloni appeared along with a text message: >>Mrs. Marsh is well enough for discharge. We will arrange transport home. She should arrive by 8pm.<<

In an hour! He gave up his plan to sneak into the back

office and went to speak to Vaira. After scoping out the club, Vaira had settled onto a seat at the bar with Honk. With both legs wrapped around the outside of her barstool, she swiveled back and forth to the rhythm of the dance music, giving Treva the impression that she was at home in the Blue Pixie.

She smiled at him. "Whatcha doing?"

"My mom is being discharged from hospital. I need to get back to the apartment for when she gets home."

She glanced at Honk, who sat precariously on the barstool. "Don't worry about us. We'll see you at the apartment later."

Treva was relieved. He hadn't thought they'd want to go with him, but it had been possible and was an added responsibility he didn't need right now.

"Right, see you later." Treva couldn't get out of the place quickly enough .

Once outside, the security guard watched with too much interest as he walked away. Treva decided not to go back. *Time to leave Glaendor and never have to deal with Ava, Nash, or the Blue Pixie again.*

He would have to find a way to explain his plans to the band. Part of him felt guilty abandoning them in a dodgy situation, but they might want to leave once he told them. If not, they could stay in the apartment for as long as they wanted; he could write a letter or whatever was needed. With access to his father's wealth that he's inherited, he could buy off world transportation for everyone, if it came to it. However, Treva had a terrible feeling that his mother wouldn't want him to use his father's credit at all. She would want him to walk away from anything touched by the Steyn family, even though it wasn't realistic. They needed those credits for a new life, or else the only place they'd be able to afford would be in Starhills. His mother didn't yet know that they didn't have their old living quarters.

Treva made good time getting back to the apartment,

which still didn't feel like home; and now they were leaving, it never would. It was similar to the way he hadn't had chance to get to know his father before that connection, too, was cut short.

Inside, the apartment was silent. Treva resisted the urge to tip-toe down the hall to his bedroom.

While he waited for his mother's imminent arrival, he searched job postings on nearby planets, hoping to find work. The problem was that Glaendor was one of the wealthiest planets in the Outer Colonies. It was designed to attract tourists and had plenty of legitimate work. Treva couldn't see his mother agreeing to the circumspect employment that was available elsewhere. Perhaps he could use father's credits to get to one of the middle worlds.

In the end, he settled on booking tickets off Glaendor to one of the major transit hubs, and decided they could figure it out from there. Selecting the 'purchase' icon was more satisfying than he'd anticipated.

The screen flashed—*Credit declined!*

A quick check showed more than enough credits in his account. *What's going on?* Either he'd inherited his father's estate, or he hadn't.

Ice coated his spine at the realization that his fears were about to be confirmed. He remembered Nash's smug expression. Was Ava trying to get control of his father's assets? He wanted to call someone, but who? Kali had told him to contact her if he was in trouble. She was TSS. They would have to listen to her.

Treva put the call through. Nothing happened. Was his handheld faulty? He tried again with the same result. The bad feeling grew worse. Treva couldn't move. His mother would be here soon and he had the awful feeling they were trapped.

Surging to his feet, he raced through the empty apartment until he reached the kitchen. He tried the apartment's central comm unit, intending to call Kali.

"All calls will be recorded," an automated voice

intoned.

"Stop!" Treva was sure that if he made contact with anyone in the TSS, it would put them all at risk.

Ignoring his shaking hands, he tried Ava. The automated voice sounded again but the vidcall connected.

Treva scowled. "Ava?"

"Hello, Treva. I wondered when you would want to talk."

Treva couldn't think. "I..." He didn't know what to say now she was in front of him. "I can't buy anything."

"Now, that's not true." She smiled. "You can buy food and essentials."

It was true, Treva had stocked up food, ready for his mother coming home without any issue. "And..."

"Who would you need to contact?"

Treva knew better than to answer the question honestly, although, he had a feeling that she already knew.

Ava's smile disappeared. "I guess you've discovered that you're not as free as you thought. Neither was your father."

Treva gaped, feeling more stupid than when the purchase had been denied. Since his return, he'd felt he was missing something but had hoped it was his imagination.

Ava glanced off-screen before returning her attention to him. "You will have to excuse me. I'm busy." Treva was about to argue, but she added, "Be careful. You're only in such a comfortable cage for appearance's sake, although we are grateful to you for bringing more hostages. If you do not cooperate, and I mean *fully*, you are liable to discover our ruthless side."

They were trapped on Glaendor! Why? Too many questions but he focused on what mattered the most. "My mother?"

"Will join you. Is there anything else I can do for you?"

He probably should have said 'yes' and tried to get more out of her, but he needed to make sense of everything and consider what it meant mean for the future and so, he ended the call.

The apartment had to be under surveillance. They were watching him.

Was that why Ava had wanted him to use the transport she'd arranged the other day? She wanted to know where he was all the time.

Is it Ava, or is it the Steyn family? Treva knew what his mother would say.

He considered checking for surveillance equipment, but it would be impossible to find it all. Needing space to think, he headed outside. When he reached the front door, he found that it refused to respond to his palm print. The small screen remained blank. He was a prisoner.

Stupid, stupid, stupid. The clues had been there all along. Restraints on his mother's wrists at the hospital and the way he couldn't get into the Blue Pixie. He'd never been in control of anything.

— — —

Anissa hadn't believed that she would ever leave the hospital until she did. When Doctor Haeloni had told her that she was going home, she'd clutched the sheets, knowing for sure that they would never let her go. It wouldn't be difficult for someone to administer the wrong dose of a drug or for her condition to take a turn for the worse.

Except, here she was now, outside Glaendor City Hospital with a single guard. She glanced at him again. It would be pointless trying to escape while ever they had her son. Besides, she didn't have the strength.

The guard caught her gaze and smiled. "You can call me Jon, if you like."

She turned away. That would never happen, since she had nothing to say to him.

Anissa was a little disappointed when he didn't say anything else. It felt like a missed opportunity, but she just wasn't strong enough to outwit an amoeba. The effects of the drugs still lingered, making her mind sluggish, and although she was steady on her feet, she felt as weak as a newborn.

Anissa climbed into the transport shuttle with one hope-—that her son would be at the end of the journey.

They traveled in silence, except when Jon commented on the lack of tourists and what it meant for the planet's economy. When she didn't respond, he trailed off. He might not know what was going on, and so she shouldn't be too harsh on him.

Anissa tried not to gape as they passed through a redundant gatehouse into what appeared to be a park with an apartment block in the center, overlooking a lake. She'd known Marco would have a nice place, but this was so far removed from where she'd raised Treva that she couldn't see how she was going to get him away without a fight.

"Nice place," Jon commented.

She looked at him sharply, but he was craning to see the extent of the landscaped gardens.

"It belongs to my dead, estranged husband." She clamped her lips together to prevent hysterical laughter from escaping.

"Oh."

As they pulled up, she said, "I can get inside just fine on my own."

"I'm sure, but my orders were to see you inside the apartment." He climbed out of the shuttle and waited for her to exit.

She took her time, trying not to let annoyance at her weakness show. When Jon offered his arm, she accepted, afraid it would take her longer to reach Treva if she didn't.

She was vaguely aware of two guards in the reception area as they accessed the elevator. Of course, Marco's apartment was on the top floor. It had to be the grandest.

Then, nothing mattered because Treva was opening the door and whatever happened, they were together again. Her vision was hazy with tears as she hugged her little boy who had been taller than her for the last year.

At some point, the door closed and Jon was gone. She felt a pang of regret at not thanking him, but it paled into insignificance at reuniting with Treva.

"Mom, you're okay, and you're here." He squeezed too hard, letting go when she gasped.

So, he'd been as worried as her. She wasn't sure how she felt about that. On the one hand, she was grateful that he was taking the situation seriously, but on the other, what had happened to frighten him?

"You need to tell me everything."

His eyes skittered around the hall—they were under surveillance! Now, why wasn't that a surprise?

"Oh," she said, nodding as their eyes connected and noting his relief that she'd understood.

A surge of renewed anger caught her by surprise, and it took some effort to control her voice. "Come on. You can show me where I'm sleeping. I'll look around properly tomorrow."

"Mom, I need to tell you something."

For a moment, it was like stepping back in time to when nothing was seriously wrong in the world and Treva was about to confess to ruining another pair of shoes. "What have you done?"

"Nothing bad, and besides—"

"Just spell it out."

"I invited some people I know in a band to stay for a couple of days. They might be a bit... erm... loud."

She patted his hand before he could say more. "I understand. You must have been lonely."

In the scheme of things, this was something they could deal with, especially as they wouldn't be staying.

"That's not all." Treva's worried expression pulled at her heart. "We can't buy tickets off-world."

It had already occurred to her that she would have to confront the Steyn family if they were going to get away.

She didn't know how she was going to make them listen, but somehow, she would. Treva was still a child. The responsibility couldn't rest with him.

"It's okay. We'll sort it in the morning." For now, she needed sleep, and then, when she was feeling better, she would take on the might of the Steyn family. She'd done it once and escaped. She could do it again.

CHAPTER 14

HERJA HID HER guilt behind a cool exterior. Mac looked as if she'd punched him in the gut. How could she adequately explain the sacrifice she needed? Mac and Pesta didn't belong to her—not like Idra and Kinder—and yet, she felt responsible for them. Not that she liked Pesta. The level of destruction the entity could cause made her think of the planet they'd lost.

Mac met her gaze. "I understand what you're planning, but this is dangerous. Not just for us, but for everyone." He stood near the doorway. "We don't really know what Pesta can do. Stars, she doesn't know what she's capable of, only that she can cause death inadvertently if threatened. One thing's certain, her death would unleash the whole of her power in one go, causing untold devastation."

"I cannot think of any other way." Herja's eyes slid from a spot next to him, which had to be Pesta. "I am sorry."

"They can't attack while we're on board."

"This is a huge vessel, and Vaughn only needs to damage a part of it to board us. We have no defenses." They'd been helpless during the initial attack, and Herja couldn't believe she'd managed to buy them any time at all.

Mac stepped toward her. "So you're going to trust him to do as he promises? I know Vaughn—"

"No." She cut him off. "I cannot tell you more than that." Herja paused, not wanting to make promises, especially, with Gosta listening, but it was inevitable. They weren't her people, but like with Treva, she had an obligation to them. "I need you to go with the *Vector*, but we will come for you. If I could think of another way..."

Mac's shoulders slumped, and he looked at the spot where she was sure that Pesta lurked.

Herja let her eyes slide away, not wanting to see what the abomination looked like. "I have to check on the damage. Stay here. I need you to talk to Vaughn when he calls back."

She walked away, ignoring Gosta's scowl. As she passed the spot where Pesta stood, the fine hairs all over her body stood up and she suppressed a shiver. Once in the corridor, she broke into a run while also putting a call through to the control center, which acted as enforcement and emergency services for their small community.

She didn't need to announce herself. "What's the damage?"

A male voice responded immediately, "The hydroponics are burning."

Shite, it could be worse but not by much. Their supplies were dwindling and they had no assets except for the drugs she didn't want to sell.

"Make sure everyone available helps to tackle the blaze. We need that produce." She ended the call before he could tell her what she already knew—they had too many volunteers.

Fire might not burn in the vacuum of space, but it sure could get out of control in the pressurized environment of the ship. She took a couple of deep breaths. While the loss of food was disaster, it wasn't a threat to her current plan.

Vaughn might only have intended to hit them as a warning, but she couldn't afford to let him find out how easily he could destroy them. It was clear he wanted revenge, but securing Pesta had to be more critical to him.

At a guess, he would be in trouble for losing her in the first place. Herja was betting everything on that being the case.

The corridor was still full of people, running one way or another. Where did they think they were going?

"Anyone not working, get in your quarters and stay there until you are told that it is safe."

Some stopped, turning in her direction. It might have been better to make the announcement over the ship-wide communication system, not bellowed it down the corridor, but it was too late now.

Herja spoke into her handheld, "Gosta, get everyone doing none-essential work into their quarters." She cut off communication before he could ask a pointless question.

It wasn't far to Engineering, and she burst through the door a couple of minutes later. "Peter," she shouted. "Get us ready to move."

Herja stopped in front of the wall of pipes and circuitry. Unable to see anyone, she listened for any sign of movement.

She was about to shout again when Peter appeared with a large white mug in one hand and a puzzled expression on his face. *Stars, hasn't he heard that we're under attack.* A young man followed, picking his way through the wires.

By the time they were both stood in front of her, Herja was ready to strangle the pair. "We need to move in thirty, no," she checked the time, "twenty minutes." She put on her captain's face. "Understood?"

They both nodded, neither spoke to confirm that they could do what she ordered.

"Can you do it?" She desperately tried to contain her frustration since it wouldn't do any good to slaughter her engineers when she needed them the most.

Peter looked at the young man. "Go on then. Get started." He returned his attention to Herja. "We will try, but it'll take at least forty-minutes and we aren't going to get far once we set off."

Herja detected the hint of an accusation in his tone but let it go. "Do it quietly and in a maximum of thirty minutes. The enemy ship doesn't need to know anything. I will tell you when we need to move."

She didn't tell them that her signal would come in the form of Gosta brandishing a whip if they didn't make an effort. Despite Peter's half-hearted agreement, she wasn't confident that he understood the ramifications of not being ready. By the time she left, he had at least managed to put his mug on the shelf.

She raced back to the flight deck to find that Mac and Gosta had taken seats. She couldn't see Pesta until she caught sight of a deeper, darker shadow out of the corner of her eye. When she turned to look, her eyes slid away again.

She checked the time. Fifteen minutes left. It was tight, but they should be okay.

She called the control center, "How's that fire?"

"It will be extinguished soon, but we've lost most of our food—"

Herja cut off the call. She did not need to be overwhelmed with problems she couldn't do anything about right now.

She turned her attention to Gosta. "Can I have a private word?"

He stood immediately, looking wary and followed her into the corridor. "What's going on?"

"I don't have time for explanations. After you've escorted them," Herja waved her arm at the door, "to wherever Vaughn wants them. Get to Engineering and make sure they can get this rust-bucket moving."

Gosta looked at the floor. "I see."

Herja wondered what the issue was but supposed that she would no doubt hear about it soon enough. She returned to the flight deck and waited in uneasy silence for Vaughn to make contact.

A proximity alarm sounded. Herja checked the

readouts—a shuttle.

Oh no! She hadn't expected Vaughn to send one before they'd spoken again. At least forty-minutes, Peter had said. She'd stupidly assumed they would have the transport time on top of the thirty minutes Vaughn had given them. She would just have to keep him talking for at least *fifteen-minutes!*

There had to be someone better equipped to do this. The computer chimed with an incoming call—Vaughn. *Right on foking time.*

Herja took a deep breath and answered the call. "We're ready," she said before he appeared.

When his face sharpened into view, his expression was amused. He didn't fool Herja. She felt the cruelty beneath his civilized exterior and didn't trust him for a second. *How the hell am I going to keep him talking for fifteen-minutes?*

"I've sent a shuttle to pick up our guests. Where are they?"

Mac got up without being asked and stepped into view. He didn't smile and made no attempt to pretend to be happy about what was happening.

"Ah, Macadema, I can always rely on your cooperation, can't I? What about your charge?"

"She's here."

"Although, I do have a few questions about the way you left the *Vector*. Your old quarters have been cleaned and are waiting."

Mac's face lost some of its color, and Herja could only guess at the threat behind the words. Mac returned to his seat and sank back out of Vaughn's view.

"What about Pesta?" Vaughn said.

"Come where he can see you," Herja waved at Pesta, not at all sure that the entity would respond, but with Vaughn watching, she pretended to be confident. The bastard would attack any weakness. Even now, he watched as if everything they did was a spectacle put on to amuse him. Herja was aware of the entity moving, but despite her determination to see, she couldn't detect anything.

"Is this a joke?" Vaughn's face had gone red. "Nobody can see it, except him." He pointed Mac's direction.

"Really." Herja looked at Gosta who shrugged.

She hadn't realized that Vaughn couldn't see the entity. Herja couldn't see what Pesta looked like but she knew if the entity was present from the way her eyes slid away. She would ask Gosta about his experience later.

"That's why we need Macadema." Vaughn closed his mouth, probably not wanting to tell her something she didn't know. "The shuttle should be with you in two minutes."

Herja suspected that he was more reluctant to have Pesta on the *Vector* than he would admit. "We can't let the shuttle dock." It was the first excuse that came to mind. "I mean, you could have armed personnel ready to board our ship?" She scowled.

Vaughn's narrowed his eyes. "What game are you playing? If that was my intention, then I would just blow you into dust."

"But then you wouldn't have Pesta." Realizing as she spoke that it was true, her plan didn't seem so desperately stupid. "And, from what Mac has said, you would die as well."

They would check the shuttle before they opened the hatch. Herja's eyes met Gosta's where he stood at the other side of the console. He nodded once and left.

"I don't have a squad waiting to board your ship." Vaughn sounded irritated.

Herja raised an eyebrow. It was too easy to rile Vaughn. Negotiating was turning out to be more fun than she anticipated.

———

Herja watched the shuttle leave with Mac and Pesta on board as she thought through their options once again.

Nothing new came to mind. She consoled herself with the knowledge that everyone would have died if she hadn't given up the pair. Now, they might all die anyway, but at least they had a chance.

She whirled, pulling out her handheld, and almost smacking Gosta who had returned once the shuttle had departed. "You are supposed to be in Engineering. Go, get this ship moving."

"They will catch us within minutes."

Herja gave him a hard look. "Do you think that I'm stupid? Now, move." She knew Vaughn might well come after them since this was personal for him, but they were not going to wait for him to destroy them.

"I'm going," he grumbled as if she'd deliberately offended him. "Should follow foking orders," she muttered.

Satisfied once he'd jogged to the door, she returned to the central console, hoping that she'd bought them enough time. Engineers always overestimated the size of jobs, didn't they? Herja refused to think about how they didn't have anywhere to take her people even if they did escape. Nor was she going to think about how they had no way to repair the damage, or about the rash promise she'd made to Mac and Pesta. Perhaps if she just concentrated on one thing at a time, she wouldn't implode.

She put a call through to the *Hyperion*. "As soon as that shuttle returns, hit the *Vector* with the Catch-All." She'd considered striking immediately but they were slow and would need time to get away. There was no visual.

Idra's voice sounded small and scared. "Yes, Captain. We're almost there."

It was good that she was afraid. It meant she would stay focused and not take anything for granted. Herja couldn't guarantee that Vaughn hadn't worked out a contingency plan for the *Hyperion* turning up.

"Timing is everything. And Idra, I don't need to tell you how everyone is relying on you."

"No, Captain."

"Good."

Herja had no idea if she was putting too much pressure on the girl. She was young, but at least she had some experience.

There was no sign of the preparations she'd ask Peter to make, but she had told him to do it quietly. She just hadn't known that it could be silent.

Since Herja had chosen their current location carefully, they weren't far from a nav beacon. It was possible they'd get within jump range before the *Vector* could follow but only if Idra timed the attack to give them the time. Then they needed Vaughn to give up now that he had Pesta. Herja planned to force him to choose between coming after them and holding onto the weapon.

She put a call through to Engineering. "Gosta, how are we doing?"

"We're ready. Just give the word."

Herja couldn't stop irritation from coloring her voice, "What are we waiting for— Vaughn, to announce he's going to blow us up? Let's go."

Suddenly, she had power but this was not the compact bridge of the *Hyperion*. The flight deck controls for the city-ship were set far apart since the ship had never been designed for a single pilot, just like it had never been designed to house so many for such a long time. She needed help; she couldn't fly *Storm's Breath* alone.

"Gosta, get back here now."

Silence.

She didn't panic and tried not to berate herself for not thinking of this when she'd sent those young pilots away or Gosta to Engineering. There were things she could do to prepare. Gosta was on his way back. His life revolved around anticipating her needs; he'd be back in time.

She forced a stiff lever away. Something deep under her feet groaned and she tried not to think about the ship shaking itself to pieces as it failed to set off.

According to the readings, the massive bulk was

moving. Herja was afraid it was going to take an hour they didn't have to travel a few millimeters. She couldn't accelerate and steer on her own, so settled for traveling in any direction as long as it was away from the *Vector*.

Vaughn had to have noticed they were moving by now. The door opened, and Herja didn't need to look to know that it was Gosta running onto the flight deck

"Where are we heading?" He asked, taking a seat at the nav console, which was located a good ten meters away.

"To the nav beacon."

Gosta didn't ask for any more details and set about plotting a course.

There was an incoming call. Herja glanced to see that as expected, it was Vaughn and ignored it.

An alarm sounded. The Vector's weapons had a lock on them. Where was the *Hyperion*? Was Idra trying too hard to get the timing right? If she didn't hurry, it would be too late.

The entire ship shook as they were hit. Another alarm blared. Herja glanced at the readings. *Fok.* The shield had failed in patches across the whole ship.

"Shields are useless," Gosta announced as if they weren't about to explode.

Herja muttered another stream of curses—Idra's name was in there. We can't survive another hit and being so huge, we're hard to miss.

Gosta was staring at the viewscreen. "The *Hyperion*." He smiled. "I don't think Vaughn saw her coming."

Herja sagged and allowed her eyes to close for a second. They might just have gotten away with it, but it had been too close.

The crisis had been averted, but Herja didn't dare celebrate yet. She still had to prevent the next potential disaster and hope that Vaughn didn't come after them.

"Tell me when you have our course plotted and locked." She moved to initiate the jump to subspace. "And, don't forget to send Idra our destination coordinates."

Gosta grunted in response.

On his mark, she executed the jump. A terrible shudder ran through the ship as they made the transition to subspace.

It was only once the front viewport was flooded with ethereal light that she try to ease her tense muscles. "I need to check the damage." Gosta was busy so, she knew better than to wait for an acknowledgment.

As she walked to the hydroponics, which were two decks down, she mused that no matter how much damage they had sustained, things could have been much worse. They were alive, and the ship was still flying.

She rounded a bend in the corridor and came across a scorched area. Five people had already started the laborious process of reinforcing the hull where it had been weakened. Their repair equipment was outdated and the metal they applied looked as if it had been recycled from internal fixtures. Someone she didn't recognize in a protective suit approached.

"Any casualties?" she asked.

"No, but we need to be out of subspace to make effective repairs."

She thanked him and relayed the information to Gosta before continuing to the hydroponic gardens, thinking it was a miracle that *Storm's Breath* had got as far as it had.

She sucked in a breath as she surveyed the damage. The fire had been extinguished, but most of the area set aside for growing had collapsed, damaging and killing many of the plants. It was worse than she'd expected. No matter what they did, they would need an alternative food source in the short-term.

The entire crop was decimated, except for some very young plants. Aydan, the head horticulturalist, sat with his head bowed. When he finally looked up, she saw tears in his eyes. Herja patted his shoulder helplessly.

His slender assistant approached, her voice soft, "We're leaking atmosphere very slowly. With better equipment, we might be able to repair it, but we're waiting for them to finish on deck three."

Herja was so tired that she couldn't remember the woman's name for a full three seconds— Erica. Just a consequence of stress and too many people relying on her to get this right.

"Okay. Send me a list of the items you need. Somehow, I'll get them."

She turned from the twisted metal, unable to get the sight out of her mind as she walked down the corridor. For some reason, it made her think of Treva, and she wondered how he was doing. There was no way she could check on him despite the sudden urge, but at least, he was better off on Glaendor than with them.

Getting past Glaendor security would be a problem after they'd left the planet in a hurry the last time they had visited, but perhaps... No, she was needed here and was just searching for a way to escape the crushing responsibility.

Herja returned to the flight deck and Gosta. They exited subspace and waited for the *Hyperion*. If the *Vector* had followed them, there was nothing they could do and they wouldn't get far if they tried to run. Herja had gambled everything on Vaughn's need to secure Pesta rather than come after them.

The *Hyperion* appeared on the monitor. Herja went to look out the viewport, needing to see that her ship and crew were in one piece.

Next, she put a call through to Idra. "Well done."

"I'm sorry, I didn't mean to let them get in another shot. Is everyone okay?"

"You did well."

Gosta raised an eyebrow, reminding her without words that she had cursed Idra's name a short time ago. She ignored him; the girl didn't need to know about that, as it wouldn't do anything for her confidence.

"You always manage it," Idra was saying.

Herja laughed at the slight whine in her voice. "There were no casualties, but I have some difficult decisions to make." She paused before saying, "Return to *Storm's Breath* when ready."

Herja ended the call and met Gosta's eyes. They both knew what she'd meant when she'd said that she had some difficult decisions to make.

He held her gaze. "Have you decided, then?"

"That makes it sound like I have a choice." She couldn't keep the bitterness from her voice. "We have the drugs. If we sell them, we'll be able to buy some of what we need."

"We don't owe anyone anything. Nobody helped our people," Gosta said sullenly, but they both knew it wasn't that simple.

Nobody knew why or how their people had been destroyed, and their nearby neighbors had feared that they were contagious. Well, that had been the rumor going around, and nobody had wanted to take the chance that the same could happen to them. Forced into piracy, it was easier for others to believe they deserved their fate.

"Give me a few hours to make arrangements, and then we can leave."

"Our position here is unsafe."

"It's safer than it was," Herja snapped. She took a deep breath. "Sorry, it's just there aren't many options. I'll try to make arrangements to sell the drugs close by so we can get back quickly."

Gosta cleared his throat.

Herja glared at him. "Don't you say it. I'm well aware of my promise, but first thing's first. It would be better to be blown up rather than die through starvation." How had she ended up responsible for the remnants of her entire people?

CHAPTER 15

PYRA TRIED TO work out why Steyn had sent him to deal with Pesta. Not that Steyn had told him what Pesta was, but he'd heard things. He was unsure whether to believe some of it.

"Pesta, as in 'pestilence'," Ava had said when he'd asked.

Like an overlooked child, Ava couldn't resist the opportunity to show off what she knew, which Pyra used to his advantage whenever possible. From what he'd gathered, Pesta was a genetically engineered weapon, unique in the amount of devastation it could cause. He didn't have a complete picture, but he'd discovered enough to make him nervous.

Pyra walked the wrong way along a powered walkway, which was no longer operational. He hadn't expected the station to be closed to everyone, except those, like him, with authorization. Pyra wasn't clear why Steyn had closed down the spaceport on a planet that relied on tourism, but Avon security personnel controlled all entrances and exits. They had been the ones to direct Pyra the wrong way down the one-way system, although he had already worked out that this route was quicker.

Colored lights cast patterns on the walkway as he covered the short distance to the Avon Security Station located within the spaceport. Pyra didn't see anything but knew weapons were trained on him. He showed his face and ID to the outer camera. A loud bleep made him jump as the door swung inward.

There was no going back. If he tried, they would probably shoot him for suspicious behavior. Paranoid—perhaps, but Pyra didn't think so.

He approached the reception desk where an armed guard scanned his retinas before checking his authorization for the second time. The big man pointed to a seat in the small reception area.

Pyra sat and tried to get his racing heart under control. His palms were sweaty and he was just thinking about asking to leave when the door opened and a burly man with enough cosmetic enhancements that he appeared plastic walked out.

"Raffia Barrendi, head of Avon Security," the man announced, clearly forgetting that Pyra had met him before at one of Steyn's meetings.

Raffia was involved in the innermost circle of SPEAR, which made Pyra wonder how many organizations SPEAR had infiltrated.

Pyra stood, swallowing and trying not to look nervous. "Mr. Barrendi?"

Raffia nodded once and spoke in a low voice, "You've come for the Commander..." he looked uncomfortable, "I told him, my people would do it, but he isn't happy."

Raffia clearly thought that Pyra was important to Steyn, which couldn't be further from the truth. Then Pyra understood why Steyn had chosen him. There was no chance of anyone reading his mind, plus, he was expendable.

Not knowing how to respond, Pyra asked, "What do you want me to do?"

Raffia frowned. "The Commander said you were coming to check on their condition and ensure they have no medical needs. I fear that in ignorance, my people were a little rough."

What's wrong with people that they immediately resort to violence, no matter the situation?

"Ah, I see. The Commander didn't give me any details, only telling me that Pesta was essential to his plans." Pyra watched Raffia plucked the sleave of his jacket.

"It's fear, you see." Raffia stared at the duty desk. "Thank you for doing this. I'll let the Commander know that you carried out the task bravely."

Pyra thought that was a bit premature since he had yet to do anything, but saw that a man in protective gear had arrived to escort him. It was on the tip of his tongue to ask if he should be similarly attired when he realized that if any of the rumors were true, no amount of protection would help.

Pyra rose and with a nod to Raffia followed the man through a door at one side of the desk, where they entered a warren of tunnels. The station was much larger than it appeared from the outside, and they passed a series of closed doors, labeled with numbers. Pyra followed the silent guard up a flight of brightly lit, broad stairs. An ornately carved wooden bannister stood out against the clinical white walls and clean lines.

They followed a corridor until Pyra thought he'd spotted their destination at the far end where a massive, reinforced door blocked the way. It was halfway down, where two guards also wearing protective gear, flanked another door, that they stopped. A ripple of tension went through the men on seeing the approaching visitors. Nobody spoke, and one opened the door, holding it wide while the other trained his weapon on the opening. Pyra realized they expected him to go inside. Tentatively, he stepped over the threshold, telling himself that it was no worse than walking in on Steyn in a bad mood.

The door slammed behind him, reverberating through the building. Pyra closed his eyes. From the sound, it was not a standard construction like it first appeared but a heavy, reinforced door.

Questioning his ability to move, Pyra concentrated on breathing. When he opened his eyes, the first thing he saw was a tall man with a black left eye and a bruise to his cheekbone. He looked normal and so, Pyra glanced around the room. It was furnished like a cheap hotel room and even had a comm unit and viewscreen, although Pyra guessed they wouldn't work.

Neither Pyra nor the man spoke, and it took a minute for Pyra's refined senses to pick up an abnormality in the center of the room. Even then, he couldn't identify any details, as it blended so perfectly with the natural shadow. Pyra found that he was reluctant to stare too hard at the spot.

The lock turned, startling Pyra out of his stupor. There would be surveillance, but he'd prepared for that. He scratched his left bicep, activating a device that was strapped to his arm and would disrupt any signal within a seven-meter radius.

Pyra asked. "Mac, can anyone read your mind?" He knew the name but couldn't remember where he'd come by it. It was the sort of mistake he hardly ever made.

Mac frowned, looking confused.

"We have about five minutes before they check on us." It was impossible to get anyone to trust him within the time he'd had and so, they wouldn't. "Steyn is a telepath. Will he be able to read your mind or does that," he nodded at Pesta, "protect you?" It was a hopeful guess that smacked of desperation, but it was all he had.

The man's expression cleared. "No, he would not be able to break into my mind with Pesta keeping watch."

"That's good. I want to help, but it's difficult when I'm unable to explain what I'm doing."

Mac frowned. "Won't he just read your mind?"

"Let's just say that he cannot." Pyra tried not to let his impatience show, but it was difficult when they had so little time. "I've disrupted the surveillance, but someone will be in soon."

Mac smiled. "They won't. Surveillance doesn't work around Pesta. I think she has some sort of— "

"Okay good," Pyra interrupted, since they were going to run out of time one way or another.

Pyra slipped his pulse gun from inside his jacket to his hand. He had expected them to search him, but he'd thought it was worth trying to get a weapon inside. After all, Avon Security were used to dealing with theft and minor crime. They had never operated as a real police force, and Pyra hoped to use that to his advantage.

Pyra passed the weapon to Mac, who took it. "I will do what I can to get you out of here, since I suspect that whatever Steyn wants you for cannot be good."

"I'm no good with weapons but will do my best." Mac held up the gun. "And, there's only one use for me as far as people like Steyn are concerned."

Pyra could not help himself. "Me?"

"Pesta and I are one now. I cannot remember what it was like to be separate."

A high-pitched squeak came from the shadows, causing Pyra to suppress a shiver. Pesta was alien and dangerous.

Mac slowly nodded before speaking to Pesta, "It's okay. I have no intention of allowing them to take you away."

Pyra hadn't known what to expect when told that a Taran acted as the creature's keeper. It was logical that the two had to be bonded for Mac to exert any control over a creature powerful enough to destroy a planet.

With the important stuff out of the way and nobody ordering him to come out, Pyra asked, "Why did you agree to bond with Pesta?" He glanced into the shadows as it occurred to him that Pesta might take offence.

Mac laughed. "I didn't volunteer." The dim lighting deepened the bruising across his face. "It's a funny story."

Pyra didn't believe that. "I'd like to know more—it might help."

"I'm a scientist." Mac laughed again but this time there

was a hint of bitterness. "I haven't always found it easy to get employment. When a company called Arma-Tech got in touch and offered me a job, I was suspicious but desperate, and so, I accepted."

A grinding noise caused them to look in the direction of the door. Pyra wasn't worried about his questions being overheard since it was natural to be curious. When nobody entered, Mac looked toward Pesta was as if for permission to continue.

"I worked on the Pesta project not realizing it was intended that I play such an integral part until the day I woke with her here." Mac tapped his head and then looked to the side. Something disturbed the dust motes and he smiled. "She's the sweetest thing you can imagine. I later discovered that she wasn't supposed to be sentient and I should have been the one changed by the procedure. It didn't work out like that."

Dozens of questions filled Pyra's mind, and he struggled to put them in order of importance. "She?"

"That's just the way I think of her. Obviously, she isn't male or female, but thinks she would like to be a girl." Mac touched the stubble on his face. "She doesn't like this." He grew more serious. "But, the important thing is that she needs to feel safe. The only times I've worried about control have been when she's felt threatened or I've been in danger. I was more worried about her when I got this," he pointed to his black eye and raised his t-shirt to display dark bruising across his chest, "than the pain."

Pyra nodded. "Steyn is clever and will turn everything to his advantage. I can't work out what he is going to do next and know I'm missing something."

Mac shrugged. "I can't help you with that."

Of course, he can't. Pyra nodded. "So, she doesn't want to destroy everything?"

"No, but she has little control over her power. That's why she needs me. If she wanted, she could take her freedom, but she isn't—"

The door handle moved, and Pyra scurried toward it. One of the guards appeared in the doorway with his colleague close behind. Best, that they believe that Pyra was in the process of leaving.

Pyra didn't acknowledge either as he slipped by and followed the staircase down without waiting for a guide. He heard the door slam and was sorry that he hadn't said goodbye to Mac and Pesta.

Raffia waited on the stairs. "Well?"

He thought about lying to cause the man some stress but suspected Mac and Pesta would rather have some peace. "Nobody needs medical attention."

Raffia let out a breath. "That's good. I wouldn't want the Commander to feel disappointed in the service we offer."

So, Raffia was afraid that he wouldn't get paid if Steyn was unhappy.

Pyra lowered his voice in a conspiratorial tone, "Between us, I would be very careful that nothing happens to the Commander's property. He can be very... er... possessive."

Satisfied with the way Raffia leaned in, nodding rapidly, Pyra smiled once more and left.   He set off to the Blue Pixie on foot.

The journey was going to take a lot longer than in the shuttle Steyn had waiting for him. No doubt there'd be questions as to why he'd walked, but he'd tell Steyn that he needed time to think. After all, he'd just survived a scary encounter, which gave him another idea. Pyra knew precisely how to behave to get a repeat trip to see Mac.

The walk gave him time; he otherwise wouldn't have to make a report. With Steyn's suspicious nature, this would be the only opportunity he got. There were too many people on the walkway, and he didn't dare slow as someone was sure to be tracking him. With a deep breath, he casually put through a vidcall. Nothing happened, which was what he'd feared. He sighed, resigning himself to finding another way.

On his return, Pyra immediately went to see Steyn, knowing that he'd still be sweaty from his walk. It was a look planned to use.

Steyn was in the back room, engrossed in reading a document on his tablet. He didn't look up when Pyra knocked and entered without waiting for a response.

Pyra dropped his handheld on the desk and knocked into Steyn as he tried to retrieve it. "Sorry... sorry... sorry."

Steyn's eyes narrowed as he focused on Pyra. "You seem nervous."

Pyra banged into the table again, taking a small amount of pleasure from the way Steyn's coffee slopped over the edge of his cup. "So, sorry."

Steyn pushed his chair out of the way as Pyra made a futile attempt to mop up the excess liquid with his long sleeves. He succeeded in getting droplets everywhere.

"Fok." Steyn stood. "I have a meeting in fifteen minutes." He glared. "Pyra, I need you to return to check on Pesta again tomorrow. Do you understand?"

Pyra ducked his head. "I'll get something to clean that up." He smile as he turned and walked away.

CHAPTER 16

OWEN HELD UP a hand in front of his face. He couldn't see anything. At the back of his mind, he thought panic would be an entirely reasonable response. It was sad that he didn't have the energy. Did his captors expect him to freak out?

Owen, in his skin-tight jeans and genuine Rolling Stone's t-shirt, exported from Earth for a month's worth of credits, tearing at his hair or breaking his fingernails on the walls as he tried to dig his way out. Perhaps he was slowly going mad.

Owen didn't know how much time had passed. They'd moved him after Narda's visit, but as they'd drugged him and covered his head, he didn't know where he was or even which planet he was on. Rather than terrify him, the lack of knowledge made him feel disconnected, as if it was happening to someone else.

Who would have thought that he'd miss that dank cell? Unfortunately, the conditions had deteriorated. Instead of bars, heavy chains encircled both ankles and wrists before being attached to a brick wall. He could only shuffle a little in three directions, clanking and clanging with every movement. Comfort didn't appear to be high on his captor's agenda; the shackles rubbed his skin, adding to his numerous aches and pains. He'd exchanged the cot for a wooden pallet half a meter from the floor. The slats dug into his back and he hadn't discovered a single position that was tolerable for longer than a minute.

The air was cool and dry with the faint smell of spirits. Days or hours ago, there had been a long period where all Owen had heard was the boom, boom, boom of bass. It sounded like he was in the toilet at a club, but as that didn't narrow down his whereabouts, he didn't waste too much time trying to work out what was going on overhead. He clung to the hope there were people nearby who might care that he was a captive, not that he had a way to let them know he was here.

Owen Bruiser would never have gotten himself in such a situation. He would have told his interrogators what they wanted to know and wet himself if threatened. *Now, if I can come up with another idea, there's a song in there somewhere.*

Where was his handheld? Of course, they wouldn't let captives keep anything that allowed communication with the outside world. He wanted to laugh, which didn't seem healthy considering the circumstances.

He slumped against the cold brick wall. The rough surface scratched his skin through his t-shirt. He leaned forward, wondering if Narda would visit again. Perhaps he could give her part of the truth, although, something in him rebelled against the idea. He still couldn't figure out why they cared about the singer in a band. They must have worked out that Kali was TSS. Still, what did they think he knew?

Next time, I'll pretend to be asleep or working on a song. They won't expect anything else from a spoiled rock star. A melody kept circling around in his head, making it difficult to think of anything else.

In the past, Owen had been accused of treating everything as a game, so he decided to play to his strength. His needed to find out where he was.

Footsteps reverberated overhead. Owen tilted his head to listen. It sounded as if people were walking across a wooden floor. Owen had tried shouting, before he'd become afraid of attracting the wrong sort of attention, but if anyone heard, they didn't come to investigate.

Now, a rattling came from overhead. When the sound was followed by the creak of a door opening, Owen realized that it had been an old-fashioned key turning in a lock. A lump formed in his throat. He should shout and ask who it was but found that he didn't want to. The chains around his wrists and ankles prevented him from hiding, so, like a small hunted animal, he remained still and silent. Wherever he was being held, the place was primitive and he hadn't worked out whether that was good or bad yet.

He couldn't see the entrance but guessed it was out of sight above him. He'd heard Narda's approach last time, but wait. Hadn't that been elsewhere? He was confused.

Suddenly, Owen could see the walls. The door must have let in light. The walls were made of bare brick but he'd guessed that. On one side a stack of boxes was as tall as him. It looked like he was in a combined storage cellar and prison.

Just what every home needs! He was slowly going mad.

As the brightness grew, the sound of boots on stone got louder. The way the shadows danced was like a scene from a horror movie, and it made Owen feel dizzy after so long in the dark.

A pale face drifted into view. Owen was sure he'd never met the man before, and wondered if this was the 'boss' that Narda had mentioned. She'd seemed frightened of him, although, he couldn't remember what she'd said.

He listened for clues and only heard one set of footsteps. He was alone. Surely, he would bring backup. Although come to think of it, Narda had come alone, confident that Owen couldn't escape and attack her. Not that he would have.

The man laughed, making Owen jump. Stars, it was as

if the stranger had read his mind.

Get a grip. He knew for certain that telekinesis and telepathy were real because of Kali and Mika, but he didn't think anybody had ever been in his head. Kali had never found it awkward after he'd had inappropriate thoughts about her. Now, that was one way to check if she read his mind, and it likely worked for Mika, as well. Not that Owen had inappropriate thoughts about Mika, but his friend was bound to take issue with any fantasy that involved Kali. None of that meant that anyone else would respect those boundaries.

The shape of a large man came into view. As he got closer, Owen could see that he was smiling. It cut through the fog protecting Owen's sanity. For the first time since Narda left, he was afraid.

As the man got within a couple of meters, his pale face stood out in the glow from his flashlight. "Indeed, Mr. Bruiser, I do not have any restrictions when it comes to delving into another's mind. Although, I'm surprised that the TSS didn't teach you any basic blocking techniques."

With the realization that he'd been right about the man reading his mind, Owen was paralyzed for a few seconds. What *had* Kali said about protecting his thoughts? Something about it being incredibly difficult without years of training—not helpful. She'd said to fill his mind with something else—the nastier, the better.

"Wh…" The word caught in Owen's throat. He hadn't spoken to anyone in such a long time. He tried again, "Who are you?"

"How rude of me. My name is Andrei Steyn, and I'm the man who holds your life in my hands."

Owen shook his head. "Sorry, I don't know you, but I'm not at my best. Perhaps if you tell me a bit about yourself, it might jog my memory." The name meant nothing and he didn't want to think about what else the man had said.

Steyn sighed. "Unfortunately, I don't have the time for this. I need information, and you will supply it."

Owen pressed his lips together before it sunk in what Steyn meant. The man was going to rummage around in his head. Owen had no idea how to fight him; he vowed to get Kali to teach him ways to try to protect himself in the future, even if it took years.

Steyn cleared his throat. "That's all well and good, but it won't help you now. I am sorry to have left you in the dark for so long, but I've been busy. I'm not a callous man and did ensure you received the care you needed."

Have I eaten or drunk anything? He couldn't remember anyone bringing food or water. But, while he was hungry and thirsty, he wasn't desperate.

"We gave you supplements when you were brought here. Enough to keep you alive, but no more than the minimum since there are no benefits to you being strong."

Owen hadn't spoken aloud since those first few words, which meant Steyn had picked the thoughts out of his head. With that realization, he tried to concentrate on the same melody that kept coming and going. It had such a lot of potential to become a song.

Steyn laughed. "You don't have the skills to keep me from taking what I want."

Owen added some lyrics to the melody. Perhaps he could use his experience of the living in the dark to produce something meaningful. Except the melody was too upbeat for that. Could he weave Steyn into a song. Something about a master villain with a love of chains.

A noise came from Steyn's pocket, which had to be an alert from his handheld. *Where's my handheld? Has anyone tried to call me? Are they searching for me?*

Steyn growled in frustration. "When I return, Mr. Bruiser, I will take your mind apart." He turned, taking the only light with him.

Owen leaned back against the rough wall. *One more master villain... to turn the ordinary into heroes.* If only he had a guitar.

CHAPTER 17

PYRA STAYED INVISIBLE at the edge of the room. Long ago, during training, he'd learned that trying too hard made him stand out. It was a balance he'd mastered, but the way that Steyn watched him told him that wasn't the case.

His boss took note of everything even when he appeared to focus elsewhere. Steyn would be upset to discover that while it made Pyra's job harder, it didn't stop him from doing what he had to do.

Pyra was impervious to telepathy, and while Steyn liked that his adversaries could not break into his servant's mind, it made him a risk. Pyra had never demonstrated any loyalty and so, it was natural that Steyn would be suspicious. The only thing in his favor was a lack of opportunity to betray SPEAR.

Fortunately, most people saw Pyra but failed to truly *see* him. Every time someone laughed at his clumsiness and dismissed him as stupid, they were taken in by his act. He wondered whether Steyn would be surprised to know Pyra had discovered a TSD arch in the cellar. Not that he knew what it was for or where it went, but give him enough time and he would discover all Steyn's secrets.

Steyn smiled, in a good mood for once. Probably, because SPEAR was generating a great deal of interest amongst citizens and governments in the mistaken belief that they would be protected against further attacks.

Pyra was supposed to return to check on Pesta again today. But, so far, there hadn't been any time and now, he had to be present for this meeting. It had clearly been planned but this was the first Pyra knew about it.

Ava entered the room, unsurprisingly, her eyes passed over him. She only respected power, which helped as she ignored him.

He took his seat next to Steyn ready to record the meeting and mark any change in subject matter as they went along. It would make editing to reflect whatever Steyn wanted easier and there couldn't be any mistakes if he wanted to remain useful. In the short time he'd worked for Steyn, he discovered far too much, which meant that his job wouldn't be the only thing he'd lose if no longer needed.

Steyn's gaze settled on him for a moment. Pyra focused on setting the recording levels, grateful for his natural resistance to telepathy.

Steyn cleared his throat. "If everyone is here, we will start the strategy meeting. Nothing that occurs in this room will be repeated—ever." He met the eyes of every one of the eight people seated at the table." The man knew how to set a tone to ensure that everyone paid full attention. He glanced at Pyra. "What's the first item on the agenda?"

Steyn knew the agenda backwards, but Pyra was ready. "The next attack, Commander."

"Ah yes. We will announce our intention to attack Glaendor, but whether the TSS takes the bait remains to be seen." He paused and turned to Pyra. "What do you think?"

Pyra jerked, almost knocking over a jug of water, which would've been a genuine accident if he hadn't caught it in time. "Me?" Pyra squeaked, making no attempt to hide his distress at being singled out. "I don't understand."

"I wonder if that's true."

Pyra wisely did not speak. If he denied knowing what was happening, he would appear stupid and if he admitted it, he would be accused of paying too much attention to Steyn's business.

Steyn turned back to the others. It would take a few minutes for Pyra's heart rate to drop back to normal but at least, he could breathe again.

"Let's start with our troops." Steyn switched direction at a dizzying speed. "Raffia, how are they?" He directed the question to the head of Avon Security.

The man twitched. "Everything is under control. There was the usual trouble-makers but they are cooperating nicely now. As you know, Avon Security strives for a culture where staff follow orders."

Steyn scanned the faces around the table. "Vaughn, you were sent for Pesta and the drugs. Can you update us on the current situation?"

The man at the far end cleared his throat. "Hey, now, don't get annoyed. I had to deal with Herja, and she's a slippery one." He was sweating profusely.

Steyn looked down his nose. "All pirates are slippery?" When Vaughn didn't respond, Steyn said, "Now, tell us again, why you didn't get the drugs."

Pyra wondered if Vaughan knew Steyn's could read his mind. It wasn't something the man advertised, but enough people were suspicious that it wasn't a well-kept secret. Vaughn struggled to get his words out and no doubt his mind broadcasted what had actually happened.

"They live on the biggest city-ship I've ever seen, but they didn't have any defenses and the drugs didn't show on our scans. They might have been on the *Hyperion,* which was nowhere in range until it attacked us."

"You didn't expect the *Hyperion* to attack?" Steyn's tone was pleasant, and yet, it made Vaughn fidget.

He'd gone pale. "Herja," he spat the name out, "was on the city-ship. I didn't think she'd let anyone else fly the bomaxed ship. Knowing how important Pesta is to our plans, I decided to get it back instead of going after them. Believe me, I really wanted to go after them."

Steyn started to say something, but Ava interrupted, "The pirate will sell the drugs, and since it doesn't matter how they get out on the streets, I say let them. The results will be the same."

A smile slowly spread over Steyn's face. "I like the idea. Okay, Captain Vaughn, it looks like Ava has gotten you out of trouble this time."

With a sense of dread, Pyra understood the pirates had stolen drugs designed to kill, but there was something else going on that he didn't understand involving Pesta.

Illegal drugs that kill people would not create the immediate panic that SPEAR wanted. If the population of the Outer Colonies were to look to them to keep them safe, they had to demonstrate power.

Since the TSS had displayed extreme competence in dealing with the last attack, and the news was full of heroic efforts to save lives, Pyra thought that SPEAR would have to pull off something spectacular. Some had gone so far as to say that SPEAR had inadvertently provided an opportunity for the TSS to promote their work. He'd seen a news report that said applications to join had gone up. Pyra could see how SPEAR had to escalate their attacks.

While Pyra's priority had always been to maintain his cover at all costs, and his role did not extend to preventing crime, he couldn't ignore what he'd discovered. If SPEAR wasn't stopped, a lot of people were going to die.

The boy, Treva, had said something about the pirate captain when he'd been talking to Ava. Perhaps there was a way to warn her through him, if she would listen. There was a chance that she might not care about the potential loss of life, but it was worth a try.

Pyra had missed part of the conversation as a young woman entered the room. Everyone went silent, looking from one to the other. They were mystified as to how she had been allowed into the meeting. Steyn initially appeared as surprised as everyone else, but he smiled and beckoned her over.

— — —

Caryanne couldn't recall why she'd come back to the Blue Pixie today, but she knew it wasn't her first visit. For some reason that she couldn't now remember, she'd been searching for somewhere to hide for an hour or two. Unfortunately, she had interrupted some sort of meeting.

Where am I? The journey was fading already and so, she focused on what lay in front of her.

Nine people sat around a large table. They all stopped when she entered the room and she was about to turn and leave, when one man waved her forward.

Commander. Caryanne remembered his name. He'd been nice the last time they'd met, but she wasn't stupid. She sensed the hostility emanating from the rest of the group and knew she'd walked into something she shouldn't have. Weirdly, her instincts told her to stay, and since she relied on them above everything else to navigate the world, she obeyed.

After hesitating, she went around the table to him. "Why don't you take a seat?" He motioned to an empty chair at his side.

Why is this chair empty? Are people afraid of him? It was hard to judge since she found most people scary.

She sat and whispered, "Really, why would you want me here?"

"Because you fascinate me, my dear."

Caryanne shuddered inside at the use of the endearment. Her sense of survival, which had been sharpened by a life she chose not to remember, was too strong not to understand the meaning behind his words. On some matters, her brain functioned better than most people's, and she knew the Commander thought of her as an object to possess.

Nevertheless, she smiled and took the seat without allowing her vacant smile to slip, but something had changed. For a start, it wasn't normal to be aware that her smile was vacant but all she could do was pretend there wasn't anything wrong and carry on as usual.

Nine faces stared at her, holding an array of emotions from confusion through to outright hostility. Caryanne didn't meet anyone's gaze. As far as she was concerned, there was only one thing to do—keep smiling. Thankfully, the murmur of voices soon filled the room, which was far better than the judging silence.

"Don't worry," the Commander announced, "Caryanne can't tell anyone what we discuss today. She has an incurable brain disorder."

Caryanne looked down the expensive mahogany table that had to have been imported from somewhere large trees grew. As far as she was aware, nobody had ever tried to cure her, although, she couldn't be certain.

She let her mind fill with whichever song came to mind—*Dark Matter.* That was her favorite.

Someone at the far end of the table said, "I think you like taking risks."

Caryanne expected the Commander to explode but he ignored the comment. He smiled and nodded as if knowing what was going on in her head, but she had the feeling he was afraid of her mind.

The little man on the other side of the Commander leaned forward to catch her eye. He looked at her differently from the others. It was like he saw her as an individual and his expression was concerned.

When he sat back, only one arm and the side of his head remained visible. *Why does he feel like an escape shuttle on a burning ship?* She suppressed the desire to move nearer to him.

Men made up most of those around the table, but there was one woman besides her. Caryanne allowed their conversation to wash over her. She had the impression they were selling something and wondered if there was a way to leave without being rude.

Steyn banged on the table, making her jump. "Let's get on with it. We have a lot to get through in the next hour."

Everyone stopped talking instantly and the man opposite nodded in approval.

Caryanne tilted her head in Steyn's direction like she was paying attention along with everyone else, when really she was doing the opposite.

"Can I assume that everyone now agrees with the plan?"

It was on the tip of her tongue to ask—what plan? But she caught herself in time.

"You need to get rid of any loose ends. We don't want a repeat of what happened—" The voice came from a man at the far side of the group with both elbows on the tabletop. He was the one who'd gestured at Caryanne earlier.

His words penetrated her lazy peace, and she didn't like it. She didn't like him. She frowned. *I shouldn't remember him!*

The Commander said, "I will arrange for all our loose ends to die together when it is convenient."

He said it so casually and with such a broad smile that it was easy for Caryanne to ignore her uneasy feeling and return his smile as if nothing was wrong. While she gave no outward indication that anything was wrong, her finely honed self-preservation instinct kicked in again, shoving the threat violently into her consciousness.

"You cannot talk in front of her," said a middle-aged man with a scowl that made him ugly.

There was an audible intake of breath when Steyn cleared his throat but didn't speak.

Caryanne continued to smile while everything around her felt superficial. *Kill, kill, kill...* She would remember.

"Why are you doing this?" she whispered to the Commander as everyone watched them. "I don't understand." She didn't think he'd tell her, but he'd think it odd if she didn't ask.

He patted her hand in a fatherly gesture. It was such a

contrast to what he'd just said that it triggered another alarm in her head. Caryanne didn't like it one little bit. Her protective shell had cracked.

She resisted pulling away, knowing how precarious her situation had become. If she showed any understanding of what was happening, she would not leave this room. Anxiety grew in the pit of her stomach and it wasn't because of the death threat that hung over her. For once, it was the fear that she wouldn't remember.

The Commander laughed. "Don't worry. She won't remember anything when she leaves this room."

"How can you be so sure?" someone asked.

"I've been in her head, and let me tell you; it's a scary place."

Caryanne felt panic grow. He could read her mind. If he did that now, he'd know that she might remember. With nothing else to do, she focused on her hands. It would be dangerous to let her fear show.

While Caryanne couldn't read minds, growing up, she'd learned to read her father's moods so well that it acted as a substitute for being telepathic. As there was always a price to pay if she got it wrong, she learned never to be mistaken. She'd escaped that life only to live out the same scenario time after time until she discovered how to forget. And now? She didn't know. The Commander was right. She shouldn't remember any of this, and yet, she decided that she would.

A kind-faced man to her left didn't look so friendly when he started to speak, "We won't get the Outer Colonies on our side without a good reason, and that's going to take some major disruption. The planets value their independence."

"What greater disruption could there be than wiping out an entire planet?" The Commander's voice had hardened. "I admit that we've had a disappointing start because of the intervention of two Agents, but those attacks were just the warmup." The Commander directed attention to the viewscreen at the far end of the room. "I have a little demonstration."

Caryanne didn't know who or what they discussed. Her mind was fixated on his talk of doing away with a planet until images appeared on the screen. She had never seen anything like it. She closed her eyes, not wanting to see more. Someone in the room gasped and she peeked to see an aerial view of a city with bodies in the streets.

The Commander spoke, "We are grateful to the team for making this recording. By the time we located Pesta, all mammalian life on the planet was gone and we wouldn't have understood the full extent of what happened because the bodies dissolved."

The screen went blank and there was an explosion of voices in the room until the Commander held his hand up for silence. "I understand your concerns, but we have moved on from when this happened, and Pesta now has a handler who exerts control over the creature."

The man with the ugly smile said, "And this is what you intend for Glaendor?"

"It is," his words hung in the air, "which is why most of you need to leave."

Caryanne didn't listen to the debate that followed, she was too busy, trying to make sure that she remembered what she'd seen even though she really wanted to forget.

Millions more could die if I forget. I need to tell Mika and Kali what I've seen.

"Caryanne," she jerked as the Commander said her name, "how well do you know Mika Hendi and Kali Wietris?"

Her head spun, and the table rocked at the mention of the two people she'd just been thinking about. It had to be a coincidence. *Don't give him a reason to look in your head.*

She forced a smile. "Mika is our band manager."

"I think he's more than that."

Caryanne looked at him blankly. In that moment, she didn't know what he was saying. There was information inside her, waiting for her to retrieve it but she didn't want to, not now.

The Commander seemed disappointed as he turned back to the table. She let out a slow breath and shook her head slightly, trying to clear it. Everything became solid and real and back in the right place again.

The little man who she liked at the other side of the Commander leaned back in his chair far enough that he was able to make eye contact. *Is he checking on me?* If he was, he was subtle, but there were too many eyes around the table, and so, she didn't speak to him.

Steyn banged on the table again. "While some of this is relevant, it's not as important as my original question. Is everyone happy with the plan?" Caryanne heard the undercurrent of impatience loud and clear.

The blonde woman that Caryanne had seen around the club spoke, "We shouldn't trust anyone." Her full attention was on Steyn. "Nobody can find out that we have Pesta or what's going to happen."

Steyn glared at the woman, making Caryanne's anxiety grow again. "Many will die, but our aim is to neutralize the TSS. Let's not forget that for a single moment."

"If that's true, why not attack them directly."

Steyn banged the table yet again, making one man at the other side almost tip over his chair. " Enough! I will answer you on this occasion. They are too well protected. Besides, they would just send more, and before you know it, we'd be overrun."

Caryanne tried to process what she was hearing but wasn't sure she understood everything correctly. They were talking about wiping out an entire planet as if was easy. She dug her nails into her palms. *It cannot be easy to kill that many people, can it?*

The woman pressed her lips together, clearly not convinced and wanting to say more, but she didn't. Soon after, the meeting ended.

Caryanne had the furthest to go to reach the door and

her way was blocked. She moved from the far side of the table when there was only the little man and the Commander left. During the walk across the floor, Caryanne forgot to be frightened. She was too consumed by repeating important facts over and over in her head so that she wouldn't forget—murder, planet, Mika, Kali. She made it as far as the small office. The exit lay a few steps ahead, but with every step, the information in her head became less and less critical.

Nearly there.

She'd almost reached safety when the Commander said, "Caryanne." She froze. There was nowhere to run. "Come this way. I want to show you something."

She turned to find him watching her like a predator watches a small bird. He smiled, and she was sure that he had purposefully let her believe that she could leave, only to catch her at the last second.

Caryanne's heart raced, and she couldn't breathe deeply. Too many memories swamped her until she didn't know who she was.

"It's okay." A male voice and warm hand on her arm, guiding her. It was the little man with kind eyes.

"Bring her this way, Pyra."

Pyra's face darkened, and she knew instinctively that he didn't have any choice but to obey, which meant that neither would she.

CHAPTER 18

THE RETURN JOURNEY had been just as tense as the one to Kaldern but for entirely different reasons. Mika had opened his mouth a couple of times but couldn't find the words. *I shouldn't have kissed her. It was selfish.* Except, they had survived impossible odds and that had made it seem like a good idea.

As soon as they'd arrived at the new TSS base on Fureron, Kali left Mika to secure the *Sepiantia* while she went to find Andy. At least, that's what he thought she'd mumbled about where she was going.

After securing the ship, Mika decided to check on the band. He knew something was wrong when he couldn't get hold of Vaira. Honk and Caryanne were erratic, but Vaira was as reliable as Kali. There was no way she wouldn't respond to a message, unless she couldn't.

Mika headed to what had become Andy's control room in the former hangar. On the way, he tried to stamp out his irritation at Kali, although knowing that she would sense it in a heartbeat didn't help.

Mika burst through the door without bothering to knock. Andy and Kali were sat, side by side at the table. They were staring at the holoprojection of a woman. Mika blinked on recognizing her—Saera Alexri!

Oh no! He considered apologizing, but since they were probably taking about him, he decided that she didn't deserve it.

Kali scowled.

Mika felt her irritation loud and clear. He swallowed the urge to shout at her to listen because that would not end well.

Instead, he said, "I can't get hold of anybody."

Kali stood, and in an overly controlled tone, said, "Excuse me."

Mika didn't need to connect to Kali's inner world to know how angry she was. Tough—this was important. She walked his way with a forced smile that always meant trouble.

Mika backed out of the room. Perhaps he should have said 'hello' and given a full explanation or tried to be polite, but it was too late now.

As soon as Kali was outside and the door was firmly closed, she spoke into his mind, *"Why didn't you just speak to me telepathically—like this?"*

Because he'd wanted an excuse to interrupt their meeting, but Mika didn't say that. An argument wouldn't get him what he needed. Not that it mattered when she saw everything he hadn't said on his face.

Mika crossed his arms. "I didn't know you were talking to the Lead Agent." He frowned. "You don't have to keep everything a secret."

"It's not a secret, and you're not in a position to demand that I keep you informed of TSS business." Kali folded her arms, matching his stance. *"Besides, it's hard to keep secrets, which is a problem."*

Mika glared. "Are you blaming me?"

She rolled her eyes. *"We still have to deal with what happened, and I'm trying to argue your case."*

"I'm sorry," Mika said, although he wasn't sorry at all. What did Andy and Kali see when they looked at him—an outsider, a maverick? *"I knew you were having an important* discussion," he didn't say, 'about me', *"but this was more important."*

"It was a meeting about your future, which should be as important to you as it is to me."

Mika knew that he shouldn't respond, knew that he didn't need to. *"If it concerns me, then don't you think that I should be there?"*

"No, because..." She searched for the words.

"I'm not TSS?"

"Well, yes. That's part of it, but if you really want to know—you are liable to make matters worse."

Mika knew she was right but he wasn't about to admit it. The fact that he still had to face charges and might end up locked up for a significant period didn't help. He'd hoped the SPEAR crisis would delay any trial. Surely they'd take into account the risks he'd taken and everything he'd achieved with Kali. If not, he could disappear in the Outer Colonies. Except, what about his mother? She might never wake but he had to be sure before he abandoned her. Then there was Kali. He needed her, and she'd never leave. The foking TSS was more important than he would ever be.

Mika took a deep breath. "I understand how you feel about the TSS."

"No, you don't, not really," Kali said immediately. "You don't have any claim on me."

She was right, but that line of thinking made him angrier. Mika had hoped that, with time, Kali would choose him, but it didn't look as if that wasn't going to happen.

She glared. "You are trying to ruin my career so that I have no choice? It won't work."

Mika took a step back. That wasn't true. And besides, they had more pressing matters to deal with.

Kali seemed to realize it at the same time. "What did you want?"

"I can't get hold of anyone in the band."

Kali checked the time. "It's early for them."

That was true but Vaira was always easy to contact, and

he felt that something was wrong. "Kali, we've already lost Owen. What if something has happened to them?"

Her tone softened, "It's different with Owen. He went off alone on Red Ghost when it was teeming with the enemy. There's nothing to make us think that anyone is actively targeting the band."

"You say that, but as we've been plastered all over the media, it isn't hard to find out that the band have a link to us. SPEAR is likely to go after anyone connected to us."

She thought for a few seconds. "You might be right, but they are with Treva. He'll have security. Have you tried contacting him?"

"No, I don't have his details, and they aren't public." Mika was annoyed at having to ask Kali to sort out something so simple. "Are you going back into that meeting?"

She responded telepathically. *"Probably not. They'll ask me what's happening, and we don't even know if there's anything to worry about."* Kali set off in the direction of their rooms.

Mika overtook her and picked up the pace. "Can you tell me anything about what you talked about in there? You know, about me?"

He thought he'd done well to keep the resentment out of his voice, but the look she gave him told him it had been an epic failure.

"Most of the meeting consisted of me trying not to tell them about our bond or what happened on the transit hub."

"Why didn't you tell them?"

He asked the question because he was curious as to what she'd say. He understood why she didn't want to dwell on the bond. She wished it hadn't happened in the first place. He tried not to feel hurt, knowing it wasn't something she had consciously sought.

She glared at him. "Do you want to be poked and prodded and examined. You've seen how everyone reacted when they found out what we did on the Antaris." She switched to telepathy even though they were alone. *"How do you think they're going to behave if they find out how we contained the explosion?"*

Perhaps due to the stress and uncertainty or because of the ridiculousness of the situation, Mika started to laugh. "Who would've thought that we'd be in this position?"

Kali scowled. "It's not funny. How will I explain any of it to my family?"

Mika thought about her trying to explain why she glowed in the dark, and it only made him laugh harder. Tears rolled down his face, and his stomach hurt.

"I don't... know." He tried to get his breath. "But, we... ate a... bomb."

"Shh, not out loud. Besides, we didn't really, even if that's what it felt like." Kali half-turned. "Stars, I should have known."

Mika straightened on seeing Andy jog down the corridor toward them. It suddenly wasn't so funny that they might have been overheard.

"What's going on?" Andy asked as he reached them. When neither answered, he looked at Kali. "I expected you to come back into the meeting."

"Er, well, Mika is worried that he can't get in touch with the others." At Andy's puzzled expression, she added, "The band."

Andy grimaced. "Let's not panic. They're safe on Glaendor, aren't they?"

Fed up with being ignored, Mika said, "They were on Glaendor. As to how safe they are, who knows."

Andy met Mika's eyes, which was an improvement. "They'll be fine. Probably, acting like rock stars, that's all."

Kali jumped in before Mika could have an angry outburst, "We're going to try to get in touch with Treva."

"Marco Steyn's boy? Okay. I was just checking that you understood that it's in your interest to get this sorted as soon as possible."

Mika hadn't considered what it would be like for Kali if he was locked up. It wasn't fair that it would affect her. She hadn't broken any rules.

Kali cleared her throat. "About that. I think Mika should be there."

Andy raised an eyebrow. "I will reschedule with that in mind, but Kali," she'd started to turn away but stopped, "come and find me as soon as you know the band are safe and let me know if there are *any* problems."

Mika wasn't sure if that last was a reference to him. He wouldn't be surprised, but they had to find out what was happening on Glaendor. Once Andy had gone, they went to Mika's room where Kali used the comm to put a call through to Glaendor.

Treva's face appeared onscreen. "Oh, hi, Kali. Um... nice of you to call." He looked older even though it had only been days since they'd last seen him.

"Treva, are you okay?"

He looked over his shoulder as if expecting someone to walk in and find him doing something he shouldn't. "Yes, it's just, uh... been difficult..."

Mika didn't know Treva, but it was clear he didn't want to talk to Kali, which was strange. They'd been through a lot together on the space station, and he had the impression that they liked each other.

"I'm just checking on the band." Frown lines creased the center of Kali's forehead. "Are they okay?"

"I think so." Treva had a distant look that Mika didn't like. He was thinking too hard about something instead of concentrating on the conversation.

Mika bit his tongue so as not to interrupt when Kali didn't immediately respond. *Don't be stupid. She's leaving space on purpose.*

Eventually, Treva answered as if suddenly remembering they were waiting, "They're at the Blue Pixie. They should be back soon."

"So, why aren't they answering our calls?"

"I don't know." There was a pause. "Sometimes they're a bit odd."

Mika had to concede that was true, but he wasn't happy. His gut insisted there was something wrong, and Treva's behavior wasn't making him feel better.

"Is there anything you wanted to talk about? You seem... tired."

Treva looked more nervous than tired, but Kali would have reasons for not pointing out the obvious. This time it was easier to stay quiet.

"No, I'm fine."

"Okay." She paused. "I'll be in touch. If you see Varia, get her to give Mika or me a call."

That was a sensible plan. They would be none the wiser if Treva gave the message to Honk, who would be too drunk to call, or Caryanne who would forget as soon as she was told.

Kali hung up and looked at Mika, who was formulating an argument for them to go to Glaendor. It almost didn't register that she was talking to him.

"What?"

"I said that you were right. There's something wrong. That didn't sound like Treva at all, and it was obvious that he couldn't talk freely. Let me speak to Andy."

"I'm coming with you."

Kali was already at the door, but she didn't argue when he followed her down the corridor.

Just to be sure she understood, Mika said, "We need to go to Glaendor."

Kali sighed. "It isn't going to be that easy. I don't think anyone is going to let us go off on our right own now, not when an attack could happen at any time."

"Kali, none of this is right. I know we might be able to help save people, but at the moment, we're just waiting for something to happen. Nobody ever won a war that way."

"I know. I feel frustrated as well, but I don't think it's down to us to win the war. We are one part of a whole effort to defeat SPEAR."

"But if the band is in trouble and we sit here doing nothing while we wait for something to happen, I'm not going to feel very good about it."

He saw that she was about to answer and then changed her mind. Good, at least she was thinking about what he was saying.

CHAPTER 19

PYRA DID AS Steyn directed and led the young woman—Caryanne—into the back office. She didn't resist, but he could tell that she wanted to.

The Commander seemed pleased, whether from the outcome of the meeting or their current situation, he couldn't tell. Pyra didn't know why Steyn wanted to play with Caryanne, particularly if she had something wrong with her. It occurred to him that Steyn was used to relying on his ability to read people and he'd become lazy. Perhaps, Pyra could use that to his advantage.

Caryanne looked up at him. "I'm in a band. You should see us play sometime. We could play here if we had our bass player and singer."

Steyn laughed. It was a proper belly laugh and startled both Caryanne and Pyra. They shared a look, unsure what it was that he'd found so amusing.

"Sorry, it's just that I think we might be able to do something about that. Give you a reunion so that you can play, what is it you call it—a gig?"

She nodded slowly, her voice small, "When we are together, we play gigs across the Outer Colonies."

"You just need your singer and bass-player, right?"

Caryanne relaxed a bit, and Pyra realized how tense

she'd been. "Owen is missing, and Kali is... I don't know."

"I find it fascinating how you remember some things and not others."

She shrugged. "I'm a mystery."

"Come this way. I hope to reunite you with a least one of your lost bandmates." Steyn turned to the door.

When Caryanne went to follow, Pyra hung onto her arm until she looked at him. Her eyes were full of questions that she knew better than to ask with Steyn within hearing distance. Reluctantly, he released her because there was no choice. She gave him a grateful smile and as trusting as a child, followed Steyn into the cellar.

Pyra didn't know what was down there, but he didn't think that it could be anything good. All he could do was be the silent witness and so, he too, followed.

By the time Pyra reached the head of the stairs, Steyn had switched on an overhead light. It wasn't bright, but they could all see a steep descent down large stone steps. Though it wasn't cold, Caryanne shivered. With the door wide, the dank smell leaked into the office.

When Steyn looked at Caryanne, she smiled as if she didn't have a care in the world, but Pyra saw beneath her mask. It took one actor to spot another.

Steyn led the way down the steps and after a slight hesitation, Caryanne followed. She was probably wondering what torture implements were down there, because that was what Pyra was thinking. He was also trying to work out how he was going to get them out of this situation. It was one thing to know about Steyn's crimes and quite another to witness them.

Pyra knew what his real boss would say, "It's not your job to interfere, only to record and report." In reality, it wasn't always that easy, especially as he'd liked Caryanne as soon as she'd wandered innocently into the meeting. She might not be what she appeared to be, but there was no malice, and her child-like quality brought out his protective instinct. Intellectually, he knew that he couldn't afford to interfere, not when more than his life hung in the balance.

They'd reached the bottom of the stairs, and Steyn was grinning from ear to ear. Pyra had never seen him so happy but the man was corrupt so it couldn't be a good sign. Whatever was going on appeared to be personal. At least, he was enjoying himself too much to notice that Pyra shouldn't have accompanied them down without checking that he was needed.

Caryanne grabbed Pyra's hand, surprising him with her strength. She was like a drowning woman, searching for rescue. Fortunately, Steyn couldn't see anything from his position at her other side, or else they might both have been in trouble.

Pyra squeezed her tiny fingers, trying to let her know he was on her side. Then, he realized that somehow she'd recognized that the first time they'd set eyes on each other, less than twenty minutes ago. Whatever Steyn had in mind, Pyra wasn't going to be able to stand by this time, no matter what his job required.

Someone shouted. The sound bounced off unforgiving brick and stone. It seemed to come from around the corner in the darkest part of the cellar.

Caryanne abruptly let go of his hand, moving deeper into the cellar. "Owen?" She broke into a run.

Steyn still had that stupid smile on his face, and it took all of Pyra's self-control not to punch the man. When Steyn gave Pyra a conspiratorial wink, he hurried after Caryanne into the dark before he could give himself away.

Once Pyra had moved beyond the light, he found that it wasn't pitch black and he could see. Against the far wall, Caryanne embraced someone. They whispered in that way only people who know each other well do.

Pyra felt a stab of envy. It happened so quickly that it took him a moment to recognize and discard it as inappropriate. He didn't even know Caryanne.

As he approached, the pair stopped talking. When they turned together, Pyra had to stamp down on a renewed surge of jealousy. They looked like they were one against the world. Pyra had never experienced anything like that since he worked alone, and there was a part of him that longed for that sort of connection.

Pyra didn't have to look to know that Steyn was behind him. He could hear his heavy tread on the rough concrete floor and see the expression of anger on Caryanne's friend's face as he looked beyond Pyra.

Steyn stopped next to Pyra. "See, Caryanne? I told you that I had a surprise for you. I bet you never guessed that it was Owen Bruiser."

Caryanne stared at him. Her smile had vanished and he could see the tension in her body.

The man—Owen—looked as if he wanted to rip Steyn's head from his shoulders. That's when Pyra noticed the heavy chains. It wasn't as if he hadn't known that Owen was a prisoner. That much had been obvious by the fact that he was living in a cellar. Nonetheless, the crude system of containment made Pyra worry for them all.

"What do you want with Caryanne?" Owen asked. "She's no use to you."

Steyn tutted. "There's no need to be like that. She's already been incredibly useful. In trying to work out how she came to be here, you've just run through a number of possible scenarios, which has showed me that you don't know anything useful."

Nobody spoke. The implication that Owen was of no more use to Steyn and therefore, disposable, hung in the air.

Steyn laughed. "I know what you're thinking, quite literally, but you might still be of *some* use to me."

Pyra frantically tried to find an argument for letting them go, but he couldn't think of anything that would sway Steyn. Nevertheless, he couldn't leave them in a dark cellar, even if it meant returning when the club was empty.

Steyn started to turn away, just as Pyra thought of something. "Wouldn't it be better if they were all in one place?"

Steyn swung back to stare at him—no doubt trying to read Pyra's mind, which he would never do. He'd tried to it a lot before remembering that it was pointless. Steyn didn't know that Pyra was a null and therefore impervious to telepathy, and so he had kept trying for a long time. Pyra didn't move, resisting the urge to say more, knowing that it would be counterproductive.

Finally, Steyn said, "You might be right; they can't go anywhere. If they try to run, I will get security to sort out the problem. I'll leave it to you." He strolled back to the exit.

Pyra went to release the chains, overwhelmed by the stench of body odor and urine as he got close. He had no means of freeing Owen and needed to find a key.

"I won't be long."

He located Ava at the bar where after some pestering, she reluctantly handed over the key. "Are you sure Steyn's okay with this?"

"Of course." Pyra met her gaze. "You can always blame me."

She nodded and turned away. Finally, she gave him a small key, although she was careful that Pyra didn't see its hiding place.

On his return, Caryanne grabbed his arm. "Thank you."

Pyra nodded. It was killing him that he couldn't explain, but while his mind was protected, there was nothing to stop Steyn from reading Owen or Caryanne. That was probably the real reason that Steyn agreed to release Owen into a larger, more comfortable prison in the first place. He was also providing Pyra with a myriad of opportunities to give himself away. Fortunately, Pyra had spent nearly two years getting close to Steyn and he wouldn't be baited into blowing his cover so easily. For now, he needed to get Owen and Caryanne to safety.

CHAPTER 20

OWEN THOUGHT HE was dreaming, but if he was, it was vivid—different to the usual confused mess that went off in his head. *Why would he let me go?*

When Caryanne had walked into the cellar, Owen had thought that he was hallucinating until he'd felt her soft, warm hands and smelled the faint floral scent of the hand cream that she preferred. Then, he'd worried that she'd been captured as well.

Now, he was dirty and stinky but free. Although Pyra said they weren't free, it sure felt like it after the hours or days or months in the dark. His eyes hadn't fully adjusted to the brightness, which had resulted in a dull headache that made every movement painful. Not only that, but he was so weak that he could hardly walk.

It must have been adrenaline that enabled Owen to climb the steep steps from the cellar to the remarkably innocuous office. He let his head fall back against the cool headrest of the chair. Caryanne had gone off to tell the rest of the band to return to the apartment where they were staying with Treva. He vaguely remembered the boy from Red Ghost, although it felt like a lifetime ago.

Owen raised his head to look at Pyra who perched on the desk, staring at the door Caryanne had gone through a few minutes ago. "Why can't we go together?"

Pyra frowned. "We don't want to draw any more attention than necessary."

The door swung open, causing Pyra to jump to his feet, but it was only Caryanne. She slipped inside, pressing her back to the wood as if her slight body could stop anyone entering.

Her eyes went straight to Owen. "I couldn't tell them why because they would have charged in here so I told them that."

Owen nodded, although the truth was, he was finding it difficult to follow what was happening. At least he was out of the cellar. He could cling to that fact.

Caryanne moved to Owen's side as without a word, Pyra left. A minute later and he was back, hustling them out of a fire exit into a shuttle he must have arranged to meet them around the back. It was evident that Andrei Steyn could get anything he wanted and it appeared that Pyra had used that to his advantage.

Owen looked out of the window of the transport shuttle. They were on Glaendor where the band had played a couple of gigs what felt like a lifetime ago. The planet hadn't made an impression on him the first time, and after his captivity, he would be happy to leave.

The shuttle stopped outside a tall building, surrounded by landscaped gardens. Owen had the feeling that if he were to walk in the grounds, they would disintegrate into dust.

Caryanne climbed out and waited to help as if he were a hundred years old. He gathered his energy and heaved himself onto the paved area at the building's entrance.

Pyra had already paid for the shuttle ride, and now led the way into the chrome and glass building. Owen stumbled over his feet and was grateful for Caryanne. She had his arm trapped in the bend of her elbow. He hated to admit that he needed the support, but each step was a struggle. His legs shook like a quivering mess. Caryanne murmured her usual nonsense, which he found it comforting.

When in the confined space of the elevator, Owen became aware of how badly he smelled. Neither Pyra nor Caryanne gave any indication that they were offended by the stench.

"I need to get clean."

Pyra spoke for the first time since they'd gotten into the shuttle. "I'm sure Treva will be able to help."

Owen leaned against the side of the elevator. "Can you tell us what is going on?"

"No."

"Worth a try." Owen found it hard to think past his immediate needs and so didn't force the issue.

Pyra didn't look at them as he said, "Steyn could want me at any time."

Owen suspected that Pyra was trying to warn them of Steyn's telepathy. The monster had been in Owen's head and so, he understood the danger, which was why he didn't ask any more questions and tried not to think at all.

The elevator was super smooth and quick, but Owen still sagged when they reached the top floor. Doors opened onto an expanse of tiles with floor to ceiling windows at either side. Owen barely took in the details, only seeing the vast distance to cover before he reached the one apartment on this floor.

Caryanne helped him across the sandy-colored marble while he tried not to lean too much on her small frame. After a few steps, he couldn't support his own weight. Fortunately, Caryanne was stronger than she looked.

Caryanne stared at the closed doors of the elevator for a long moment, while Owen was only half-aware of it disappearing with Pyra.

"Why does it have to be so far?" he muttered.

"Come on. You can do it."

Apparently, he couldn't. One minute the floor was beneath him and the next his cheek was pressed against the smooth tiles.

People suddenly surrounded them. He picked out Vaira and Honk's legs before someone strong lifted him, carrying him into the apartment where he sank into softness. It did little to ease his aching muscles, but he was so tired that his eyelids fluttered.

Despite the grime and dried sweat, Caryanne continued to hold one of his hands in a gentle grip. He saw her mouth move but couldn't hear what she said. Honk, Vaira, the boy—Treva—and a woman he didn't know were talking at once, drowning out Caryanne. The woman had dark skin and brown eyes like Treva. Even with one hand over her mouth, Owen knew she was Treva's mother.

Nobody paid attention to Caryanne because they were used to her inability to say anything meaningful. If she hadn't been trying so hard, Owen would have ignored her, too. She wouldn't remember anything but who knew what she'd been through and besides, it was cruel when she was trying so hard. Even if she didn't remember anything, he wanted someone to listen to her.

Owen raised his free hand. Vaira grabbed it, leaning in close to find out what he wanted.

"Listen to Caryanne."

Vaira straightened, releasing him before clapping and shouting in a deafening voice, "Everyone, Caryanne has something to say."

Caryanne's shoulders sagged slightly in relief, and she smiled gratefully at Vaira. It wasn't her usual vacant smile, which was why Owen forced his eyes fully open.

Treva shook his head. "No, it's not safe."

Vaira's eyes widened, but she quickly recovered. "Play some music."

"Does that actually work?" Treva looked skeptical.

Vaira shrugged. "I don't know, but if Caryanne is going to tell us something, I can't wait long to find out what it is."

"Computer," Honk said, "play *Dark Matter* by the Higgs Boson Bruisers."

The familiar intro to the song Owen had written filled the room. He wanted to object. His song should be played at a higher volume, but he didn't have the energy to get anyone's attention. They huddled close, except for Honk who leaned against the wall.

With nowhere to sit, Vaira crouched. "What do you want to tell us?"

Caryanne stared at her hand. The one still holding Owen's and opened her mouth. Nothing came out and it took another try for anything to emerge, but by that time she had everyone's attention. "I had to... force myself... to remember. Memory is sometimes important." She looked at the faces of those standing above her. "The Commander said my brain was broken, but he was in my head at my worst. You know how I can be," she didn't wait for a response, "and so, I think it convinced him that I couldn't remember, but I had to."

"In your head?" Vaira scowled.

Honk looked as if he was going to slide down the wall at any moment. "What is a commander?"

Everyone shared puzzled looks, but Owen knew some of what she was talking about. He willed them to listen because he didn't have the energy to intervene.

Caryanne continued, "Owen can't tell you because he wasn't there, which is why I had to remember."

His mind filled with questions. It was amazing that Caryanne was speaking for longer than a sentence and might be why people continued to listen.

Caryanne looked down. "I don't remember everything. It's a jumble." Owen squeezed her hand, and she smiled before continuing, "The Commander reads minds." She stopped and Owen was about to tell her to go on, when she started talking again, "I needed to warn you. We are in a prison and there is something about, something about..." Her face screwed up in concentration. "Something called Pesta." She waved a hand. "I think they want to take control from the TSS."

Treva's mother ran from the room. Honk slid down the wall with both legs stretched out in front of him like a drunk deer. Although his eyes were open, it wasn't clear if he'd heard any of what Caryanne said.

Vaira collapsed on the bed. Owen couldn't see her expression but imagined she was as shocked as everyone.

Owen's eyes drifted shut. He would just close them for a few minutes before they made plans.

— — —

Where is she? The apartment was large, but Treva had checked every room while searching for his mother.

True, he wasn't able to concentrate as he was still reeling from Owen's arrival, but he didn't think he'd missed any rooms. He struggled to believe that Owen had been a captive at the Blue Pixie when Ava had shown him around the club. Did she know? Who was the Commander and why hadn't Treva heard anything about him? It was as if he was skimming the over the surface of life, never seeing what lay beneath.

"Sorry," he muttered, shutting the bathroom door quickly, not wanting to see what Honk was doing in there.

His mother wasn't anywhere in the apartment. Treva's throat felt tight. She could be reckless, but she wouldn't, not now, would she?

They couldn't leave the apartment, never mind take a ship off-planet. All attempts to book passage had failed.

None of the band had seen Anissa Marsh. After one last check of the bedrooms, he stopped in the hallway. She was gone. Somehow, she'd disappeared, but to where?

He checked again, this time looking for anything that might tell him where she was headed. It was another seven minutes before he thought to check his handheld and found her message.

My dearest Treva,

I know that you will worry when you read this, and for that, I am genuinely sorry. You have tried to find a way off this planet but your father's family is blocking passage. I need to try to reason with them as there is nothing to be gained from keeping us as prisoners. It might be foolish but I have to try. I am not strong enough to sit here and wait.

I will do my best to come back to you but if something happens, I want you to leave with the others. I have sent you the address and contact details of your aunt, my sister. You won't remember her but she will take good care of you. Under no circumstances are you to come looking for me.

Please forgive me.

I love you more than life,
Mom xxx

Treva closed his eyes, trying to hold in the terror so he could think. *Where did she go?* The only place he could think of was the Blue Pixie. Perhaps, the Commander would send her back, or lock her in the cellar!

She must have gone before Treva was awake! Did she really think that he wouldn't go after her? *She thinks of me as the fifteen-year-old child I was before she was kidnapped.* If only she'd known what he'd done, there was no way she would expect him to wait at the apartment. He should have told her instead of trying to protect her.

There was no time to waste. He didn't want to draw attention to the fact that she was missing any more than he already had by telling the others when they were being watched.

Treva slipped out, glancing over his shoulder to make sure the door locked behind him. The elevator arrived with a soft beep and he stepped inside, ignoring the growing tension between his shoulder blades as he watched the numbers on the digital display count down.

Eight, seven—

Treva racked his brain, trying to think of something to tell security.

The elevator beeped at the ground floor, and the doors opened to reveal the lobby. Treva's mouth was so dry, he couldn't swallow.

Act as if you are entitled to leave. He straightened and tried to relax the muscles of his face while thinking this was the stupidest plan he'd ever had.

He stepped out and was immediately confronted by a couple of security guards, wearing the uniform of Avon Security. With both guards' full attention was on him, he tried not to feel intimidated. They were a good deal taller than him.

"Good afternoon, sir. Can I ask where you're going?"

Treva opened his mouth while his brain worked frantically to come up with a plausible answer. "Blue Pixie." As the truth slipped out, he realized that it was as good an answer as any.

The nearest guard consulted his handheld. "I'm sorry it's no longer on the list of approved destinations."

Treva didn't have to fake surprise since he hadn't known there was a list. "It's not? I went there yesterday."

"I can see that, but the situation changed when your latest friend moved into the apartment, too."

"What *is* on the list?" Treva asked in desperation.

"Nowhere." There was no apology in the man's tone.

Treva started to ask why he'd bothered to check but stopped. He considered demanding that they treat him with respect but doubted that he could pull it off. It probably wouldn't do any good and could get him confined somewhere worse than the apartment. Better to play along.

"Can you ask the Commander if I can go to the Blue Pixie, please? I'm sure that it should be on the list. I need to keep an eye on my business interests."

The guard stared at him without blinking.

Treva couldn't give up; he had to find his mother. "I mean, Ava has been teaching me about the business."

Perhaps, it was Ava's name or maybe the man took pity on him, but the guard sighed before speaking into his headset. "Unit 102 requesting permission for—" He looked Treva in the eye. "Name?"

"I thought you knew, which is why you stopped me."

The guard frowned. "We have orders to stop anyone from leaving the eighth floor."

For the first time, Treva noticed a digital display above the sliding doors that identified the floor where the elevator stopped. It occurred to him that they might sneak out if they walked to another floor. Surely, it couldn't be that easy. The guard was staring at him.

"Treva," he almost choked out, "Steyn." He would become Steyn if it got him what he needed.

"Roger." The guard turned his attention to Treva, "That will be acceptable."

He let out a relieved breath. "Thank you."

The guard glanced at his colleague. "Jon will have the shuttle brought around."

Treva had known he wouldn't be allowed to go alone and was just pleased to get an agreement to leave the apartment, even if the Blue Pixie was the last place he wanted to go.

The transport shuttle was one of the small ones that were designed for quick transfers. Fortunately, only Jon sat up front while Treva leaned into the plush seat at the rear. He stared at the apartment on the top floor, wishing he'd told the others what he was doing. Too late for regrets now. As they set off, his eyes were drawn to a dark line against the side of the building. It took his brain a second to catch up.

A fire escape! Perhaps there's a way down after all.

The journey passed quickly with Treva alternating between wanting to kill his mother and worrying that he wouldn't find her. On arrival, there were more Avon security guards outside but they allowed Treva to pass without comment. Communication between the groups must be better than expected.

Once his eyes had adjusted to the change in light, he scanned the bar. Nash wasn't there and neither was his mother. Treva hesitated. He didn't want to go to the back room, but he had to check.

Treva crossed to the back corridor, trying not to dwell on how nobody took him seriously because of his young age. He was surprised to see yet another guard outside, a sure sign that something had changed. It was too late, he couldn't return to the apartment without knowing and so, he squared his shoulders and approached the door.

This guard stepped to meet him. "Is the Commander expecting you?"

Treva hesitated a moment too long, trying to decide between a lie and the truth.

The guard didn't wait for an answer. "I will ask." He slipped through the door. Treva didn't have time to turn around before the man was back, saying, "You are expected."

Blinking in surprise, Treva entered the familiar room, wondering what he was doing. There were four figures but he only saw his mother.

The surprise on her face must have mirrored his own. She started to stand until the large man next to her put a hand on her arm. From where he sat in the middle, Treva decided that he must be the Commander. The little man—Pyra—he'd seen three days ago stared at his handheld while Ava winked, sending a shiver down his spine.

Treva's mother scowled at the Commander as she shook off his hand, coming to Treva's side. "I told you not to follow me." She looked more scared than angry.

The Commander leaned into a pool of light cast by a

desk lamp, causing Treva to suck in a breath. The man's features were similar to his father's and the same as his own. With a resemblance that strong, Treva didn't doubt he was a close blood relative.

Why is he treating us this way?

Treva stepped into the room. "Who are you?"

"Ah, yes." The Commander stood and moved around the desk so they were within touching distance. "I've seen your picture." There was a pause before he added, "I'm your uncle, Andrei Steyn."

"But why?" Treva's mind whirled.

Treva didn't doubt the family connection, but there was nothing friendly about the man in front of him. His father had told him little about their family and had promised that he would meet them at some point. There'd been no mention of an uncle, but his mother was full of warnings about Marco's extended family. It was something he couldn't ignore any longer. They needed to get away from the Blue Pixie.

"You have everything you need?" Andrei—Treva couldn't think of him as the Commander—said with a smile full of teeth. "All you need to do is stay out of my way. It's not difficult, is it, Anissa?"

His mother tugged on Treva's arm. He wanted to ask more but knew that she was right and they should get out.

"Treva," Andrei said as his mother pulled him through the door. "If you speak to any pirates, I want to know everything they say."

Why does he need me to tell him anything when he is monitoring us?

The door close and Treva ran with his mother into the club. It was louder than a few minutes ago, although it could only be mid-afternoon.

"Are you okay?" Treva asked.

Anissa stopped with one hand on the empty bar and took a deep breath. "Yes."

Treva's head was spinning as he spotted the guard

from the apartment. He pointed. "That one brought me here."

There was a faint smile on her lips as she said, "Jon—he transported me as well. I will see if he'll take us back." She strode off.

Before he could follow, someone touched his arm. He turned to see Pyra and there was something different about him.

"I want to help." Pyra scanned the bar but only his eyes moved. "Walk to the door as if I'm escorting you."

Treva frowned, unsure whether to trust him. "Why?"

"I'm out of time." He started toward where his mother was talking to the guard. You know the pirates?"

Treva was about to deny it when he felt something hard press against his leg. He froze. A weapon? Some sort of bomb?

"Keep walking."

Treva forced his legs to move.

"Take this." Something hard hit Treva's leg. "It will jam third party signals. Once on, it covers seven meters."

No threats, but it doesn't mean I can trust him. Have we got anything to lose? He grimaced because he'd seen firsthand that things could always get worse. His hand curled around the small object, and he slipped it into his pocket.

"Tell the pirates not to sell the drugs. They are designed to kill over time." Treva opened his mouth, but Pyra interrupted. "I know you have no reason to trust me, but I'm out of options."

"What—"

"There isn't time. Steyn is a telepath. You need to hide what you know."

Treva was stunned. *What did I think about just now?* What could he have given away? They were almost at the door. "How?"

"Fill your mind with everything that he expects and hope he doesn't look further."

As they reached Jon and his mother, Pyra stumbled

over something on the floor. "My life is in your hands."

Treva couldn't see what he'd tripped over. The little man chuckled as if he did it all the time. He looked so different from the intensely intelligent man from moments earlier that Treva didn't know what to think.

—   —   —

Time was running out for Pyra even if he chose not to act. He only had a few minutes to established a comm link if he was going to do it. Still, he waited.

Is this the only option?

Until a day ago, Pyra expected to continue working undercover for the TSS for another few years. Although his cover remained intact, he was now going to blow it.

Perhaps he could escape through the TSD arch hidden in the cellar. He dismissed the idea. Although, he hadn't managed to find out where it went, it would be somewhere under Steyn's control.

Steyn had to monitor all outgoing communications, and even if Pyra had the scrambling device, they would have picked up the unauthorized destination. Since he'd given the device to Treva, there was no chance of using it. Someone would discover him, if not immediately, then soon. Pyra couldn't disappear for a short period without drawing suspicion, and it wasn't for lack of trying.

After meeting Pesta, when Pyra had known the situation had become too desperate to ignore, he'd tried to get out information but found his handheld blocked. This would be his only report, and it would have to be enough because this ultimate, unspoken sacrifice had to be given freely. Nobody could ask him to give up his life to fight the power intent on enslaving his people.

Pyra had waited until he'd was sure there was no choice and he had reached the point where he simply couldn't live with himself if he didn't do everything to stop Steyn.

This is really happening, and soon. I won't be able to take it back. A film of moisture coated his hands, and dry dust clogged his nostrils, making him feel nauseous. He found it hard to think beyond the words that made up his report.

The call went through and as with previous missions, it was answered immediately. Pyra didn't know the woman on the other end and didn't bother asking her name. Instead, he relayed the information quickly. Since he could be discovered at any time, it was important to convey only the facts. Finally, he sent through the horrendous recording that Steyn had played during the last meeting, showing the effect of unleashing Pesta on a planet. Once done, he felt a profound sense of relief.

When the woman asked if he could wait, he agreed. *Nothing matters now.*

The next voice he knew, even though he'd never spoken to her directly.

"I'm Saera Alexri, and I wanted to thank you. I don't need to tell you how vital your intelligence is in this war." Her voice was soft. "Do you need help to get out?"

Pyra straightened and his throat felt thick as he prepared to address the Lead Agent. "Thank you, but there's no way off-planet, as far as I can tell."

"I understand." She paused before saying, "Do you need to end the call?"

Pyra smiled sadly. "It doesn't matter what I do now."

"Please say 'no', if you would rather not, but would you speak to one of our operatives near to Glaendor?"

"Mika and Kali?"

"No, but how do you... forget it. We don't have time."

"I'd be happy to tell you what I know." Pyra couldn't believe that he hadn't been discovered. It was essential to provide as many facts as possible to help the TSS in their fight against SPEAR. The scale of his betrayal wouldn't matter as the outcome would be the same.

The Lead Agent didn't try to pretend that he would be okay as she said, "We will always be grateful for your sacrifice."

After a couple of clicks, a male voice came through, "Hello, I'm Andy Rentaria. Thank you for speaking to me. Did the Lead Agent explain that we can have people on the way? Anything you can tell me about the situation on Glaendor would be useful."

Pyra had accepted that his own death was inevitable, but now, he started to wonder if he could stay alive long enough for help to arrive. Reality returned in a rush. *Wishful thinking. Steyn isn't going to let me slip away.*

"Nobody can dock on Glaendor. It's under the control of SPEAR. And Avon, the private security company, do whatever they want. I doubt that they will allow your ships anywhere near," Pyra said.

If the news impacted Andy in any way, it didn't come through in his voice. "That is really useful. Are you safe enough to answer some questions?"

Pyra snorted and glanced at the door. "It's only a matter of time until someone spots the call."

"I'm sorry. Your information will save many lives."

"What do you want to know?" Pyra didn't want to hear anything more about his sacrifice. It was too much like talking about a terminal illness.

"What is SPEAR's objective?" Agent Rentaria asked.

"To show that the TSS is an enemy of the Outer Planets and offer an alternative leadership."

"Is there anything you haven't already told us about Pesta?"

"I can't see Pesta, but her handler says that she is sentient."

"What about Steyn?" Andy would not have heard his report.

"He seems to be the mastermind behind SPEAR, and he wants operatives Kali Wietris and Mika Hendri either killed or captured, as he blames them for the failure of his plans."

"Thank you, Pyra. Your—"

Pyra cut the call as he couldn't stand more talk of

greatness or sacrifice. If his life was going to be short, it was better not to dwell on death.

The door opened, spilling noise into the room. Ava was silhouetted in the doorway. He couldn't see her expression as she sauntered across to stop at the other side of the desk, leaning against it with one hip jutting out. Ava was beautiful, but Pyra saw the way she watched for any sign of weakness. Apparently, even Marco Steyn had fallen for her charms at one time.

Now, as she cocked her head to one side, letting her blonde hair fall across one cheek, he wasn't fooled. The posture was contrived, and yet, he could see how some might be too blinded by their desire not to notice.

Pyra stood, unsure what he was going to do. His heart pounded as he wiped his palms on his pant legs. He hadn't expected to feel so afraid.

"Pyra," she caressed his name, "what are you doing?"

"I was thinking about making a call." As always, he stayed as close to the truth as possible.

She forced out a laugh. "Who would *you* have to call?"

"I'm not totally alone." Sometimes he enjoyed making a game of telling the truth without revealing anything but today, not so much.

She considered before shaking her head. "Who would have you?"

Pyra smiled. Ava would never understand what it was to be part of something bigger. He almost felt sorry for her.

Some of that must have shown on his face because she turned away. "I want to see this Pesta for myself."

Pyra hadn't expected that. She must have found out that he'd been to see Pesta.

Perhaps he should seize what circumstances offered and see where it led. "I would love to help, but even though I went to see the creature, Steyn... Commander didn't tell me much. What do you know?"

CHAPTER 21

THE SHUTTLE SKIMMED over vast forests interspersed with patches of agriculture. The sky was bright, and it would be easy to believe that there was nothing wrong. Unfortunately, Herja's gut told the truth. She felt vulnerable in the tiny craft but had wanted to leave the *Hyperion* with its cargo out of range of Jeolla's planetary defenses.

She couldn't settle, and Gosta's heavy breathing was annoying. So far, she'd managed to keep her irritation to herself, but they needed to get on with it.

"Take us lower," she instructed. "I want to see exactly what we are dealing with." What she couldn't say was that she wanted to see those who might be affected by the new drug. Gosta, quite rightly, would point out that she was torturing herself.

His contact had eagerly set up a meeting when he'd found out where the drugs had originated. It didn't surprise her to learn that he was a Governor on one of the planets that had refused to help her people a year ago.

Herja couldn't shake the uncomfortable feeling that dealing drugs was going to bring them trouble. "It's always those with the least that suffer," she murmured.

Gosta looked up. "What?"

"Never mind."

People working in the fields turned to stare as if they didn't see many ships. There were a handful of transport shuttles over the city but nothing out this far.

Why do they use manual labor to harvest? It didn't make any sense with technology so freely available. Makaris Corp practically handed out harvesters to anyone willing do the groundwork for a farming operation.

"Let's get the meeting over with," she said.

Gosta turned them toward the capital, following directions from air traffic control before descending to the private station. The high fencing and excessive security at the perimeter did nothing to improve Herja's mood. Armed troops awaited their arrival.

Gosta's expression was grim. "Are you sure about this?"

"Now he has doubts." Herja raised her eyes. "If we turn away, they will probably shoot us down."

This whole operation was wrong, but at least the *Hyperion* was far enough away to not be in danger. Unfortunately, that meant no backup; they had no choice but to brazen it out now.

Once on the ground, they waited for clearance. Herja glared at Gosta, who wisely stayed quiet. The whole situation was an indication of how desperate they were. Something had to change soon.

"They deserve it," Gosta mumbled.

She gave him a sidelong look, wondering if he was trying to convince himself. He was right, nobody in the Outer Colonies had agreed to help. The richest planets were the worst. When her world and people were in trouble, some thought that they might be infectious, but they could still have offered aid. Herja and her people had been forced into their current role, but that didn't make her feel any better about what they were doing.

The hatch opened, and they stepped out into the smell of fruit—although, it might be that she'd been in artificial environments for so long that the scents in natural atmosphere felt alien. Herja touched the sample she'd brought along to makes sure it was still there. The last thing she needed was to go into a negotiation off-balance.

An official smiled as if greeting a delegation, not a pair of drug dealers. Herja forced a matching smile, feeling that the whole situation was a bit bizarre. Despite the additional security, she would have been more comfortable in a seedy bar. Better to take a chance with witnesses present rather than behind a fence, surrounded by armed guards.

Despite the friendly greeting, the man didn't offer a name as he led the way to a large hangar past row upon row of ship parts. They made their way to a small office at the back with a sofa, chairs, and a small bar. Either, these people entertained dubious people regularly, or it was a great place to work. Nothing stood out as suspicious, but she didn't like it one bit.

Why did I let Gosta talk me into this?

For a brief second, Herja thought there was a child by the bar, but on closer inspection, it turned out to be a tiny woman. The shoes gave her away, which also meant she couldn't be as frail as she initially appeared, since she needed more strength in her calves than Herja had in her entire body to balance on the massive heels.

When she raised a glass in their direction, Herja shook her head and glanced at Gosta, who was staring, narrow-eyed, at the official who'd led them here. It made her feel better that he didn't trust the situation any more than she did.

Another man followed them into the room. He was almost an identical copy of the first, except that he was as tall as Gosta. *Brothers?*

Nobody had checked them for weapons, and yet, Herja was certain they had no chance of getting off the base until allowed to leave. Without speaking, she took a seat. Gosta raised an eyebrow and she took a small amount of pleasure in knowing that he'd have to remain standing. There needed to be enough distance between them that if attacked, they wouldn't go down together.

Next, two big men filed in, flanking the door they'd entered—as if more security was necessary. This was more like what she'd expected, which made her feel better.

She closed her eyes briefly, before smiling. "You know who we are."

The first brother spoke, "There's no need to tell you more than you already know."

The new brother crossed his arms. "What have you got for us?" His voice was surprisingly high for such a big man. "We need something new to keep our people entertained."

The first brother looked at him sharply.

Yes, you wouldn't want those words to get out, would you?

Herja thought of the people working in the fields and wondered why they bothered to lie, not that it mattered. She just needed to get this done as quickly as possible before she changed her mind.

Gosta flashed her a look.

She sighed and pulled out the small packet.

"I'll be honest." She smiled, knowing they wouldn't believe her. "This came into our possession... by accident."

"But you've checked it?" Brother two's voice went an octave higher.

"Umm." It was obvious that they hadn't.

The other brother muttered, "Amateurs."

He intended it as an insult, but Herja didn't care. It was true, they *were* amateurs in the world of drug dealing, and she wanted to keep it that way.

The tension in the room increased. Herja knew these people thought that they were at their mercy, but she had a few tricks to show them.

Brother one signaled to the man on the left. Without a word, he stepped forward to snatch the packet before jabbing a device into the bag to draw out a sample, which he then injected under his skin.

It happened so fast that Herja only made sense of it

afterwards. They'd not asked what drug was on sale before he'd pumped it into his body. She couldn't imagine anything that could induce her to do the same. *Just what sort of people are these?*

The drug took effect immediately. Everyone watched as he swayed from side to side before toppling to the floor.

Herja was halfway to her feet when brother one said, "He blissed-out so fast." The awe in his voice worried her. "You have some decent shite."

"He looks unwell," Herja said, wondering if 'decent shite' meant they had a sale.

She'd moved to Gosta's side for a better look at the unconscious man. He was pale and his eyes were closed, but his face was relaxed. Had he sustained a head injury in the fall? If he'd expected to keel over, why hadn't he sat down first? He blinked a couple of times and lurched upright, causing Herja to grab Gosta's arm.

Gosta dug an elbow into her ribs, and she suppressed a grunt at the sharp pain. Now, wasn't the time to retaliate but he would pay, even if he was right and she wasn't working to sell the stuff. This was definitely her last drug deal.

Her handheld alerted her to a call, which she fully intended to ignore, except the code that flashed up meant it was Treva. She stared at the screen for a long moment while the dainty woman brought their test subject a drink. From the smell, the fumes should be enough to revive him.

Herja glanced at her handheld for a second time. Thing was, Treva wouldn't be calling for a chat. Something was wrong.

She looked up. "Sorry, but I need to take this."

Gosta stared with wide, disbelieving eyes and shook his head, attempting to signal to her. Since she didn't need to be telepathic to know he was telling her not to fok this up, she ignored him.

The brothers frowned, but she didn't give them a chance to do anything before she was back in the hangar, taking in a great lungful of hot grease and oil.

"Treva, this isn't a good time."

"Don't sell the drugs you got from my dad."

Herja stared out through the wide-open doors, not seeing anything. She was trying to work out if Treva knew where she was and what she was doing. If not, it was an uncanny coincidence that he'd contacted her now. She shook her head—it had to be a coincidence.

"Why?"

"They're designed to kill."

She couldn't make sense of what he was saying for a moment. "You're wrong. I've just seen someone take some and he's fine. Better than fine, blissed out." *Whatever that means.*

"They don't kill immediately. It takes time."

"That's drugs for you."

"No, I mean one dose kills but not straight away."

Inside, she cursed but it didn't help. She'd known that this was a bad idea, no matter how desperate they were. She was going to kill Gosta if they got out alive.

"Herja?" Treva's voice sounded far away. "Are you still there?"

"Thank you, I heard and understand." She hung up.

It didn't change anything; all their reasons for being here still applied. They could sell the drugs regardless of the effects, except her foking conscience wouldn't let her. It wasn't the population of Jeolla that had refused to help Herja's people, it was those in power. The same people who would make a profit.

Even with the decision made, she still didn't know if they could escape the base. *How did I end up in this position? It is Gosta's fault.*

Herja palmed her pulse gun, hiding it in the long sleeves she'd worn for this very reason. She swept back into the room. Everyone, except the woman and man by the door, were seated.

Smiling, she plucked the bag containing the drugs off

the table. "Something's come up. We will have to rearrange."

Gosta surged to his feet. At least he wouldn't question her in front of those who had the potential to pose a threat.

The others stood, confused.

She had to keep them off-balance.

"We can't let you leave with the goods," the first brother said.

Herja tossed the small bag on the table. "That's all we have with us." They were desperate. She hadn't even taken payment. "The price will be acceptable." She had to offer something.

Brother two took a step in their direction. "It's a deal then."

Herja knew she shouldn't agree but didn't see another way out. "It's agreed." One way or another, it would cost them later.

Brother one nodded to the man at the door while his colleague remained slumped. Herja saw that his color had returned and wondered how long he had to live. She pushed away guilt and hurried out with Gosta. Once outside, they ran before anyone could offer an escort.

"Are you going to tell me what happened?" Gosta panted at her side.

"On the shuttle."

Every step, Herja expected an armed guard to stop them. As soon as they were on the shuttle, Gosta sealed the hatch and Herja ran through the pre-flight checks, only remembering at the last second to request permission to leave. Only once it was granted, she bent forward in relief.

Gosta planted his palms on the console. "We're in trouble, aren't we?"

"You could say that."

CHAPTER 22

AFTER ENDING THE call with Herja, Treva did his best to get the others together. Owen suggested the kitchen, as it was where people were most likely to congregate. It was also big enough to accommodate everyone comfortably. Whoever monitored them was going to be suspicious whatever, which meant they might only get one shot at a private conversation.

"I hope that jamming thing works." His mother waved at the grey box sitting in the middle of the marble table where Treva had placed it.

Straps came off each side like it was designed to fly or be secured to a limb. When on, it emitted a soft buzzing but only when touched. Even with the noise, Treva wasn't sure that it was doing anything. It was risky trusting Pyra when they didn't know anything about him.

Treva waited until everyone, except Vaira, had filed in, which took a frustrating amount of time, before switching on the device. *Where is she?* Everyone talked at once, making Treva want to shout for order like Mr. Rothi at school.

Vaira hurried into the room. "Is it on?"

"Yes."

The room went quiet.

"We were acting like normal, even if some of us overdid it." Owen said from where he stood over at the counter, glaring at Honk, who leaned back in a chair with both feet on the table. "So that nobody would get suspicious."

"Oh, that makes sense." Treva should have thought of that. "We don't know how closely they are monitoring us so, it's best to be careful."

"Speak for yourself. I went to see if there was a way to get to another floor. We might even get someone to help us or, at least, let us use their—"

"That's a good idea," Treva interrupted her. "It might be possible to sneak out from another floor."

Vaira snorted. "Forget it. I couldn't budge the interior stairway door. Someone's secured it to trap us up here."

Treva muttered, "Of course they'd think to do that."

Owen cracked a couple of eggs into a bowl. "We don't know how much time we have before they investigate; might as well have lunch ready in case anyone turns up."

Owen was almost back to his old self, except for a haunted look that he got from time to time, when he would stare into space. He couldn't have been given much food at the Blue Pixie because he'd done nothing but sleep and eat since arriving at the apartment.

Caryanne leaned against the counter close to Owen. "I'll help."

How can they think about food? Treva was too anxious but agreed that it made sense to behave as normal as possible. He moved back his chair to see everyone.

Vaira frowned. "Omelet?" She hovered near the door as if reconsidering the decision to join them.

Before they could get into a pointless discussion, Treva said, "We need to decide what we're going to do."

His mother leaned forward, placing both hands palm down on the table. "These people are ruthless. We need to get out of here."

"I agree," Owen said, patting Caryanne's arm as she wrinkled her nose at the pan's contents.

Vaira came to sit at the table where she picked at her nails. "We'll never get past the security." She looked at Owen. "They didn't bother us last time we were here for a gig on Glaendor, did they?"

Owen chopped something green. "We have to try to leave."

"I'm working on it," Honk said, balancing his chair on two legs at the far end of the table.

Treva had no idea what he meant and, like the others, ignored him. He caught his mother shaking her head, lips pinched.

Giving her nails a break, Vaira leaned back in a mirror image of Honk. "What are we going to do?"

Owen handed Caryanne a spoon, although it wasn't clear what she was going to do with it. "We ask Kali for help, and failing that, go to someone else in the TSS."

Caryanne looked up. "But, we have everything we need here."

Treva's mother shook her head vigorously. "Only until they decide to kill us." She put her hand over Treva's. "I know it's hard, but we can't just wait for rescue. I'm pretty sure I can distract one of the guards even if we can't get off planet."

Treva frowned. "How do you know that Jon's going to be working?"

"Because I asked about his shift pattern." Her eyes challenged Treva to make something of it. "I'll do whatever it takes to get you away from here."

Treva glared. "Not anything!"

Vaira laughed. "Caryanne is good at… making friends."

Caryanne smiled. "I like people, but not the Commander—he's not nice."

Honk started to snore softly, distracting Treva who couldn't understand how he was asleep while balanced so precariously.

Treva forced his attention back to what mattered. "Do you want me to try to get in touch with Kali? I was too scared to tell her anything when she contacted me."

"Yes, do it," Owen said.

When nobody objected, Treva tried to initiate a comm link but there was no response. Owen left Caryanne with the cooking and wiped his hands before trying Mika. Nothing.

Treva shouldn't have been surprised since external calls hadn't worked before, but he'd thought the jammer would allow them to call out. "I'd hoped we'd get hold of one of them."

Vaira said, "Perhaps, they aren't available. Andy—Kali's boss—might help."

Caryanne sat at the table. Her forehead was creased and she plucked at the sleeve of her top while looking off into the distance.

The smell of burnt egg wafted from the pan and Owen rushed over. "It's okay, Cary."

"I don't think it is," she murmured. "We don't want to make the Commander angry. We could stay here and hope that he forgets about us."

Vaira made a face to show what she thought of the Commander. "I'll try Andy." She got up and activated a comm link.

Treva didn't expect a result but after a few seconds, Andy's face appeared. That was when Treva realized he'd seen him arrive with TSS reinforcements on the space station after his father died. He'd spoken to Kali at length. It was just that Treva hadn't paid much attention at the time.

"Vaira, what's happening? Are you okay?" the Agent asked. He couldn't see them where they sat at the table and there was silence, except for Honk's soft snoring. Thankfully, Honk changed position and cradled his head in the crook of one arm.

"We're mostly okay." Vaira said. "I'm going to let Treva talk since he knows more of what's going on."

Andy nodded and Treva moved to the screen. If he

wondered why he was talking to a kid, he didn't let it show. "Good to see you. What's happening?"

Treva wasn't sure where to start but knew he needed to talk. "We're probably being monitored."

Andy frowned. "Then, be careful what you say."

Treva shifted the position of the viewscreen so that Andy could see the table. "I was given a device to block surveillance."

"Are you sure it works?"

"No, but it's all we have."

Andy must have accepted that, because he said, "Are you at the apartment?"

Treva nodded. "Planet security is acting on my uncle's orders so we can't leave."

"Uncle?"

"Andrei Steyn. I don't know anything about him and have only just met him, but he had Owen chained in the cellar of the Blue Pixie." Treva sent Owen an apologetic look.

"Owen Bruiser is with you? Is he okay?"

Owen leaned into the camera's range. "Hi, Andy. I'm alive. Although it got nasty for a while."

Andy's expression darkened. "What happened?"

"Andrei calls himself the Commander. He's very interested in Kali and Mika, but I didn't tell him anything." He smiled as if just realizing it himself. "Not that it mattered. He took what he wanted from my mind, anyway." Owen frowned. "Come to think of it, he said he trained with the TSS."

Andy glanced to the side as if someone else wanted his attention. "We don't have commander rank in the TSS, aside as an honorific for starship captains." His gaze returned to them. "Thank you for the information. I'll see what I can find out about him. If he's the same person who is behind..." Andy stopped himself from saying more. "Can you get out?"

Owen looked at Treva, who answered, "No, we're

trapped in my apartment."

"Your dad's apartment," corrected his mother.

Treva let out a loud sigh. "Yes, Mom, I know, but it's ours for now." Annoyed at how much like a kid his mother could make him look and feel, Treva returned his attention to Andy. "We'll try to find a way out." They hadn't actually agreed on a plan, but it was a minor point.

Andy smiled grimly. "Okay. I'll see what we can do to help."

Caryanne waved, distracting Treva from what he was going to say next. "Tell him about the Commander's plans to destroy the planet."

Andy straightened in his chair. "Was that Caryanne? What did she say?"

Caryanne flushed. "I forced myself to remember and now, I can't forget." Her eyes lost focus, causing Treva to worry that she was going to sink into herself again.

Andy leaned forward. "What can't you forget? What did Andrei Steyn say? This is important, Caryanne."

Her eyes were solemn. "I know. I told you. The Commander said that they were going to destroy Glaendor with something called Pesta."

Andy was silent for a couple of seconds. "Thank you, Caryanne. You've done remarkably well to remember. I know how hard it is for you. Can you recall anything else?"

"He scared me. I think he looked in my head and whatever he saw made him sure I wouldn't remember. That's why I had to, but now I don't know how to shut it off. I'm scared."

"We will help. That's all I can say to offer hope."

Caryanne shuddered. "He hates Mika and Kali."

Andy spoke gently. "Let me talk to Owen again."

Caryanne nodded and Owen stepped into view, holding a steaming pan wrapped in a towel.

Before Andy could speak, Treva asked, "Why would he do that?"

A chorus of voices sounded from behind him: "I want

to know that," and "Yes, tell us."

Andy sighed, looking tired. "All I can tell you is that they are attacking certain targets in the sector." He held up a hand, forestalling the questions that Treva felt needed answering. "We don't know why, but suspect they want to take over the Outer Colonies."

"Why now?" Owen asked.

"It doesn't matter. Andrei is a threat regardless." Andy looked at Owen. "We're running out of time, so no more questions. Is there anything else you can tell me?"

"Not really. I don't think he got much from me, since I didn't know anything. Although, it was weird how fixated he was on Kali, and he's keeping us in this apartment for a reason. I just don't know why."

"You make good bait. I need you to concentrate on getting out."

"We'll try."

Andy nodded. "Okay, let's talk again as soon as you're somewhere safe." His smile didn't reach his eyes. "Thank you for everything you're doing to stop these criminals and stay safe." He ended the call.

Owen placed the pan in the sink. "Okay, it's probably best we leave. Five minutes to grab anything you need. Let's go."

Vaira muttered something under her breath, while Caryanne shook Honk's arm until he woke. Vaira and Owen shared a look but Treva didn't know what it meant.

He picked up the jammer. "Before I turn this off, remember that we won't be able to carry much."

"It sounds like you have a plan," Owen said.

"I do." All of a sudden, Treva felt much older than his fifteen years.

— — —

Owen had only ever been a singer, which meant he should have been passed out at the kitchen table, like Honk, but he hadn't been the same since Luca's death. Part of that was because he knew that he could have easily been the one to die. When he thought about what he'd achieved, there was the music, but something in him said that he could and should do more.

What a joke.

Who else was going to get these people out of here? Certainly not Honk, Vaira, or Caryanne. Treva was too young, despite the way he acted, and Owen didn't know enough about Anissa to judge.

The kitchen reeked of burnt food. Owen stared at the congealing mess. What had made him think that he could cook? Sometimes Vaira cooked, but nobody else bothered. They relied on food deliveries, eating out or the prepared meals stocked on the *Sepiantia* for extended space travel.

Owen considered packing something, but his most vital possession—his handheld which contained his life—was missing, and everything else was on the *Sepiantia*. Driven by a desperate need to get out of the apartment, with or without a clear plan, he worried they were doomed to fail.

There was no point trying to clean up. He left the pan to soak in the sink as the comm unit announced an incoming call. Startled, he answered, wondering who wanted Treva or Anissa as it never occurred to him that it might be for him.

Andrei Steyn's fleshy face filled the large screen, making Owen want to throw up. For a few seconds, his body remained trapped in the dark at the mercy of the tyrant.

It was the smirk on Steyn's face that freed him from the memory. The cruel curve of his lips sent a surge of rage through Owen as he realized that his greatest fear was Steyn inside his head. *The man can't read my mind through the viewscreen. Come on. Luca would have given him an argument. Besides, the others are relying on me.*

Steyn stayed silent, and since Owen didn't want anyone to blunder into the kitchen and give anything away, he spoke, "What do you want?"

"I've been informed that we lost a part of your apartment on our monitoring system. I need to know why."

Owen didn't pretend to be shocked that the apartment was under surveillance. "Why is that our problem?"

"It's your space. We need to identify the faulty equipment."

"What does that mean?"

Out of the corner of his eye, Owen saw the small grey jamming box in the middle of the table where Treva had turned it off.

"I'm glad you asked, Owen Bruiser." Steyn smiled. "I'm sending over a team. You need to let them in to avoid further action."

Owen suspected the real reason for the call was because Steyn couldn't come over himself and wanted to see what he could find out. Before he could respond, Steyn focused on a spot over his shoulder and abruptly ended the call. They had to assume that the team was already on their way.

Treva stepped into the kitchen with the others behind. "We heard."

Even Honk looked worried.

Owen snatched up the jamming box and turned it on. "Well, at least we know it works."

Steyn might have spotted it and known what it was but since they had to escape before his people arrived, it didn't make any difference to their plans.

"Any idea how long we have?" Anissa asked, fastening the straps of a small backpack. When there was no answer, she said, "What's your plan, Treva?"

The boy went pale. "We need to get onto the roof."

Anissa frowned. "I know we're desperate, but I'm not ready to throw myself off."

Owen thought she was trying to lighten the mood, but Treva said, "That's not what I meant."

Anissa's frown deepened. "If we get to the roof, how are

we going to get down to the ground and avoid security?"

Treva started towards the door. "The security is supposed to pass through the grounds regularly, but I haven't seen them patrol since Avon arrived. There's nobody at the Gate House, so we should be okay."

"But, how are we going to get to the ground?"

"I spotted a fire escape on the outside." Everyone stared at Treva, who shrugged. "It's all I've got."

"We'd better get to the roof, then." Owen needed to focus on action. "We don't have time for debate."

Treva nodded. "We'll go onto the office balcony where we can climb onto the roof and get to the ground from there."

Anissa disappeared, presumably heading to the office.

"Are you sure we can get down from the roof?" Vaira asked, voice strained.

Treva shook his head. "I've seen something from the ground, but don't know for sure." When she stared at him with her mouth open, he said, "Look, Dad was paranoid about security. He wouldn't have allowed anyone to go through the apartment for repairs and so, they must have access from elsewhere. Even if we can only get to another level, it will increase our options."

It sounded logical and tenuous at the same time. One thing was certain, they would only get one chance, and it was unlikely that there would be time to climb up and back down.

"How does getting to a lower level help?" Vaira asked.

"The guards can see which floor the elevator comes from. If we go down from another floor, there's a small chance we might sneak past."

Owen couldn't see how that would work. Their group was too large. Then again, what were the guards going to do? Shoot them?

They joined Anissa outside the office. Owen stared up, realizing that the architect had wanted the penthouse to have vaulted ceilings. *It's going to be a long climb.*

Anissa said. "I'll distract the guards."

"How will you get away afterward?" Caryanne asked. "We can't just leave you."

"I'll persuade them to let me go shopping. It isn't as if I'm the one they want. Even if a guard comes with me, there's bound to be a chance to run away."

There was no uncertainty in her voice but Owen noticed the way she gripped the strap of her rucksack. She wasn't as confident as she sounded. *Good, it's a terrible plan.*

Treva scowled. "No way. We stay together."

"He's right," Owen said. "We should stick together. It's no good if some of us escape and others don't."

"I didn't mean to…" Treva looked helplessly at Anissa. She smiled. "It's okay."

Anissa straightened her shoulders. "Let's get on with it. None of this will work if Andrei's people turn up first."

"I'm ready. It's better than sitting here," Vaira agreed.

Honk stared at the wall. "Leave me. There's no way I'll survive the drop."

Vaira shook her head. "There's no way anyone would survive falling thirteen floors."

Treva was already heading to his father's office, where he threw open the doors. Owen still held the grey box in one hand, and now Treva grabbed Honk's arm with the other and steered him to the office. "Come on. We aren't leaving anyone behind."

CHAPTER 23

KALI KNEW THAT there was something wrong on Glaendor. Treva hadn't sounded right, and the way he'd looked over his shoulder during the conversation, it was as if someone had been listening.

They needed to find out what was going on, but she wasn't free to take off for the planet and she didn't want to leave the TSS. Her job had been a route back to sanity after she was free of the Priesthood. It gave her purpose, but she had no idea how to convince Andy to send them to Glaendor. Unfortunately, Mika had interrupted the meeting before she'd gotten a sense of what Lead Agent Alexri intended.

Andy was seated at the table in the middle of his makeshift office. Kali knocked and entered with Mika close behind. He looked up.

"You wanted to know as soon as we discovered anything," she said, trying to read his mood. "There's definitely something wrong on Glaendor."

Mika came in behind her. "We need to check out what's happening."

She flashed him a warning look, knowing that he was probably already on route in his head. This would be difficult enough without his impatience.

She spoke telepathically to Mika, *"Let me do the talking."* When Andy raised his eyebrows, she said aloud, "I was just telling him to shut up."

Andy shook his head. There were fine lines around his eyes that hadn't been there when she'd seen him earlier and a distant expression.

"What's wrong?"

Mika moved to her side but thankfully, stayed quiet.

"Treva just contacted me to tell me that Glaendor is in the hands of the enemy. The band is with him, for better or worse—and they have Owen."

Mika breathed a visible sigh of relief.

Thank the stars the band is okay! As relieved as she was, Kali dreaded the conversation she'd inevitably need to have with Owen about how she'd left him on Red Ghost.

Andy didn't miss a beat. "Do you remember that private security firm when we were investigating the missing women?"

Kali would struggle to forget. "Avon Security. I thought the TSS was going to deal with them?"

"Other things took priority for us, and now they are working for SPEAR." Andy paused. "Or, perhaps they were always working for them. You will have to return to Headquarters."

Kali shook her head. "It sounds like we need to be on Glaendor. We can't just let them kill all those people. It's the sort of gesture that would suit SPEAR's aims. Then, there's Treva and the band..." She looked to Mika for support.

"It's not just that," Andy continued. "SPEAR is on a mission to ramp up the pressure on the Outer Colonies to bully people into supporting them."

There was a pause as he let the information sink in. There had always been a danger of SPEAR escalating their attacks if they didn't achieve their goal and their campaign hadn't killed the numbers they'd wanted.

Mika and Kali spoke at the same time, "How?"

Andy echoed Kali's thoughts. "Based on new

information, it looks like Glaendor is the next target." Andy paused. "We think they're going to use Pesta."

Kali shook her head. "Pesta is with Herja. Isn't she?"

Andy shrugged. "Perhaps, not."

Mika interrupted, "What does anyone know about Pesta?"

"The name seems to be inspired by folk legend," Andy replied. "There are older Taran variants, but the closest match is a tale from Earth, of all places. Pesta traveled on a ghost ship filled with rats. Not only was Pesta the harbinger of grotesque suffering, but sailors were also the carriers of the plague and victims of Pesta."

"Whoever engineered Pesta based it on that legend?" Mika muttered.

Kali sat. "But, why?" She shook her head. "Sorry that was a dumb question. Why build any weapon?"

Mika hesitated before sitting beside her. Andy stared off into the distance. When Mika opened his mouth, Kali put a hand on his arm before he could speak. She had never seen Andy like this, which meant it was bad.

Andy turned away. "It'll be easier to show you." He directed their attention to the holoprojector.

It remained blank for a few seconds before blurred images flickered across the screen. The picture sharpened and a man's face came into focus. He had the sort of appearance often chosen to represent the Taran race, a symmetrical face and too straight teeth and a golden skin tone that was nearly but not quite natural. He could have been an actor or news anchor.

He stared into the camera and a female voice said, "Begin." His eyes flickered to where Kali imagined the woman stood just out of shot before returning to look at them.

"We succeeded in creating the impossible—a weapon to wipe out animals and people alike, while leaving structures and vegetation intact," he said, sounding older than he appeared, "and then, we lost control."

Kali noticed delicate equipment on benches with workstations and one darkened window. The background was bright and clean.

"It's too late for us. We cannot risk the infection spreading." His face became drawn with a grey tinge crept over the golden shade. "I'm..."'

The female voice cut in, "This is a record of our creation. We have deployed drones.

The man's eyes remained on his silent audience. "There was a moment," he looked down, running a hand through his hair, "one stupid moment where the creature felt threatened and we lost any semblance of control. That's why we are dying. I think it was an accident, but when they gave us the keys to this discovery..."

The camera panned to show a man in a bio-suit on his back. It was obvious by the way that his head was twisted at an unnatural angle that he was dead.

The camera approached, and Kali glimpsed the rest of the laboratory, which appeared undamaged. She was tempted to close her eyes before they reached the man's visor but she needed to see.

At first, she thought that there was something obscuring the visor. It looked as though the edges of his face had disappeared.

The female voice was low, almost a whisper, "It's as if he is being erased."

Kali blinked as he gradually disappeared. It was easy to believe that it was an effect used to scare whoever reviewed the footage but she knew from Andy's reaction that wasn't the case. The recording jumped to a shot taken above the planet, panning out to show bodies in the streets.

There was silence.

It was one thing knowing that Pesta could cause devastation and another seeing the result. She had never considered the level of testing that would have been necessary to ensure that the weapon delivered. No wonder Andy didn't want to watch it again.

Kali had to swallow a couple of times before she could speak. "Where?"

Andy took a deep shuddering breath. "A planet in the Outer Colonies called Roana. The Enforcer's investigation put it down as a natural disaster."

Kali frowned. "They were too afraid to investigate fully?" While she understood their fear, it was difficult to believe that they wouldn't have asked for help.

"There were rumors that the inhabitants were infected by some sort of microbe."

"Everyone died?"

"It seems that way." Andy turned off the holoprojector. "And, there was nobody left to demand answers." He took a deep breath. "The incident happened some time ago, but this footage just surfaced. It was sent to the media earlier today, not to us. It was only when they asked us to confirm the footage was genuine that we became aware of it."

Kali didn't ask if it was real. "And they're targeting Glaendor in a new attack?"

Mika responded immediately. "We have to go." There was a challenge in his eyes. "I already wanted to go find the band but, but now we *really* need to get there as soon as possible."

Kali let her head fall to the table. As if things weren't bad enough, they had delivered their friends into the hands of the enemy.

Andy nodded. "I suspect that's exactly what they want—you two on the planet."

"They might not know that we know." Kali tried to loosen her shoulders.

Andy stood. "No, too many information sources have been filtering back to us and you. They *want* you to know what's going on, so you'll try to act. It's a trap."

"It might be a bluff," Kali said, even as her heart told her something different. "We know that Pesta went with Herja, which brings into question how she got into enemy hands. If she did."

Mika scowled as he looked from one to the other. His expression hardened. "We can't abandon our friends."

Andy sighed. "I need to get clearance. But I have to warn you that it is unlikely a request to go to Glaendor will be granted. We don't have the resources to provide adequate backup, and SPEAR wants you there."

Mika stiffened but Kali hadn't given up. "Wouldn't it be better to do the unexpected?" she asked. "SPEAR will expect us go to Glaendor en masse. They won't expect us to slip in quietly."

"Glad you agree," Mika said to Kali.

She ignored him to focus on convincing Andy. "We can't ignore the threat. It's a whole planet, and SPEAR will say that the TSS doesn't care about what happens to the Outer Colonies..."

Andy stared at his desk, and she could almost see him cataloguing the options. "Give me ten minutes. Do not even think of going off on your own, because I will come after you, resources or no resources." Andy looked at Mika. "Whatever happens, you cannot take the *Sepiantia*. It is too visible and the security services are acting for SPEAR."

Mika glared but didn't speak.

"Mika, it's just a ship," Kali said. "Some things are more important."

His expression went blank and she knew he was thinking about how his mother remained in a coma.

She felt compelled to respond. *"You have me."*

He looked away, and she couldn't tell if it was because he'd accepted what she'd said or whether he didn't believe her.

CHAPTER 24

TREVA STOOD IN his father's office with the double doors wide. It wasn't long ago that he'd leaped across the balcony to get inside. Back then, he'd almost slipped and fallen and while they didn't have to break in that way now, it would involve a risky climb.

Treva was worried his mother wasn't going to listen. It hadn't been long since their reunion, and he wasn't ready to lose her. While she wasn't much use to his uncle as bait, Treva wasn't so sure that didn't place her in more, not less, danger? If Andrei thought to use her as a hostage, Treva would be in trouble.

Andrei's people could arrive at any moment and they had to be gone. Treva chose to ignore that he had no idea how to get off the grounds, never mind the planet. If he thought about all their problems, he would be paralyzed with fear.

He walked onto the balcony and looked over the edge. Far below, the artificial lawn stretch out with no sign of any security patrols. Andrei's people had to come through the gatehouse, as the apartment block had air defenses; his father had said it was the sole reason he'd chosen to buy the penthouse. *At last, a piece of luck.*

Treva turned to look at the group assembling behind

him. None were capable of climbing the smooth wall to the roof, and it looked like they'd have to haul Honk up there.

Treva took a deep breath. "I'll go first."

His mother grabbed his arm and Treva thought that she was going to try to stop him. Instead, she pulled him in for a hug. She felt solid and warm but smaller than she should be. Everyone stared, and his face grew warm. He resisted wriggling out of her grasp, giving her a final squeeze before releasing her. She kissed his temple and stepped away, hiding her face.

"If I can let you do that," she pointed at the wall, "I don't want to hear any arguments about me playing my part when the time is right."

Treva wanted to rub at the tears that started to form in the corners of his eyes but was afraid it would draw attention to the fact he was crying.

"I'm going inside so that I don't have to watch you climb." She blew Treva a kiss that would have been funny in other circumstances.

Treva pushed everything from his mind and stared up at the wall. He only had to scale four meters, but it was smooth and there was the potential of falling to his death. The layer of sweat coating his palms would not be helpful.

Owen ordered Vaira to keep watch over the balcony and went to stand at Treva's elbow. "I'll do it."

It took Treva a few seconds to realize that Owen was offering to climb first. He really wanted to accept but remembered how weak Owen was. *He looks stronger than me and he wants to do it.*

Sadly, Treva shook his head. "I'm younger and lighter."

Owen pretended to frown. "Are you calling me old and fat?"

Treva was about to deny it when Owen winked. "Okay, I would give you a lift up, but it will be safer to get you something to stand on."

Caryanne appeared with a chair and Vaira called, "If you drag that," she pointed at a metal table near the edge of the balcony, "to the wall, we can put this on top, and he can stand on both. Keep watch. I need to fetch something." Vaira returned to the study.

Treva eyed the table and chair, thinking it looked precarious, but he couldn't come up with a better suggestion.

Owen and Caryanne dragged the heavy table to the wall and lifted the chair on top. It looked about as stable as balancing on the nose of a moving shuttle but at least it made the climb to roof shorter.

Vaira reappeared with a coil of belts she'd linked together. "We can use these if you can fix them to something."

Treva nodded, realizing that he'd been so focused on getting to the roof that he hadn't thought about how everyone else would follow. Thank goodness, he didn't have to think of everything.

Vaira had him wrap the belts around his waist, and then Owen helped her hold the chair steady while Treva climbed. He wanted to check how far he'd fall if he slipped but knew better.

Now that he was centimeters from the wall, he could see that it wasn't as smooth as it had first appeared. There were small cracks where he could jam his fingers. It stung as he scraped off skin. *It hurts but not as much as falling.*

Treva wished he'd climbed more than that one day with the school. If he was going to do it, he needed to stop thinking and start doing before he lost his tiny bit of courage.

He shifted his weight and the chair wobbled. Owen grabbed it with both hands but Treva's heart was already hammering.

One hand rested against the wall and he reached up with the other, jamming his fingers into two cracks. He hardly felt the pain as he pulled his right leg up, letting his left take all his weight. His toes scraped down the side of the wall until they caught on something and he had to resist the impulse to look.

Feel the way. If I fall, I will land on the balcony.

Treva pushed with his right leg, using all his strength as the other leg came off the chair. His stomach lurched while his head filled with images of falling.

Owen was speaking. Something about being okay and taking it steady, but all Treva heard was the rushing of blood in his ears.

It felt as if he was leaning backward, even though he was firmly against the wall. His right leg shook as his toes took his full weight. He was going to fall. *Land on the balcony. Land on the balcony.*

An image of his body broken laid at the base of the building was difficult to erase. His breath was coming faster and faster until he was dizzy. He reached for another handhold, fighting not to look down. His toes scuffed the wall in a continuous judder as he failed to find purchase. Frantically, he tried again. Finally, his toes caught but the crack didn't feel big enough to hold his weight. A tremor was growing in his other leg. He couldn't hold on much longer.

He reached up slowly. With everything counting on this one hand, he searched for a grip. There was nothing but air and then, his hand came down on the lip of the roof.

Treva had never felt so relieved. *I'm almost there.*

He pushed up, straining from his toes. Both calves burned as he grabbed the edge with the other hand. His left foot flew free. The momentum ripped his right foot from the wall.

Treva gasped in shock and pain. His arms burned as they took his entire body weight. He caught a glimpse of the ground beyond the balcony and instantly squeezed his eyes shut. Moving with agonizing slowness, he pulled himself up a centimeter at a time. His feet scrabbled, giving him a little traction. Eventually, he got his chest over the ledge and wriggled the rest of the way.

It felt as if he took a layer of skin off his stomach on the sharp edge of the tiles but he hardly cared as he collapsed onto the safety of the roof. A few seconds later when his racing heart had started to slow and he'd taken a couple of steadying breaths; he uncurled the belts, securing them and dropping them over the edge. Leaving Owen to organize the others, he went to check out the roof space.

Treva leaned over the side. *Oh, stars, it's a long way down.* Over in the far corner, he spotted the fire escape. He ran over and stared at what was left. It hung as it should but had been sheared off a few meters down.

Treva ran around the roof, checking each of the walls but there was no other way down. Someone had made sure that nobody could leave the roof.

Treva raced back to the others, feet crunching on the gravel. Vaira and Caryanne were already up and in the process of pulling Honk over the edge.

His mother was saying to Owen, "You go next and then you can help me over the difficult bit."

Treva was about to explain that there was no way down from the roof when he caught sight of movement out of the corner of his eye. "They're coming."

Two cars zipped through the entrance. They were traveling well beyond the sedate speed limit for the drive.

Owen scrambled up to kneel beside Treva. "Everyone get down. We don't want them to spot us."

They couldn't go back. Trapped, it would only a matter of time before Steyn's people found the doors wide with a table and chair pointing the way.

"Anissa, what are you doing?" Owen questioned. "Get up here."

Treva looked down to see that his mother had returned the chair and was now dragging the table away from the wall. How was she managing to move it on her own?

"Mom, don't."

"It's the only way. Get as far away as you can and take good care of each other." She blew Treva another kiss and disappeared inside.

Treva felt numb as he turned to Owen. "There's no way off the roof."

He was aware of the others listening, but they were out of time. The enemy had arrived and he strongly suspected that his mother had gone to meet them.

Why would she do that? But he knew that she did it for him, so that he could get away with the others. It had always been a stupid plan.

Owen stared into space for a long moment. "They might not find us up here now that Anissa has moved the furniture."

Nobody pointed out that they would be stuck until someone rescued them. And, what about his mother?

"We have the belts," Vaira finally said. "If we can think of a way to make them longer. Perhaps by tying our clothes together, we might get to the ground."

Treva wanted to laugh at the ridiculousness of the idea, but they were that desperate.

Caryanne cocked her head to one side and sniffed. "Can anyone smell smoke?"

"Oh no." Owen looked at Treva. "I bet Anissa set fire to the apartment. She thinks we have a way off the roof."

— — —

Anissa didn't give into her worry; all that mattered was getting Treva out of the building safely. The hardest part, escaping her son's overprotectiveness, was already done. When had he started to think that it was his job to protect her? He wasn't grown up yet. It was part of a mother's job to persuade her children that she was superhuman, all while being petrified inside.

Anissa deactivated the sprinklers, which turned off the automatic alarm. Stars, she hadn't meant for that to happen. There might be others in this apartment block.

Anissa was well aware that her chance of pulling off this deception had been slim. If Treva had known that she'd had no intention of going with him, he wouldn't have climbed onto that roof.

The heat from the fire warmed her back. It had been easy to start, thanks to the bottles of high-proof vodka in Marco's study that Honk hadn't discovered. The alcohol had given her the idea, although she hadn't expected it to work so quickly or so well. She tried to ignore how satisfying it was to set fire to Marco's stuff. She'd started the fire on the balcony so that Treva had no choice but to go without her. She hoped the fire would create enough of a distraction for them to get off the roof and stop Treva from coming after her.

She had no idea whether the jammer was still working or if someone may have watched her set the fire. She needed to head to the ground floor where she would either get past security or not. As an added precaution, she put through an emergency call, reasoning that the more chaos, the better the opportunities to escape.

Anissa tried not to think about where Treva and the others would go next. Their plan hadn't extended beyond getting out of the building. There'd been no time for more, but Treva was smart enough. He would get to safety and if she wasn't around, the others would look out for him. *But, not like me.*

Anissa couldn't afford to think like that. Better to focus on what she needed to do next.

She stepped into the elevator, which immediately set off for the ground floor. The journey was quick, yet it gave her enough time to doubt her ability to do what needed to be done. After everything she'd been through, surely she could do this final thing.

She tried to wipe smudges from under her eyes. She felt old, but Jon—the security guard who had taken her to the Blue Pixie—had seemed to like her. Deep down, Anissa hoped that he would look the other way while she slipped out.

The elevator chimed. She had reached her destination.

There was nothing she could do about her pounding heart or the sheen of sweat on her forehead. Instead of worrying about it, she plastered on a smile. Full of energy, she stepped out of the elevator. As expected, the two security guards turned towards her.

An alarm shrilled from the control panel to the left of the entrance and exit. Both men turned to the viewscreen. The guard Anissa didn't know put one hand on his weapon as if it would do any good to shoot at fire.

Anissa approached carefully, a new plan forming. "There's a fire in the apartment. I don't know how it started but the others are still inside."

Jon straightened as he strolled to meet her. "What happened?"

"I don't know. When I came out of the bedroom, the hall was on fire and I was forced to leave or burn." She looked into his concerned eyes. "My bedroom is next to the exit." She pressed her lips together, letting him see that she was close to tears. "Treva, my son is trapped in there. Can you help?"

"It's okay. We'll get them out."

"Thank you!" She smiled at him.

The other guard, whose name she didn't know, walked toward the elevator. Anissa hung back with Jon, unsure why she felt so relaxed with him. She needed them both to go to the apartment.

The guard stopped by the elevator before looking back. "She has to come with us."

Jon opened his mouth and she thought he was about to protest, but he smiled and gave her an apologetic look. "Sorry, but he's right. It's procedure."

Her plan wasn't going to work. She'd known that it wouldn't be that easy, but at least she'd tried. The others should be far away. Anissa nodded, letting Jon know that she understood as they joined his colleague at the elevator.

"Shouldn't we use the stairs if there's a fire?" Jon asked.

His colleague didn't look at him. "Can't," he glanced at

Anissa, "I'm not saying more in front of her. Besides, there's no alarm and probably no fire."

Jon frowned, clearly not happy with his colleagues attitude but unwilling to challenge him.

The man's eyes lingered on her chest, and she couldn't help the blush that heated her cheeks. Although she wanted to pretend she was in control, her experience of men had been severely limited by caring for a child without any support.

Anissa paid attention to her intuition and thought she'd have a sense of when the others were clear of the building, but she felt nothing. She'd been kidnapped because of her potential ability. If she'd known when she was a good deal younger and without a child, she might have joined the TSS.

Anissa stepped into the elevator and swallowed, suddenly aware of a tension between the two men. *Oh no!* They stared at each other as if one was about to throw a punch. Anissa's impulse was to get away as fast as possible but as the doors closed, she realized that wasn't an option.

She spoke to Jon, "Perhaps I should stay…"

Hadn't they already established that she couldn't stay in the lobby alone? What could she suggest that they might consider? This was ridiculous. She'd imagined they would contain the fire before it became a threat to the other residents but at this rate, the building would be ashes first.

"You do know there's a fire, don't you?" She kept her attention on Jon because despite her better judgment, she liked him. She would have to be careful; it wouldn't be a good idea to relax too much with him.

The other guard snorted and turned away. Anissa wondered if she'd made a mistake by being obvious that she liked Jon.

Surely, Treva had gone by now. Why did she have an insistent niggle that he wasn't far away?

— — —

Treva was having a hard time believing he'd managed to make their situation worse and they were now stuck on the roof of a burning building. Not only that, but his mother had been the one to set fire to the entire apartment block. It would have been a good plan if there really had been another way off and someone hadn't sabotaged the fire escape.

Treva had had an inkling that his mother might have been planning something, but he'd been too scared of the imminent climb to pay attention. Perhaps they should be waving at Andrei's people to come and rescue them rather than hiding. Then again, while he didn't want to burn to death, he'd promised not to allow himself to be used against the TSS. Besides, it was too late now; Andrei's people had disappeared into the apartment block's reception.

The other four looked just as shocked, even Caryanne was peering over the edge as if contemplating the distance to the ground.

Owen sat with his back to the lip of the roof, expression determined. "As I see it, we have three choices."

"Choices?" Treva couldn't see one never mind three.

"Do nothing. Try to climb down the outside of the building—"

"Eight floors!" Honk stared at Owen like he was mad.

"—or jump to certain death." Owens face was grim. "Have I missed any?"

Vaira sat on the edge as if there wasn't a massive drop behind her. "A fair assessment of the situation." She sounded relaxed, but the paleness of her face and the way she pressed her lips together suggested otherwise.

Honk lay on flat, gravel covered roof but now levered himself into a sitting position. "I'm not going anywhere." Just as he spoke, an air current brought a stream of smoke in their direction, causing him to cough violently.

"I choose option two." Caryanne was leaning out to study the outside of the wall in a way that made Treva nervous. "But, I might as well jump for all the good trying to climb down would do."

"He didn't tell us about option two," Treva said in an attempt to distract himself.

"No, but it was obvious." Caryanne looked at Owen.

He shrugged. "She's right."

Treva and Vaira rechecked all four walls in the futile hope that they'd missed something. Smoke billowed out of the building in a continuous stream, hanging in dense patches over the roof. Treva's eyes watered and he was finding it increasingly difficult to breathe. They would suffocate before they burned.

Owen coughed as he encouraged Honk to move away from the thickest of the smoke. Honk choked as he struggled to his feet. Everyone was so focused on Honk that they didn't noticed the small shuttle until it almost landed on top of them.

Treva gaped as smoke obscured it for a few seconds before it cleared. How had it bypassed the no-fly zone? Andrei probably had the power to do whatever he wanted, but how had they known the group was on the roof?

Treva coughed and looked around frantically. He could jump, but there didn't seem much point unless everyone died. Honk would need help to get over the side. Besides, he was too traumatized by the climb to consider jumping to his death.

A hatch slid opened, and Treva raised his hands in case the people inside were trigger-happy.

Owen grabbed one of Treva's arms, pulling it down. "It's a medical shuttle. Act cool."

The smoke cleared enough for Treva to see the green symbol that denoted Glaendor City Hospital on the side. He hastily dropped his arms before his behavior aroused suspicion. It was difficult to breathe, and he covered his mouth in an attempt to get more oxygen into his lungs.

Another, larger shuttle touched down next to the first. People in protective suits climbed out. Were these Andrei's people? Treva didn't know.

One of them came over, his voice clear despite a helmet. "Where did the fire start?"

Owen answered, his words muffled by coughing. "On the floor below. We don't know what happened or why the sprinklers didn't work."

Treva realized that the fire responder thought they'd come to the roof solely to escape the fire. One of the medics slid a mask over Honks face as another helped Caryanne into the shuttle.

The man nodded his thanks, moving toward the balcony where they'd climbed onto the roof. Someone joined the man. They each carried cylinders, which Treva knew from school would extinguish the flames.

Owen had set off to join the others when Treva remembered the restraints on his mother's wrists at the hospital. It might be more dangerous to go there than Treva had first thought. Owen stopped to have a coughing fit, allowing Treva to catch up.

Treva grabbed Owen's arm. "The hospital will contact the Commander." They both bent over, trying to stay beneath the worst of the smoke but it was impossible.

Owen's eyes streamed with tears. "Understood." He gasped. "We need to get out of... here first." He grabbed Treva's shoulder. "Then, get out... of there... at the first opportunity."

Relieved that Owen agreed, they helped each other to the shuttle. Treva had lost track with everyone and hoped they were okay.

Inside the shuttle, a medic in protective gear fitted a mask over Treva's face. The oxygen-air mix was cool and smelled faintly of disinfectant, making him cough more. He resisted the impulse to pull it off, knowing that it was the smoke not the mask causing the problem.

Something was clipped to his finger—a tiny device that provided readings about how his body was functioning. From the way that the medic was studying a handheld monitor, the readings weren't normal. Treva couldn't see the medic's face. After a couple of seconds, he nodded and directed Treva further into the shuttle.

The others were already there, wearing identical masks. Caryanne waved, while Vaira looked relieved to see them, and Honk's wide, staring eyes didn't appear to see anything.

Once settled in a seat, Treva thought about his mother. What would Steyn's people do to her when they found out that the rest of them were gone?

Treva pulled off the mask, ignoring the medic's gesture to put it back on, and leaned close to Owen. "I have to go back for Mom."

He couldn't help thinking that he would never see her again. She had decided to sacrifice herself for him, again.

Owen nodded to show that he'd heard but kept his own mask in place. His chest rose and fell as he breathed deeply, occasionally bursting into another coughing fit. His face had turned red and blotchy.

Treva patted his arm, feeling helpless as he put his mask back on to stop the medic's agitation. There wasn't anything he could do for now.

The medic held up his index finger in a sign of approval as if he were a kid, and Treva sat back to focus on what they needed to do next. As soon as they got away from the hospital, he would contact his mother—one way or another—and take it from there.

What if she never intended to escape? He knew her, she would try to get free eventually. They had to slip away as soon as they arrived at the hospital before anyone could run their details through any systems. Treva just hoped that it was going to be that easy.

CHAPTER 25

ANISSA HAD PLEADED for the two guards to save her son, since to do anything else would have been suspicious. While there was no sign of the flames that undoubtably raged inside the apartment, as soon as they stepped out of the elevator, the smell of smoke was unmistakable. Anissa didn't dare look at the guard who had questioned the existence of the fire.

Treva and the others should have been safely away, and she felt guilty watching as the two men debated opening the door and risking making the fire worse. They'd disagreed about contacting the emergency services, and Anissa didn't tell them that she'd already alerted them. After the guard that she couldn't name had spoken to someone, he'd gestured them back into the elevator.

Jon had looked about to argue until his colleague had said, "She's here."

"Shite," his colleague said, heading back in the elevator.

Jon hung back. "Shouldn't we take the stairs?"

"Can't it's locked."

Jon shook his head. "This place is a foking deathtrap."

They'd returned to the lobby with Anissa biting her tongue. If Treva had really been in danger, she would have tried harder to get them to act but at the same time, she didn't want them to risk their lives when it was unnecessary.

She watched for any sign that they were suspicious, but both seemed preoccupied. Anissa didn't know who *she* was and didn't dare ask in case it drew their attention. She guessed it had something to do with the arrival of Andrei's people.

As soon as they reached the lobby and the outer door slid open, the sound of shouting and booted feet reached them. Five people crowded the small space.

Anissa stayed as far back as possible, trying to blend into the background, which was impossible and so, she settled for remaining behind Jon. There was no smell of smoke in the lobby.

A loud, female voice bellowed, "Detain that woman."

Someone grabbed Anissa's arm. It was Jon. He didn't speak or look at her and his attention didn't waver from whoever was giving the orders. She couldn't see with his bulk in the way.

Her rather simple plan of sneaking off when everyone was busy tackling the fire felt foolish. She tried to calm the thundering of her heart. They might let her go when they discovered that she was no use to them. She tried not to think about how the Steyn family operated.

She'd been young and naïve when she'd believed Marco's promises. Looking back, she supposed he'd never had a chance after being born into the Steyn family.

The woman in charge marched over, looking nothing like Anissa had imagined. She'd expected a soldier, but this woman wore a tailored black pantsuit and red shirt. Blonde hair was tied back with a headband to stop any stray hairs from escaping. Red lipstick matched the shirt and made her even more striking than she was naturally.

Jon's colleague and Andrei's people, except for the woman and one man, piled into the elevator and went up to the top floor according to the elevator indicator.

Anissa stayed quiet, worried the woman might know

something of her if she worked for the Steyn family. She might even be related to Marco.

Taking some comfort from knowing that Treva and the others had to be away by now, she just hoped that he didn't worry what was happening to her. It wasn't that she'd given up trying to escape, but she didn't want him to undo what she'd achieved with her sacrifice.

The other man watched the elevator as if it posed a threat. Nobody would expect her to do anything. *What if I ran for the doors? Would Jon shoot?* She hoped that he'd think twice before shooting her in the back but she didn't know for certain. Although, Jon would have to release her arm before she could run. All thoughts of escape disappeared when the woman approached. Anissa couldn't suppress the sense of dread as the woman stopped a meter in front of her, the full force of her scowl claimed all of Anissa's attention. *Why is she so angry?*

"Where are they?" the woman demanded.

Anissa started to ask who when her head whipped to one side and pain exploded in her right cheek. *She hit me!* She would have fallen if Jon's grip on her arm hadn't made it impossible. Worse than any pain was the realization that she might die.

Ice-green eyes came back into focus as the woman continued to glare. "You know exactly who I'm talking about."

She's reading my mind. Treva run!

Jon frowned. "They're trapped in the apartment, aren't they?"

"Are they? How do you know?"

"Well..."

"I need to be sure."

Anissa sagged in relief. Nobody had read her mind. While trying hard not to think about Treva, he'd been at the forefront of Anissa's mind. Thankfully, the woman could no more read minds than Anissa, else she'd have known where they were.

Jon glanced at the surveillance screen over by the door. "They have to be. Nobody left this way, and there is no other way down."

What did Jon mean—*there's no other way down? There's the fire escape.*

"The stairs were removed, weren't they? For... er... security reasons? That's why we had to use the elevator."

The woman glared at the guard. "This happened because you weren't doing your job. I need to see all the footage."

Anissa managed to keep her mouth shut, but the woman swung back to face her. "What did he see in you?"

She was confused. *Who? Jon? Marco? Surely not Marco!*

Anissa was too distracted to seriously consider the meaning behind the question. If they found out about the fire escape, they could still catch Treva. *There has to be a fire escape.* Else, she'd killed Treva and the others when she set fire to the apartment.

Why didn't I check before setting the fire?

The woman moved away to look at the viewscreen behind a small counter. Anissa couldn't see the footage, only observe the reaction of the others.

The woman broke off to glare at her. It occurred to Anissa that with that level of hatred, she must have been close to Marco—a girlfriend?

Anissa went hot. That couldn't be it. This woman was jealous of Anissa's relationship with a man who'd had her kidnapped and put in storage. How sad and desperate was that? Something else might have triggered the woman's anger, but Anissa thought she was right.

Sirens sounded in the distance as the woman looked at Jon. "Shoot her."

Jon's hand tightened on Anissa's arm, making her winced. She resisted the urge to pull away and make it worse.

The other man spoke for the first time. "Let me do it." When he smiled, the heat that had risen moments earlier in

Anissa turned to ice.

"No." The woman glowered. "This is *his* mess." She turned her attention to Jon. "Let him sort it out."

Anissa couldn't keep quiet any longer. "Who are you?" She couldn't say why it was essential to know since it wouldn't do her any good.

The woman's glare intensified, and Anissa was sure she wasn't going to answer, but then she said, "Ava Funshi. I want you to know who took your life."

It was a shame that the name meant nothing to her, but Anissa wanted to spit in her face anyway. "I'm sorry that my *husband* rejected you." Jon shook her arm, but Anissa continued, "You deserved him." It was on the tip of her tongue to say, "you can have him," when she remembered that he was dead.

"On second thoughts, I'll do it." Ava snatched the gun from the guard.

The sound of sirens directly outside the building made Ava turn, cursing at the sight of emergency vehicles.

Jon yanked Anissa toward the door, making her stumble.

"Where are you going?" Ava demanded, swinging the weapon in their direction.

He paused, before answering, "I can't kill her here."

"Make sure you get rid of the evidence."

Jon hauled Anissa out before Ava could say anymore. Anissa stumbled, straining to see the roof. There was nothing but great billows of smoke.

Jon hissed, "Move."

Anissa couldn't get air into her lungs. Was Treva safe or was he stuck up there, choking to death?

Jon shoved her into the waiting shuttle before clambering in after her. She paid no attention as he programmed in their destination. If Treva really was dead, she didn't care if Jon shot her. How could she live with what she'd done?

She should have fought getting into the shuttle. Jon was

going to murder her! And, she was making it easy. Better to force him to kill her somewhere public rather that than nobody knowing what had happened to her. Each breath came faster than the one before. She caught the edge of the seat as her head filled with cloud and the world tilted. *I will not faint.*

Jon sounded strained. "We need to get out of here."

He glanced anxiously behind. Maybe he didn't want to kill her. If so, it wasn't too much of a stretch to think that he might help.

Anissa fought to think. "Do you know how long ago I left that man?" Jon didn't respond, but she carried on because anger felt better than fear. "It's been fourteen years. After that amount of time, nobody should have to deal with that shite. I didn't want anything to do with him, and still he screwed up my life. If he wasn't dead, I would kill him."

Jon didn't seem to be listening but then, this man was supposed to murder her. *Why should she care what he thought?*

"I should've told Ava that Marco would've done anything for me back when we were together. Never mind that I ran away and hid for fourteen foking years."

Why am I telling him this?

"Their relationship must have been shallow for her to get so jealous over nothing. Were they living together?" It wasn't what she wanted to know. "There was no sign of a woman in the apartment."

Jon didn't respond as they passed through the gatehouse. His expression hardened and she realized he expected someone to stop them.

Talk was better than silence and so, she continued, "Ava might be pretty, but she's too forceful, too insane for Marco." She thought for a second. "If he wasn't dead."

Jon chuckled.

She glanced at him, but he was focused on the street outside the shuttle. They were speeding, which was good.

Someone might pull them over and then she remembered, he was the police.

She rubbed her right bicep, which was still tender where he'd gripped her. Dare she hope that he didn't want to kill her? Could she persuade him not to hurt her? While she was feeling a bit calmer, it would be a bad idea to relax. Where were they going?

She checked the door and was unsurprised to find it locked. The override switch for emergencies was above her head. Her hand drifted toward it and then fell into her lap when Jon cleared his throat.

He said, "There's only so far I can go for a job, and I never signed on for murder." He stared at the road ahead. "We need to get away before she sends someone to make sure I've carried out her orders."

Does he mean that he's not going to kill me? Can I trust him? She shouldn't, but why bother to lie when there wasn't anything she could do about it? She allowed herself to feel relief for a moment.

"Treva," she managed to say, "was on the roof. What did you mean when you said there was no way down?"

He glanced at her before continuing to scan their surroundings. "The fire escape was destroyed to make surveillance easier."

The shuttle sped past the largest hotel on Glaendor, but Anissa hardly noticed. "I set fire to the apartment and killed my son."

"I don't think so," Jon said, not at all surprised by her revelation. "The emergency services were on the roof when we left."

Anissa grasped the lifeline. "They took them off?"

"If they did. They'll be taken to Glaendor City Hospital." Before she could shout that they needed to go there immediately, Jon said, "We will arrive in three minutes."

Anissa gripped the seat and tried to control the spiral of 'what-ifs' that wanted to drag her down. She was a ball of knotted tension.

The hospital came into sight, towering over the lower buildings, and she leaned forward to join Jon in staring out the vehicle's windows. They pulled up outside the main entrance and Anissa remembered that she couldn't trust the hospital's administration. She turned to Jon, about to share her fears when he swung the shuttle down a side street.

"What?" Anissa's heart leaped as five figures ran across the street, heading for the nearest walkway.

Jon took the shuttle over the group, causing them to duck with hands over their heads. He came down in front of them, blocking their way.

Anissa spotted Treva, turning back the way they'd come. Three armed security guards broke into a run at seeing how close their quarry was to escaping.

Jon released the door. Anissa didn't need him to tell her what to do. She dropped the short distance to the ground, waving and shouting frantically.

One of the security guards aimed a weapon in their direction.

Anissa shouted, "Hurry up."

A ramp lowered from the side door of the shuttle. Not waiting for it to reach the ground, Anissa pulled herself up and scrambled inside. Honk was in the lead, despite a lumbering gait that should have put him in last place. Caryanne and Vaira climbed the steps with Owen shoving them ahead. Of course, Treva was last.

Something scorched the side as Treva reached her, shouting, "Go."

She leaned out but other arms hauled him all the way in as the door started to close. The shuttle shuddered as weapon's fire hit it. Jon didn't have to do anything as the shuttle initiated emergency maneuvers, taking them straight up, above the buildings.

Jon mumbled, and she guessed he wasn't happy with how close they'd come to being killed.

It was a tight squeeze in the back. Anissa managed to

collapse into a seat next to Vaira, clutching her chest in relief. Treva crouched in the aisle, making sure the door was sealed.

Their speed ramped up. A warning flash up on the control panel: 'Excessive speed!'

Anissa wanted to close her eyes but felt too responsible for the risk Jon was taking for them. She was hardly able to believe that they were all together again.

Her son grabbed her hand. "Are you okay?"

Anissa locked eyes with him. "Jon was supposed to kill me but didn't." She turned to Jon, needing to make sure. "Instead, he helped rescue you. Thank you."

He smiled grimly. "I think I'm insane. Else, why would I be piloting a shuttle like a maniac?"

"See," she turned back to Treva, "we can trust him. If not, he would have shot me already."

Treva raised his eyebrows, clearly not happy with her logic and yet unable to argue it. "Where are we going?"

They sped across the city. Nobody had stopped them yet, but that wouldn't last. Jon took them higher, well above the pedestrian walkways. Only then did he engage the automatic pilot and turn to Treva.

"We can't get off-planet with SPEAR controlling all the ports. Even if we stole a ship, we wouldn't get far. There's only one place that I can think of that isn't controlled by SPEAR."

Treva's eyes widened as he understood what Jon was proposing at the same time as Anissa.

"Starhills," she said.

Jon nodded. "It's going to be risky, so if anyone has any other suggestions, speak now."

The others stared at them with blank expressions. Except for Treva, none were from Glaendor and were probably unaware that the notorious Starhills was controlled by gangs who lived by their own rules.

Treva shook his head.

"That's what I thought but don't worry, the people

there owe me." Jon said and turned his attention back to the controls. "Starhills, it is."

CHAPTER 26

KALI SCANNED THE flight deck of the *Vanguard* from where she sat on a ledge in the front viewport with one knee drawn up for balance. It was much smaller than the *Sepiantia*, which was only one of the problems according to Mika.

Since it was supple enough not to impede her movement, Kali already wore her protective suit. She glanced at Mika before turning her attention to the view outside. It wasn't the first time she'd wanted to break the silence between them but was still building up courage.

Fascinated by the kaleidoscope of subspace, no matter how many times she saw it, she said, "I like feeling insignificant."

"Not me." Mika's voice was tense. "If you are small, you get trodden on." She glanced over to see him studying the readout far more intently than was necessary. "I don't like this control interface."

She rolled her eyes, having no intention of allowing him to shut the conversation down. "Is that what's important to you—power?"

He spoke without looking at her, "And if it was? Would you blame me?"

Kali had the feeling that he was trying to provoke a

reaction. Then he could retreat into himself. She preferred to argue.

She returned to the colors outside the viewport. "I like that planets, forests, and lakes will be here when I'm gone." She saw from the reflection in the window that he was staring at her. "I need to tell you something." She cringed, not meaning to build up things. "What I'm trying to say is, I can't give up the TSS."

"No," he let the word hang in the air, "you wouldn't." His voice was flat. "Of course, you want to find a way to reverse the bond."

She hadn't meant that, had she? Except, she couldn't have both Mika and the TSS. There was no anger from him like she'd expected, and she found that she was disappointed. *He's making it too easy.* Although, it didn't feel easy. It felt like he'd accepted defeat.

She turned to face him. "I just want you to understand how important the TSS is to me, that's all."

"I will try to let you go." His voice was devoid of emotion.

Panic rose. It felt as if she'd broken something precious. "Mika, talk to me."

He looked at her. "I don't deserve you and should have let you go already."

"Why, not because of the charges?" She knew that wasn't it.

Mika's eyes went cold. "I don't pretend to remember everything he did, only what he allowed me to know."

Kali frowned, not understanding.

"As my father, he had access from when I was born. My mother had never learned to use her abilities, and even if she had, she wouldn't have been able to protect me." Mika stared off into the distance. "As I got older, he taught me to use my abilities, but not before ensuring that he had ways through any shields—a backdoor into my mind. But then you know about that." A brief glance in her direction and she knew what he was thinking, about how she had almost died as a result of that backdoor.

He avoided her gaze. "The worst was the things I did to placate him, like with those women. He'd hurt her so many times, you see."

She didn't know who he meant at first, and then guessed, "Your mother."

"Yes. He soon learned that it was a far more efficient way to force me to do want he wanted."

Kali jumped off the ledge and went to stand in front of him. "It wasn't your fault."

Mika didn't acknowledge her. "I didn't know he had access to my mind at will. Of course, there were clues. Sometimes he said things or answered a question that was only in my head, but I didn't guess the truth—at least not until that final time, just before we killed him."

She placed her hands on his arms. He didn't pull away, but he wasn't with her either. His mind still sifted through the past.

"Sometimes he made me do things. Joelee, my mother, knew it wasn't me, but it didn't matter."

Kali stilled in horror. "What sort of things?"

"I'd cut until her blood ran bright down the blade..." He trailed off, his mind returning to the things he'd done. No, been *forced* to do. "That's why it was almost a relief when she disappeared, at first, until I started to think of all the things he could have done to her."

"It wasn't your fault." A furious anger boiled up in Kali. That anyone like Tregaren could be given access to any child. "What happened to those women wasn't your fault, and neither was anything with your mother."

"That's why it would be cruel if she dies without ever knowing that he was gone."

"Because we killed him." Kali had never been happier that anyone was dead, and she felt no remorse for being the one to end Tregaren's overly long life.

Kali decided that the ghost of Tregaren couldn't have Mika; he was hers. She stepped in close until she was almost standing on his toes and kissed him. It was a gentle, coaxing kiss.

Unbelievably, he didn't respond. But instead of allowing the stab of rejection to grow, she deepened the kiss. *"No, the past can't have you."* Mika wasn't much taller than her and she pulled his head down to make it easier. *"You belong to me now. I need you."*

His hands came to her sides, cradling her. She sighed in relief that she had him back. Kali wouldn't allow the darkness that Tregaren had created to have him.

His mouth covered hers in a slow searing kiss that melted her body and made her forget that she was on a flight deck, heading into danger. Energy flowed from Mika into her through her lips, before spreading throughout her body.

This is where I belong.

Mika broke off the kiss and she moaned in protest, pressing into him. "Don't stop."

"I need you to think about this." His voice was rough. Whereas before there'd been nothing, now she felt an uproar of emotion. "Once we go down this path, there will be no turning back."

She pushed closer. "I need..." Except he was right, there would be no turning back in more ways than one. "I'm sorry." She stepped away, breathing heavily. "You're right."

It felt as though something had been torn out of her. *How can I do this after everything he's been through? After everything I've been through?* Because it would be worse to regret it.

She expected him to get angry, but his expression softened. "I don't want you to regret anything. Besides, we have to survive this trip first. Afterward, we can decide what to do, if there's anything to do."

With how she felt, Kali suspected that it might be too late by then, anyway, and the bond would be permanent. She returned to her perch, her body pulsing with an energy that hadn't been there before.

She desperately tried to think about what they might find on Glaendor—anything to distract her from the way Mika's eyes glowed brighter when he looked at her. This trip might be a waste of time. It would be an excellent strategy to get them out of the way for whatever SPEAR planned to do next.

Kali gasped as a jolt went through her and she almost fell off the ledge. The transition from subspace to standard space was more jarring than what she'd experienced previously. Usually, she barely noticed. From Mika's expression, he'd felt it, too.

"What was that?" she asked.

Mika shook his head. Before he could respond further, the comm unit chirped. Kali accepted the incoming transmission.

Andy sounded stressed. "Thank goodness I managed to get you before you reached Glaendor."

Kali went to stand next to Mika at the console, careful not to touch him.

"I can't get hold of Treva or the band." Andy revealed. "I hoped to get a message to them but they've disappeared. It is possible that they've successfully escaped."

"We'll find them," Kali said with more confidence than she felt.

Mika gave her a small nod of agreement, then directed his attention to Andy. "Let's see if there is another way down to the planet. If not, we might still be useful in orbit close by."

Andy considered his proposal for a few seconds. "Okay, but be careful. If Steyn does trigger the destruction, you don't know how far and fast disease will spread. It might wipe out the planet in hours."

"We won't take any unnecessary chances."

"Kali, take the word 'unnecessary' out of that sentence, please. It gives you far too much wriggle room."

Kali smiled. "We'll stay in touch."

"Oh, I almost forgot. I recently learned that we have an

operative deep undercover with Steyn. If he's still alive, you may be able to help each other. His name is Pyra."

"We'll look out for him," promised Kali.

Andy hung up, and Kali looked at Mika. "What now?"

Before he could answer, the comm bleeped again. Mika checked the screen. "It says it's Treva."

Kali frowned. "Well, that was easy. What's going on?"

"We'll know soon enough." Mika answered, "Hello."

Treva's face appeared on-screen. "Hi, guys." He sounded more like himself than when they had last spoken.

Kali scanned his face. "Are you okay?"

"It's a long story, which I won't go into now. I'm so glad to speak to you." Treva managed a weak smile. "I'm going to send you coordinates and clearance codes from Avon that should get you through the planetary shield without being questioned."

Mika checked the viewscreen. "I've received the coordinates and codes. We will be there soon." Mika ended the call and looked at Kali. "If the codes are wrong, we'll be destroyed by the planet's defenses."

She frowned. "It's still our best option."

Kali contacted Andy. "We've been in touch with Treva. He says he's safe and thinks there's a way down to the planet without us being detected. We're going to go for it."

Andy didn't look happy. "Kali, be careful." He looked as if he wanted to say more, but the screen went blank.

Mika directed the ship to the control point through the planetary shield closest to the destination coordinates. Kali involuntarily held her breath as they approached the security outpost.

"Sending codes now," Mika said, his voice tight.

Kali resisted the urge to bite her nails while they waited for a response.

Both of them let out long breaths when the codes cleared. The console pinged and lit up with a blue indicator light showing they were cleared for entry.

"It seems Treva has made some new well-connected

friends," Mika commented.

"I'll take any help we can get."

Mika peered at the monitor. "That's weird."

Kali moved to look over his shoulder but couldn't see anything out of the ordinary. "There's plenty of traffic. So, what?"

"Yes, but it's only going as far as that orbital station." He indicated an icon on the screen. "Nothing seems to be coming from the planet's surface."

"Do you think we're too late?"

Mika shook his head. "No way to know for sure, but we'd better hurry."

He kept the ship at a high altitude to reduce the likelihood of detection until they were right above Treva's coordinates. As they began the descent to the surface, a series of protective domes shielding the metropolis came into view. One central dome had smaller domes intersecting with it, creating different neighborhoods outside the central city. Kali held her breath, waiting for the ground-based planetary defenses to detect them.

Mika read out information from the screen. "We're heading to a neighborhood called Starhills. I have no idea why no one has asked for additional authorization, but we are now heading straight for the dome." He looked at her, clearly wanting conformation that they were going to risk causing catastrophic damage.

Kali felt lightheaded but nodded. They were trusting a fifteen-year-old with their lives.

Decision made, Mika didn't hesitate any longer. The ship skimmed the surface of the dome, and Kali flicked off the proximity alarm.

Mika grunted. "There's an opening. I can see it."

Kali stared at the fracture in the smaller dome's surface. "There must be some sort of force field in place." Atmosphere should leak from the fistula, except there was no sign that was happening.

"I'm going through."

They dropped into the gap. Alarms reset as the ship's readings returned to normal.

Mika slowed and pointed to a building missing its roof below. "That's where we're heading."

There was no greenery in the vicinity. Ugly, dark buildings surrounded their landing site, acting like a tunnel. Mika was forced to descend meter by meter as the *Vanguard* headed to their destination.

— — —

Mika's chest tightened as soon as they passed inside the dome. Despite all their precautions, they could have flown into a trap. If they had, it would be hard to get off the ground now they were enclosed. Mika wasn't a coward, but he wished they were somewhere safe for once.

Despite his best effort to get off the *Vanguard* first, Kali was ahead. She exited through the airlock.

They were greeted by an odd assortment of people who didn't seem like they should be working together. Treva stood at the front of the rough-looking group of men and women. Each had a pulse rifle or some sort of homemade weapon slung over their shoulder; Mika was thankful that none were pointing in their direction. Most of the people were loud and full of bravado. One young man and woman showed far too much interest in the *Vanguard,* and Mika made a mental note to lock down the ship before leaving.

As usual, Kali appeared to take everything in her stride. When she talked about the TSS being her home, he believed her. If only he'd felt the same. He had hoped that she'd change her mind. Now, Mika knew that had been a mistake and she'd break what was left of his heart first. Then again, he might not survive the next few days so why worry about it?

Mika brought his thoughts back to the present. Treva was, what, fifteen-years-old? They were asking a lot of a kid that age. But, if they were going to stop Steyn, they needed his help.

Mika caught sight of Caryanne running toward him. He couldn't help breaking out in a smile.

"Mikaaa!" Caryanne screeched.

He caught her in a hug. "It's good to see you."

She whispered in his ear. "I have so much to tell you." That didn't sound like Caryanne.

"Am I missing something?"

"Mika," she lowered her voice, "I had to remember."

Mika frowned, not understanding, and finding it hard to concentrate. He could see Kali approaching a man in uniform and strained to hear their conversation.

"Jon? Jon Del-Awai?"

"That's me." The man's expression was puzzled as he turned and then his eyes lit in recognition. "Ah, it's my favorite shiny new TSS Agent. Did you find your abductee? Was that only weeks ago? Because it feels like months."

"It was a few weeks ago but stars, a lot has happened since then!"

"Tell me about it. I've gone from zero to hero." His ripped uniform and stuck-up hair, made it look like Jon Del-Awai was having a bad day.

Caryanne tugged on Mika's arm, and he couldn't help smiling. She was like a small child who wanted attention. "Are you listening? I remembered what the Commander had to say so that I could warn the others."

Her words penetrated. "The Commander? Is that Steyn?"

"Yes, Commander Steyn wasn't very nice," her eyes widened, "and he kept Owen chained in the basement."

"Owen. Is he okay?"

She smiled with an innocence that, if he didn't know better, he would think was affected. "Owen is with us—me and Vaira and Honk. We managed to escape, and so did Treva's mother." She pointed to the man talking to Kali. "Mr. Del-Awai was supposed to shoot Treva's mom, but he ran off with her and rescued us instead."

Mika checked to see if she was serious, but she'd already moved on. He wasn't confident that everything she said was right. At least they were together, which was a relief.

"Where are we, exactly?" Mika asked.

"It's called Starhills."

"Caryanne, you remembered!" Maybe she *did* have genuine memories of those other things too. Mika hadn't believed it until she'd said the name of the place where they'd landed.

She frowned. "It's not good, is it?"

Owen and Vaira dashed through the group. Vaira hadn't changed, but Owen was different; older and more serious. When he smiled, he looked more like the old Owen.

Mika grinned in return. It was good to finally see everyone. Mika hugged Owen and then Vaira.

Owen said, "I guess Caryanne has got you up to date."

"Yes, well, that was a surprise in itself." Mika shook his head. "When this is all over, I want to hear all the details but you can start by explaining who these people are."

Owen leaned in, lowering his voice. "The security guard over there," he nodded at Jon Del-Awai, "had previous dealings with this section of misfits who don't conform to Glaendor's capitalist agenda."

Vaira hit Owen on the arm. "Hey, if it weren't for them, we'd be chained in some cellar by now."

"I'm not being horrible. It's just Glaendor's second biggest secret, that's all."

"The biggest being that the planet is home to SPEAR?" Mika asked.

Vaira gave him a one-armed squeeze. "We've missed you and have a lot of catching up to do. But first, we have to save the planet."

"Indeed." Mika didn't feel like laughing, but his mood had lightened. "Where's Honk?"

Vaira smiled. "Sleeping off today's excitement. It was all too much for him, as usual."

Mika saw Kali hop from one foot to the other as she tried to contain her eagerness to get on with the search for Pesta. The kid she was talking to couldn't have been more than eighteen-years-old. One side of his face was covered in a tattoo and the pulse rifle slung over his left shoulder looked like a newer model.

Kali waved Mika over. "We need a plan."

CHAPTER 27

KALI FELT AS if they'd landed in the middle of a gangster movie, and not one of Treva's companions looked older than eighteen.

They left the hangar or factory or warehouse— whatever it was—and walked across open ground toward a walkway that was familiar from Kali's first time on Glaendor. She peered into the sky and could see the faint arc of the protective dome. She still wasn't sure how they had come through unscathed. The dome would make Glaendor City an excellent place to unleash Pesta. It would cause catastrophic damage but might be contained within the enclosure, or not, she had no idea.

Kali could see how the devastation would serve as an example of Steyn's power. Although, he must have made plans to leave the planet, if he was still here, before the disease was released.

Owen explained that Starhills was controlled by gangs and the only place safe from Avon Security.

"Why doesn't Steyn do something about it?" She asked. "He must have the resources to take back the area."

" 'Cause Steyn likes what we do for him." One of the young men sauntered over. A plasma gun swinging from his shoulder. "There's things he likes to keep unofficial and it buys us the freedom to do what we want."

"This is Tommi," Jon said.

Kali sighed, thinking that anyone who knew how to use a weapon didn't generally advertise they had one. Tommi was a gangly kid with tattoos covering both arms so that they looked like sleeves, a mop of ginger hair and smattering of freckles, he looked about fourteen. She guessed that he was older.

He nodded. "Tommi Bear-Pants."

Kali blinked. "Pleased to meet you. Glad you're going to help. Local knowledge is always useful."

Tommi let out a snort of laughter. "That's not likely." He slapped Jon on the shoulder. "He helped us out, he did, though, he owes us now." He swung away almost hitting Kali with his gun, "hey, wait," he shouted to a group.

Kali shook her head and scanned their surroundings. It was very different from what she remembered. The high-rise hotels and casinos, accessed from the main walkways were missing from this neighborhood. Before, everywhere had appeared safe and well lit, and the central walkway was very different from this one. Here, the buildings climbed so high that they blocked out most of the light, making the walkways feel dangerous.

Jon Del-Awai saw her expression. "They knock out the lights, and security avoids this sector." He nodded at one of the high-rise buildings to the left. "I had a missing person case and so had reason to be down here." He grimaced. "It's why I dared to bring your friends when we were out of options."

Kali frowned. "Did you find them?"

"Who?"

"Your missing person."

"Ah" He smiled. "Turned out she wasn't missing after all." After a few seconds of silence, he said, "I think you worried my bosses last time you were on Glaendor."

"Why?"

"They didn't want you looking too closely." At her

questioning look, he said, "Places like this aren't supposed to exist in a modern metropolis."

"Unless, it's deliberate," she muttered.

Del-Awai looked at her with a question in his eyes.

"You heard what he said about a mutual arrangement."

He sighed. "Yeah, but there's only so much one man can do."

Kali didn't agree but there was no point making enemies, she had too many of those. Instead, she let him go on without her.

She looked up at the compact, uniform buildings; they reminded her of an anthill. The windows facing the walkway were covered with piles of clothes and packages. Tattered curtains hung in some, and a strong odor permeated the air. Why did some of the population live in such poor conditions compared to the rest of the planet?

Treva came from behind. "It's different, isn't it?"

Kali nodded, knowing that he too was comparing it to the rest of the city. "I didn't see anything like this when I visited before."

"I used to come to the outskirts to pick up packages for... well, I later found out that it was for dad."

"Drugs?"

Treva met her gaze. "I think they were part of something bigger." He stopped himself from saying more and then must have thought better of it. "Herja ended up with the shipment, but I warned her not to use them." He pointed back the way they'd come. "That must be why they have another way onto the planet."

It wouldn't take much for the TSS to uncover this operation. This way, the authorities could deny any knowledge of what was going on while letting these people take the risks. They probably didn't even know who they were dealing with half the time.

Kali lowered her voice, "We can't trust anyone."

Treva shrugged. "I don't. We were just glad to have somewhere outside of my uncle's reach, even if it's only temporary."

Kali suspected they weren't safe. There was no telling what the arrangement was between SPEAR and the gangs.

Kali said, "We need to find Mac and Pesta before everyone dies."

Treva gestured toward Tommi. "He says he can get us into Glaendor City without being detected for a price, but I don't know how we will find where they are being kept."

Kali raised her eyebrow at the mention of a price. She doubted they'd get in without being detected with the amount of surveillance she'd seen when last been in the city, but they had a job to do.

"Do you know someone called Pyra?" she asked.

Treva's eyes brightened. "He works for Andrei. He helped us."

"He might know something if we can get to him."

Treva shook his head. "I have no way to contact him."

Kali doubted that Steyn could hide Pesta's presence from Mika and her now that they knew what to look out for. They just needed to get close enough to sense her.

"You want treasure?" Tommi wandered over with a smirk, and Kali half expected him to point to his groin.

When she stared blankly, he looked away and said, "I can take you into the city if the boss okays it."

Mika joined them. "I can't sense anything that might be Pesta."

She shook her head. "There's nothing close."

"We can't trust him." Mika jutted his chin at Tommi.

Kali considered asking Mika to stay behind. She wasn't sure that he wouldn't do something stupid while trying to keep her safe. She dismissed the idea. He would refuse and she'd need the boost of power he gave her.

"No, but if he knows how to get across the city, we need to take advantage of it." She hoped she was right. *"Steyn is likely to expect us, since he knows about this alternative way onto Glaendor."*

Mika ignored Tommi who stood staring at them both.

"You think it's a trap but Steyn won't be able to hold us. We're too strong together."

"We don't know that, and he has to have a plan in case we show up."

Treva looked at them both. "Do you want us to stay here?" He didn't sound happy.

"It would be safer."

"It might be better to take them with us," Mika said.

"They're not trained."

"Neither am I."

"Well, you don't have to come either." Kali was getting annoyed. *"I don't have time for this."*

"Okay." He hesitated and then put a hand on her arm. *"I'm sorry."*

Kali sighed. *"I'm sorry, too."* She was more worried than she wanted to admit to anyone, even herself. *"We just don't know what we're going to face once we find Pesta."*

A small, wiry boy pushed Tommi to one side, his eyes narrowed in suspicion. "Our services aren't free."

"Who are you?" Kali asked.

"The one you need to deal with. I'm Rox, and I make the decisions."

She wanted to laugh because he looked like the youngest but noticed the way the others looked at him and moderated her tone, "Everyone will die if we don't stop SPEAR. Isn't that reason enough to help us?"

He laughed. "Why should we believe what you say when you threatened our trade?"

Kali frowned. "Trade?" *Does he mean the drugs?* She resisted the urge to point out that they should be doing better if that was the case. In a way, these people were more of Steyn's victims.

Rox thrust out his chest. "You want our help, then you pay. Simple."

Well, at least they had gotten to what mattered, and Kali was more than happy to operate alone. She would walk away.

Rox pointed to a group made up of Owen, Vaira, and Treva. "Don't forget your friends."

Kali stopped. They couldn't take everyone into danger.

Mika put a hand on her arm. *"Let me try."* His eyes glowed a little brighter. *"Sometimes being TSS is a disadvantage. These people have probably fought authority all their lives."*

She nodded, annoyed she hadn't anticipated that herself. It wouldn't do any harm to let Mika try since she couldn't sense Pesta yet.

Kali stepped away, giving Mika space to try to reach an agreement. "Just be quick."

Mika spoke in hushed tones while Rox shook his head and gestured toward the city.

Kali tried to contain her impatience but it was hard when they didn't know how long they had before SPEAR unleashed Pesta on the planet.

Mika appeared at her elbow. "There's a problem."

"What?" Impatience colored her voice despite her best effort.

"They want something in exchange for help."

Kali rolled her eyes and it took all her discipline not to point out that they had already gotten that far. "We don't have anything to barter with."

"They've suggested we take Tommi, who will claim payment from whatever we find."

"They want to use us as an opportunity to steal. No— that's not going to work."

"I thought you'd say that." Mika paused, and she could tell that he thought he had the answer. "Or, we could contact Andy and get him to send some credit."

Kali couldn't believe that he would suggest paying criminals, but she realized they didn't have much choice. Whatever they did, there were risks.

"It's the only way that we can leave the others here." Mika folded his arms.

Of course, Mika would think that it was okay to give

them what they wanted, because he didn't have to think about the consequences. "And, what happens if they end up killing half the population of Starhills in a turf war, which would never have started without the finances to buy weapons?" *Although, the seriousness of the current situation might justify it.*

Mika dropped both arms to his sides. "I hadn't thought of that."

She softened. "I have to consider all the possible consequences, or else we can easily cause as many problems as we solve."

Mika looked uncertain. "There is another way, but I don't think you're going to like it."

"Just tell me. We're going to be out of time soon."

Mika still didn't answer straight away and then blurted, "We could influence them." She was about to refuse when he added, "Just think about it. Everyone on this planet is going to die unless we do something soon. What is worse? Breaking the rules and messing with some gangsters or letting the entire population die?"

What he said made sense. It crossed a line, but was that selfish? They were out of time and this would be the quickest and safest way, and she could ensure that no harm came to the others.

"Let me speak to Andy first."

She didn't want to bother him at a time like this, but it wasn't a decision she could make alone.

Mika nodded. "Okay, but hurry."

Kali contacted Andy on her handheld.

"You made it then?" He spoke so casually that she knew he'd been worried.

She moved further from the others, not wanting her conversation to be overheard. "Yes, it's a weird situation. We're in a region called Starhills, which is run by gangs."

"There is no information about that at all," He sounded distracted as he checked, "but I do have something for you. Andrei Steyn has links to the SPEAR Corporation, which has been around for many years. Obviously, the source of the terrorist's name but amongst other things, they've contracts for weapons."

Kali put everything together. "That must be where Pesta came from?"

"We don't know for sure, but I suspect so. But there's no record of a living weapon quite like Pesta before that footage of an attack on the planet. It's suspicious timing with everything else going on."

None of that mattered to Kali with the current mission at hand. "I should've spoken more to Mac when I had the chance." Unfortunately, the circumstances had been impossible on Red Ghost. "Treva told me that Mac was employed by a laboratory who experimented on him and he ended up bonded to Pesta."

Andy interrupted, "You told me in the debrief, but who is behind the SPEAR Corporation's development of Pesta?"

Kali frowned. "You don't think that Steyn is in charge?"

"I don't know. It would be nice to find out, but your priority remains to stop Steyn using Pesta to destroy Glaendor."

When she explained what she wanted to do to get the criminals to help, Andy shrugged. "Dangerous times call for unusual measures."

She knew that he shared her sense of urgency but couldn't help thinking that his ready consensus was partly due to Glaendor being insignificant and far from anything that mattered.

Kali ended the call, more disturbed than she wanted to admit. She hadn't had time to think about how the threat might go beyond Steyn.

With Andy's agreement, the task of influencing Rox was easy. TSS Agents were all trained in mental manipulation techniques, though such practices were reserved for critical situations; upon further reflection, she couldn't think of many occasions more desperate than this. Her spoken and telepathic influence allowed Rox to believe that he was gaining something essential. Even though she knew the action was justified and sanctioned, it didn't stop her from feeling that she'd done something bad to mess with his inner mind.

"You should have let me do it," Mika said.

"I would have felt as though I'd shirked my responsibility."

If Tommi was surprised by his boss's change of heart, he didn't show it. He led them through Starhills and out the other side. They followed him down alleyways and under the walkways to avoid surveillance.

"He doesn't seem bothered about risking his life, taking us across the city." Mika's voice sounded in her head.

"He's following orders."

"He might not be taking as big a risk as we think."

She stopped. *"Wait. Have you looked into his mind? Just because we did it once, doesn't mean we can do it all the time."*

Mika gave her a small smile. *"It seems even someone as stubborn as me can learn about boundaries with the right motivation."*

For some reason, his confession made her smile as she ran after Tommi before he moved out of sight. *"I'm scanning surface thoughts and there's nothing I wouldn't expect so far."*

Mika laughed, startling their guide. "Sorry. Just had a funny thought. Nothing I need to share."

Kali raised an eyebrow, wondering how either of them could find anything amusing with so much at stake. Despite what she'd said earlier, she hoped that Steyn wouldn't pose too big a threat against their combined power. After all, he was a *failed* TSS Agent, allegedly, and she was a high-ranking Primus graduate.

Mika grabbed her arm. *"Can you feel that?"*

Kali halted, trying to identify what had piqued Mika's interest.

Tommi noticed and was forced to backtrack to their

position under a walkway. "What are you doing? It's not safe to stop."

Kali held up a hand, cocking her head to one side.

"What you listening for?" Tommi frowned. "It's too noisy."

Tommi was right—it *was* noisy. Footsteps clattered, combining with the creak of the walkway overhead and shuttles whooshing past just out of sight. Kali wasn't listening with her ears but nevertheless, she dropped her gaze to better concentrate. Could Mika sense Pesta already or had it been a more general question?

There—Mac came through stronger than Pesta. Did Mika sense the same? She would try to remember to ask him about it when they had time. She lifted her head and Mika grinned, setting off in the direction she would have indicated if he hadn't already known.

"What...?" Tommi asked.

Kali shook her head, staring after Mika. Pesta was ahead, and they would have no choice but to join the walkways as they followed their enhanced senses to find Mac. She quickly realized that Tommi wasn't going to be much help from this point. They would have to hope that the volume of people in the city kept them hidden.

"Tommi, it's time to go back."

"I'm going with you." He folded his arms across his chest. "I have no choice."

She saw that he wasn't going to change his mind. He was obeying orders. She considered influencing his mind but recognized the impulse for the slippery slope that it was.

She sighed. "Okay, but it'll be dangerous and you will have to follow us now that we know where we need to be."

Mika had slowed to wait for them. They couldn't move too fast without drawing attention, so they continued along the wide walkways with their bright advertisements until it became clear that they were heading to the docking station. It was too much of a coincidence and was probably a trap.

"I need to tell Andy where we're going."

Mika nodded and she saw in his eyes the knowledge of what she hadn't said. Andy needed the location in case they didn't make it out alive.

She found a quiet spot, relieved when Andy's face appeared on her handheld. "I just need you to know that we think Pesta is at the docking station, but it could be a trap."

"How's Mika?" Andy asked.

She looked over to see Mika glance in her direction. "It's complicated."

"Kali, be careful. Don't do anything foolish."

"Like using our abilities together?" She refused to consider that Andy might be referring to anything else.

"Exactly. Steyn wants you out of the way, and you could end up in a position where you have no choice."

That was all she needed. "Thank you, I will bear that in mind."

"Take care."

"And you." Kali didn't know why she was reluctant to end the call.

Stop being silly. You've faced worse. Except, she wasn't sure that she had. Tregaren had been bad, but at least she'd known what to expect. Conversely, they knew very little about SPEAR. She ended the call and joined the others.

Men wearing Avon Security uniforms stood at the entrance to the docking station. There was nobody going in or out, which was weird—unless Steyn had trapped the entire population to ensure that they all died. That was a hideous thought.

Kali was in the process of considering their options when Tommi tugged on her arm. "This way."

She shared a look with Mika. He shrugged and she agreed. What did they have to lose? If they killed the guards, Steyn would know that they were there and if she attempted to influence them and they were protected, the result would be the same.

Tommi took them to a ventilation shaft that appeared too small to fit inside until they reached it. Mika went in first, followed by Kali and then Tommi.

Inside, the docking station was deserted. Tommi kept glancing over his shoulder and even though he didn't say anything, she knew that he felt something.

Mika jumped a barrier and dropped into shadow. Tommi and Kali followed. This had to be a trap.

"We're heading the wrong way," Mika said into Kali's head.

She nodded. "I know precisely where we need to go."

Tommi stared. "Are you two doing freaky shite?"

Kali ignored him, vaulting the internal walkway and running to the other side, aware of the other two behind. She followed the wall back the way they'd come until she could get onto the moving walkway running the opposite direction. Fortunately, it was switched off, allowing them to move against the normal flow.

They took the exit off the walkway at the Avon Security Station, where Kali had last been with Jon Del-Awai. They had to have been picked up by surveillance now.

"In there?" Tommi didn't look happy.

"You can go back," Kali said while trying to work out how to get inside.

Nothing moved, but Kali felt people inside the building. She wondered how many Steyn could shield from her telepathic reading. It was unnaturally quiet in an area that was usually full of people. Mika squeezed her hand, no doubt sensing some of what she was feeling.

She motioned to Tommi who strolled over. "Is there another way inside?"

His eyes were wary. "Are you mad?"

Kali needed to check that there weren't possibilities that she hadn't considered. Doing nothing wasn't an option..

"He's waiting for us," Mika said.

Tommi's eyes widened, reminding Kali how young he was. Whatever he'd learned on the streets, this was outside his experience.

Kali kept her voice low even though Mika would hear regardless—Tommi didn't know that. "We will take it from here."

Tommi stiffened. "I'm not afraid."

How can I convince him to leave without losing face?

Mika's voice came from behind. "What Kali meant to say was, we can't look after you and ourselves."

Kali raised an eyebrow, barely resisting shaking her head.

Tommi rose a couple of centimeters, his face full of color.

"You have the physical strength," Mika continued, "but unless you can protect your mind against attack, they will use you against us."

Tommi opened his mouth to argue but nothing came out. He finally understood what they were up against.

Kali patted him on the shoulder. "Don't worry. We all have limits."

Tommi nodded and disappeared over the other side of the walkway.

Steyn knew that they would sense Pesta if they got near enough and he hadn't taken precautions, which told Kali everything. They were expected. Now, it was up to her to find a way inside that didn't get them immediately captured or killed.

CHAPTER 28

"PYRA!" ANDREI YELLED.

Where was the little man? He was far too evasive and if Andrei hadn't already been suspicious, he would be now. Hurried footsteps sounded from down the corridor. He couldn't sense anyone, so it could only be Pyra.

The little man tripped over his own feet on entering the room. Andrei narrowed his eyes. *Did he do that on purpose?* It wasn't the first time Andrei had thought Pyra exaggerated his clumsiness but now, he was certain.

Pyra bowed as if expecting trouble, and Andrei couldn't shake the impression that he was more intelligent that he appeared. When he'd brought Pyra through the TSD arch to Red Ghost, he'd never planned to allow him to live so long. It had been a mistake to forget that. Now, he would keep him close to ensure that nothing upset his plans.

Andrei's eyes bored into the top of Pyra's head. "Stay close."

When Pyra raised his face, his expression was confused but he wisely didn't ask for clarification.

Andrei's handheld announced a vidcall, and he struggled to find patience. He glanced at the screen. *Oh no. Not now!*

Even though he desperately wanted to, he couldn't

ignore his mother. She'd trained her children to respond when they were too defenseless to fight Maggie Steyn's monumental will.

"Andrei, I've been trying to get a hold of you." His mother's crisp voice gripped something inside and forced him to pay attention.

He didn't point out that it was a bad time. "Hello, Mother. What can I do for you?"

Her large, brown eyes stared into his through the screen, and he noted that she'd allowed streaks of grey to lighten her black hair. "Even knowing what I'm going through with the loss of my youngest child, you've been remiss at keeping me informed."

The twinge of guilt was overshadowed by anger that even dead, Marco continued to be her favorite.

"I want to see my grandson."

How does she do it every foking time? Maggie Steyn's secret power was her ability to disrupt his plans with the most inconsequential demand. It would have been a reasonable request when he had Treva, but not now... He would have to find and retrieve the brat, which would seriously upset his schedule. Still, he knew from bitter experience that there was no point arguing with her.

She narrowed her eyes. "Don't think that I don't know what you were planning to do with him."

There was no way that she could have known that he'd planned to let Treva die. Nobody on Glaendor knew of her existence, so they couldn't have told her.

She smiled. "You see, I don't need spies—not when I know you so well. No excuses. You have two days to bring him to me." Someone off-screen said her name but she kept her attention on him. "Don't make me your enemy, Andrei. You have been warned." She disconnected the call.

Andrei fumed. She hadn't even asked after him, as if nothing he did mattered. Well, he would show her, but first, he had to find Treva.

Almost immediately, he had to change his plans again.

Only this time, he felt calmer after seeing the message from Raffia. As expected, Kali Wietris and Mika Hendi had turned up at the station. As a senior member of SPEAR as well as the station's commander, Raffia was capable of delaying them but as it was those two, he would need help. Andrei took some comfort in the way his plans were coming together despite his mother's best effort to disrupt them.

Andrei strolled out of the room with Pyra trailing behind. Pyra didn't speak on the journey in the oversized shuttle that Andrei used to travel on Glaendor. He was so quiet that Andrei almost forgot that he was there. *How many times have I forgotten that he was listening?*

Pyra's betrayal wasn't unexpected, although Steyn hadn't seen it coming because the meek man didn't seem capable. Even now, as Pyra watched the city slide past, there was nothing to suggest that he was a spy. Worst of all, Pyra had betrayed him to the organization Andrei hated the most.

The TSS had failed to see Andrei's potential once, going so far as to say that his temperament was unsuitable. If Andrei hadn't met Tregaren, how would he have developed his natural abilities? They would have condemned him to a half-life, and Andrei would not forgive that. The more he thought about it, the angrier he got until he couldn't contain it any longer.

"I'm curious." He kept his voice low despite what he felt. "How did you think you'd get away with using my communication system to report to the TSS?"

Pyra turned to look at him. There was no alarm or fear in his face, only resignation. That wasn't what Andrei wanted. He needed him to suffer before he died.

Pyra sighed. "You wouldn't understand."

He was no longer the frightened little man he'd been a few minutes ago. He should be *more* afraid, not less. Andrei should kill him because it was too dangerous to add an unknown factor into the mix at this stage—not when he was so close to getting what he wanted.

"I will show you how little the TSS cares about whether you live or die." Andrei watched out of the corner of his eye, but if Pyra was nervous, he still didn't show it.

The shuttle swung under an archway, heading for the rear entrance of the station. Not many people knew that a back way in existed.

Once inside, it was gloomy but not dark. A light flickered, making shadows dance wildly until there was nothing to see but rock walls.

Andrei shielded his mind. It wouldn't do to be discovered before he was ready. Everything was going to plan, but he couldn't let go of the fact that Pyra had acted against his own self-interest. It didn't make any sense, and if Pyra could do it, so could someone else. Andrei wanted to ask why, but the shuttle's navigation system announced that they'd arrived.

Andrei took a vial of what looked like smoke from a hidden pocket. Eyes closed, he inhaled the contents. Not a wisp escaped. Within seconds, he became aware of a shift in consciousness and he could see more than ever before.

The grey minds of the station's inhabitants were scattered. He dismissed them, focusing on the two colorful minds, one predominantly purple and the other turquoise. He could know more but was afraid of losing track of time in this state.

Andrei exited the shuttle, suddenly eager to test his new abilities. Things were changing in his body—like before—except, he'd taken more of the gas and the intensity had already doubled. He ignored the murkiness that had come over his normal vision

It had only been in the past couple of weeks that he'd accepted that his natural ability hadn't been so special. Tregaren had told him as much years ago, but without an alternative, he hadn't wanted to listen. There was no need to worry about the price when he felt so strong. SPEAR would ensure the downfall of the TSS.

SPEAR should have captured the imagination of the

Outer Colonies in the way that Kali and Mika had. They represented everything he hated about the TSS, but once they were eliminated, people would have no choice but to turn to SPEAR.

Raffia Barrendi waited as planned. "They're inside already." He sounded anxious, but there was no need for nervous.

Andrei swept past Raffia, with Pyra close behind. He was so intent on locating the colorful minds that he didn't hear Raffia's directions. Kali and Mika had attempted to shield their presence from him, but their abilities were too strong to be easily hidden. They were as powerful as anyone Andrei had come across.

Pesta lurked amongst the maintenance equipment in the basement where Andrei had instructed they be held in order to minimize the number of people likely to see anything. There were reasons that he didn't want to reveal his new power too soon. A niggling at the back of his head said that he should have seen what Pyra was up to before now.

Andrei could activate Pesta at any time by freeing it of its Taran keeper. Then he would wipe out the entire planet, forcing the Outer Colonies to flock to SPEAR for salvation.

Andrei couldn't remember how he'd felt before he'd inhaled the smoke. Even with practice, he couldn't use the full extent of this Gift, which disappointed him. For now, he needed to concentrate on the task at hand, especially as this was another test and he had a lot to prove.

The floor and walls were less solid, more like drawings, than before he'd inhaled the smoke. He could see through to the people moving around. The whole world was less substantial than it had been minutes before.

Andrei walked in a straight line toward the bright auras. He stepped through a wall, which tickled but couldn't impede him.

Shouts and screams sounded from far away, as if being played back at a low volume. He waited for Pyra, who had to run through the building, using the doors. *He hasn't tried to escape.* Andrei couldn't work out why that bothered him. Pyra arrived, panting as if he'd run a long way.

Andrei frowned. "What did you mean when you said that I wouldn't understand?"

Pyra blinked rapidly. "Some things are bigger than one person. I discovered what truly matters."

What could be bigger than this. *I'm the savior of the Outer Colonies.* This was his destiny. The Outer Colonies would become a force to be reckoned with and then, even the TSS would have to take him seriously.

SPEAR's enemies would not sense him in this state. His entire body tingled as he passed through another wall.

A woman shrieked, causing Andrei to shake his head in annoyance. He was thankful that the noise sounded farther away than it should. He wouldn't let anyone see his new abilities. He reached out a tendril of power and crushed the woman's brain. Raffia would be annoyed, but better to deal with him rather than allow his plans to fail.

Andrei's targets were on the other side of the wall. Now that he was close, he felt something unexpected—one of them was familiar. An image of Tregaren appeared in his mind. He was dead and yet, there was no mistaking the ex-priest's signature.

Andrei stepped through the curtain that had once been a wall. The man who stood a couple of meters away wasn't Tregaren but his son.

What's he doing here?

Mika resembled his father, and Andrei remembered that Tregaren had been training his son to contribute to their cause. It was a shame to kill him without knowing how he came to be a TSS operative.

Kali Wietris was further away, but they were both startled by his arrival. A blast of energy passed through his body.

He struck Mika at the same time as the Wietris woman hit him with another bolt that made his head ring.

Andrei instinctively stepped back through the wall but not before he saw that the spot where Mika had been was empty. *Something has gone wrong.*

Wietris shouted, "Mika!" once, and then she was running.

Andrei retreated. He wasn't sure what had happened and didn't want to repeat the mistake. Despite his intention to kill Tregaren's son, Andrei hadn't done it. Instead, he'd sent him far away. Now, to deal with Kali Wietris but she could wait. He couldn't disappoint his mother.

— — —

Kali froze for a fraction of a second before her training kicked in.

Mika was gone. Their connection remained, which meant he was alive—somewhere. It might be possible to reach him, if she tried, but she didn't dare take her attention off her surroundings. Steyn had walked through the wall as if it weren't there, and he'd been so quick to attack.

They'd known this was a trap, and had knowingly walked into it anyway, but nobody had guessed that Steyn was that powerful. How could the TSS have failed to know about the strength of his ability?

She had no sense of Mika attempting to contact her, but perhaps he was afraid of putting her in danger. She refused to consider anything else. Retreat or continue? There was no decision to be made. *Stay calm. Find Pesta, then Mika.*

Steyn would attack again. Soon. In fact, she had no idea why he'd left, unless he'd used up his power. Possible, but she wouldn't bet her life on it. Kali skimmed the minds in the vicinity for any sign of Steyn, but there was nothing. Pesta was ahead and stationary, which was suspicious.

Movement at the door caused her to bring her pulse gun up, her mind primed to attack.

A little man appeared in the doorway with both hands

raised. Kali had never seen him before and couldn't sense him.

"I'm Pyra and I want to help."

Andy had mentioned Pyra working undercover for the TSS. He had infiltrated SPEAR.

Kali slowly lowered her weapon. She couldn't be sure it was him, but it seemed unlikely that Steyn, as powerful as he was, would bother to resort to such subterfuge.

"Where did Steyn go?" she asked.

"I was about to ask you the same question. I've never seen him walk through walls or show much more than a bit of telepathy." He scanned their surroundings. "Where is Mika Hendri?"

Kali couldn't afford to think about Mika right now. "He disappeared, as in 'poof', but he's not dead." Before Pyra could ask any more, she said, "I need to find Pesta." She saw him frown. "I can sense her whereabouts, but haven't learned to walk through walls."

"Oh, I can take you to where he was keeping her."

Kali allowed Pyra to lead the way, through the room into a corridor, which was deserted. When Pyra started to go upstairs, Kali stopped. "She's down, not up."

Pyra shrugged. "Steyn may have had her moved."

"Let's try down." Kali led the way.

"There's only the basement below."

"How come Steyn didn't read your mind when you were spying on him?" Kali asked.

"I'm a null. Nobody can read my mind."

Kali had heard of nulls in passing, though she wasn't sure why one would have anything to do with the TSS. She didn't question what Pyra told her since he would have needed a way of protecting his mind from Steyn. He moved silently, making her wonder how much of their training had been similar.

Kali prepared for Steyn to appear at any moment, from any direction. When he didn't, she became concerned that he was waiting for them to get into position before he attacked again.

When they reached the basement, they were directly over the spot where she sensed Pesta. She touched Pyra's arm and pointed down.

He frowned, but she saw that he understood. It obviously wasn't where Steyn had kept Pesta until their arrival. Pyra indicated that he wanted to go right. She nodded, trusting that he was searching for access to below.

"There!" he exclaimed. "I knew there was a door somewhere."

There was nothing written on the wide double blue doors. Pyra opened the one on the left before disappearing through.

I have a bad feeling about this.

After checking for Steyn, Kali followed, only to find Pyra waiting at the head of stairs leading to a sub-basement. Crisscross red laser beams blocked their way.

Lasers to delay us, but why? Steyn knows we're here already. Unless we will trigger an alarm.

She bit her tongue as she'd been about to ask if there was another way, but logic told her it was unlikely. A memory arose of someone in her training group manipulating the electromagnetic energy currents of an alarm. He'd borrowed a ship to impress a girl; though he'd been caught, it wasn't because of the alarm.

The information was third-hand, but Kali understood the theory. She needed to transfer the flow of electricity from one side to the another without setting off the alarm. In theory, she could trick the receptor to think that the beam hadn't been broken. Mika would be better at this. She clamped down on the wave of emotion. Mika wasn't here.

She focused on one of the beams and visualized its operation in her mind, assessing its intensity and energy flow. When she felt she understood enough to replicate the beam, she tentatively reached out her hand to interrupt its path. It continued to pulse, and there was no sign that she'd triggered anything.

"Hurry." Pyra almost made her lose her concentration. He probably thought she was mesmerized by the pretty patterns, but her technique was working.

"Stay here," she said to Pyra, glad to have an outlet for the tension building inside her.

She focused on tricking all of the beams that barred her path and started to move through. Against her orders, Pyra followed. She dismissed the impulse to warn him a second time. It was more important to get to Pesta and stop what was about to happen.

CHAPTER 29

ANDREI STRUGGLED TO contain the growing power. It was hard to make it do what he wanted. He had intended to kill Tregaren's son, not send him away, but something had slipped in his mind at the crucial moment. He hadn't been prepared for how hard it would be to concentrate and now, thanks to his mother, he had to take a detour from his plans.

It helped to remember that this was just another test. He had to embrace every challenge if he was going to maintain his position.

He was tempted to let Treva die, but his mother would know. She already blamed him for Marco's death. It was as if she saw inside him and nobody could save him from her anger. Time was running out; he had to capture the brat and get back before anything vital happened.

Wietris was nothing without the reservoir of power that lived in Tregaren's son—not that he had seemed aware of his potential, despite it being immediately obvious to Andrei. Wietris was busy, trying to get into the maintenance room. If she left, he would let her go, since Pesta would kill everyone except those who left through the TSD arch in the Blue Pixie to the orbital station.

With the new power coursing through him, all he had

to do was focus on Treva to find him. He smiled. Of course, there really was only one place the boy could have gone.

Andrei took his private shuttle to the invisible border with Starhills, sure that he was wasting time using conventional transport. He could have stepped there in a moment if only he could work out how. So full of power and no instruction on its use.

The spotters sent up the alert as soon as he arrived at the edge of Starhills, but this time, Andrei didn't wait for an invitation. The gangs had served their purpose by successfully transporting the drugs. It wasn't their fault that Vaughn had lost the cargo to pirates.

Each and every one of them were waiting upon his arrival, including the lovely Caryanne. He'd forgotten about her until he strode down the center of the walkway, enjoying the wave of fear his presence generated. Not one had the courage to attack him as he arrived at their traditional meeting place.

A buzz of activity centered around the building as they frantically prepared for a minor war. It wouldn't do any good.

"Rox," he shouted, staring at the precise window where the boy hid. "I want to talk."

Starhills should have been called Greyhills. Graffiti was the only visible marking on the high-rises that packed people in like a storage facility.

Andrei suspected he could ride the energy to the top of the buildings where it dissipated under the protective dome. The image filled his mind so completely that he was surprised when, Rox came out of a door opposite, forcing him to gather his thoughts. The gang leader walked with shoulders back and chest out as if he wasn't quivering in his boots. Andrei felt the truth.

When Rox was close enough not to have to shout, he said, "You're trampling our agreement by coming here. Starhills belongs to us."

Andrei scowled. "But what am I to do when you shelter

my enemies?"

Rox swung the rifle from over his shoulder and pointed it at Andrei. He positioned the scope and squinted as if lining up a shot.

Andrei laughed. "Go on. It won't do you any good."

No weapon could injure him, he was too far gone in the change. He wasn't sure if it was permanent and found it hard to care.

"Why are you here?"

Andrei studied the boy, seeing that he was determined not to cooperate. There was something else. Someone had messed with his head.

I'm a fool. What am I doing wasting time?

Andrei took hold of the gang leader's mind. Rox resisted, dropping his weapon, but there was nothing protecting his mind. He didn't have the skills to produce a shield, so he never stood a chance. As he fell in a crumpled heap, his heart fluttering as it failed to pump blood through the chambers and his tissues starved of oxygen started to die, Andrei smiled. Power felt good.

Andrei shouted to everyone listening, "I want Treva Steyn in ten seconds, else you all die."

There was a commotion as the singer in that useless band tried to stop Treva. Then, the boy ran from the building toward Andrei with a woman close behind. Treva looked taller and even more like his father than when Andrei had last seen him a few weeks ago. Andrei recognized the woman as Marco's estranged wife. He didn't want to deal with her, so he stopped her. Treva paused, ready to run back to his mother, but Andrei forced him to come to his side.

Marco had always been the family favorite because he was the youngest. It was annoying how much that still rankled. His mother better not decide to keep this boy and make things even worse.

"You will follow me," Andrei stated.

He set off back to the shuttle, prepared to use force if

the boy resisted, except he didn't. He'd made up his mind to go. Andrei saw it in his head. Then, he saw something else; they had a ship. Nobody could be allowed to leave the planet.

Andrei turned back after taking the ship's location from the boy's head. The warehouse where it had been parked wasn't far. He went to it, not sure if he walked or simply glided. Inside, he found the beautiful sleek ship, less than three years old.

Yells of surprise sounded, but he ignored them; he was on a timeline and had to get back to deal with Wietris. He briefly considered how best to disable the ship. It would be easy to destroy the power distribution cells, but there might be replacements. And besides, what would be the fun in that?

While Andrei would have preferred the drama of an explosion, he didn't know how. So without a clear plan, he expanded his mind until he surrounded the ship, and then he squeezed. Nobody had shown him how to use the power to destroy, but it came more naturally than anything else. The metal twisted and bent, making him smile while everyone ran from him. There was nothing left but a twisted block of metal by the time he'd finished.

When he went back to the alley, he found that his nephew hadn't moved, despite the urgings of others. They wouldn't understand that the boy belonged to him now.

Andrei turned his back on Starhills as some of the gang members scrambled to block his way. He admired their courage even as he waved a hand to send them flying as if a tornado had lifted them into the air.

Andrei muttered to himself, half aware that the boy could hear. There was no doubt that Treva would take whatever he could and use it against him if Andrei was stupid enough to give him a chance. It is what he would have done in Treva's position.

"Are you really my uncle?" Treva was studying Andrei's face and comparing it to what he remembered. "You sort of look like my father."

Unlike the last time they had met, the boy seemed more curious than afraid. Andrei saw Treva as the reason his brother had betrayed their family.

"You weren't satisfied with what Marco offered," Andrei said, watching as his words hit their mark.

Treva spoke, but Andrei had already stopped listening because something was bothering him. He wasn't sure what it was until his handheld chimed. It took longer than it should for him to remember how to answer the device.

Once he did, Raffia's face appeared on the screen. "She's in the basement."

That wasn't right. It should have taken a lot longer for her to get past the security safeguards. "You must be mistaken—there hasn't been any alarm."

"You need to return before she takes off with our greatest weapon."

Andrei didn't argue, although he had taken note of Raffia's lack of respect. It was something he would address later by denying him access to the Blue Pixie. He ended the call and looked at the boy.

Treva didn't have any trained ability and should be incapable of causing trouble, but Andrei had witnessed the problems this boy had created with nothing more than determination and luck. If he took him back to the station, there was a risk that he would get in the way. There was also a chance Andrei would inadvertently kill him.

"Accidents happen—remember that, boy."

Treva frowned, and Andrei saw that he was thinking about the ones that he would leave behind. It reminded Andrei of Caryanne. There wasn't time to force her to come like the others; as, even now, he was reluctant to enter her mind.

As if on cue, Caryanne ran down the middle of the walkway after them. Andrei hadn't called and yet, she came. Perhaps he was destined to bring her, despite the danger.

Had he killed any of the others? He couldn't remember.

"Your grandmother wants you safe," Andrei said to Treva, his tone making it clear that it was not his preference. "The only safe place is the Blue Pixie."

When Treva opened his mouth to argue for the others, Andrei stopped him from speaking all together. The boy was afraid now, which felt right. It might not be so bad taking his nephew home, after all.

Andrei smiled. "I will leave you at the Blue Pixie where Nash can keep you out of trouble."

Treva fought harder but Andrei stopped him and held out a hand for Caryanne to take.

"I'm glad you made the right choice."

She hesitated but took his arm, looking at Treva with a concerned expression. Andrei forced Treva's facial muscles into a smile. It was the least he could do to try to make her feel more comfortable about accompanying him.

When they reached the shuttle, she stopped. "Take me instead of Treva."

Steyn laughed. "I would like nothing better." He forced Treva into the shuttle. "See, he wants to go."

Of course, she didn't believe him, and it made him sad to watch her back away. It was such a shame that she was going to die when Pesta's destructive force ravaged the planet.

Climbing into the shuttle, he blew her a kiss. "Goodbye."

By the time they reached the Blue Pixie, he'd already forgotten about the girl with vacant expression and crazy mind.

— — —

Treva wanted to cry. He shouldn't be back at the Blue Pixie. When he'd left, he'd been sure it was for good, and now, here he was and nothing had changed.

What did his mother think about the way he'd left? Did she know that he hadn't had a choice? It hadn't looked like that. All he could do was hope she'd guessed the truth. Treva hadn't known that someone could take control of another's mind. He had to find a way to stop Andrei because there was no way that he could leave his mother to die on Glaendor—not after he'd tried so hard to get her back.

A constant drumbeat pounded in the background as Treva scanned his surroundings. Only a handful of people sat at tables, sipping liquor. Ava was by the bar, talking to one of the staff who leaned away as if she were shouting.

Treva still sensed the taint of Andrei's influence in his mind. There was no way he was waiting for him to return. He'd never felt so helpless, trapped in his own body. If Treva had held any notion about fighting, he now knew that Andrei was too strong to go up against. He hadn't been able to so much as scratch an itch when under his thrall.

Treva closed his eyes in an attempt to shake off the numbing fear. When he opened them, Nash stood in front of him with a broad grin. He closed his eyes again but on opening them, Nash was still there. Nobody was going to save him, so he had to get out of this himself, and quickly.

Nash's grin grew impossibly wide. "You're back."

Treva grimaced. "I wanted to come back." The lie rolled off his tongue. "There's something I have to do."

Nash sneered. "You've already found your mother."

Treva was struck at the animosity, and it made him wonder about Nash's home life. They'd never spoken about his family in all the time they'd spent together. He let it go. The knowledge might have been useful earlier, but there was no time for that now.

Use your brain.

Nash was older, stronger, and more confident, but Treva had one advantage: Nash expected Treva to behave like the boy who had been desperate for his approval. After everything, Treva was no longer weaker. He'd survived worse than anything Nash could throw at him. Plus, he knew Nash.

"Yeah, but…" What could he say that wouldn't set the older boy off? "I couldn't handle the responsibility."

Nash glared, and Treva knew he'd made a mistake. "I hate people who are given everything and then waste it."

Oh, that was it. Treva hadn't had to work for his father's regard, unlike Nash. It had come automatically with the sharing of blood. Treva saw that it would be a mistake to point out any disadvantage that came with that same blood. Nash would see how he could have taken advantage of the situation if their roles were reversed.

All Treva could do was offer part of the truth. "Mom didn't want to stay, and I couldn't risk losing her again so soon."

Nash's expression didn't alter, but Treva saw his fingers uncurl a little and his glare lost some heat. "What made you come back now?"

Had Andrei told Nash that he planned to bring Treva back? On second thought, he didn't think Steyn would bother to explain himself to Nash. If the other boy knew, he'd found it out for himself.

"Andrei forced me."

"Well, don't think you're coming back to be in charge."

Treva blinked, not knowing what Nash was referring to since he'd never tried to take charge, but he forced a smile. "It's terrific to see a friendly face—you wouldn't believe where I've been."

Nash didn't smile in response, and internally Treva cursed at the suspicion in Nash's tawny eyes. The other boy had never been good at hiding how he felt, and Treva wanted to kick his younger self for ever thinking that Nash was a friend. He'd been too desperate and only cared about the way other people saw him rather than what mattered. He thought of the way he'd ignored his mother's disappearance for the chance to get to know his father better. The glamour of money and status had blinded him, and Nash had taken advantage of his naivety. No, he couldn't blame anyone else for his choices.

"I'm sorry," Treva said to Nash and meant it.

Nash grinned, sensing weakness and opportunity. "I can't wait to hear why."

Treva glanced down, surprised to find that he was going to say more. "I wasn't very fair to you. You were my friend, and I didn't help you when I could have."

Treva had no idea where that had come from, but it felt the right thing to say. The reason he'd never helped Nash was because he hadn't understood his position.

Nash looked unsure. "You're a Steyn, and that makes people care what happens to you."

Treva was about to argue that everyone had that, but perhaps Nash only had the fragile bonds he'd built at the Blue Pixie.

"I'm sorry—I should have done more."

Nash frowned, clearly unsure what to do now that Treva was behaving unexpectedly.

Treva asked, "Do you believe people can change?" Nash's frown deepened, and Treva thought that he might have gone too far. "Never mind. How about I show you where Dad kept a stash of Blue Delight?"

"Okay, that way, you can start to make it up to me."

Treva laughed. It was too easy.

Nash added, "This doesn't make us right, unless there's a whole year's supply. Ava watches the stock like it matters if she loses a drink or two." Nash turned to check that she was out of earshot, before saying, "You'd think she'd want to keep everyone happy."

Treva couldn't see Ava. She might prove to be a bigger problem than Nash.

"I'll make you show me." Nash stepped toward Treva and it was as if their conversation a few moments ago had never happened.

"I *said* I'd show you." Treva set off for the back room before Nash could grab hold of a sensitive body part.

Thankfully, the door was unlocked and no one was present. Nothing had changed; it even still smelled faintly of Ava's perfume.

"This way." He walked through the office to the door leading to the cellar where Owen had been kept a prisoner. When Caryanne had described where Owen had been, Treva had wanted to kick himself for the missed opportunity to rescue him.

Treva memorized the number of steps to cross from the office door to the cellar. The lock was easy to operate from the outside, but Treva would only have seconds if he was lucky. The mechanism was stiff, and he wanted to recheck it, but he couldn't without risking making Nash suspicious. Inside, the light switch was to the left of the door, but it didn't work.

Treva looked at Nash. "I don't have a handheld."

It was a lie. Andrei hadn't taken his handheld, but as he was sure it had been an oversight, he didn't expect Nash to question it. He needed the other boy to go first.

Nash sighed. "I'll use mine."

The first step into the cellar was narrower than the rest. Treva's chest tightened at what he was about to do. Nash descended without a second's thought.

Treva hadn't lied—not wholly about the alcohol. He frantically scanned the space for the crates that Caryanne had described in her eagerness to impress everyone with her newly discovered memory. They were in the furthest corner.

Nash glanced around as if he'd never been in the basement before. "Is this where that singer spent a few days?" He stared at a pair of discarded shackles, and Treva held his breath. "Bet he's not so cocky now."

Treva pointed to the crates, hoping that they weren't empty. Nash hurried over, not noticing that Treva didn't move as he let out a gasp of delight and plucked out a bottle.

"Let's drink to friendship." Treva kept his voice steady by a sheer force of will.

Nash glanced over his shoulder with a scowl, obviously not ready to take things that far. "This isn't blue delight."

The bottle dangled from his thumb and forefinger. "Hey."

"Perhaps not," Treva muttered.

Shadows closed around him as Nash focused the light on the crates.

"It's whiskey." After a pause, he started to take out another bottle. "It'll do."

Treva forced himself to stay still until Nash was busy trying to remove the top from the bottle.

"I was a bit disappointed with your dad," Nash said. Every muscle in Treva's body stiffened as he continued, "You know, with the way he died."

Treva's nails dug into his palms as he bit back a response and stepped backward, banging his calf on another crate.

Nash's head whipped around. He must have caught the movement out of his peripheral vision.

"Sorry." Treva uttered on seeing Nash's face turned from confusion to determination.

The bottle fell. Before it smashed, Treva was already on the stairs, taking three at a time.

Nash roared.

Treva bashed his left shin on the concrete, barely feeling the pain. Running blind, he couldn't afford to trip. Nash would be on him before he could rise.

The thunder of Nash's feet behind was drowned out by his own labored breaths. In their many races, Treva had never beaten Nash and now, his life depended on doing just that. His feet skipped over the disintegrating concrete. Nash grunting like an animal, too close behind.

What if Ava is waiting in the office? At least, she would stop Nash from killing him—maybe.

Treva leaned forward, risking smashing his face into the concrete should he miss a step. Then, his hands scrabbled at the door. *Where's the handle?*

He couldn't see a thing. Flashes of light from behind did nothing to help. Nash had to be centimeters away from closing a hand around Treva's ankle and hauling him down.

There. His fingers closed around cool metal and he threw himself into the office, catching sight of Nash's red twisted face before he slammed the door and flicked the primitive and yet effective bolt into place.

"I'm not that sorry," he breathed out against the solid wood.

A thud reverberated against the door and Treva stumbled backward, unable to trust that it would hold. Nash's threats and curses came through, making him thankful that the wood was thick and the lock solid. Worried that someone might hear, Treva hurried across the floor, wanting to get as far away as possible.

The office door swung open to reveal Ava. Treva froze. The pounding on the cellar door increased in vigor, although Nash couldn't know that anything had changed.

Ava blocked the exit. With both hands on her hips and her hair disheveled in a way he'd never seen before, she glared through narrowed eyes. And she was so very still.

Treva didn't know what to say, since there was no denying what he'd done. The sound of Nash pounding away was enough to condemn him. His mouth was too dry to form any words but he had to try.

Ava spoke through gritted teeth. "He's not coming back!"

What?

Treva thumping heart didn't let him think, but when she still didn't move, it slowly dawned on him that she was mad at Andrei. She didn't care about Nash, and she certainly didn't care about Treva.

He didn't know where he found the audacity to say, "My uncle's not the sort of man to sacrifice himself." Perhaps he could convince her to find Andrei instead of whatever she'd been told to do. "He told you to take me somewhere, didn't he?"

Her eyes snapped to his face just as Nash went quiet. "I'm supposed to take you through the TSD arch to the orbital station, where we are to wait for him." She frowned, arms falling to her sides. "But he will die, won't he? If he stays when he releases the disease? Unless it's all a lie." She muttered something under her breath. "He will have a way of saving himself, but the rest of us—Raffia and me—we're expendable."

"What's a TSD arch?"

She frowned. "A Telekinetic Spatial Dislocation arch."

When Treva's expression didn't change, she said, "It's a short-distance portal through subspace, connecting the cellar to the orbital station."

"How did I miss that?" Treva wouldn't know a TSD arch if he fell over one, but if it was big enough to walk through, he couldn't see how he'd missed it.

Ava almost smiled. "You had a chance to see it, but you were too scared of spiders."

Treva could have kicked himself. They'd had a way off-planet all this time and he hadn't known—not that it was any use now. He couldn't abandon the others. "You would have shown it to me?"

"Why not? You wouldn't have known what it was, and at the time, I was trying to distract you from what was in there." She indicated the door that held Nash.

Treva didn't want to remember that Owen had been kept as a prisoner under their feet. He forced himself back to the present. "My uncle hates me, wants me dead. Why would he want you to take me somewhere safe?" Andrei had told him it was because of his grandmother but Ava was unlikely to know that.

She went still again. "That's right. He couldn't even look at your photo."

"We could go and ask him what's happening," Treva said as Nash started to shout something that was muffled by the door. "I agree that he wants us out of the way permanently, and we shouldn't make it easy."

Her expression hardened. "In that case, we should go ask him."

"You know where he is?"

"He will be with that creature, ready to kill everyone."

"I'll help you." He didn't expect her to believe him, but when she turned and left, he followed, and she didn't send him back.

CHAPTER 30

MAC'S HAND WAS outstretched. The palm that faced Kali had two straight lines drawn in red across the center. *He's trying to hide Pesta.* She tried to see past him, into the shadows.

Pesta had traveled with Herja's crew without causing any harm; at least, nobody had reported anything. So, was Mac overprotective, or was it something else? If he'd known her better, he wouldn't have bothered, since even as a child, Kali hadn't responded to 'no' and not much had changed in the intervening years.

Kali automatically catalogued his injuries—a cut on his forehead, bruising to both forearms, and from the way he held one arm over his middle, an injury to his torso. How bad? She couldn't say, but he was on his feet so he could walk.

Since she was short on time, Kali used telekinesis to lift Mac into the air. He squeaked in surprise, waving both arms frantically as if trying to find balance. As she placed him to one side, she realized the telekinesis had taken more effort than it should. *It's because Mika's gone.* Although she could feel him, the strength she'd come to rely on had drained away.

Oh, this can't be good.

Steyn had to be on his way back from wherever he'd gone, and he'd sent Mika away in the blink of an eye. Kali knew that despite her training, she wasn't any stronger than him and so she couldn't expect the results to be any better.

She peered into empty space, but the light from her handheld glinted off something wet. There was a brighter setting on the device—an all or nothing option. Pesta clearly preferred the shadows, and until now, Kali hadn't wanted to use it and blind them all, but she needed to see what she was dealing with to make an informed judgement.

She stepped closer, selecting the high beam but keeping it pointed at the ground and partially covered with her hand. It was dangerous for Pesta to feel threatened, but in this situation, she wasn't overly worried.

She took an involuntary step back and it took a couple of seconds to make sense of what she saw—nothing. Yet, there was an impression of form—a tingling in the center that faded at the edges.

"If you sense her, it's because she lets you."

Kali glanced at Mac, remembering that he didn't have any enhanced abilities of his own. "It feels like a forcefield."

"She," Mac corrected. "Referring to 'her' as 'it' suggests that she's nothing more than a thing, when she is, in fact, a sentient being."

There was nothing to indicate that Pesta was feminine, although Kali understood his desire to mark her as more than an object. Kali didn't sense any malice, and Pesta didn't attempt to follow when she backed away. If anything, there was a sense of sadness that couldn't have come from her as she was too full of adrenaline.

Kali frowned. "What do you do?" At his puzzled expression, she said, "You don't have any ability that I can feel, and so you cannot stop... her from attacking—"

Kali cocked her head to one side. Did he know that Pesta was in him? Probably not.

"She's peaceful." Mac shuffled his feet and looked down

for a moment before meeting her eyes. "We are bonded so we can communicate, and I know where she is." He looked away. "You aren't going to help us, are you?"

"I'm going to try." It was all that she could say. "We need to go out before Steyn comes back." Kali was already moving toward the exit.

"We can't. There's no way off the planet... you could..." he looked away again, "kill me in a way that doesn't make her lose it, so that he can't find her."

Kali shook her head, still moving, resisting the temptation to sympathize with him. "I think with Steyn's power, he'll find her without you." They didn't have time for doubt. "Now, move."

Kali felt Mika in her mind just before he spoke, *"What's happening?"*

She was relieved that he sounded fine. *"Are you okay?"*

"A little weak, but not dead."

She took his attempt at humor as a good sign. *"I'm with Mac and Pesta—we need to get off the planet, but I have no idea how we're going to get back to the ship."*

"Kali, don't hesitate to do whatever you have to." He paused, but she knew he'd tell her, no matter how reluctantly, *"Andrei is somehow stronger than Tregaren. There was no warning, and I think although he intended to kill me, he didn't want to, which is why I'm here."*

She tried not to let what he said affect her. *"Where are you?"*

Again that pause before the bad news. *"I don't know. There's no form. It isn't anywhere on Glaendor or any planet."*

She closed her eyes. For a second, the weight of responsibility and impossibility of the task was too much. How was she going to stop someone that powerful?

Mika must have sensed her mood. "Sorry, I shouldn't have said."

Kali forced her eyes open and squared her shoulders. This was what she had signed on for and if she didn't succeed, a lot of people would die.

"It's okay—I need to know what we're dealing with."

"What are you going to do?" When she didn't answer, he said, *"Kali?"*

"I'm glad you're okay, but my... our options aren't good."

Mika went quiet, and Kali's mind raced. Steyn would be back in any minute, and if they were still in the basement, they wouldn't stand a chance. To make matters worse, she could feel people congregating near to their only exit. She reached out telepathically to find that none had any abilities, so perhaps they still had a chance.

Ignoring Mika's question, she moved silently, the way she'd been trained. They had been forced to repeat the exercises so many times that her body knew how to move without conscious thought.

Mika remained nearby and she felt better with his mental proximity. She focused on what they needed to do next to get to safety.

A shout came over the hiss and rattle of machinery. "Avon Security, come out with your hands where we can see them."

Kali's first instinct was to avoid using her abilities against members of a planetary security force. *They are our enemy.*

Pyra hid to one side of the door. He remained calm as they locked eyes.

She didn't know him but had to trust him. "Take Mac," she didn't say, and Pesta, "and find a ship in the docking station. I'll be right behind you."

He nodded, reminding her again that he had undergone similarly rigorous training.

She had to give Mac and Pesta every chance, which was why she broke her own rules. Mika had taught her that sometimes all that mattered was the result. It wasn't as if she couldn't justify her actions, but it still felt wrong.

She tapped into the leader's mind, noting that he'd sent a message to alert Steyn. That gave her the strength to invade his private thoughts and made it easier to force him to order the other six to leave the building. She sensed their confusion and eased it with a part of her mind that was not engaged with the leader.

Then, she called over her shoulder, "Mac follow Pyra."

It was a risk, but she worried that Steyn would catch them before they got anywhere and at least this way there was a chance they could steal a ship.

Mac stumbled, sounding confused, but then he saw Pyra and the two shook hands, reminding her that they had met before. She would have told them to hurry if she hadn't been concerned that it would lead to more delay.

Her senses told her that Pesta was so close to Mac that she was virtually on top of him.

The way out of the security station was clear. Now she had to deal with Steyn.

— — —

A promise was a promise, and Herja had made one to Mac. If they couldn't sell the drugs and save their people, she would do her best to free Mac and Pesta before she was forced to do something even more desperate.

Gosta had made it very clear that he was not impressed with her decision to fly straight to Glaendor. Even so, she was caught off-guard when he pulled the ship hard to port on their approach, making Herja's head spin. Two plasma beams in quick succession shot past the hull, lighting the hull in a silent blaze.

"They don't seem to want us here," Gosta said without looking up from the controls.

Herja closed her eyes briefly and shook her head, wondering why she put up with him. *I should have brought Idra.*

"Gosta, stop tempting me to order you out of the airlock and come up with a plan that gets us down to the planet in one piece."

He snorted. "That's your department."

She couldn't argue with that. As usual, it would be up to her to come up with an ingenious solution, except, she was out of ideas.

"Stars, just what we need."

Herja went to look at what Gosta was complaining about and saw the *Vector* on an intercept course. In two minutes, the ship would be close enough to fire on them with their energy weapons. She should have known Vaughn would wait for an opportunity to get revenge.

The comm unit chimed. Gosta looked over and at her nod, flicked it on.

Vaughn's smug face filled the screen. "So, you came."

Herja frowned but didn't rise to the bait.

"I knew that you'd come," he said. "I saw how reluctant you were to lose Pesta."

He knew less than he thought, but she wasn't about to give away an advantage by bragging. Herja had no intention of wasting time sparring with Vaughan. She'd made a promise, and they had tried to fulfill it. Honor was satisfied. And yet, she found that she wasn't.

Gosta muted the comm. "We're close to the planet again. At any moment, planetary defenses are going to start firing on us."

Herja grinned, suddenly knowing what they had to do. "Do you trust me?"

Gosta sighed. "It's going to be like that, is it?"

Vaughn was saying something that she couldn't hear. Gosta unmuted the comm and she wished that he hadn't.

Talking over Vaughn, she asked, "Why bother? You retrieved Pesta. Why come after us now?"

Vaughn stared at her like she was insane for asking. "You made me look bad. It's a matter of pride."

"Well, I'd let it go if I were you." She frowned at her nails. "It would be for the best."

Vaughn's scowl deepened. It was the last expression she saw before she ended the link.

Smiling at Gosta's strained expression, she said, "I'll take over now." She switched to manual control, ignoring the warnings automatically generated by the ship.

Gosta clambered into one of the flight chairs and very deliberately fastened the straps. Herja saw but had bigger things to worry about than his non-verbal comment on her flying skills.

Gosta leaned forward, making the chair tilt alarmingly. "He's powering up weapons."

She didn't need him to tell her, since she could feel the *Vector* in the same way as she could feel the planet's defense weapons were trained on the *Hyperion*. Each was like a burning spot in her mind. It wasn't something she'd ever thought about before and was only aware of now because of the weird shite they'd been through recently. As always, she let her body lead and tried not to think too much.

Using the single-handed control that was as familiar as her bed, she sent the *Hyperion* sharply down toward the surface of the planet while increasing their speed. Vaughn fired a fraction too late. Two missiles grazed their shields, doing no harm.

I warned him. There's nothing more I can do.

Within seconds, they were within range of the planet's defenses. As she'd known he would, Vaughn followed, matching their trajectory.

Herja held steady, fastening one strap with her left hand, while Gosta muttered under his breath. He might be praying, except she knew he was more likely to be uttering a stream of curses.

The edges of the dome that protected Glaendor became visible. An opening lay directly below but they had yet to bypass the defenses that were concentrated in that area. Once they were close to the surface, the large weapons would be rendered useless.

Beams came at them from all directions. Herja didn't look, letting her body take over as she jinked the *Hyperion* from one direction to another in a zig-zag pattern while continuing to head for the opening. The ship shuddered as it picked up speed. With millimeters to spare they shot through with Vaughn close behind. Sandwiched between the planetary defenses and the *Vector*, Herja felt the moment the other ship fired and knew there was nothing she could do. Both blasts hit their shields at the same time.

By some miracle, their shields held.

Vaughn followed into the planet's atmosphere. His ship took hit after hit.

The muscles in Herja's right arm tightened and jerked, sending the *Hyperion* spinning back toward the domed enclosure.

"Too fast," Gosta shouted.

Herja's stomach flipped over. The single strap holding her to her seat threatened to give way as she clung to the console with her left hand.

Now. Her body responded before she recognized the word. She changed direction—straight down.

An explosion lit up the sky as the *Vector* was reduced to burning debris. Herja stared, not quite able to believe that her plan had worked and the *Vector* had been destroyed.

Gosta struggled to right himself in the chair. "Stars, how did we manage that?"

"Luck." Even as she said it, she knew it was more than that.

"It'll be us next," Gosta grumbled.

Full of the joy that came with unexpected survival, Herja laughed. "Not likely. We're too close to the planet now. It'll be too dangerous to shoot at us."

If she'd expected Gosta to cheer, she would have been disappointed. "Just ground security for the two of us to deal with, then," he said, releasing himself from the chair's restraints.

Herja turned her attention to their next objective. *Now, if I was a planet-killing bioweapon, where would I be?*

— — —

Despite almost two years of undercover work, Pyra hadn't discovered the entirety of Steyn's agenda. It frustrated him that he still didn't understand what SPEAR hoped to achieve—yes, they wanted control of the Outer Colonies, but to what end? Nobody would allow them to stay in power, regardless of how much support they drummed up from the population of the Outer Colonies.

Steyn wasn't stupid, which meant that Pyra was missing something vital. There was a tug at the back of his mind. He recognized the feeling and knew that if he could just find a few minutes' peace, he would put everything together. Unfortunately, he'd never felt less peaceful in his life.

It occurred to him that if Steyn unleashed the disease from Pesta that he'd seen destroy a planet in the footage they'd watched, he would die along with everyone else. That couldn't be right. Steyn would never sacrifice himself. While he might have become stronger than anyone that Pyra had ever known, that would mean nothing against the wave of disease that Pesta would release.

The sensible thing to do would be to slip away and get as far from Steyn as possible. Except, nowhere on the planet would be far enough and Pyra's only hope was Kali. It was a desperate situation.

They raced past station personnel, who paused whatever they were doing and stared. Nobody tried to stop them.

It didn't surprise Pyra when Kali shouted, "He's here." She waved to the handful of men and women that remained. "TSS. Get out."

Pyra wasn't sure whether it was Kali's instruction or if people were already spooked, but they abandoned their posts and ran. Kali halted and faced back the way they'd come. She was prepared to cover their escape, but Pyra knew they wouldn't get far without her. Pesta only had one talent, as far as he knew, and his own was not going to serve anyone in these circumstances.

Pyra dared a glance over his shoulder and saw Steyn. He wasn't moving, and Pyra had a sinking feeling that he didn't have to get close to use Pesta.

Kali stood, legs apart and he wouldn't have been surprised if she'd announced, "You have to go through me first." Instead, she silently watched Steyn.

No. Run! Pyra stopped, as well—too afraid to shout his warning. She wouldn't listen, anyway. Mac was breathing heavily and his body was almost bent double. He had too many injuries to sustain any sort of pace. Pyra hadn't known Kali long, but he didn't think that she would leave him behind.

Kali faced Steyn. His old boss was so powerful that she didn't stand a chance. For the first time in his life, Pyra wished he had some ability so he could help them escape.

There was a remoteness to Steyn's gaze that was new, as if all this was beneath him. Had he'd lost his mind? Pyra wasn't sure whether that would make the situation better or worse.

A movement behind Steyn had Pyra's heart leaping in his throat. His eyes picked out Ava. She was the last person he'd expected to see and the last to offer any help. She hung back. Steyn either hadn't noticed or didn't care.

Pyra waited for his opportunity to make a move. All of their futures would be decided by what Steyn did next.

CHAPTER 31

KALI WAS EXHAUSTED, but she couldn't afford to show it. Something had changed drastically. Mika? She'd lost him. She felt drained of energy.

Mika's voice came through in her head, making her sag in relief, *"Why can't I feed you my ability anymore?"* He sounded more distant than before, and she tried to grab hold of him.

"I don't think it works like that. Together, we amplified each other's abilities, which was why we were stronger combined. Now, you're too far away for that to work." As she spoke, she understood that if she died, that would have a devastating effect of Mika. *"I need you to let go."*

There was silence, and she wondered if he'd heard. Did he suspect why she wanted him to release her?

Steyn's attention turned to her. Could he hear what they were saying? She didn't think so. It was something else—a result of too much power when he wasn't used to it.

"I can't," Mika said quietly.

"You're holding on too tight." What could she say that would make him let her go? *"It's affecting my ability and right now. I need everything I've got."* She tried to keep the strain out of her voice, worried he would sense the lie.

Mika had to know that if their amplified abilities hadn't been enough when they were together, then her mind alone wouldn't be enough now. Yet, she had to try, because as far as she knew, there was only her standing in the way of this planet's destruction and everything that would come after.

"I'll try," Mika acknowledged.

Kali needed him to be quick but she resisted saying so, knowing there was a danger he'd refuse. *"You can only do your best."* That sounded like what her mother would say.

There was a roar. *It's only in my head.* By the time she'd realized, Mika was gone, leaving her emptier than at any time in her life.

"Mika?"

There was no answer. What had she done? What if, she'd been the only thing keeping him here, and now he was really gone? She tried to think through the panic because it wasn't helping. Her chest hurt and she could feel the rapid beat of her heart in her throat.

"Please, Mika. Please be okay."

Steyn laughed, which brough Kali back to the present danger. She sensed a woman in the shadows but kept her attention on Steyn, who had changed. She couldn't pinpoint how exactly.

"You're weak," Steyn said with a frown. "It's too easy."

Did he really care? Although, she hadn't anticipated that he'd sense the change; she had intended to bluff, but that seemed pointless now.

His eyes rolled into the back of his head. At the same time, Kali felt power surge through him. She frantically tried to think of a way to get the others out of the way, but if there were ships in the allocated docking bays, they would hardly be waiting open and ready to go. SPEAR had obviously prepared well for this attack. Steyn must have an escape route planned.

To her left, Pyra stumbled, his face confused as he muttered to himself. Then, louder, Pyra said, "It's true." She looked over to see that his face was slack in shock. "I didn't believe it—thought it was the ramblings of an unhinged mind."

"What?"

Kali wanted to shake him. He should be trained to share information in a clear and concise manner.

Steyn's eyes were cold, but there was something else— a distance that hadn't been there before. "You didn't think I trusted you? Really, Pyra, you always were the wild card, although I admit that I hadn't imagined that you were working for the TSS."

Kali frowned. "Never mind that. What are you planning to do? If you activate Pesta's power," she barely managed to say it, "you will kill yourself as well as everyone else on the planet."

"Mika, are you still there? Please don't be gone," she pleaded telepathically. There was no response and she sensed nothing. The terror that he was gone forever was almost worse than the imminent destruction she faced.

Pyra grabbed Kali's arm, his face intense. She wanted to send him away but managed to hold it together and pay attention. "He—"

Steyn interrupted, "Tregaren claimed to know the way to immortality but couldn't, or wouldn't, deliver. He did, however, introduce me to the Erebus, who offered God-like powers."

"He won't die. The Erebus protect him," Pyra got out.

Kali withered. "He's working with them?"

The aliens had appeared two years before, and keeping watch over their activities had been keeping the TSS fully subscribed since then. It was how Kali had found herself largely on her own as a green Agent and why backup was always in such short supply. But Tarans were maintaining a tenuous peace with the Erebus. Why would they be protecting a mad man? She took an unsteady breath. "What does the Erebus have to do with any of this?"

"It's what all of this is about." Pyra hands moved in

agitation. "SPEAR's lack of purpose never made sense. I should have thought more about it, but didn't have the chance." He looked at Steyn. "Nobody was supposed to know, were they?"

Steyn looked... different, more translucent, and it occurred to Kali that he was in the middle of some sort of transformation.

"I needed to create Pesta before the Erebus would help me. There were many failed attempts before this one. Who'd have thought that the solution was to tie it to someone like him?" He pointed at Mac.

Kali had pushed the unknown woman to the back of her mind, but now she moved closer to Steyn. One look at her furious face was enough for Kali to decide to invade her privacy.

The woman stared intently at Steyn. "Why didn't you tell us?"

When Kali touched her mind, the flood of bitterness, jealously and anger swamped her. Thankfully, Ava didn't have any abilities, just a pulse gun, which in the scheme of things was good news.

Steyn didn't answer, and it didn't surprise Kali when Ava brought the weapon up to point at him. "You're the same as your brother. I swore I'd never be used like that again. In fact, you're worse—happy to let us die like we're disposable."

She squeezed the trigger and the blast hit Mac squarely in the chest. Kali blinked. The weapon had been aimed at Steyn but it had gone straight through him.

Of course, he can walk through walls!

Ava didn't seem to notice as Mac toppled. She continued to shout, "If I'm going to die, so are you, Andrei Steyn!"

Pyra tried to catch Mac, and the two went to the floor together. Kali ran to them, even though it was too late. She felt life leave Mac's body but something was wrong.

Pesta!

In the same way that it had been instinct to contain the bomb blast on the station, Kali threw a shield around Pesta. Triangular sections of her shield came together to form a pyramid. It was better and took far less energy than the first one, which was just as well since she didn't have the strength. Even now, she had no idea whether it would contain Pesta.

Steyn laughed at Mac's crumpled form. "So dramatic, Ava. Thank you for getting things moving. I keep getting distracted." Crouched at Mac's side, Kali saw Steyn look at her. "Of course, I won't be affected, but everyone else will, including you."

"No," Ava screeched.

She ran at Steyn looking as though she was intent on killing him with her bare hands. She'd only gone five steps when she slammed into an invisible wall with such force that she collapsed.

Steyn stared at her. "The Blue Pixie is protected. You would have been safe."

A high-pitched screech rattled Kali's brain. She staggered, covering her ears, only to discover that it was inside her head. Steyn cringed before his expression smoothed out.

Raw grief slammed into Kali. She couldn't stop the pain. It wasn't the first time she'd experienced grief, and her experience helping others with loss had taught her that a willingness to share the pain couldn't be underestimated. She had just lost Mika and so she understood. It never crossed her mind that Pesta might be different when she reached out to do it again.

Kali felt the alien presence calm and resisted the impulse to pull back. The agony in her mind receded before something pushed against her shield. It was a more inquisitive than a forceful attempt to get into her head. She saw Pesta now that Mac was dead, although she suspected that her imagination created the image and it probably had little to do with Pesta's actual appearance.

Pesta spoke—at least that's what Kali thought the rise and fall of the sound was intended to be. *"Let me in."*

Kali pushed back, remembering what it had felt like to have Tregaren in her mind. *"I can't."*

"I need a base."

"Can you hold it together, or are you going to kill us all?" Kali asked a little more abruptly than she intended.

She didn't expect Pesta to understand, but the entity shivered. *"You hear and see me!"*

Kali frowned to hide her confusion. Mismatched eyes stared back. The longer she held that gaze, the more she felt a soul-wrenching sadness that was only partly to do with Mac's death.

Kali wasn't sure if Pesta actually had a physical body. Mac had always talked as if she was corporeal, but that didn't mean it was true. That might just have been his understanding.

Pesta's voice buzzed in her head, *"I will dissolve into disease if you don't let me in."*

"Dissolve?"

"I cannot hold my form in spacetime. If I unravel, everyone dies. I will die."

"Can you choose not to kill everyone?" Kali was worried that wasn't how it worked since Pesta had been created to be a weapon.

"There's no scent or sight or taste. Everything I experienced was through Mac. If I'd been born... I should not be aware... I want to live."

They weren't dead yet, despite the worst happening. Perhaps SPEAR didn't understand their weapon as well as they thought they did.

"Let me in," Pesta implored again.

Kali shook her head. She'd expected the request as soon as she'd understood that Pesta controlled Mac rather than the other way around. She had allowed Tregaren into her mind and that had been bad enough. It had been different with Mika. Her throat tightened. She couldn't afford the indulgence of grief, but they had shared something special.

Pesta's power shifted and, although it was like nothing Kali had experienced before, it smelled and tasted similar to Steyn's energy. *They're infused with the same energy!*

Kali's eyes snapped to Steyn. "You created Pesta with the help of the Erebus?"

He didn't respond, but she knew she was right. It was the only thing that made sense and explained why he wasn't worried about dying—he was changing into something else and would not be affected. Kali squinted.

He was fading. Halfway to becoming transparent. His clothes hung from his body as if he were shrinking.

Steyn sold his soul to the Erebus! Hyperbole aside, he had struck a deal for something that Kali would not have thought possible. She knew that the Erebus existed in a realm outside of normal spacetime reality, but she didn't realize it was possible for a normal Taran to be transformed—despite what the Priesthood had attempted to achieve through their experimentations on her and others. She'd always thought they were insane, but now she was watching a man fade before her very eyes as his power grew.

Thankfully, Ava was still in a heap on the floor near to Steyn. She shouted and cursed, but Kali ignored her as the shield she'd thrown around Pesta was growing thin. Without Mika's abilities to enhance her own, she just didn't have the strength to maintain it for any length of time.

Kali tried and failed to send a telepathic message to Andy to let him know that the docking station was empty. Although, if she died, she didn't know what he could do. Perhaps they should run, but there was nowhere to go and besides, it took all her energy to hold the shield.

Pyra's eyes were wide. "We're in trouble, aren't we?"

"I want you to go."

He looked around wildly. "Where?"

Kali didn't know. She just wanted one less person to worry about. As if the universe wanted to remind her of how little her desire mattered, something tickled the edge of her perception where she had extended her reached. *Treva! What's he doing here?* It was the last thing she needed.

Pesta spoke, her words were much clearer than they had been. *"I need him. Do not let him go."*

Kali shook her head. *"What do you mean? You need Pyra?"*

"Without an anchor, I will dissolve, and then everyone dies. He can be my anchor."

Kali shook her head, not sure whether it was an option. *"What will happen to him? Will it be like with Mac?"*

"I want absolute control this time."

Kali had no idea if it was possible, but releasing her was a big risk. She shook her head in an attempt to clear it. *Face facts, I'm not going to hold onto this shield much longer.*

Pyra swung to her. "We need another option."

Kali explained what Pesta had proposed and saw the color drain from his face. He stared at the ground before meeting her eyes.

He swallowed. "I won't be any good—I'm a null."

Before Kali could respond, Pesta interrupted, *"It doesn't matter, I can still use him."*

Kali told Pyra, who paled further before nodding. "I will do it."

She wanted to say that she understood what a difficult decision it was, but there wasn't time. Though the offer was a lifeline, it felt wrong. A chance to save the planet and millions of lives, so why was she reluctant to lower her shield? She felt Pesta's impatience and guessed that she could break through if she tried. In fact, Kali wasn't sure why she hadn't already. Her attention snapped to her surroundings. Something was happening. Although she couldn't see Pesta, she could sense her.

"Hurry," Pesta urged.

The single word went through Kali. It wasn't her decision. She looked at Pyra, who was frozen to the spot, glassy eyes stared into space. He'd agreed, hadn't he? So why couldn't she shake the feeling that she needed to protect him as much as everyone else.

What would Mika do? She knew instantly that he would accept Pyra's sacrifice for the greater good. Would Andy? She didn't know but suspected that the TSS might.

Kali looked over at Steyn, who was well on his way to his new form. Whatever she decided, they didn't have long.

She jerked as someone brushed her mind.

"We've just exited subspace. I can sense you but not Mika."

"Andy, thank the stars! Steyn did something to Mika." It took everything she had not to break down. *"I've lost him. We're not connected anymore."* It hurt, and she was so grateful when Andy didn't ask for details.

"I'm on my way, but we have to be cautious. It won't do any good if the automatic planetary defenses blow us up before we reach you."

"There isn't anyone else here. Hurry, something's happening to Steyn. It has to do with the Erebus. Plus Pesta's handler is dead so... well, you know what that means."

"Kali, hang on."

Andy was gone from her mind, but she felt his presence slowly—oh, so slowly—coming closer.

CHAPTER 32

IT WAS FAR easier to land at the docking station than Herja had anticipated. The army she'd expected to be waiting was nowhere in sight. In fact, according to the sensors, the place was deserted. It felt very wrong. They'd be wise to leave, and despite what Gosta thought, she was generally sensible.

"What are we going to do now?" Gosta asked, unaware of how much judgement that one question held.

"We find Mac." Herja's gut told her they were running out of time.

They armed themselves before leaving the ship. Herja held her plasma gun in her right hand as she crept from the *Hyperion* and took in the surroundings. Though she stayed low as a precaution, the station was deserted. One look at the tension in Gosta's face, and she knew he felt it was wrong like her.

He muttered something that sounded like, "All I've ever wanted was a quiet life." It wasn't true, else he wouldn't hang around with her. "How are we even supposed to find Mac?"

Herja didn't have the first bomaxed clue, except her uncanny ability to find whatever she was looking for. Her inexplicably perfect timing might yet serve them well.

"Let's find out what's going on. The planet was well-defended when we entered their airspace. It makes you wonder why everyone left, doesn't it?"

"Not me. I'm quite happy living with mystery. There's no need to look for what happened. It's not our business."

"Vaughn could have told anyone about our people. We need to check what information he passed on."

Gosta couldn't argue with that. Their goal was always to protect their people, and at this time, that meant the city-ship.

Herja concealed her weapon and led the way to the ground-level. Once there, she followed the exit signs, aware that they were being watched, although by who—or what—she didn't know.

Enormous screens silently advertised hotels and casinos, while the shops and bars in the station were silent and empty. Doors stood wide while half-eaten food congealed on tables with glasses almost full. A tray lay on the floor as if it had been discarded when its owner had been zapped away. Nothing moved across the expansive floor, and every footstep echoed despite their attempts to walk silently.

She shared a look with Gosta, and they continued with caution. They hadn't gone far when they heard raised voices. Continuing at a steady pace, there was nothing they could use as cover, and there didn't seem to be any point in dragging out their approach.

Herja drew her weapon, and Gosta did the same, moving to her left and leaving a stretch between them. It was a feeble attempt to make it more difficult for anyone targeting them.

Herja recognized Kali but she didn't know the small man at her side. Mac was on the ground and something about the angle of his body told her that he was dead.

We're too late. Herja pushed away the sadness and despair that rose with practiced ease.

It had been a difficult journey only to find out that they

hadn't arrived in time, but regret would have to wait until they were safe. The small hairs at the back of her neck stood to attention. They were in danger, even if she hadn't pinpointed the source.

Further away, she made out a woman on the ground but very much alive. Another figure stood close, and at first, she couldn't decipher what it was. Slowly, her brain made out that it was the form of a man, and there was something wrong with him.

She took in a sharp breath as, at her side, Gosta faltered. The figure was missing substance so that he resembled a ghost from lore. Unable to take her eyes from him, she felt, rather than saw, Kali half-turn toward her. Like her, the Agent was focused on what was happening fifty meters away. Herja gave Kali a nod of acknowledgement right before things got crazy.

— — —

Kali wasn't surprised by Herja's sudden appearance, since it seemed that everybody she'd ever known was going to show up. It make her feel better when she realized that the pirate had to have arrived in a ship, which meant there might be a way of getting Treva past Steyn without him ending up as part of the drama. If she was aware of Treva's presence, then Steyn had to have sensed it, too— although he didn't appear bothered by anything.

Steyn had faded and was definitely metamorphosing into something non-Taran. As she contemplated what to do about it, a shockwave went through her, powerful enough to hurt her teeth.

The shield containing Pesta had shattered. Kali instinctively threw a shield around Pyra, and felt Pesta bounce off.

Pyra ducked and threw his hands over his head. Kali hadn't realized that she'd decided not to sacrifice him, and so her behavior came as a surprise.

"I've got you," she told him.

Oh, stars above. She hoped that Pesta was not becoming the disease. Her new shield spluttered out as she failed to find the strength to hold onto it. Fortunately, Pesta had already moved on.

Kali tracked her position. Their intimate contact, having opened a channel between them. She seriously doubted that she would have been able to produce another shield, but she prepared to protect Herja and her man. There was no need. Pesta headed in Steyn's direction.

Oh, no. The last thing they needed was for Steyn to get hold of Pesta. Even if Pesta could stop herself from releasing the disease, Steyn would force her to do it.

Kali was hardly aware of moving toward Steyn as Pesta neared him. He didn't give any sign of awareness, but it felt like a vortex sucking at her. She struggled like a fish trying to escape a whirlpool.

Kali wanted to help, driven by the fear that Steyn was moments away from taking control. Then it would over for the planet, and possibly the Outer Colonies. She clenched her fists, nails digging into her palms, unable to think of a way to help.

Come on—you can do it. You have to do it!

Suddenly, Pesta broke free and like a shooting star, hit Ava in the center of the chest and disappeared. Kali blinked, and stared at Ava, searching for any sign that she was now host to Pesta.

Ava pushed up from the ground, her expression blank.

Treva chose that moment to run toward her. Kali wanted to shout for him to go back, but the words died in her throat as blaster fire hit Steyn in the chest, causing whatever was happening to him to falter like a broken shutter before the transformation resumed at the faster rate.

Kali swung to see Herja's weapon pointed at Steyn. The pirate had an expression of deep concentration, giving Kali the feeling that if determination alone could end Steyn's life, he would be dead.

The shots seemed to have passed through him, and apart from a flicker of pain on his face, they did nothing. If anything, his transformation had sped up.

There wasn't much left of the man he'd been, and now he was becoming solid again. Could the transformation have failed? No, she had seen too much to hope that was the case.

Gosta shouted to Herja, "Incoming TSS ships. We have to get out of here."

Andy's almost here. Kali tried not to feel relieved, since the TSS didn't have a cure for Pesta and would struggle to deal with Steyn.

Kali expected Herja to go, but she continued to empty her weapon into Steyn. He looked mildly irritated but it was clear that it wasn't having any effect despite him no longer being translucent. Herja must have realized it as well, but she didn't stop firing until Treva had reached her.

A wave of frustration went through Kali. Surely they could do something. If only she could injure Steyn, in any small way, it might make a difference.

Kali tried to find something inside, but her body was drained. There was no way she could scratch him, never mind deal a lasting injury. Although, she clearly remembered the sphere of energy she'd created with Mika on the space station, she didn't have the power to do more than conjure a spark. She automatically reached for Mika, and gasped with renewed pain when it was as if he had never been there.

Suppressing the hopelessness that threatened to consume her, she reached out to Pesta. *"Help! If we don't stop him, you'll always just be a weapon to be used by the Erebus."*

"He is Erebus."

The words chilled Kali. She knew few details about the aliens that had appeared recently, only that the TSS didn't know how to defeat one. Steyn had returned to a fully solid form that looked like himself, except that his eyes now shone with a grey light.

Pesta held up Ava's hands, twisting them to study the backs before examining each finger. Kali couldn't help thinking that if Pesta's grief for Mac had been real, it had been short-lived.

She knew that Pesta heard her and tried again, "*I can't stop him—it—without help.*"

"*You are too weak.*" Pesta cocked Ava's head to one side. "*They are coming.*"

Kali had no idea whether Pesta was referring to Andy or someone else. "*Then there's no time.*"

"*I will not be a prisoner.*"

"*Okay.*" Kali was ready to agree to anything at this point.

Just the thought of using her ability made Kali want to curl up from exhaustion, but she took a deep breath. There wouldn't be another chance—it was now or never.

Steyn looked around. "*Pesta?*" His voice sounded deeper, but it might have been her imagination.

While he looked like the old Steyn, Kali felt was a buzzing sensation from him as Pesta's words played in her head—*he is Erebus.* That was impossible; one certainly couldn't *become* one of the ancient, metadimensional aliens. However, it was possible that they were somehow using him as a vessel. Didn't he know that Pesta was inside Ava?

Before Kali could do anything with the information, a blast rocked Steyn off his feet. Herja must have found another weapon and set it to maximum firepower. As Steyn struggled back up, his face twisted in a grimace, again there was no sign that the blast had done any significant damage.

Kali tried again, "*Pesta—*"

"I am beautiful." Ava stroked her left forearm.

"*If you don't help, it won't matter. You will still be used before you die.*"

Pesta or Ava—was there anything of Ava left—looked

at Kali. *"You are not as beautiful as me. That is good."*

"Help me?" Kali tried not to beg.

Pesta pointed at Herja. *"Male or female?"*

Kali realized that it was a question. *"Female, now—"*

"Interesting. I would like to find out more about her."

"Pesta, we need to—"

"I know—stop Steyn. I understand."

Herja's gun stuttered and she cursed as it was ripped from her hands. She was already moving, but there was no cover so she threw herself to the ground.

"Ah, there you are." Steyn's eyes fastened on Ava.

Kali felt heat flow through her and looked around wildly. *What now?*

"Use my energy wisely." Pesta's words sounded in her mind.

The heat was unlike anything that Kali had ever experienced. She formed a ball of energy to rival anything she had ever created and threw it at Steyn, hitting him center-chest.

He froze, eyes closing.

Kali watched, thinking that she had actually done it— had hurt him enough to matter.

His arms moved, rising from his sides as he held them out wide and smiled. "How?" He looked from Kali to Pesta. "Interesting, we never anticipated anything like that." Steyn's face hardened as he focused on Pesta. "You belong to me."

Ava stumbled backward and Kali had the impression that Pesta was afraid for the first time.

From Herja's side, Treva shouted, "Uncle, stop!"

Steyn had to have known where Treva was, but he made no move to attack the boy. Probably because he was beneath his notice. Kali wondered if Treva understood that there was nothing of his uncle left in Steyn.

Treva recoiled as Steyn's grey eyes locked onto him, saying, "I should have killed you."

"But, you said—"

The rest was drowned out by a high-pitched screech. Kali slapped hands over her ears as the everyone staggered and fell. A shriek that Kali had already experienced from Pesta. Helpless to stop the noise, anger and frustration threatened to overwhelm her. It was as if she was back in the cells of the Priesthood without skill or ability to fight. She'd sworn never to feel like that again.

All her experience and training had to count for something. She would not die a victim, unable to help those around her.

Kali gritted her teeth, ignoring a splash of bright blood that fell from her nose and landed between her feet. There had to be a way—she just needed to find it.

Blasting energy didn't hurt Steyn, but what about the opposite? Drain him of energy.

"Pesta, don't let him take your beautiful new body."

The high-pitched wail increased. Kali hadn't meant for that to happen. Warm liquid slid over her top lip. If Pesta didn't stop—they would all die, except Steyn who was unaffected.

"You were created by the Erebus." Because who else could have created her? *"But they made a mistake and allowed you to be sentient."*

"I don't want to die."

"Take his power—" Kali scrabbled at her neck as she suddenly couldn't breathe. It was Tregaren all over again, but she *had* killed him once.

"You will stop," Steyn voiced in her mind.

Kali couldn't breathe, but the pain in her head had stopped. She didn't know what it meant as darkness closed in at the edges of her vision.

CHAPTER 33

MIKA HADN'T HAD any choice but to release Kali, not when more than anything, he wanted her to live. That, in itself, would have been enough, except he'd sensed her pain and it was fear for her that drove him out of darkness that had closed over him.

Mika saw that Kali intended to fight Steyn, even knowing that she would fail. Irritation brought him fully to the present. If only she wasn't so full of self-sacrifice, she could have escaped.

But, that's one of the reasons I love her so much. There was no part of her that he wanted to change, which was only one reason he wouldn't allow her to die.

Mika didn't know where he was. It hadn't been dark at first, but it was now, and if he listened carefully, he could hear something far away. He was left with a huge hole where his soul should have been. *Kali kept the darkness back.* Now, he was alone. Friendships with Vaira, Caryanne, Owen, and even Honk sat on the periphery. They would continue without him if they survived Steyn.

For years, Tregaren had tried to make Mika stronger. *You aren't trying. There's more. Why do you hide your power?* As a child, he'd resisted Tregaren's influence the only way he could, by denying the strength of his ability. As he grew and became stronger, he'd continued to suppress his ability to defy Tregaren, never realizing that it gave his father the means to control him.

"Don't worry, you're nothing like him," his mother had said.

Mika had never believed that, but now, after Kali, he wasn't sure. Without her, there'd been nothing to anchor his conscience. It hadn't occurred to him that it was wrong to raid that boy's mind. All that had mattered was obtaining the information he needed.

Mika wasn't stupid. When he examined the situation, he was more like his father than not. For the first time in his life, Mika didn't run from the thought because Tregaren had an ability that would leave most trained Agents gawking. What could Mika achieved with the same ability?

Only one thing mattered. He could help Kali defeat Steyn. Together, they would have a chance. He finally saw what he'd been doing. Instead of owning his ability, he'd given it to Kali as a way of unleashing its full extent without fear he'd become Tregaren.

Now he had a choice: he could stay trapped in the dark or acknowledge what he was and what he could do, return to Glaendor, and save Kali.

What if Kali hates me for being like Tregaren? But at least she'll be alive. That would have to be enough.

Mika breathed deeply. He couldn't feel his lungs, which was only to be expected when he was trapped by his mind.

Steyn was something alien, which meant that Kali was in even more danger than he'd anticipated. Reaching out to her felt as normal as breathing, and yet, Mika couldn't do either. Something blocked his way.

What would Tregaren do?

Mika shrank from the thought. It felt as if he'd betrayed Kali and himself. *I'm not him, but I can use what he taught me.*

This time, he did put himself in Tregaren's place. *He would reach into his enemy's head and exert the control he'd had all of his life!* It was because of Kali that Mika had broken free.

Mika saw what he'd hidden for too long. He'd always had the strength to stop Tregaren. Fear had allowed his father into his mind from the start and kept him there. Mika could have stopped him; he'd just been too afraid to do it. Mika would have cried out if he had voice at the realization that he was guilty of contributing to the suffering that Tregaren caused.

Mika deserved to stay lost in the dark until his body was gone. Wasn't that the easy way out? Hadn't he been a coward for too long. It wasn't a coincidence that it was only by embracing his abilities that he could save her.

Mika heard Tregaren's voice as if he stood at his shoulder. *"See the white line."* Mika saw a line of light pulsating as if connected to his heartbeat. *"That's your well of power, use it..."*

Mika allowed his power to fill him. This time when he reached for Kali, he felt her presence, faint but there. Using the driving need to join her, he clawed his way, bit by dark bit, back to the world.

Mika blinked open his eyes to see the same room where Steyn had attacked him. His body was one large ache as he rolled onto his side and gasped. Pain knifed through his chest. After everything, he might not be capable of standing, never mind fighting Steyn.

—   —   —

Kali raised her head from the ground. How was she still alive? Her whole body felt as though it was on fire, every nerve ending raw and her throat clogged so that she doubted she could talk. She put her hand to her neck. It felt normal but she knew without the shadow of a doubt that she'd suffered damage inside.

Kali focused on her surroundings and dragged air into her lungs. She didn't have long left, but she would make it count. Then, she blinked, where were the others? How long had she been unconscious? Her head was foggy but something had happened with Pesta and Steyn.

She must be imagining things. "Mika?" For a second, she'd felt him, but then he'd gone. Sometimes, if she wanted something badly enough, her mind tried to give it to her even when it wasn't true. That's all that had happened, and now was not the time to dwell on her loss, so she gritted her teeth and tried to focus.

Her mouth was dry. She felt three of them: Herja and her man, as well as Treva, but where was Pyra? It took longer than it should for her to work it out. Of course, he was a null. She wouldn't feel him.

She had nothing left. It was tempting not to move, let everything wash over her, but she couldn't. Not while the others were alive and the entire planet was still in danger. That's why she'd fought to become an Agent instead of living as a victim. She needed to fix broken situations.

Kali pushed herself up into a sitting position, one side of her face was numb from the cold floor. The world was unstable and the ground less solid than usual. She hung on until the sensation eased.

Herja turned to her. "Glad you are still with us."

Kali tried to respond but the words were slow to come. She swallowed. "I need you to get out of here while you still can."

Herja stared at her for a long moment, and Kali saw that she understood the hopelessness of their situation. For a second, she was afraid Herja was going to stay but then the woman nodded.

Herja issued orders in a clipped tone. Both Treva and Pyra looked Kali's way but she motioned them to go, willing them to recognize that there was nothing they could do to help. They reluctantly moved away with Herja.

Kali didn't want to think how weak she was when everything rested on her. Vision hazy, she saw that Pesta had lost the battle and Steyn was in control. Poor Pesta had been reduced to a weapon in the same way that Tregaren had used Mika.

The only positive was that Steyn was consumed by whatever was happening to him. She didn't know how much time before the transformation was complete.

What can I do? There was no way to fight Steyn directly but there had to be something she could do. *Andy!* She could tell Andy what was happening. She could share, let him see everything. Reaching out to find his warm familiarity was easy even in her depleted state.

"We're almost there," he said as soon as she made contact.

She refused to allow herself to think about how torturous it was to know that he was so close and yet would be too late. *"I've got nothing left except—"*

"Then get out of there."

"Andy, just listen. I'm going to share everything in the hope that you can use it to help stop the Erebus." Andy went silent as he must have realized that it was pointless to argue.

Even now, part of her resisted, arguing that it wasn't safe to expose her innermost secrets, except it didn't matter with Mika gone. She would soon be dead.

Kali slowly opened her mind and was immediately back on the ship with Tregaren as he took everything, invading and seeking control. *Just a flashback.* This was Andy. She could surrender because he knew her as well as anyone, except for Mika, and accepted her with all her flaws.

Andy was silent, a gentle presence, careful not to intrude too deeply. Despite that, he would see more than she intended.

Perhaps that was why she sensed Mika again. It was a longing that despite the danger made her eyes burn, which was why she doubted what she felt when his presence didn't flicker and disappear. She looked at the tunnel that led back to the city.

"Mika?!"

"It's okay. I'm here."

Then she saw him. A deeper shade of black against the dim tunnel and she had to fight not to cry. Did the universe want to destroy her? To make her watch as people she cared about died while she was helpless to stop it.

She saw his face now, and he was smiling. As her strength faded, she wasn't sure if any of what she was seeing was real. Tears clouded her vision as she felt herself slip away.

"I need to stop him," Mika said, *"like I should have stopped Tregaren."*

"You can't." Even her mind was weak. *"He's invincible as Erebus, but part of him is still Steyn."* And, then she could only watch as if from a distance.

Mika punched through Steyn's shield before he knew what was happening. Kali felt as if she were fading as her eyes became too blurred to see. Steyn sagged, but she felt him reach for Pesta.

"No." She couldn't let it all be for nothing. Perhaps she'd taken some strength from Mika, she didn't know, but when she threw a shield over Pesta, something happened. "Go!" she shouted.

Free from Steyn's control, Pesta didn't hesitate. Still wearing Ava's body, she ran after Herja, arms and legs flailing like it was the first time on her feet.

Mika didn't hesitate, destroying what was left of Steyn's mind. She felt it, even though she lacked the strength to lift her head from the cold floor.

Then she recognized the danger. She remained linked to Andy, letting him see that Mika was as strong as one of the fallen Priests. Even though it was too late, she severed the connection with the last of her strength.

— — —

Andy exited the hatch first. His ability and the sensors

told the same story. The planet had survived unscathed, without any disease, and Pesta had gone, although, that created another problem—one he didn't have the capacity to consider right now.

All Andy truly cared about was getting to Kali and Mika. He needed to be sure that they were okay after his connection with Kali had ended so abruptly.

Andy was surprised to see a small figure waiting, as he hadn't sensed anyone. Then, he realized why. The man's face was streaked with dirt, while the hands he held high in obvious surrender, trembled.

Andy lowered his weapon and unfastened his helmet, removing it from his head. "Pyra?" He recognized him from the one time they had spoken over a comm link. "Please lower your hands. Steyn is dead and you are in no danger from us."

Pyra sagged in relief . "I guess I can finally drop this bomaxed undercover assignment." He swallowed hard. "I'm afraid it's going to take some time to accept that I'm alive, but there are things you need to know. Steyn might be dead, but there are others involved with SPEAR and the Coalition."

Andy pushed down the irrational impatience he felt at being asked to consider the wider situation when all he wanted to do was check on Kali. He nodded to Sabrina, who was in charge of the Militia for this operation. They fanned out to check the immediate vicinity for any threat. Thanks to Kali, Andy knew what had happened prior to their arrival. It was unlikely that SPEAR would be waiting with Steyn dead, but it wouldn't do to get complacent.

Andy turned his attention back to Pyra, having made a decision. "There's not enough of us to secure the planet, only the station," he already knew that there was another way out, "which makes your knowledge of who's involved essential in ensuring that individuals are brought to justice in the future."

Pyra stiffened, and Andy saw that he needed

reassurance that they would listen to him once the immediate situation was under control.

"Your information is important," he put a gentle hand on his arm, "but, right now, I need to find Kali."

"Of course."

"I suggest you check in with the onboard medic." Andy started to walk away as he added, "Pyra, welcome back to the TSS." At Pyra's nod, Andy signaled to one of the Militia to escort him onto the TSS ship.

Now, to find Kali and Mika. As it turned out, it wasn't difficult. They had remained in the same spot where Andy last had contact with Kali.

He sighed in relief as he approached figures made tiny by the vastness of the empty station. However, his concern grew as he got nearer and made out Mika standing over Kali, who was propped on one elbow. She looked like she would need to be carried out.

Andy ran the rest of the distance to them. "Is she hurt?" he asked Mika.

Mika opened his mouth to answer but Kali spoke, "I killed Steyn."

Mika frowned and hesitated before adding, "With my help."

Andy had seen enough while in Kali's mind to know that she was trying to protect Mika. What had happened wasn't something he could ignore, but he intended to deal with it later once he had made sure they were safe. He scanned the area, both with his vision and mind, but the place remained deserted and he doubted there were any more nulls like Pyra.

There was one matter that he couldn't ignore. "Where did Pesta go?"

"She's just gone," Mika didn't sound sorry.

Kali shook her head. "I didn't see what happened to her." He followed her gaze to see that she was staring at what was left of Steyn. "She didn't destroy the planet, even when Steyn killed Mac."

"I don't understand. I thought that in itself would set her off?" Andy wandered over to examine what was left of Steyn, repulsed and fascinated in equal measures.

Kali's breathing was shallow as if it hurt. "So did everyone, but I guess we didn't know as much as we thought we did." She paused to catch her breath. "When Steyn and Tregaren created Pesta to be a weapon, they didn't expect her to be sentient. Nobody knew that she would have the ability to exercise choice."

"She's still dangerous," Andy said.

Kali managed to sit with Mika's help. "Perhaps, but we can't neutralize all risks."

Andy didn't think she was talking about Pesta. He turned his attention to the body, which had lost all color and started to sink in on itself. It took Andy a few seconds to recognize that it was its very unnaturalness that disturbed him. He forced himself to crouch and scrutinize everything.

Even now, the organic matter that was Steyn slowly disintegrated, reminding Andy of the horrific images from Pesta's attack on Roana. Curiosity overcame his aversion to the decaying body, and he pressed a finger to Steyn's chest. Other than a slightly cool sensation, there was nothing.

Steyn's clothes remained intact, appearing oversized on the disintegrating frame. That's when he spotted a glass vial with a gold stopper in the shape of a dragon. He picked it up and peered at what seemed to be traces of a gas inside.

"What is that?" Mika asked from behind.

Andy clutched his chest with his free hand. "Shite, you startled me."

"It's a funny color."

Mika was right, the gas had a yellow tinge, and Andy had never seen anything like it before.

"I'll send it for testing." Even as he said it, he wondered what measures would need to be in place to make it safe.

There was a challenge in Mika's eyes as he asked, "What happens now?"

From everything Andy had seen of Mika's abilities, it would be difficult to subdue him if he chose to resist, but he was too powerful to let loose. They'd have no choice but to try to work out a deal together.

Before Andy could answer, Mika returned to Kali's side. She put a hand on his arm. He looked at her and there was the familiar buzz of telepathy that generally annoyed Andy, but today, he was grateful that Kali was able to calm down the situation.

Both looked at him and Andy responded, "Nothing's changed." Everything had changed, but his responsibilities remained the same. "I need you both to return to Headquarters with me."

Mika tensed before helping Kali to stand.

"I can get..." Andy started to say.

Kali waved off the offer of medical transport, allowing Mika to support her as they walked to the waiting TSS ship. Andy would make sure they both saw a medic before they set off for Headquarters.

It seemed the mission had been a success overall. Not without its loose ends and issues, but he'd seen worse. They'd lived to fight another day, and in the end, that's what mattered.

CHAPTER 34

TREVA KNEW THAT nothing would be the same again. They were back in his father's apartment despite the ongoing repairs for fire damage. Trouble was, he couldn't work out if it was good or bad. How could everything go back to normal after what he'd experienced?

It was easy to look back and think that his life had been good before his mother had been kidnapped, but the truth was, he hadn't been happy. Something had been missing. He'd thought that it was his father, but during the short time they'd had together, Treva had realized that it wasn't that simple.

He didn't want to go back to who he'd been before, because while he hadn't known anything of life, he'd been desperate for approval—whether from Nash or his father. Now, he recognized that his mother was the most important person in his life.

The comm unit chimed and his mother answered. "Okay, you can send him up." She hung up and turned to see Treva loitering in his bedroom doorway. "It's someone here for me."

Why does she have to treat me like I'm a child? Not wanting to sound like a whiny kid, he retreated. Sometimes, it was better to be sneaky.

When he heard the door open, followed by the murmured voices, he went to peek, sure that they would have to pass his door. He was wrong. She took the man into the lounge as his father's study was still undergoing restoration. He sighed, having resigned himself to not finding out who was visiting until later, when his mother called his name.

Not wanting to appear too eager, he took his time crossing to the lounge. He went in without knocking to find them opposite each other on the overstuffed chairs. Treva hadn't expected to know the man but he recognized Kali's boss.

He stood. "Andy Renteria," he held up his hand in greeting to Treva, "we've met before, but it's always been under difficult circumstances." After they'd both sat, Andy said, "I need to ask you some questions."

Treva reluctantly nodded. "I'll answer if I can."

"I understand that you don't want to get Herja in trouble, but it's important that we find her. She took Pesta with her."

Treva frowned. "She only took Ava and me. Pyra didn't want to go."

Andy paused, seemingly trying to decide whether to say more. "Pesta is inside Ava."

"Oh." Treva struggled to remember anything that had happened at the end with his uncle. "I don't know where they went. She dropped me at Starhills. I was worried, you see..." He looked at his mother.

She smiled. "He was worried that I thought he'd gone willingly, but I knew something unusual was going on when I couldn't move until they'd gone."

"Ah, you are sure that you have no idea where they were going?"

Treva shook his head, relieved that it was the truth. "No."

"Well, thank you for your help." Andy stood again, and Treva understood that it was his cue to leave.

Treva rose and slowly went to the door where he paused. "I don't think it was just me that didn't know about Ava. Herja didn't either."

Andy pressed his lips together and nodded. "Probably not. If you hear from her, I need you to let me know."

Treva nodded but he didn't meet Andy's eyes as he said, "Sure."

Herja had saved his life too many times for him to betray her. Regardless of what Andy thought, that's the way she would interpret him giving away her location.

Treva headed toward his room but stopped a short way down the corridor to listen. His need to know what they were talking about outweighed his fear that Andy would sense him.

Andy's voice carried clear enough, "Treva is Marco Steyn's official heir. I need you to think about working with us to uncover all of his assets."

"We don't need anything from the Steyn family."

"I understand how you feel, but if you don't work with us, it's going to be incredibly difficult to identify where, for instance, the laboratory that created Pesta is located."

There was a long silence. "Would there be any compensation?"

"I'll be honest, we're likely to seize all of Steyn's company assets, what with others in the family working against us, but the apartment and personal items would be yours to keep."

"What about Jon?"

Treva rolled his eyes. He liked Jon well enough, but why did she have to be so obvious?

"Jon Del-Awai?" There was a pause. "We didn't arrest him."

"He was helping you—"

There was a smile in Andy's voice, "Indeed, he did help, and I'm sure he will be in touch later to check that you are okay."

There was a long silence before Andy said, "I want you

to consider sending Treva to the TSS academy for training in a couple of years' time."

Treva froze, hardly daring to believe what he was hearing. It would mean everything to learn to use his Gifts and put them to use like Kali. *Could I do it?*

Even if his mother said no, surely he could change her mind within a couple of years.

Her voice was weary with resignation, "Since I cannot see him settling down to a 'normal' job, that might be a good idea. I dread to think what trouble he'll get into if left up to his own devices."

Treva grinned. Perhaps his mother knew him, after all.

— — —

Herja glanced at the viewscreen on the flight deck of the *Hyperion*, which showed the lounge or more precisely, a young blonde woman staring at her hands. "Who is she?"

"No idea, but she's bound to be trouble," Gosta said. "I don't understand why you didn't dump her along with the kid."

"Because we were in a hurry to get away as fast as possible." She watched her for a minute longer. "There's something odd. You will have to keep an eye on her."

"We've got bigger problems."

Herja couldn't help but laugh at Gosta's glum expression. *Doesn't he know by now that we always find a way?*

"What can you possibly find funny at a time like this?" Gosta grumbled.

"How can *you* be so depressed. Things are finally looking up!"

He gave her a dour look, not the least bit amused by her lighthearted response. In all fairness, the situation did seem hopeless. The power grid of the *Storm's Breath* was failing, their food stores were in dire straits, and their people had nowhere else to call home.

She smiled. "Don't you see? Andrei Steyn is gone. Sure, another will no doubt rise to take his place in the organization, but there's always disruption during a transition like this. We still have the information from Treva about all of the Steyn ship routes. Without a leader to say otherwise, they'll no doubt continue business-as-usual to keep product flowing."

"You want to attack a ship. Now?"

"Oh, no, not the ships. They'll expect that, but with those routes, we can pinpoint where those ships go."

Gosta sighed. "A storehouse. You've lost your mind."

"Oh, my friend, you know it's brilliant. They'll never see us coming and they are bound to have everything we need."

"It's madness that I listen to anything you say." He shook his head.

Herja patted him on the shoulder. "It's because you know I always have a plan."

— — —

Mika found it hard to meet Kali's eyes. In fact, every time he looked at her, he felt the loss of what they'd had for a brief time and it hurt. He wouldn't change anything, not even letting her go but... well, it was hard to accept living a life with less color.

They were back at the temporary base on Fureron. He didn't know what was happening and why he wasn't on his way to TSS Headquarters. Nobody seemed to know anything, or if they did, they weren't telling Kali and Mika. This was the first time they'd been alone. Kali sat with her leg brushing his on one of the firm bunks in his room. Although basic, at least it wasn't a prison cell.

Kali looked a lot better after seeing the medic on the return journey. Mika had heard him say that only time and rest would restore her back to full health.

"What's wrong?" she asked.

In the heat of her gaze, it felt like nothing had changed. He shook his head, reluctant to attempt to put his feelings into words, too worried about making a mess of it. *Everything is different now.*

Kali put a hand on this forearm, lighting up his skin with a shock of electricity that almost convinced him to forget his resolve to let her go.

"I was thinking." She cleared her throat.

Is she nervous? Mika gave her his full attention, listening carefully.

She continued, "Only if you want. But I thought that perhaps, we could spend the night together."

He stared, wondering if his mind had conjured some sort of illusion to make up for all the misery it had piled on over the last few hours.

"I mean, now there's no danger..." She trailed off, probably convinced that he wasn't interested.

"You can't know that there's no danger." Internally, he cursed himself for a fool, but now more than ever, he didn't want her to make a mistake. "It's still there," he blurted, and more softly, "for me, it's still there."

"I'll take that chance. If it happens, it's meant to be."

"Really?"

It occurred to him that she was doing this to save him, but it had to be what she wanted. This time, he was determined not to overthink things since he'd given her every opportunity to walk away.

He studied her face. She really was beautiful, and best of all, there were no doubts clouding her eyes. Like him, she knew what was certain to happen and she didn't care.

He asked, "Are you sure?" Then added, "Ignore that. I need to keep my mouth shut. My answer is, yes."

"Sometimes you have to lose something to find out how important it is," she said just before he silenced her with a kiss.

— — —

Andy grinned and Kali felt her face grow warm. *He can't possibly know.* It had to be her imagination because Mika hadn't changed. She glanced over to him standing stiffly with his arms folded while awaiting judgment.

Kali didn't think that Andy was going to say anything bad because he was too jolly.

He looked at her. "I spoke with Lead Agent Alexri."

Well, that explained why they were still cruising the Outer Colonies rather than on their way to Headquarters.

Andy continued, "And, we agreed that you should monitor Mika."

"What does that mean?" she asked immediately, hoping it meant what she thought.

"Well, it's obvious that we need someone to keep an eye on things here and," he glanced at Mika, who hadn't altered his position at all, "since you two are determined to bond, we might as well make use of it."

Kali let out a relieved breath. She wasn't sure how she felt about continuing to serve in the Outer Colonies, but she knew that things could be much worse.

Mika's scowl had deepened. "What if she doesn't want to?"

Andy sighed. "Then we will have to reexamine the situation. We can't cover every eventuality, but I suspect that we will need your ability at some stage." Andy glanced down to read a message on his handheld. "You might want to go to the hospital first. It seems that your mother is finally awake."

"About time," Kali muttered before asking, "What about the band?"

"Owen signed a six-month contract with a hotel on Glaendor, saying it will give them time to decide what they want to do without their bass player and manager."

"And Herja?"

"Ah, she is turning out to be elusive. Dropped Treva off at Starhills, as requested, but the boy reckons he doesn't know anything."

Mika raised his voice, "So, you're just going to let her take Pesta and disappear?"

He's doing a terrific job of hiding his feelings. It was a good thing that they had renewed their bond, or she would have thought that he was miserable about the situation.

"Not likely," Andy was still smiling. "I think it sounds like the perfect job for the both of you, and it might even keep you out of trouble for five minutes."

Kali locked gazes with Mika and finally his eyes softened. He belonged to her in a way she couldn't articulate, the bond between them unbreakable. Even so, she had no illusions about him—the scars of a lifetime tied to him to a monster. Not even Kali, could predict where that would lead them. Wherever it was, she looked forward to the journey.

ADDITIONAL READING

Cadicle Space Opera Series by A.K. DuBoff
Book 1: Rumors of War (Vol. 1-3)
Book 2: Web of Truth (Vol. 4)
Book 3: Crossroads of Fate (Vol. 5)
Book 4: Path of Justice (Vol. 6)
Book 5: Scions of Change (Vol. 7)

Verity Chronicles by T.S. Valmond & A.K. DuBoff
Book 1: Exile
Book 2: Divided Loyalties
Book 3: On the Run

Mindspace Series by A.K. DuBoff
Book 1: Infiltration
Book 2: Conspiracy
Book 3: Offensive
Book 4: Endgame

Dark Stars Trilogy by A.K. DuBoff
Book 1: Crystalline Space
Book 2: A Light in the Dark
Book 3: Masters of Fate

AUTHORS' NOTES

From Lucinda Pebre:

Wow, we made it to the end! Amy said that Book 3 was going to be epic, and that's certainly how it felt when writing it.

Thank you so much for reading the entire—to date—Shadowed Space Series (and if you didn't, I hope you understood what was going on).

I won't lie, I was a little worried about getting Book 3 right. There's a certain amount of pressure in ensuring the end of any book delivers, but that goes double for a series. For me, it doesn't matter how good the rest is; it's the ending I remember. I have to confess that Mika almost died on a few occasions until I discovered that he didn't want to be 'good' and it was okay to let him be who he wanted to be. Thankfully, Kali needed him even if she didn't know it, and Mika deserves to find happiness after surviving Tregaren. Despite needing to get things right and pull everything together, this book was an absolute joy to write which is perhaps why it ended up slightly longer than the others.

Co-writing with Amy has been a blast. I feel fortunate to be writing with someone who is such a good fit, and I don't want it to end. Fortunately, we left Herja oblivious to the fact that she is now a person of interest to the TSS and it has nothing to do with piracy and everything to do with the dangerous entity on the *Hyperion*. How is she going to save her people when they're out of resources and being hunted?

Our next task is to make sure that Herja's story fits within the wider Cadicle Universe, which is a challenge all of its own.

Thank you to everyone who contributed to making the series the best it could be. Without the beta readers and proof-readers, the story would be a more flawed version of itself.

I want you to know that I take all of reviews and suggestions into consideration when I receive them, so please leave a review or get in touch and tell me what you love and what could use improvement.

An additional note from A.K. DuBoff:

This books was quite the ride, wasn't it? I was thrilled to finish my first read of Lucinda's draft. It's been an incredible experience to watch how she'd grown as a writer over these three books, and I can't wait to see what she does next!

The plot threads we've introduced in these books will come into play in the Taran Empire Saga, and it's been so much fun figuring out how to fit the puzzle pieces together. Being able to work with Lucinda and my other great co-authors is what has made it such a wonderful experience. The ideas they've brought to the table have elevated the Cadicle Universe beyond my wildest expectations. I'm so happy to have this amazing team!

The character of Herja has turned into a bit of a show-stealer, so we've decided to focus the next plot arc on her. Since there will be a change in focus, we'll likely make it a new series rather than Book 4 of this one. More details are forthcoming, but I think it's safe to say that new exciting adventures are coming in 2021.

As always, huge thanks to our fantastic beta reading and proofing team—John, Steve, David, Leo, Kurt, and Charlie. You are a joy to work with, and you have incredible insights. Thank you for helping to make these books the best they can be.

And thank *you* for reading this trilogy! We hope you're looking forward to more many tales :-).

∧BOUT THE ∧UTHORS

LUCINDA PEBRE

Lucinda Pebre is my author name. Lucinda because it starts with the same letter as my real name; Pebre is a salsa from one of my favourite restaurants in Sheffield, a stunning addition to any dish. Just like Lucinda. Sorry, I couldn't resist, it's more about my love of food. I'm a part-time author living in Sheffield, UK, where I share my life with dogs and a long-suffering husband who is a part-time musician. Even though I'm a city girl, I spend my spare time in the Peak District, running and walking. Yoga and reading anything science fiction, fantasy or paranormal keeps me sane enough that I only let my insanity out in my writing.

www.lucindapebre.com

A.K. DUBOFF

A.K. (Amy) DuBoff has always loved science fiction in all its forms—books, movies, shows and games. If it involves outer space, even better! She is a Nebula Award finalist and USA Today bestselling author most known for her Cadicle Universe, but she's also written a variety of space fantasy and comedic sci-fi. Now a full-time author, Amy can frequently be found traveling the world. When she's not writing, she enjoys wine tasting, binge-watching TV series, and playing epic strategy board games.

www.amyduboff.com

www.ingramcontent.com/pod-product-compliance
Lightning Source LLC
Chambersburg PA
CBHW030605180626
46816CB00005B/1687